Praise for *Gone with a Handsomer Man*

"This debut mystery by a well-regarded novelist will please any reader, but particularly fans of Jennifer Crusie or Mary Kay Andrews."

—*Library Journal* (starred review)

"Fluffy as a buttermilk biscuit . . . Charming." —*People*

"*Gone with a Handsomer Man* is fun, funny, and fabulous!"

—Janet Evanovich

"Michael Lee West fans, rejoice! *Gone with a Handsomer Man* has a fresh, funny, and delightfully flawed heroine that you'll fall in love with from the get-go. By turns sweet and surprising, it's a wonderful, quirky escape."

—Joshilyn Jackson, *New York Times* bestselling author of *Backseat Saints*

"Great cook—though reluctant detective—Teeny Templeton keeps the pot bubbling. . . . Delicious."

—Lee Smith, *New York Times* bestselling author of *The Last Girls*

"By turns acerbic and sweet, poignant and funny, with great sex, bad boyfriends, and Do-Not-Try-This-at-Home recipes. However you slice it, *Gone with a Handsomer Man* is as addictive as red velvet cake."

—Harley Jane Kozak, Agatha, Anthony, and Macavity Award–winning author of *Dating Dead Men*

also by michael lee west

Gone with a Handsomer Man

a teeny bit of trouble

MICHAEL LEE WEST

Minotaur Books
New York

This is a work of fiction. All of the characters, organizations, and events portrayed in this novel are either products of the author's imagination or are used fictitiously.

Printed in the United States of America. For information, address St. Martin's Press, 175 Fifth Avenue, New York, N.Y. 10010.

www.minotaurbooks.com

The Library of Congress has cataloged the hardcover edition as follows:

West, Michael Lee.
A teeny bit of trouble / Michael Lee West. — 1st ed.
p. cm.
ISBN 978-0-312-57123-8 (hardcover)
ISBN 978-1-250-01402-3 (e-book)
1. Women cooks—Fiction. 2. Murder—Investigation—Fiction. I. Title.
PS3573.E8244T44 2012
813'.54–dc23
2011045369

ISBN 978-1-250-02347-6 (trade paperback)

First Minotaur Books Paperback Edition: February 2013

10 9 8 7 6 5 4 3 2 1

a teeny bit
of trouble

one

It's not every day that I bake a dozen red velvet cakes, learn that my boyfriend has a love child, and I witness a murder. To calm down, I invented a whole menu based on the Miranda warning. My favorite is Anything-You-Say-Can-Be-Used-Against-You Quiche. It calls for onions, smoked ham, and pepper cheese. Place ingredients in a deep-dish crust and add heavy whipping cream, salt, and pepper. Bake in a 400-degree oven until the filling is nicely browned. Serve with You-Have-the-Right-to-Remain-Silent Salsa and You-Have-the-Right-to-an-Attorney Pita Dippers.

Coop O'Malley is my lawyer and my boyfriend. He just started working at a big firm here in Charleston. The job comes with an ulcer, which is why I was home on a Saturday afternoon baking cakes instead of eating sweet tea scallops at Palmetto Place. We were supposed to meet there to celebrate Coop's thirty-first birthday, but he'd phoned on my way out the door.

"Hey, Teeny," he'd said. "I hate to cancel at the last minute, but my boss asked me to work overtime."

I had no reason to doubt him. Coop was a by-the-book kind of guy. Loyal, meticulous, and hard working. That's what had drawn me to him in the first place, way back when we were kids. I'm a spontaneous, trouble-prone gal, and he's a cautious, rule-following guy. His personal motto is engraved on the back of his watch, *semper paratus,* always prepared. My motto is *merda accidit*, shit happens. Opposites attract, right?

I spent the rest of the day getting my order ready for The Picky Palate—that's a café in the historic district. I'm a freelance baker. This is a dream job for a self-taught cook like myself, especially since this city is filled with professional chefs. I work at home and tote my pastries to the café, which sells everything on consignment. The red velvet cakes go into a revolving glass case with other Low Country favorites—shrimp and grits martinis, Benne Wafer Trifle, Pluff Mud Pie. At the end of the day, the shelves were empty.

Late that afternoon, I put the cakes into my beat-up turquoise convertible and drove to the café. The smell of buttered corn bread pulled me down the aisle, past shelves that overflowed with raffia-tied jars—gourmet jellies, lemon curd, pickled okra.

My boss stepped out of her office and put her freckled arm around my waist. "I'm going back to chef school," Jan said. "I'm selling The Picky Palate. Would you like to buy it?"

My knees wobbled. A few months ago, I couldn't afford a peach martini, much less a whole café. Then, on a fluke, I'd inherited the Spencer-Jackson House on Rainbow Row, along with a trust fund. I hadn't decided what to do with either one. I'd been raised by hardcore Southern Baptists, women who were deeply suspicious of earthly treasures, and they'd taught me that the Lord was a tad capricious about giving and taking. So I hadn't quit my job, nor had I sold my peach farm in Georgia.

I didn't know doodly squat about running a business, but I promised Jan I'd think about her offer. As I drove home, the August heat punched against the top of my head like a fist. The minute I stepped into my kitchen, the phone rang. Before I could say hello, a lady shouted, "Quit spying on me, Teeny Templeton!"

Each word burned my ear, as if scalding water had spurted out of the receiver. I recognized the voice immediately. It belonged to Barb Browning Philpot, Coop's high school sweetheart. They'd broken up eleven years ago, right after he'd gone away to college.

"Why are you calling me after all this time?" I asked. "And why do you think I'm spying?"

"Drop the Miss Innocent act," Barb said. Each word left a smoking imprint on my brain. "Come near me and my daughter again, and I'll hit you with a restraining order."

The only thing that needed restraining was Barb's tongue. I lifted the caller ID box. The screen showed a number with a South Carolina area code. My hand trembled as I set down the box. What was going on? I'd moved away from Bonaventure, Georgia, six months ago, but Barb still lived there with her pharmacist-husband and their ten-year-old daughter. I'd never seen the child. Or maybe I had.

Six weeks earlier, on a hot June afternoon, a little girl had shown up at Coop's beach house, claiming he was her daddy. He'd told me that his old college roommate was behind it. Barb's name hadn't come up. Nor had the child returned to Coop's house. Now, just remembering that day made my lungs flatten. I reached into my apron pocket, pulled out my asthma inhaler, and took a puff.

"Poor Teeny," Barb said. "You can't catch a break—or your breath. And you never will. Coop wants to dump you just like he did in high school. He's sick of your dead rat pussy."

I let that comment pass. "Barb, I don't have a reason to spy on you."

"No?" Her voice screaked up. "I saw you peeking through my window last night."

"That's impossible," I said. "I was with Coop last night." And I'd fed him shrimp tacos, red rice, and strawberry shortcake with lots of whipped cream.

"He'll be with me tonight," she said.

"Wrong," I said. "He's working."

"Is that what he told you?" She laughed, a blade-sharp sound that cut right to my soul.

I hung up and dialed Coop's cell phone. Not that I believed Barb for a second, but when he didn't pick up, I felt all woozy-headed and my rear end hit the floor. I just sat there, breathing through my mouth. My bulldog,

Sir, pushed his cold nose against my arm. He's brown and white, with a smooshed-in, wrinkled muzzle. A creamy stripe runs down the center of his head, as if he'd collided with a bowl of royal icing. Normally, he calms me down, but I kept shaking.

I punched in the number to Coop's law firm. The answering service informed me that everyone had left for the day. My throat clenched, as if I'd accidentally swallowed a cocktail onion. Was I reaching for trouble or was trouble reaching for me?

The afternoon wore on and wore me out. I called Coop three more times; he didn't pick up, and I didn't leave voice mail. If he wasn't at the office, where was he? And what about that little girl who'd shown up on his porch a few weeks ago? Was she Coop's long-lost child? He was an honorable man. I couldn't shake the feeling that he'd gone back to Barb so he could help her raise their daughter. And he just hadn't found the words to break up with me.

Don't get me wrong—I love children. But I hate liars. A while back, I'd promised Jesus that I would tell the truth, and I began keeping a yearly record of my fibs. Every January first, I start a new tally, and I end it twelve months later on New Year's Eve. This year, I'd told eighteen lies, and it was only mid-August. If I got cornered, my score could rise into the triple digits.

Coop was one of the few people who understood my preoccupation with the ninth commandment. When I was eight years old, my mama, Ruby Ann Templeton, had abandoned me at the Bonaventure Dairy Queen. She told me to run inside and buy two cones. When I came out, her car was gone. I never saw her again. Mama's older sister, Bluette, raised me. My aunt promised to never leave, but cancer is an asshole disease that doesn't honor promises. Last winter, she died, but she'd become my moral compass. What would she think about my dilemma?

One of her favorite mottos was "Believe but verify." That's what her hero, President Ronald Regan, used to say about the Russians. I wasn't sure it applied to boyfriends, but a little verification wouldn't hurt—just as long as the verifier wasn't caught. I'm not a violent person. But tonight might be a different story if I found Coop and Barb doing the horizontal boogie.

I waited until 10.00 p.m., when it was full dark outside, then I opened my laptop and did a reverse search on Barb's phone number. I got a hit for a Sullivan's Island rental on Atlantic Avenue, a ritzy address, just 10.4 miles from me and six miles to Coop's house on Isle of Palms.

First, I MapQuested the directions. Next, I went upstairs and dug through my closet. The rack was filled with consignment store finds: raspberry dresses, lime skirts, tangerine blouses. Unless I wanted Barb to spot me, I'd need to wear something less colorful. I pulled out a black scuba suit. A few weeks ago, I'd found it at a garage sale, and my head had filled with visions of a tropical, snorkeling vacation. Thank goodness I'd bought it, because it was my only black outfit. I put it on and stuffed my hair into a Braves baseball cap. I cringed when I passed by the foyer mirror. All I lacked was a harpoon and I could go after Moby Dick. But I wasn't gunning for a whale. I was going after the truth and a tall, blond bitch.

I drove my convertible across the Ravenel Bridge. By the time I reached Sullivan's Island, the wind had sucked out strands at my hair, and I looked like a rabid possum. I parked on the beach access road and walked to Barb's rental. The night arched above me, dark as a mine shaft. A storm was blowing in from the Atlantic, and the air reeked of dead fish and pluff mud.

It wasn't too late to turn back. I could go home and watch a Cary Grant movie, *Suspicion* or *Charade*, and plow through a gallon of peach ice cream. I didn't have to be a stalker-girl.

No, Teeny. Keep going. You've got to verify.

Barb's house sat on a jetty, a three-story brown clapboard that lorded over the cozy, old-fashioned bungalows. They were dark and shuttered, but her windows glowed with curry-colored light. I walked to the backyard and stopped beside a clump of sea oats. A wooden deck ran down the length of the house. The floodlights came on, and bright cones splashed across the grass. I moved back into the shadows, congratulating myself on my smart attire. My dark suit was the perfect camouflage.

A skinny blonde flung open a door and stepped onto the deck, her white caftan snapping in the wind. She held a martini glass, and the liquor shimmered like a melted apple. Her eyes darted this way and that way. Over the years, I'd seen Barb's photograph in the Bonaventure *Gazette*'s society pages, but I'd forgotten how pretty she was in person.

I blinked. What had gone wrong with her perfect life? Why was she living in a rental? And where was her little girl? The beam from the Sullivan's Island lighthouse circled toward me, and I dove into the oats. My cap flew off and honey-colored frizz exploded around my shoulders.

"Teeny?" she called. "I know it's you because I recognize your shitty hair. If you damage my sea oats, I'll shave your head."

I grabbed my Braves cap and stepped toward the deck. I pressed my tongue against the thin gap between my front teeth and grinned. Not because I was amused. This was my "oh shit I want to die" smile. It was involuntary, like a sneeze, and held back a slew of emotions.

Barb skewered me with a look, her eyes cold and sharp as sea glass.

"I'm not spying," I said, and raised my lie tally to nineteen.

"Then why are you here?"

"I lost my dog." Lie number twenty.

"I thought you *were* a dog." She spoke in a slurry voice. As she veered to the edge of the deck railing, the martini sloshed out of her glass. "Why are you wearing that stupid wet suit?"

"It's the latest style." Lie number twenty-one. I was on a roll.

"Maybe at SeaWorld." She laughed, a high, tinkly sound.

I dragged my shoe through the sandy grass. If only I'd brought that harpoon, I could have pinned her to the deck and force-fed her benne wafers.

She clawed her hair out of her face. "Coop just left. But he'll be back."

Her voice hit me like unripe peaches, each one piling up on my chest, crushing my lungs. What would it take to bring her down? Two harpoons and a Russian sub wouldn't be enough.

"You're making this up," I said.

"I don't care if you believe me. But you shouldn't believe Coop, either.

The truth doesn't matter to a lawyer." She put her martini glass on the deck railing, then she pulled a BlackBerry from her pocket and squinted at the keypad. "I've got proof he was here. Want to see his picture? Step a little nearer. But not too near or I'll call 911."

I squinted up at the phone and my stomach tensed. Coop's image filled the little display screen. He sat on a white sofa, red kilim pillows heaped around him. I dragged my gaze away from the phone and looked into the living room. The same white sofa. Same pillows.

Barb flashed a triumphant smile. "I'm sorry it has to be this way. But you're better off. You shouldn't be with a man who doesn't love you."

More hard, knotty peaches landed on my chest. I wanted to toss them back, but I couldn't move.

"Poor Teeny. You have such a look of pain in your eyes. But you'll feel more pain when I call the police and report you for trespassing." Barb spoke without malice, but hate blew off her in clear, wavy sheets like steam rising from a boiling soup pot. She glanced down at her phone again, her finger poised over the keypad. "You've got two seconds to get off my property."

She walked back into her living room and closed the patio door. She stood there, watching me.

Tears burned the backs of my eyes as I walked around her house, through the shadowy yard. When I got near the driveway, I heard footsteps. A tall, rangy guy in a Bill Clinton mask strode toward Barb's front door. The mask was rubber and fit over his whole head, hiding his face and hair color. The wind kicked up his black Windbreaker, showing a baggy jog suit and skinny legs. One gloved hand held a key. He opened the front door and stepped into Barb's house.

Coop? I thought. *Is that you?* My stomach cramped and I bent over double. Why did he have a key? How long had he been seeing Barb? *Believe but verify, Teeny.*

I hurried into her backyard, trying to ignore the tight, squished feeling in my chest. I was trespassing. But I wouldn't do anything crazy, like throw sand. I'd just call them assholes, which was a perfectly legal thing to say, then I'd take my bulldog and leave town.

I tiptoed up the deck staircase and peered through the glass door. Barb and the masked guy were arguing. His gloves were latex, the kind favored by surgeons. Blue paper booties covered his shoes. No, he definitely wasn't Coop. Not with those long, stringy legs.

He grabbed Barb's neck and they veered into a table. A pottery lamp crashed to the floor and shattered. The man's gloved fingers sank into Barb's throat. Her face reddened, and her eyes bulged. He was murdering her. I dug my cell phone out of my rubber pocket to call the police. Before I could flip it open, my alarm went off, playing the stupid-ass theme song to *The Twilight Zone.* I cupped my fingers over the phone, trying to smother the sound, but the man had heard. His head swiveled. He dropped Barb and she crumpled to the floor. He stepped over her limp body. Then he lunged toward me.

Holy crap. He'd killed her and I was next. I vaulted down the deck stairs as if a jet stream were coming out of my butt, and I flew into the terrible night.

two

I raced around Barb's house and skidded into the driveway. Oh, Lord. I'd just witnessed a murder. And now the murderer was after me. I glanced over my shoulder. Bill Clinton stood five feet away, right beside the trash can.

"Leave me alone," I yelled, brandishing the Nokia. It was still playing the creepy music. I tried to shut off the sound, but the phone squirted out of my hand and clattered on the pavement. I bolted onto Atlantic Avenue and cut down a side street. A shingled cottage was just ahead, and it looked occupied—lights blazing, cars in the driveway.

I sprinted across the front lawn and tripped over a concrete garden gnome. I must have blacked out a minute. When I came to, my head ached and grass was stuck all over me, as if I'd been garnished with parsley. I grabbed the gnome's ears and pulled up. The yard was empty. So was the street.

Deep breath, Teeny. Come on, honey. Just open your mouth and breathe.

A teenaged girl with short red hair turned up the driveway. She glanced at the garden gnome, then her gaze stopped on me. She jolted. "What're you doing in my yard? You trying to steal something?"

I got to my feet. What could I say? That a guy in a Bill Clinton mask had killed my rival? That he'd chased me? But I felt so dozy-headed. What had I really seen? "A guy was chasing me," I said.

The redhead stared at my wet suit. "Maybe he thought you were a burglar. Why are you dressed that way? Were you night surfing?"

"Yeah," I said, and bumped my lie count to twenty-two. I glanced at the street. Shadows leaped across the pavement, but I didn't see the man.

The redhead stepped closer. "If you're scared, call the police."

"Can't. I lost my cell phone."

"Oh, my god." She clapped one hand to her cheek. "If I lost my cell, I'd be totally freaked. It's got my Facebook password and everything."

Great. I hadn't thought about that. My Nokia was crammed with pictures of Sir and Coop and my cakes. If Barb's strangler had found the phone, I'd be dead baker walking.

"I'm sorry about your troubles." The redhead squinted at my wet suit again. "But you need to leave. If my mama sees you, she'll think I'm hanging out with bad people. She'll ground me."

I gathered up my courage and crept back to the rental. The floodlights were off, and darkness pooled in the long, empty driveway. Only the Lord knew where I'd dropped my phone. But I had to find it. I forced myself to scuttle forward. The floodlights came on, streaking down the concrete. A high-pitched girlie voice cried, "Get off my property, you freak."

A little girl stood on the front porch. She yanked two iPod wires out of her ears and glared. Her skinny legs protruded from a pink nightgown. Two dark blond braids fell past her shoulders. I gazed at the child's huge gray eyes, and all the breath rushed out of my lungs.

"What's your name?" I asked. But I knew. This was the child who'd knocked on Coop's front door all those weeks ago. Suddenly everything clicked into place. *This is Barb's child.*

"I'm Emerson Philpot," she said in a loud, arrogant voice. She moved to the edge of the porch. The wind lifted her braids and she slapped them down.

I started to introduce myself, but she cut me off. "I know who you are. You're my daddy's booty-call. If you don't get out of my damn driveway, I'll scream. It's against the law to scream after dark on Sullivan's Island."

My ears rang with one word: Daddy. I pushed my hair out of my face.

How could Barb run away? She'd been choked. But it had happened so fast, I couldn't be sure. I half-expected her to walk out that front door, her caftan billowing.

"Where's your mama?" My voice sounded high and unnatural, as if I'd sipped helium.

"Gone. Her car isn't in the garage, and her suitcase is missing. She runned off and left me. I'm not staying by myself. I'm going inside to pack. Then you're taking me to Daddy. He'll know what to do."

She darted into the house, leaving the door ajar. My collision with the garden gnome had left me with a dull headache, but I made myself go inside. Barb's body wasn't on the floor. The broken lamp was missing, and the shattered bits had been swept up. Maybe I was hallucinating. Or dreaming. I pinched my hand.

Ouch, that hurt. Okay, so this was real.

A portable phone sat on a rattan table. I lifted the receiver and called Coop's cell phone. I got turfed straight to voice mail. Next, I called his house. A busy signal. I started to punch in 911—it was the right thing to do—but my finger froze over the 9. Just two months ago, I'd been in the wrong place at the wrong time, and the cops had accused me of killing a guy. Well, actually he'd been my ex-fiancé. I'd caught him playing naked badminton with two naked skanks, and I'd attacked them with peaches. When the ex turned up dead, the police had interrogated me. I'd told the truth, but it had sounded weird and unbelievable, and I'd ended up in trouble.

Don't think about it. Don't you dare.

It wasn't my personality to dwell on the past, especially if it dredged up hurtful memories, but I reminded myself of three important facts. One, the truth hadn't set my ass free. Two, Coop had made sure that my name was cleared (and I wanted to keep it that way). Three, the experience hadn't been a total loss because I'd invented some unforgettable recipes: Keep-Your-Big-Mouth-Shut Scones and I-Learned-My-Lesson Lemon Curd.

The Sullivan's Island cop would dismiss me as a loon if I told him that

Bill Clinton had strangled a woman. But I'd be in a mess if I admitted that I'd quarreled with a woman and now that woman was missing.

So was my phone. If it was in Barb's driveway, all I had to do was call myself and listen for the ringtone. I tapped in my number, then I set the receiver on the table and ran out the front door. I waited for the quirky notes of *The Twilight Zone* to rise up, but I only heard clanging wind chimes, thunder, and distant surf.

I pushed out a long sigh, and air whistled through the thin gap between my front teeth. Emerson ran onto the porch, clutching a backpack in one arm, a stuffed hedgehog in the other. She'd changed into a blue gingham dress. On her feet were red shoes, as if she'd been off to see the wizard but took a wrong turn.

"Did you hear any strange noises tonight?" I asked. "A vacuum cleaner? Screams?"

"You are so weird. I want to leave. Now."

"I need to call Coop and tell him what's happened."

"Do that, and I'll bite you."

We walked to my convertible. She kicked sand while I put up the top. Minutes later, as we headed toward Isle of Palms, my headache shrank to a dull flicker. I cut my gaze to Emerson, studying her profile. She had a low forehead, a turned-up nose, and wide lips. The Philpots had distinctive features—high foreheads, bulging green eyes, and butterfly ears. Emerson didn't look like them. Except for her gray eyes, she didn't resemble Coop. Was he her daddy or not? And why hadn't he told me about her?

She stuck out her tongue. "Stop looking at me, you skeezer."

"My name is Teeny."

"Duh. It's a stupid name. And you live in a stupid house. Mrs. Philpot said you painted it with Pepto-Bismol."

I pinched the steering wheel. "How do you know where I live?"

"We drove by your house a hundred-million times a day." Emerson tapped her braids together. "I saw you walking a hideous mutt."

I pushed my shoe against the gas pedal a little too hard, and the car shot forward. They'd been spying on *me*? "My dog isn't hideous," I said.

"His face is all smooshed in."

"It's supposed to look that way. He's an English bulldog."

"I know what he is. But what are you? A midget? You should trade the bulldog for a Yorkie. The next time you walk around the Battery, you won't look silly. Mrs. Philpot said that a small woman needs a small dog. The scale is better."

"Thanks for the advice," I said.

"Want more? Get braces on your teeth. And cut your hair. It's so huge it deserves its own zip code. Mrs. Philpot said that you're a dead ringer for Cousin Itt, that furry character in *The Addams Family.*"

"I've been called that before." I shrugged. I'm only 5' 1¾" tall and I've got big, bad blond hair. "But why do you call your mom Mrs. Philpot?"

Emerson lifted a braid and sliced it through the air, as if chopping my question into little pieces. I wasn't ready to give up. "How old are you? Ten?"

"I'll be eleven on December twenty-third. And you're not invited to my party."

"Happy Birthday in advance," I said.

"I bet Mrs. Philpot won't come to my party." Emerson slumped down in her seat. "I ought to charge her with child abandonment. I saw that on *Laura Norder.*"

"What's that?"

"Are you serious? It's a TV show. Cops, lawyers, bad guys. It got cancelled, but you can catch the reruns."

"You mean *Law & Order*?" I asked.

"That's exactly what I said." Her chest puffed up. "You better not make fun of me. I'm a straight A student at Chatham Academy."

I was still peeved over her remarks about Sir, so I said, "Is that a reform school?"

She rolled her eyes. "A private academy in Florida. Near Naples. I live there year-round. I have my own quarter horse, and lots and lots of friends."

"Sounds like a cool place." I glanced at her. Her face was impassive.

Behind her, the dark landscape whirled by, dotted with lights from beach houses.

"Nobody but country skanks say cool," she said. "And keep your eyes on the road. I don't want to die in this butt-ugly car."

I put both hands on the wheel and stared straight ahead. The headlights cut two cones onto the pavement. Everything about Barb was an enigma. She was missing. She'd sent her daughter to a boarding school. Had mothering put a crimp in her style?

I turned into Coop's long, sandy driveway. Lightning flickered over the dunes, brightening the gray, clapboard house. The square windows blazed with a honeyed glow. Thank goodness Coop was home. I let out a huge breath and parked behind his red truck. He might be an asshole liar, but he'd know what to do.

Emerson scrambled out of my car, dragging her backpack and hedgehog. She trudged through the sandy yard to the front door. I walked behind her, taking huge gulps of air. A storm was blowing in, and I smelled the faint tinge of sulphur.

From inside the house, I heard a deep bark, then Coop opened the door. His eyes were a striking mix of gray and blue. That's the first thing I always notice about him. They skipped from me to Emerson.

"What's going on?" He folded his arms and his white t-shirt stretched over his wide shoulders, showing the outline of his deltoids. A Pepto-Bismol bottle jutted up from the hip pocket of his sweat pants.

"I was just about to ask you the same thing," I said.

Coop looked troubled. His face was finely-chiseled, with a square, masculine jaw. When he was happy, his whole face became a soft oval, but fear hardened his bones.

His giant dog skidded into the foyer. T-Bone was a giant mixed breed, a rescue with wiry, taffy-colored fur, a white belly, and intelligent amber eyes. His head reached Coop's elbow, and Coop is 5' 10". T-Bone sniffed my outfit. Dammit, I'd forgotten that I was wearing it.

Emerson leaped back. "Will it bite?"

"No, honey," Coop said. "Just let him smell you."

She held still while the dog dragged his nose over her dress. The mammoth tail began to wag, then his pink tongue shot out, the size of a corned beef brisket. Emerson squirmed away. A wide grin creased her face as she looked up at Coop.

"Guess what happened? Mrs. Philpot deserted me. I get to live with you. Isn't that super-great news?"

Coop's dark eyebrows angled up. "Barb did what?"

"She's gone." Emerson pushed past him. "And I'm hungry. Got anything to eat?"

"I just made a bowl of jalapeño dip," Coop said. "The kitchen is the first door on your right. The Doritos are on the counter."

No wonder he had an ulcer. I ached to fix him an apple-and-brie omelet, just the thing for acid indigestion. And the child was so thin. She needed something more substantial than dip. She needed comfort food: mashed potatoes with butter, cream, and sea salt.

Emerson skipped off, her braids bouncing on her shoulders. T-Bone trotted after her. The minute she was gone, Coop gave me a questioning look.

Where to begin? I studied the Ansel Adams print on the wall behind him, black-and-white trees. Ebony vases sat on a bookshelf, next to carved ivory elephants. These were Coop's signature colors. His brain was the same way. He wanted facts, no gray areas.

A knob moved in his throat. "Why are you wearing a scuba outfit?"

I didn't want Emerson to overhear us, so I pulled him onto the porch and gave a quick summary. Barb's phone call, the masked guy, the strangling, the chase, my lost phone, and my discovery of Emerson.

"She says Barb's suitcase is missing," I added. "So is her car. But how could she drive? When I ran off, she was on the floor and she wasn't moving. Maybe Bill Clinton went back to her house and got rid of her body."

"Did you see him go back?" Coop asked.

I shook my head.

"Did he have time to chase you, dispose of her body, and clean her house?"

I shrugged. "I lost track of time. But I know what I saw. He choked the life out of her."

"For how long? A minute?"

"I didn't time that, either. But it happened fast. Maybe ten or fifteen seconds? Barb's face was red as a strawberry. And her eyes . . ." I broke off and shuddered. "My phone startled him. He let go. She fell. And she didn't move."

"She probably wasn't dead."

"She looked like it." I stared hard into Coop's eyes, wishing I could see behind them, where everything had a right side and a wrong side. A place where textbooks had been memorized, all those words pushing back his scary emotions.

"It takes longer than ten seconds to strangle someone, Teeny. See, during those fifteen seconds, Barb's carotid arteries were compressed. Her brain wasn't getting oxygen. So she passed out."

"When people get strangled on TV, they die immediately," I said.

"It takes longer in real life. Three or four minutes of nonstop strangulation. A little faster with a ligature. And, it depends on how strong the guy was and how much pressure he put on her carotids. After the guy ran away, Barb probably regained consciousness."

I didn't want a lecture on strangulation. I rubbed my forehead again. The dull ache had finally vanished, but I still felt dizzy. "I just know that man went back and killed her."

"You don't know what he did."

"I can't believe that Barb got up, cleaned the broken lamp, and left her house. Left her child. Why would she do that?"

His hand circled my wrist. His lips parted, like he wanted to say something, then he clamped them shut.

I shook him off. "I wouldn't have gone to her house if you'd told me the truth. But you said you had to work late. I believed you."

"I did have to work. I stayed at the office until eight thirty."

"But I called. The answering service said nobody was there."

"There's no operator in our building. We use a service in Mount

Pleasant. I was with my boss and two other lawyers. On my way home, I stopped by Barb's house."

"Yeah, she showed me your photograph."

"What?" He looked puzzled.

"She took a picture of you with her cell phone." I crossed my arms. "So what happened after that? Did you set up a DNA test? Talk about the future?"

"She didn't want to discuss the test. She tried to seduce me."

My pulse thrummed in my ears. "Is that why you didn't answer your phone?"

"God, no. I turned it off earlier. She kept calling. I couldn't get any work done." He dragged the pink bottle from his pocket, unscrewed the cap, and took a swig. "As for the seduction, I rejected her. I told her I loved you. She said she'd gotten rid of you once and she'd do it again. She threatened to abandon the little girl. To force me to raise her."

"Barb told a different story. She said you still loved her."

"She was trying to shake you up. She lied."

"So did you. Why didn't you tell me about Emerson? She's the same little girl who showed up on your porch earlier this summer. You never said she was Barb's child. You said your old roommate was pulling a prank."

"He's done things like that before. I tried to contact him, but he wouldn't return my calls. That's how Burke is. He sets up a practical joke and makes me squirm."

"But didn't you wonder about that child?"

"No, because she didn't come back. I really believed it was a joke. I pushed the incident out of my mind. Then this afternoon, Barb phoned. She said I was the little girl's dad. I was in shock. But I wanted to talk to her. I wanted to know why she'd waited a decade to tell me about Emerson. I'd planned to tell you everything."

I narrowed my eyes. "When?"

"Tonight. I've been calling your house since ten o'clock."

I wanted to believe him, I really did. But I couldn't. "Let me get this straight. A ten-year-old girl showed up at your house. A girl with gray eyes, just like yours. And you never once connected her to Barb? Because eleven years ago, you and her were sleeping together."

"It crossed my mind. But only for a second. Barb and I broke up after I started college. We had a blow up right around Halloween. If she'd been carrying my child, she would have forced me to marry her. She wouldn't have kept quiet for ten years."

Arithmetic wasn't my specialty—I even had trouble reducing recipes. But I counted on my fingers, trying to do the math of Barb and Coop. "You and her broke up in late October. She gave birth to Emerson over a year later, the end of December. No one has a fourteen-month pregnancy. You had to know the child wasn't yours. Yet you *still* went to her house?"

Coop's brow puckered. "December? No, that's not right. Barb said Emerson was born in September."

"Well, somebody's mistaken. Because Emerson claims her birthday is December twenty-third."

"This doesn't make sense. Barb was specific about the date, September fourth."

"Even so, if Barb had been pregnant when you broke up with her, the baby would have been born in July or early August of the year."

"Barb claimed that she went six weeks overdue. I should have known she was lying."

From the kitchen, I could hear Emerson lecture T-Bone about the evils of preservatives. Coop set the Pepto bottle on a table. He took my hand and rubbed his thumb over my knuckles.

"I should have told you about Barb. But I was in panic-mode. I am so sorry. I wouldn't ever hurt you. You're the only thing that's right in my life. When I look into the future, I see us together. All wrinkled and gray-haired. Just you and me."

"But I need you to share your worries with me. Don't hide them behind a lie. Even if you're trying to protect me." Tears pricked my eyes. I didn't know much. I was too short and my grammar was all wrong. But deep down I knew that it would take more than a lie to make me stop loving him. I could identify his pine-and-cotton scent if I fell into a vat of ammonia. He had this way of tipping back his head when he laughed. And I got shaky when he gave me a lopsided smile. I am a shy person, but I felt brave whenever he took my hand and led me into a crowded restaurant.

Be a hard-ass, Teeny. The man has a separate set of rules for himself. And when he's threatened, he shuts down emotionally.

He kept stroking my hand. It felt just right. But my reaction was all wrong. A woman was missing, maybe even dead. A child had been abandoned. This touched my personal raw spot, one that had never healed.

"Coop, we should call the police."

"And tell them what?"

"That a man strangled Barb Philpot."

"But you said he used a key to get into her house."

"Maybe he stole it."

"The police will be more interested in you." He glanced at my wet suit. "They'll want to know why you were peeking through Barb's window."

"It was a door."

"As your lawyer, I'm advising you to skip the police. At least for tonight."

"Can lawyers give advice to their girlfriends?" I swallowed. Was I still a girlfriend?

"I'm not worried about an ethics violation. Barb told me she was going to leave the little girl. I believe she went through with that threat. I don't know how the masked man figures into it. Maybe we'll find out when Barb turns up."

I looked into his eyes. Why was he so calm? Normally he was a worrywart. Always scanning for danger. He kept a stash of extra batteries in the pantry, paid his taxes before they were due, and stopped at yellow lights. Hurricane instructions were taped to his kitchen wall. I didn't know what had made him this way, but I knew he longed to be different.

He stared back at me, his irises changing to pure gray. His gaze said, *Stick with me, Teeny. I'm trying to change.* Just last week, we'd driven to the Battery and traffic was backed up. He'd swerved down a one-way street, knowing full well that his truck was going in the wrong direction. He'd gritted his teeth, ignoring the honking horns. When he'd finally turned off King Street, he'd flashed a one-sided grin. "See?" he'd said. "I can break the rules."

But I just wanted the truth, not a whole different man.

"Let's get Emerson settled in the guest room." He stepped closer, and his sweatpants brushed against the front of my rubber suit. "Then you and I will sort everything."

Sort everything? Coop had lived in England for several years, and he'd picked up weird phrases from his ex-wife, a gorgeous British archeologist. I'd found out about Ava O'Malley the same way I'd found out about Emerson—by chance.

"Sort it yourself," I said, pulling away from his grasp. "I'm going home."

three

Fifteen minutes later, I was back on Rainbow Row, barricaded on the third floor of the Spencer-Jackson House. Sir was nestled beside me, the burglar alarm was set, and a walnut dresser blocked the bedroom door.

But I still didn't feel safe. I'd never been comfortable in this mansion. It's real pretty, a pink stucco with gray shutters, one of the most-photographed places in Charleston. Inside, the rooms were filled with priceless objects that dared me to break them. I was clumsy, better suited to a house with muddy floors and battered furniture. But I knew one thing: beauty isn't the secret ingredient of a warm, welcoming home. I didn't know what that ingredient was, but I was determined to find it.

Sometimes, though, when I baked supper for Coop, a sweet, butter-crust aroma wafted through the air, shimmering like notes in a gospel song, and a peaceable feeling wove through me. During those moments, I felt right at home in the Spencer-Jackson. Smells are real important to me.

Tonight, those fragrances were gone. The bedroom had a closed, musty odor. Lightning shivered behind the windows, showing a glimpse of shape-shifting rain, then the sky turned dark again.

I shut my eyes and imagined myself in The Picky Palate. If I bought it, I'd add a new recipe to the menu: I'm-Scared-to-Try-New-Things Tilapia would go nicely with Orange-You-Glad-You-Took-a-Risk Marinade. This sauce calls for 1 cup orange-flavored liqueur, ½ cup blood orange juice, and ½ cup peach juice. Whisk until smooth, then add: ¼ cup blood orange zest, ¼ cup finely chopped, skinned peaches, 4 garlic cloves (peeled and minced), 4 tablespoons stone-ground mustard, ½ cup safflower oil, 1 teaspoon sea salt, and 2 tablespoons chopped fresh pepper. Add ¼ cup chopped herbs, such as Italian parsley and lemon thyme. Serve over pan-fried tilapia.

Coop loved tilapia. But he was on Isle of Palms and I was on Rainbow Row.

Get a grip, Teeny. I opened my night-table drawer and pulled out my emergency stash of Reese's Cups. As my teeth sank through layers of peanut butter, I reminded myself that food had brought me and Coop together. When I was an itty girl, Aunt Bluette had taken me to an Easter egg hunt at the Bonaventure First Baptist Church. Even then, I could locate candy the way a bloodhound tracks convicts. I went straight for the chocolate ducks and Jelly Belly carrots.

As I toted my overflowing basket across the lawn, a big kid in a rabbit costume knocked me down. My candy spilled, and the rodent scampered off. Coop helped me to my feet. He was a year older than me, a serious boy who'd won punctuality awards. Me, I was a tardy, child slob, but I knew handsome when I saw it. And just like that, Coop had imprinted on my brain as if I were a baby goose. For the rest of the day, I'd toddled after him, trying to say his name, but I couldn't shape the words.

I didn't talk until I was three years old, mainly because I was afraid to open my mouth. If I did, someone shoved an asthma inhaler between my lips. When I finally worked up the nerve to speak, my first word was *turnip*, and I shouted it in front of everyone at First Baptist. I was sitting in the back pew with Mama, right behind the O'Malleys. Coop sat between them, dressed like a child evangelist—shiny black suit, starched white shirt, and a red bow tie.

Halfway through the sermon, he flicked a paper wad in my hair. I ate it. He laughed, a watery sound that whirled through the holy air, colliding with the preacher's dry voice.

"Hush!" Irene O'Malley hissed in her son's ear. He slumped down in the pew. I waited for him to toss another paper wad, but he held real still, as if trapped by the shrill edge in his Mama's voice. I kicked the back of the pew. He didn't budge. I opened my mouth wide, intending to shout Coop's name, but my lips wouldn't form a C. So I hollered out *turnip*, mainly because we'd eaten a batch for supper the night before, and also because Ts were easy, seeing as my name started with one.

The preacher's voice snapped off, and Mama stared down at me. I pulled away, thinking she'd smack me, but she gathered me into her arms. "My baby talked! Thank you, Jesus!"

Laughter rippled through the congregation, but Mama kept smiling like I'd found a cure for vaginitis, a word she herself had been using recently.

Coop's head popped up. He turned around and whispered, "Taters."

"Turnip," I insisted.

More laughter. Irene O'Malley pinched her son's arm. "Bad Cooper," she hissed. "Bad!"

He slid back down in the pew. I wanted to make him laugh again, and I wanted Mama to hug me. But I was also peeved at Mrs. O'Malley.

"Damn turnip!" I yelled, and threw a hymnal to the floor. I wanted to say something real special, so I threw in a few of Mama's favorite words. In my childish mind, *beets* and *bitches* sounded like the same things, foods that grew in the dirt. I realized my error when Mama's proud smile morphed into a frown. She hustled me out of church, slapping my legs with the mimeographed program.

When we reached the peach farm, she washed out my mouth—not with soap but with Some Like It Hotta sauce, which was supposedly made from jalapeños, vinegar, and brimstone. This fiery baptism was meant to correct my vocabulary while it burned my tongue, but it only proved that mixing root vegetables with profanity was a bad idea. On that day, a foodie was born, but I never forgot the lowly turnip, and each Thanksgiving, I lovingly add them to casseroles and savory pies.

Just thinking about that day calmed me down. But I was still determined to improve my vocabulary. I lifted my thesaurus from the night table, opened the book to the Ps, and the word *prevaricator* floated up. Evader, deceiver, tale-teller.

"A sign," I whispered, and tossed the book aside.

Sir placed his paw on my arm. Bulldogs have the most expressive faces, and his dark eyes looked directly into mine, as if to say, *Chill.*

The phone rang, and I leaned toward the night stand. Coop's number appeared in the caller ID panel. I lifted the receiver. "Hey," I said.

"Just making sure you got home safely," he said.

His voice sluiced over me like warm pear juice. "I'm okay," I whispered.

"No, you're not, baby. You're hurt and confused—"

His strained voice worried me, but I was even more concerned about the endearment. Baby? What did that mean? He'd always called me sweetheart.

I pressed the heel of my hand against my eyes. "Any news about Barb?"

"No."

"I was just about to nod off when you called. I'll talk to you later, okay?" I didn't trust myself to wait for his answer, so I hung up. A few seconds ticked by, and the phone trilled again. My hand closed on the receiver. No, let it ring. I'd speak to him in a few days, after I'd had time to sort a few things on my own.

I unplugged the cord from the jack. Sir's bottom teeth jutted into his muzzle. This was his "don't be cruel" look. He didn't know the half of it. We Templetons specialized in peaches and poisoned recipes. The fruit was real, but our recipes were a harmless method to relieve tension—like a punching bag, but with imaginary food. If someone pissed us off, we wouldn't spit or pull hair; we'd just mentally cook a deadly meal and pretend to feed it to the enemy. My aunts had written these lethal concoctions in the back of a spiral-bound church cookbook. Some of the dishes were paired with music and Bible verses. That had been Mama's special touch. At Coop's suggestion, I'd hidden the tome in a Charleston lockbox—after I'd memorized every last formula, of course.

If only I'd cooked a pie for Barb, a Get-Rid-of-the-Bitch Pie. The key ingredient is hydrangeas. The flowers and buds are poisonous, similar to cyanide, causing acute gastrointestinal distress. I wouldn't have fed it to her; I would have thrown it in her face. Take that, you man-stealing, child-leaving hussy.

I felt sad. I shouldn't vicariously poison a missing woman. Because long ago, for a brief time, we'd been friends.

Pink hydrangeas had bloomed in the front yard of Barb's childhood home. She'd lived in Bonaventure's historic district, and her family's white wooden house had faced Newgate Square, with views of tiered fountains and manicured gardens.

My house had also been white, but it stood at the end of a long gravel road, smack in the middle of a peach orchard. Barb had bought her clothes at the mall. I'd shopped at Tractor Farm Supply. My family was uneducated. Barb's parents were college professors. My forebears were Irish convicts and farmers. Barb traced her lineage back to Atilla the Hun. My aunt was a professional clown; Barb's great-great-aunt had worked as a cryptologist during World War II. Barb wrote encrypted love letters to Coop, and I wrote recipes to myself.

In high school, Barb had been the head majorette—poised and focused, with perfect eye-hand coordination. Never dropped her baton stick, never stumbled, never failed to dazzle the audience with her gold sequins and vertical figure eights.

Every Friday night, I'd marched behind her in the band, pretending to blow into my clarinet. During one homecoming ceremony, someone tied my shoelaces together, and I didn't have time to unravel them. I lurched across the football field and tripped face-first into the grass. The audience let out a collective gasp when the tuba player stumbled over me, followed by a jarring crash of wind instruments and drums. Barb didn't seem to notice; she kept doing arm rolls, her luscious cleavage spilling out of the sequins.

When she was a junior in high school, she talked her way into my sophomore Home Economics class. She ended up sharing a desk with me. While I read about the history of onions, she held out her hand, showing off Coop's class ring.

"Would you like to touch it?" she asked.

I shook my head.

"But you like him, don't you?" she persisted.

"He's a friend," I said, struggling to control my telltale face.

"Is that why he went fishing with you last week?" she asked

I shrugged.

"He told me all about it." She licked the ring, leaving a slick trail over the blue stone. "He talks about you a lot."

I'd been crushing on him since that long-ago Easter egg hunt at First Baptist. Every Sunday I'd made a point to sit behind him in church. And yes, I'd invited him to go fishing in the creek that bordered my family's peach farm. But I'd had no idea that he'd discussed me with Barb. A thrill shot through me, and I almost dropped my onion book.

"You're blushing," Barb said.

"No, I've got a fever."

"I hope you're well by Saturday night," she said. "I'm having a pajama party. Since you're so crazy about onions, why don't you bring a Vidalia dip?"

Sure, with a little rat poison. Why was she inviting me? I wouldn't fit in with her ritzy-fitzy friends. I politely declined. I thought I was in the clear until that evening, when the phone rang. It was Barb's mom. She sweet-talked Aunt Bluette into letting me attend the party.

Late Saturday afternoon, my aunt dropped me off at the Brownings' house. To my surprise, I was the only guest. Barb sat at the kitchen table and painted her nails, talking about her deep love for Coop. I was relieved when Mrs. Browning gave me a tour of her walk-in pantry. The shelves were loaded with gadgets and gourmet spices. She was a professor of home economics, and she knew how to make vinegar from scratch and how to take plain old canola oil and infuse it with garlic, lemon, or hot peppers.

Barb scowled at her mother. "Quit hijacking my guest," she said. "We've got better things to do than listen to food talk."

After Barb's nails dried, she dragged me into the dining room, where her father was bent over a jigsaw puzzle of the Pacific Ocean. They spent the whole evening discussing which blue piece went where. They were competitive, with strong egos, and their discussion quickly turned into a raging argument, which they seemed to enjoy.

Mr. Browning got up to answer the phone, and Barb snatched a handful of pieces and took them to her room. She hurried back before her father returned. This seemed like undaughterly behavior, but I didn't have a daddy, so what did I know?

Later that night, she dragged me to her frilly purple-and-pink bedroom. She stretched out on one of the twin beds and showed me a coded love letter she was writing to Coop.

"Looks like gibberish," I said.

"No, silly. They're anagrams. That's where you take a word and scramble it."

Just like an egg, I thought.

Mrs. Browning poked her head in the room. "Your father is in tears. He's missing critical pieces to his puzzle."

"Maybe you cooked them." Barb smiled. After Mrs. Browning left, Barb slid off her bed and peeled back the rug. A dust mote swirled up, drifting over six blue puzzle pieces.

"You lied to your mama," I whispered.

"Yes, but it's *so* much fun." She reached deeper under the rug and pulled out her diary. She licked the tip of a pencil and started writing. A few minutes later, she pushed the book into my hands.

My friend Teeny could be majorly cute if she didn't cut her own hair, eat too much candy, and shop at the Salvation Army. Her ugly brown eyes can be changed with blue contact lenses. A dentist can fix her gappy teeth, and a full-service salon can pluck her brows, straighten her grody hair, and add highlights.

I'm not sure what to do about Teeny's knees. They are yucky, way too far down on her legs, just this side of a deformity. She should throw away her cheap minidresses and buy jeans and long skirts. A hat will cover her fivehead—that's an abnormally high forehead. I can't do anything about her dwarfism, nobody can, but I can teach her to walk in stiletto heels. It's an art form, one that every girl, short or tall, must master.

I should have been offended, but I was more surprised that she hadn't written in code. I asked her about it, and she rolled her eyes.

"The point of a diary is to capture my feelings. Anagrams would take too long. They'd destroy my natural spontaneity. Besides, I will be famous one day, and I want my diaries to be read by the world."

Next, she told me about her plans for next weekend: she wanted to fix me up on a blind date with Josh Eikenberry, the son of the local undertaker. "He's a nice guy," Barb said. "Even if he's just a second-string quarterback."

I wouldn't have dated Josh if he'd been an NFL football star. He had sad, puppy dog eyes and wore too much Ralph Lauren cologne, perhaps to cover the lingering smell of formaldehyde. Plus, he combed his hair in an unstylish pompadour, which showed off his striking widow's peak. When he wasn't dry humping girls in the back of his daddy's hearse (so the rumors went), he hung out in the cafeteria with the other jocks and told Bad Granny jokes, but he always blurted the punch line a beat too soon and no one ever laughed.

"I'm not going out with Josh," I said.

"You've got to," Barb said. "Coop set this up. He thinks Josh is perfect for you."

"I don't want O'Malley picking my boyfriends."

"He's just trying to help," Barb said.

Maybe this was true. Coop had always been protective of me. I could totally see him acting as a matchmaker. Plus, if I went on a double date, I'd get to be near O'Malley for a few hours. So I let Barb fix me up with Josh.

The next weekend, the four of us went to a block party on Oglethorpe Square. It had rained the night before, and Barb got her brand-new shoes muddy. Coop carried her three blocks to his house on Hanover Square. Josh and I trailed behind in a dense cloud of Polo cologne. While he cracked jokes, I blinked up at the O'Malley's house. White clapboard. Black shutters. Six majestic columns. The kind of house that belonged on a plantation, not in the middle of downtown Bonaventure.

Coop set Barb down in the grass. He began cleaning her shoes with a stick. Josh pinched my arm. "What's red, dead, and can't stop screaming?"

"A tomato?" I said, trying to be polite.

"No, a peeled granny in a bucket of salt."

I jerked away from him. I wasn't in the mood for a joke, not when the love of my life was on his knees, scraping dirt from a goddess's shoe. Pain twisted through my chest, a real pain like acid indigestion. If only I could be a girl with straight hair and muddy feet.

Stop it, Teeny. Thou shalt not covet thy frenemy's boyfriend.

"This isn't working." Barb frowned at Coop. "Can I borrow a pair of your mom's sandals?"

"Sure," Coop said, and carried her into the house. I started to follow, but Barb pushed the door shut.

Josh spun me around. "How do you fit a bad granny into a martini glass? Throw her into an ice crusher."

Before I could pull away, his tongue darted into my mouth, fast and slick as a minnow. He smelled as if he'd been embalmed with cologne, and my throat closed. I broke loose, gasping.

"Get back here," he yelled. "Barb said you'd go all the way."

"She *what*?" I cried.

"You heard me, bitch."

Anger boiled up inside me, and before I had time to think, I jammed my knee into his groin. He howled and clutched his hands over his privates. Then he scurried off the porch, whimpering for his mama.

I sat on the porch until Coop and Barb came out. He offered to drive me home, but Barb shot him a withering look. "Teeny's spending the night with me."

I scrambled to my feet. "No, I'm not."

"But my mother wants to teach you how to make her famous three-cheese soufflé," Barb said. "Won't that be fun?"

After Coop dropped us off, Barb pulled me into her bedroom and tossed me a clean gown. I threw it aside. "I want to go home."

"Hush, you're interfering with my creative energy," she said. She opened her diary and began to write. Finally, she lowered her pencil and read out loud.

> *"Tonight Coop scraped mud off my shoes. He dropped to his knees in a worshipful position and cradled my foot in his hand. It was so rad, the bestest feeling in the whole world. Like I was the queen of a majorly cute country. I looked down on him and spit right in his hair. He didn't notice because he was overcome with love. I was overcome with an urge to whack him in the head with my other shoe and I would have shuddered when his skull cracked open like a dropped watermelon. I am not a violent girl. Plus, all that blood would have been grody and I would have barfed if it had gotten on me. But I wanted to hurt him. He's so boring. Such a goody two-shoes. Josh and Teeny were watching, so I pulled the fury back inside me and spared Coop's life."*

"What kind of writing is that?" I cried. It sounded like the run-together thoughts of a budding serial killer.

"It's fiction," she said, looking offended. "I employ the stream of conscious style. But you make Cs and Ds in English, so you can't possibly understand literary techniques."

"Ain't that the truth." I jammed a pillow over my head.

She yanked it away. "Why did Josh run off tonight? What happened?"

"I kicked him."

"Why?"

"Because he got fresh. You told him I'd put out."

"You're a liar. And you're insane. Guess you can't help it. All the Templetons are short, fat lunatics. If you ever get married and have a child, you'll run off and leave it. Just like your mother left you."

"You're nothing but a writing fool," I said. I grabbed a pillow and blanket, then I marched out of her room. If it hadn't been so late, I would have called Aunt Bluette and made her pick me up. I made a pallet on the front porch, but I couldn't sleep, so I made up recipes.

The next morning, Coop stopped by the Browning. Before I had time to move, he tripped over my legs and fell on top of me. I lay beneath him, trying to memorize the scratchy-softness of his white shirt and the mossy tang of his English Leather cologne. That's what he wore back then. I liked how it smelled. I liked how his chest pressed against mine. I counted each thump of his heart.

The front door creaked open, and I turned my head. Barb's face contorted. "Teeny Templeton, quit seducing my boyfriend!"

Coop raised up. "Teeny didn't do anything. I tripped."

Barb started crying. Five minutes later, her mama drove me back to the farm, blaming her daughter's behavior on hormones. "It's that time of the month," Mrs. Browning said. "She can't control her mood swings. But what woman can?"

If you asked me, Barb was a spoiled rotten, homicidal puzzle stealer who could eat cookies any time she wanted and never gain a pound. But I just smiled at Mrs. Browning.

That Monday, I went to school early to work on my Home Ec project. Barb was already there, putting the finishing touches on her snickerdoodle cheesecake. "If you try to steal Coop from me, I'll beat you in the head with my shoe," she said. Then she smiled sweetly.

Later that morning, when the teacher handed out the grades, I got an F because worms had mysteriously ended up in my Lady Baltimore cake.

The next day, someone wired a dead crab to my truck's carburetor. The day after that, someone wrote graffiti in the Waffle House rest room. After all these years, I could still see those words so clearly: TEENY TEMPLETON GOES DOWN ON A FIRST DATE was scratched into the paint right next to TEENY TEMPLETON HAD SEX IN THIS STALL.

Needless to say, Barb and I stopped being friends.

A whole year went by. She and Coop were voted Bonaventure High's "Cutest Couple." I assumed they'd get married after graduation, but they broke up. Not too long afterward, he asked me on a date. We went to a First Baptist cookout at the lake. The next night we went to the movie theater, and the night after that we went fishing. All my life I'd loved him from afar, but he'd always treated me like a sister. Now, he looked at me in a new way, one that made prurient thoughts fill my head.

The first time he kissed me, an unbearable pleasure took control of my brain. My limbs relaxed, and my insides filled with damp heat. Our tongues met and danced away. I didn't know kisses could make me woozy-crazy. Like a fool, I kept his hands in the Baptist zone.

The summer whirled by. I baked him peach pies. He took me to a Bon Jovi concert and to a pool party at his parents' house. In August he stopped calling. At first, I didn't worry. He was about to leave for college, and he'd shown me his mile-long to-do list. I baked a cake for his birthday and left a message with his mother, but he never called back.

One blazing hot afternoon, he showed up at the farm and said he and Barb had gotten back together. I started wheezing. *Please God, not an asthma attack. Not in front of Coop.* Aunt Bluette rushed me to the hospital. Coop's dad was my doctor, and he put me in an oxygen tent. My lungs recovered, but my heart had shriveled to the size of a peach pit.

"Don't be sad, Teeny," Aunt Bluette said, tucking a blanket around my chin. "When a door closes, a window opens."

My psychic cousin, Tallulah, drove down from Tennessee. She was on her way to Chamor Island to visit Aunt Bunny, but she spent a few nights with us. Tallulah listened to my sad story, then she squeezed my hand. "You'll find love again. And when you do, the guy will have an O, A, and E in his name."

Coop O'Malley's name had those letters. But so did a dozen other guys.

After Tallulah left, I moped around the farm until late August. Then I started my senior year. Coop went to a college in Chapel Hill, North Carolina, but he came home every weekend. It hurt my heart to see him and Barb at football games, even though I was dating Aaron Fisher, the most popular jock in high school. He had the right moves, and his name had the right letters. *He's the one*, I kept telling myself.

But Aaron had another destiny. He won a football scholarship to Clemson, and during his freshman year he drank too much alcohol at a fraternity party and died. I was ready to give up on love. Then, a year later, I met an older guy. Son Finnegan was in medical school, and just when I started to fall for him, Aunt Bluette chased him off.

All I had left was the memory of romance. It reminded me of the perfect peach pie, where your fork breaks through the flaky, top crust into the sweet, amber-colored filling and the flavors of summer melt on your tongue. But I'd forgotten to write down the recipe and I could never make that exact pie again. My life had become a Jimmy Webb song, "MacArthur Park."

The years ran by, a whole decade of loveless years. Sure, I dated. Once, I'd gotten engaged. Then, a few months ago, on a balmy June night, I walked into a Charleston pub and ordered a peach martini. I remember that evening so clearly. An Elvis song played on the juke box. And a guy with gray-blue eyes sat beside me. Coop O'Malley, a guy with an O, A, and an E in his name. Later, he told me that he'd felt an unstoppable urge for Guinness and he'd driven from Isle of Palms to downtown Charleston.

"I'm a logic-driven man," he'd said. "But I've got just enough Irish blood to believe in fate. I've known you since we were children, but when I saw you that night, I fell smack in love. I knew that I'd come to that pub for a reason."

Maybe it was fate. Or maybe it was thirst. It didn't matter. Coop and I had found each other again; but I couldn't shake the feeling that something was about to go terribly wrong. I could almost hear Aunt Bluette's doors and windows. They weren't slamming, they were being nailed shut.

four

The next morning, a pinprick drizzle fell over Charleston, glazing the sidewalks and trees. I put on a rainbow-striped skirt, a dazzle of cherry-lilac-daffodil-blueberry-and-lime, something I'd scored at a vintage shop. If anyone carbon dated the fabric, it would probably be identified as Joseph's coat of many colors. Also, I wore a lightweight red cotton jacket, a pink blouse, and high-top turquoise sneakers. It was the kind of outfit that could cause instant blindness, but I was a foodie, not a fashionista.

I grabbed an umbrella and walked Sir to the Battery. My missing cell phone was still on my mind. What if the masked man had found it? Would he turn it over to the police or run up a bill? In the distance, church bells clanged, calling Charlestonians to Sunday school.

My pulse slowed as I walked back to East Bay Street. Then it sped up again when I saw a strange yellow van in front of my house. Through the rain-speckled windshield, I glimpsed the driver's chin-length brassy hair. His broad nose lay across his face like a catfish fillet.

Red Butler Hill. Coop's private detective.

In addition to doing surveillance, Red had just started moonlighting for a repo company, and he drove a new van every week. Emerson Philpot sat in the passenger seat looking pissed off. Why were they here? And where was O'Malley?

My heart sped up a little more when the van's side door rumbled open and Coop climbed out of the rear compartment. His dark hair curled at the ends. The holes in his Levis showed flashes of tanned skin. He hadn't shaved, and dark stubble ran under his jaw. His shirt was so damp, I could see matted chest hairs beneath the wet cotton.

"I'm sorry to show up unannounced," he said. "I tried to call. But you didn't answer. So I came over."

His husky drawl made me tremble. He looked pretty shaky himself, and I repressed the urge to pull him into the house, wrap him in a wool blanket, and feed him warm apple turnovers. I don't know what it is about me, but I have this need to take care of people.

"I unplugged the phone," I said, then my throat went dry.

He cast an appreciative glance at my figure, but didn't comment about my eye-popping outfit. Sir's stubby tail wagged. He lunged over to Coop, and the leash flew out of my hand.

"Hey, little buddy." Coop's bangs flopped in his eyes as he bent down to scratch the dog's head. An unstoppable love welled up inside me as I remembered another wet morning when Sir had raced into the traffic on East Bay Street. I'd stood on the sidewalk, begging him to come back. Without hesitation, Coop had charged into the road. He'd almost gotten hit by a car, but he'd saved my dog.

The van's horn tooted, and I turned. Emerson flattened her nose against the side window. Behind her, Red gave me a thumb's down sign.

Something is going on. Something bad. I glanced at Coop. "Why is Red here? Did you find Barb?"

Coop shook his head. "Not yet. Red and I went back to her house. Her car and suitcase really are missing. I looked for your phone. Didn't find it, sorry."

"Thanks for trying." My gaze wandered back to Emerson. She licked the window.

Coop raised up. "I got a hold of Barb's husband."

My mind latched on to the phrase *got a hold of.* When Coop is upset, his Georgia accent breaks through the polish that he'd acquired in

England. *Got a hold of* wasn't something you did to a snapping turtle. My throat clenched. Now I knew why he'd come over. He was taking Emerson to Bonaventure. And he'd come to say good-bye.

My hand shook as I unlocked my iron privacy gate and stepped into the brick corridor. I leaned against the wall, just beneath the flickering gaslights. Coop and Sir were right behind me.

"Lester wants me to bring Emerson to his drugstore."

It took me a second to digest that sentence. Lester Philpot was Barb's pharmacist-husband. But why did he want the child brought to his store?

Today was Sunday, and Philpot's Pharmacy was closed.

I spread my hands along the brick wall. "Did you tell Lester what I saw?"

"No."

"Why not? Because it's hearsay?" Me, I was right fond of hearsay. I made illegal U-turns and drove through yellow lights. I lived in the gray zone. Even my front door was gray, and every time Coop passed through it, he seemed to loosen up.

"I told Lester what Barb told me," he said. "That she'd threatened to run away and leave the child. He wasn't surprised."

"But he only knows half of the story," I said. "Your half."

The firm line in Coop's jaw told me that he was doing the best he could. "Lester is arranging a paternity test, so I'll be in Bonaventure for a few days." He touched my arm. "Will you come with me?"

I shook my head. But the warm pressure of his fingers sent a moist flush through my whole body. He must have seen something in my eyes, because his jaw softened. He took my face in his hands.

"Please give me another chance, Teeny. I'll never hurt you again."

Aunt Bluette used to say that picking a man was like selecting a peach, a conscious act, but she was wrong. I couldn't choose who I loved, but I could decide how I wanted to be treated.

"I thought we could stay at your farm and eat peaches," he said.

"I'm not going anywhere," I said, but I did too want to go. I raised my lie tally to twenty-three. Then I felt so ashamed. This wasn't about me, it was about Emerson. I stole a glance in her direction. She drew an angry-smiley face on her window.

Coop's hands fell to his sides. He looked away, but not before I saw tears beaded on his lashes. I had never seen him cry, even when he was six years old and he'd cut his chin on the merry-go-round. I'd held my gloved hand to the wound. He'd been such a tough little guy, but I'd felt his pain as my own and I'd bawled my eyes out. The memory of that day pressed in around me, and I could hardly breathe.

"You had me at peaches," I whispered. This was a Jerry Maguire moment. Lies or no lies, kid or no kid, I was going with him to Georgia.

During the three-hour drive to Bonaventure, Red draped one hand over the steering wheel, his diamond cluster ring catching the morning light. Before he'd become a private investigator, he'd worked cold homicide cases, but the job had given him sleepless nights and high blood pressure.

Coop and I sat in the backseat. Behind us, in the rear of the van, Sir and T-Bone stretched out. Emerson rode shotgun and lectured us about the mating habits of hammerhead sharks. "I saw a real hammerhead at the aquarium," she said. "Its name was Bruce."

"How'd you get a name like Emerson?" Red asked.

She gave him a side-eye glance. "I'm named after a famous essayist. Ask Daddy what it means."

Coop gave me a sheepish look. "Ralph Waldo Emerson is one of my favorite writers."

"One of your favorites, well." I hadn't known this. What other tidbits was he hiding?

Emerson peered around the edge of her seat. "Let's play Me-ography. It's a game, and it'll help me get to know y'all better."

"Sure, kid," Red said. "What're the rules?"

"Describe yourself in five words. It can't be two, like peanut butter or South Carolina. I'll go first. My Me-ography is McDonald's, Chatham, hedgehog, puzzles, iPod."

"Is McDonald's one or two words?" Red chuckled.

"One." She nudged his arm. "Your turn."

He scratched the back of his neck, leaving white marks on the tanned flesh. "Detective, bachelor, fishing, psychology, biscuits."

Emerson peered over her seat. "What about you, Teeny?"

Everything I loved had a slew of words—KitchenAid mixer, bacon drippings, red velvet cake. I thought a minute, then I said, "Peaches, asthma, bulldogs, cakes, truth."

She pointed at Coop. His mouth kicked up into a smile. "Guinness, justice, chocolate, rules, dogs."

"Let's play again," she said. "Only this time, name things that start with an E."

E for Emerson. I was relieved when we finally pulled into Bonaventure. The town fathers had modeled the town after Savannah, and the nine, park-like squares were bordered with historic homes. On the main highway, the old manses had been converted into restaurants and boutiques. Bonaventure's Me-ography would be food, funerals, family, gossip, and church.

Red's forehead puckered as he glanced at the side roads. They spread out in all directions, each one terminating in a park, showing glimpses of statues, fountains, and gazebos.

"I never seen so many freaking streets," he said.

"The avenues run north to south," Coop said. "They're named after U.S. states and big Southern cities."

"Gotcha." Red lifted one hand. "But what about the east-to-west streets?"

"Botanical names," Coop said. "Oleander, hemlock, privet."

I shuddered. All poisonous. Named by my Templeton forebears, a pack of British convicts who'd settled the town, but they'd fallen down the social ladder. My family would have plunged even more if the locals had known about our secret cookbook.

The van sped around Oglethorpe Square, past buildings with wrought-iron balconies and hanging petunia baskets. A crowd stood outside the Whigs and Tories Sports Bar, and farther up the street, a man in a scissors costume walked by the Hair I Am Salon.

"It looks like a little piece of Savannah broke off and drifted west." Red's lips puckered as he steered around a horse-drawn carriage.

"It's quirkier than Savannah," Coop said.

"And no paper mills," I put in.

"Paper schmaper," Emerson said.

Red loved food almost as much as me. So I pointed out a few trendy restaurants in the historic district. "Anthony Bourdain once passed through here," I said. "He called Bonaventure quaint, kooky, and delicious."

"It's a tourist trap." Emerson flipped her hand at the souvenir stores.

Red shrugged. "People gotta buy t-shirts somewhere."

Philpot's Pharmacy stood on the corner of Rowan Street and Philadelphia Avenue, just across the bridge from Oglethorpe Square. Several years ago, the building had been renovated. Green paint had been sprayed over the red bricks, and thick, emerald-tinted windows were installed. The locals had dubbed the building "Oz," which was fitting because Lester was a bit wizard-like. He stood behind a tall desk rather than a curtain, and dispensed cures and unsolicited advice.

I squinted at the windows, trying to see into the store. Lester had been my pharmacist, and in all the years I'd known him, he'd never mentioned Barb or Emerson. He was a self-appointed drug czar, the kind who was suspicious of customers who needed pain pills or sleeping aids. Twice, he'd accused me of abusing my inhaler.

Red angled the van into a parking slot. I shifted my gaze to the door, where a CLOSED sign hung crookedly from the knob.

"Don't stop here." Emerson's fist rose into the air. "Keep going. I command it."

Coop leaned forward. "Honey, we already talked about this. Your father told me to bring you here."

Her eyes brimmed. "Mr. Philpot isn't my dad. You are. And if you leave me here, I'll hunt you down. Then you'll be sorry."

A purple flush ran up the back of Red's neck. For all of his toughness, he hated conflict. "It's too hot to sit here," he said. "Let's buy some groceries and go to Teeny's farm. After lunch we'll call Mr. Philpot."

"Or maybe never." Emerson lowered her fist. "Let's go."

We stopped at Piggly Wiggly, then we drove down Savannah Highway, past swamps, pine forests, hardwoods, and farms. This was the lower coastal plain, Zone 8 on the *Southern Living* gardening map. In this sandy soil, you could grow ginger and date palms and gardenias. Templeton Orchard was the only peach farm in the county, and the highway was jammed with billboards that advertised onions, peanuts, a butterfly hatchery, and PICK YOUR OWN STRAWBERRIES.

The tires shuddered as we drove over the bridge that spanned Connemara Creek. Years ago, Coop and I had fished here, but it looked the same, with cattails and mudflats. Way off in the distance, a flock of white birds skimmed over the water.

"Egrets," Emerson said. "They're monotonous. That means they mate for life."

"You mean monogamous." Red glanced out his window. "But I'm not sure that's true for egrets."

"Is too. The boy egrets bring twigs and stuff to the girls. They make nests. If you don't believe me, call Chatham Academy. They'll tell you about egrets."

Sir poked his damp nose against my arm and shuddered.

Emerson's lips stretched into a wide-open frown, showing pink gums and small teeth. Once again, I was struck by her unusual features. I glanced at Coop—his mouth was plush and sculpted, and not nearly as wide as Emerson's. His upper lip formed an M with well-defined peaks; hers was level. Lester's mouth resembled an anchovy, and Barb's mouth was shaped like a piece of red licorice.

I studied Emerson's expansive, cartoonish lips. Could a smile be inherited? Or was the child going through an awkward growth spurt, which gave the illusion of an overly wide mouth? I touched my own lips and wondered where I'd gotten them. They didn't look like Mama's or Aunt Bluette's. I assumed I'd taken after my dad, but no one knew who he was. According to Mama, he was either a redheaded hashish dealer or a green-eyed proctologist, but neither man had been local.

We drove past the Dairy Queen. I averted my gaze, but not before I saw a ghost of myself, an eight-year-old kid in pigtails holding two dripping cones. I'd stood outside, searching the parking lot for Mama's car, until a policeman took me to Aunt Bluette's farm.

Don't look back. You are so over this, Teeny.

I turned away from the window, trying to shake off the image, but everything was so clear. It had been a hot day. The sun had pushed between my shoulders like melted butter. A burned, curdled smell floated in the air. As the cones melted, white ribbons streamed over my wrists and tapped against the pavement.

I drew in a hitching breath. Coop's hand covered mine, as if he were blotting up that spilled cream. He looked into my eyes.

"How much farther?" Red asked.

"Take the next right," I said.

The van swerved down a gravel lane. Peaches were lined up on both sides like a welcoming committee. He parked in front of a white clapboard house. My pulse beat out a soothing rhythm, *I'm home, home, home.*

The guys opened the back of the van and unloaded the groceries. I ran to the porch, unlocked the front door, and stepped into the foyer. Sweltering air pressed in from all directions. The house had been empty for months, but it smelled the same as always, like country ham and browning biscuits. The welcoming bouquet drew me inside, as if my aunt had put her arms around me.

"This place is icky," Emerson said.

Red climbed onto the porch, a grocery sack in each arm. "Don't worry, kid. You won't be here long."

"Good," she said, but her pewter eyes held a glimmer of fear.

I moved from room to room, turning on air conditioners. Within minutes, cool air spun in eddies, pushing back the peppery heat. I made my way to the sunny kitchen. The old, humpbacked refrigerator was still running. I'd left it clean and empty. I passed by the black cat clock. Its eyes and tail hadn't moved in years, but the time was accurate: one o'clock. I smacked the tail and it whipped back and forth.

Emerson charged through the door, braids swinging. "I'm hungry, Teeny. Fix me something to eat."

"You like hamburgers?"

"Only if they're from McDonald's."

Red squatted beside Emerson. "Sure, kid. We'll feed you. Just tell us your dad's phone number."

"Bite me," she said.

After I put away the groceries, Coop and I walked to the backyard. He piled charcoal bricks into the rusty grill, humming to himself. I couldn't stop looking at his hands. He had sturdy fingers, short nails, and knuckles the size of macadamia nuts. I wanted to press his palm against my cheek. The fear and anger I'd felt last night had gone flat and shiny, too slick to catch. If we'd been alone, I would have reached for his hand, but I could hear Emerson's sassy, strident voice coming from the kitchen.

I looked toward the orchard. Egrets skimmed over the trees, flowing across the sky like spilled cream.

"Emerson's monotonous birds are back," Coop said, grinning. He lit the charcoal, and flames licked up. "Why is she so preoccupied with animal facts?"

"She's keeping her mind busy. That way, she won't think about Barb."

He watched the egrets circle back toward the creek. "Is that why she's got a sharp tongue? Because deep down, she's worried?"

"When dogs are scared, they bite. She's fear-biting. But with words." I'd done that a time or two myself, until Aunt Bluette had filled up the gaping hole that mama had left.

He laced his fingers around my neck. "I'm so glad you came with me. And you've been so kind to Emerson. You really understand children."

"Nah." I shrugged. I just knew how it felt to misplace a mother. I heard a thumping noise. I looked down. Coop's right foot drummed the grass, not an impatient gesture, but a controlled kinesis. Ten deliberate beats with each foot. It went still, and his left foot began tapping. I'd never seen him do this except when his mother called—Miss Irene was soft-spoken, but she could shake him up over silly things.

He leaned back and his forehead puckered. "Maybe I should I call Lester and let him know we're here. I don't want him to accuse us of kidnapping."

"He can't do that. Emerson might be your daughter."

"Lester is her legal parent."

The screen door creaked open and Emerson skipped out, holding a squirt gun that we'd bought her at Piggly Wiggly. Red was right behind her, gripping a platter in one hand. He stepped around us and set the patties on the grill. Flames spiked through the metal rack. He glanced at Emerson. "You, with the pistol. Douse this fire."

Emerson marched to the grill and aimed her gun. A glistening strand of water arced through the air and hit the coals. They hissed and smoke boiled up.

"Maybe you got a future as a fireman," Red told her.

She tucked the gun in her pocket. "I don't want a blue-collar career. I'm going to be a volcanologist and live in Iceland."

"That's a big word for a little girl," Red said.

"Huh, I'm not little. I've got a big brain. I know everything."

"Yeah?" He hunkered beside her and tugged her braid. "Do you remember what happened last night?"

"I went to my new dad's house and ate jalapeño dip."

I drew in a sharp breath. Why was Red quizzing her? He had an associate degree in psychology, but I wasn't sure if he knew how a child's mind worked.

"What about before?" he asked. "At your mom's place. Did she tuck you in bed?"

"She never does that."

"You didn't hear her leave?"

"Nope. My iPod was blasting."

The kitchen phone rang. Each short, decisive trill made me wonder how the gossips had figured out that I'd returned to the farm—with two men and a ten-year-old. I stepped into the kitchen and lifted the receiver.

"Hi, Teeny. This is Lester Philpot." His voice had a sour edge, making me think of pickle relish. "I heard you were back in town. And before you ask how I know, one of my loyal customers saw you and Mr. O'Malley at Piggly Wiggly."

"We stopped by your pharmacy earlier," I said.

"Sorry I missed y'all. I had an emergency." He paused. "Barb has passed on."

"Passed on?" Part of me knew what he meant, but another part imagined a BMW speeding past the minivans on I-16.

"Dead." Lester blew out a sigh. "She killed herself."

five

I lowered the phone to my chest and bent over, forcing myself to breathe. Barb had killed herself? No, not possible. I pictured that night on Sullivan's Island, her white caftan billowing around her long legs. She would never kill herself. What had happened after the guy in the Bill Clinton mask had chased me? Had he gone back to the rental to finish strangling Barb? I could totally see this happening. But what had he done with her body?

"Teeny?" Lester's voice rose up from the receiver. "Are you still there? Hello?"

I pushed the phone against my ear. "I'm here. But I'm in shock. Barb's really dead?"

"Yes, we're all stunned," Lester said in a dry-as-Georgia-dirt voice.

I didn't want to pry, but I had to know more. "What makes you think she killed herself?"

"She left a note. Blaming me, of course. She must not have been thinking clearly, or she couldn't have ended her life at the Motel 6 in Sweeney, Georgia."

That rat hole? Sweeney was a speck of a town on Highway 25, about thirty miles south of Bonaventure, noted for Vidalia onions and crystal meth. If Barb really had killed herself, wouldn't she have picked a grand hotel in Charleston? Or even a cozy bed-and-breakfast in Bonaventure? Why would she drive to Sweeney?

Maybe she hadn't. Maybe the masked guy had gone back to her house. Maybe he'd squeezed her neck for four minutes. He could have tossed her body into the truck of her car. Serial murderers did this all the time. Still, he'd picked a strange place to dispose of her body. The land between Charleston and Sweeney was filled with wetlands. Wouldn't it have been easier to dump her in a marsh?

I almost blurted my theories, but I stopped myself. I couldn't tell him about Bill Clinton, not without discussing it with Coop. Not without incriminating my damn self.

"I've got to plan my wife's funeral," Lester said. "Please tell Mr. O'Malley that I pulled a few strings for the DNA test. Georgia Genetics will swab Emerson tomorrow morning at my drugstore. The problem is, I don't have time to fetch her tonight. I'd send my mother, but she's in a tennis tournament. Can Emerson spend the night with you?"

"Why, of course."

"I knew I could count on you. Just bring her to the pharmacy at seven thirty in the morning. We'll need Mr. O'Malley's saliva, too. One more thing. Don't tell Emerson about her mother. Or the test. She'll run away. She's done it before."

"I won't." My feet prickled, as if ants were biting my ankles. The sensation spread up the backs of my thighs, changing into a pants-on-fire burn. I kicked out my leg. No ants. No bites. Nothing but nerves and shock.

I didn't remember hanging up the phone. The air turned grainy, swarming with tiny black dots, as if the ants had sprouted wings and were flying out of my ears and mouth. Had Barb really and truly killed herself?

A sick feeling waved over me. Bile hit the back of my throat. I darted to the sink, yanking the phone cord behind me, and spit into the stainless-steel bowl.

The screen door creaked open, and warm air blew into the kitchen, smelling of hickory smoke. Red gripped a platter of hamburger patties, each one scored with grill marks. He set the dish on the counter, then he turned his pockets inside out. "You seen my handcuffs?"

Coop stepped around him, carrying the buns. "You probably left them in the van."

"They were right here." Red squinted at me. "Sheesh, are you okay? Your face is green."

Coop put the buns on the table and glanced at me, his brow puckering. "What's wrong?"

"Barb's dead." As I repeated my conversation with Lester, Coop leaned against the counter, looking a little green himself. The screen door opened, and Emerson skipped into the room, trailed by the dogs.

"If I eat a mad cow burger, will you take me to McDonald's?" She tossed the water pistol onto the counter and twirled around.

No one answered. Red piled lettuce and onions on his hamburger. Coop rubbed his face.

"Sure, we'll take you," I said.

"Pinkie swear me." She hooked her little finger around mine. "Break your promise and I'll take a contract out on you."

Coop lowered his hands. "Teeny doesn't break promises."

"You should bronze her. When y'all finish eating, come get me." She grabbed a burger and ran back outside with the dogs.

Red lifted the mustard jar. "Poor kid. She don't know what's coming."

Coop walked to the door and shut it. "I can't believe Barb killed herself. Maybe we should call the Sweeney police department."

Red nodded. "Good idea, Boss."

I handed Coop the phone book, then I left the room. I didn't want to know the details of Barb's death. I wanted to believe that she had regained consciousness and decided she'd teach everyone a lesson. Then maybe she'd driven to Sweeney and mixed pills with alcohol, an accidental death.

I put one hand on my stomach. I felt jittery inside, like I'd swallowed tadpoles. I forced myself to think of practical matters. Emerson was spending the night in an icky house. I had three bedrooms: one downstairs, and two on the second floor. I needed to dust, put clean sheets on the beds, and crank up the other air conditioners.

I ran up the stairs and pulled linen from the hall closet. I passed by the hall window and saw Emerson run across the backyard, her braids bouncing on her shoulders. I thought about pushing open the window and telling her about the birding hot spots. The orchard was home to the endangered red-cockaded woodpecker. She'd like that. But I couldn't pull in a breath. My throat was no bigger than a saffron thread. Emerson thought her mama would come back to her. Tomorrow she would learn the truth from Lester. Until then, I could only offer soft words, a feather pillow, and a Happy Meal.

Gripping the sheets to my chest, I walked to the end of the hall, past Mama's old art gallery. I stopped in front of a giant replica of *The Last Supper.* Mama's Jesus bore a strong resemblance to Elvis Presley, with Colonel Parker and Joe Esposito as disciples. Scattered on the table in front of them was fried chicken, cheeseburgers, mashed potatoes, peanut-butter-and-banana sandwiches.

I opened the door to Mama's door and turned on the air conditioner. Musty air kicked up the plaid curtains. I'd only spent eight years with Ruby Ann. Most of that time had been unbearable for us both, yet her loss had been palpable, a living thing, like a benign tumor that grows just beneath the skin, hard and inoperable.

No, Teeny. Don't think about that. Think about all the food you'll cook. The peaches were ripe and juicy, brimming with sweetness, just begging to be made into a salsa. It's an easy recipe. Peel and chop peaches. Add chopped red bell pepper, diced onion, minced garlic, and jalapeños. Chopped cilantro gives a fresh zing. Mix ingredients with oil and vinegar. A pinch of salt brings out the flavor. Serve with pork-and-pepper tacos.

Dust swirled up as I stripped Mama's walnut bed. The filaments drifted past the wall mural that featured PG-rated sketches of the King. Emerson couldn't sleep here. I hurried across the hall, into my old room. It was the same as ever. Twin beds with white ruffled pillow shams and log cabin quilts. Bookcases stuffed with cookbooks. Mama's paintings hung on the walls, normal pictures of layer cakes and meringue-topped pies.

I made up the beds, then I ran down to the kitchen. Coop was still on the phone, but Red filled me in. "Nine thirty this morning, a maid found Barb's body hanging from the shower rod. I don't know the actual time of death. But we should hear something soon. The Sweeney coroner is fast-tracking the autopsy."

"Why?" I sat down at the table and folded my hands.

Red shrugged. "Apparently the coroner has a golf game."

Emerson burst into the kitchen. "Someone take me to McDonald's right now or I'll do something bad."

I didn't want the dogs roaming around the house until I'd scoured the rooms for toxic items. When you own a pet, you have to dog-proof, because ordinary things like raisins and onions are fatal to canines. If T-Bone or Sir found my ancient stash of chocolate, I'd never forgive myself. I lured the dogs into the parlor. It was a cozy, old fashioned room. A carved settee. Piano. Old hi-fi. Nothing that could hurt a dog. I firmly latched the pocket doors, hurried onto the porch, and locked up.

Ten minutes later, Red angled the van into the McDonald's parking lot. Emerson dove into the backseat and grabbed Coop's arm. "Daddy, will you sit next to me?"

He smiled, his eyes crinkling at the edges. "I was fixing to ask you the same thing."

A lot of guys wouldn't be this accommodating to a bratty kid, even one who'd lost her mother, but Coop wasn't just any guy.

Emerson scarfed down two Happy Meals and a vanilla shake. In between bites, she quizzed us. "Which animal is *not* in the Bible?" she asked, dangling a fry over her head.

"Hamsters," Coop said.

"Y'all need to go to church. Cats are the *only* animals not in the Bible." She dropped the fry into her mouth.

"What about mountain gorillas?" Red asked.

• • •

On the drive home, Emerson kept yawning. When the van pulled up to the farmhouse, she flung open her door and jumped into the gravel.

"Wait, honey, the door's locked," I called, fumbling in my purse for the key.

She ignored me and sprinted toward the porch. Coop helped me out of the van, and a gust of wind filled my striped skirt, shaping it into a bell.

Emerson pushed open the front door and ran inside. The dogs trotted onto the porch and shot down the steps. T-Bone loped in circles, but Sir waddled over to me and rubbed his flat face against my legs.

Red pointed at the door. "I thought you locked up, homegirl."

My stomach tightened. "I did."

"Maybe the wind blew it open," Coop said, draping his arm around me.

It was indeed a blustery night. The trees moved against the dusky sky, the heavy branches whispering like ladies in church. T-Bone's ears perked and he gazed off into the shadowy orchard. I looked, too. A ripple of light cut through the tall buffalo grass. T-Bone padded into the clearing, his fur bristling.

"Don't you go chasing rabbits," Coop told him.

Red's hand dropped to his holster. "That's no rabbit."

Way off in the shadows, the light bobbed. A grainy shape darted between the trees. It was a man. And he was running toward the creek. T-Bone sprinted into the weeds. Sir was right behind him, but I drew him back. "You're no match for a burglar," I told him. Just saying that word made me sick.

Red pulled out his Glock. In the distance, a human howl rose up. The light zigzagged violently, bouncing against the trees, then it dropped and went still. A few seconds later, the beam levitated from the weeds and moved toward the house in a quivering dazzle.

"It ain't the prowler," Red said. "The light is too low."

A blinding radiance cut through the buffalo grass. T-Bone ran into the clearing with a flashlight in his mouth. He dropped it at Coop's feet.

"Sheesh." Red shoved the Glock into the holster.

Coop snatched the light and aimed it at the trees. No movement. Nothing.

Sir twisted around, trying to escape. Coop passed the beam over the orchard again. "Teeny, you ever had prowlers before?"

"Someone broke in last December. Aunt Bluette was in the hospital." I let go of Sir and stood, brushing dirt off my skirt. "A guy stole her pain pills and a portable TV."

"I'm checking the backyard." Red waved at the house. "Y'all go in and see if anything's missing."

My heart pounded as I followed Coop to the porch. The dogs padded behind us, their nails scritch-scratching on the cypress planks. Coop bent down to examine the door. The lock was intact, and the wood didn't have gouges or scratch marks.

"You've got a spring lock," he said, and pointed at the knob. "A credit card could pop it open."

We went inside and checked the rooms. Nothing was disheveled. Aunt Bluette's Hummels and Precious Moments figurines were lined up in the curio cabinet.

"Maybe he didn't come into the house," Coop said.

"Yes, he did." I pointed to the pocket doors. I'd closed them before we'd left and now they stood ajar.

"I bet T-Bone nudged them open," Coop said. "He's an escape artist. I should've named him Houdini."

While Coop circled through the rest of the house, I went upstairs to check on Emerson. She sat on my old bed, unbraiding her hair. The stuffed hedgehog lay on the ruffled pillow. I glanced around the room. Either the prowler was a neatnik or he hadn't entered this room.

"Why was T-Bone barking?" she asked.

The truth would scare her, but I didn't want to lie, either. I felt my "oh shit" smile snap into place. "He was chasing something."

"Stupid dog." Emerson sighed. "I'd love to chitchat, but it's been a long, crappy day and I'm sleepy."

I knew she wanted me to go, but I lingered in the doorway. "You want a glass of warm milk?"

"Ick, no." She turned on her iPod and reached for the earphones. I wanted to put my arms around her and hold her the way Aunt Bluette had held me, but all I said was, "I'll be downstairs if you need me."

"As if."

I found Coop in the kitchen. "Emerson's fine," I said, though he hadn't asked.

"But you aren't," he said. "You're shaking all over. Should I get your inhaler?"

"I'm fine, really." Our eyes met. The air between us was spiked with electrical charges, and we stepped toward each other. Coop wrapped his arms around me. The heat from his body radiated through his thin cotton shirt, flooding me with a warm sweetness. I rested my cheek against his shoulder. It felt just right, solid and sheltering. And I knew that I'd already forgiven him for not telling me about Barb. Like Aunt Bluette used to say, "Nobody's perfect. When you forgive others, you forgive yourself." I think maybe she got that from Dr. Phil, but it was true.

Footsteps clapped in the hallway. Coop and I broke apart. Red strode into the kitchen, his cheeks flushed. "You missing anything, Teeny?"

"No. Everything's fine."

"I bet it was a kid. He probably thought the house was unoccupied." Red's voice sounded blunt, as if he'd sanded the edges of each word. He grabbed a beer from the fridge and twisted off the metal cap. "Big day tomorrow. What happens after the DNA test, Boss? You and Teeny gonna stick around and wait for the results?"

I walked to the sink and folded a tea towel. I wished I could be more like Red, moving effortlessly between prowlers and practical matters.

I felt the pressure of Coop's hand on my elbow. "What do you think, Teeny? You want to stay in Bonaventure?"

"That would be nice." I wasn't in a hurry to get back to Charleston. I had plenty to think about. If Coop was Emerson's dad, would I be a part of her life? Would she ever warm up to me? If so, I shouldn't buy The Picky Palate Café. If Coop needed my help, I'd be there. Just deciding this made me feel calmer.

Red took a swig of beer, then he sniffed his armpits. "Does this house have a shower?"

"Upstairs," I said. "First door on your right. Your bedroom room is across the hall. Hope you like Elvis. You're sleeping with him."

"You got 'the King' hid in the closet, girlie?" He winked. Then he went upstairs.

Coop put his arms around me. "Your heart is beating so fast. Are you still worried about the prowler?"

"No." It was the truth. My pulse always went haywire when I smelled pine, cotton, and Aqua di Parma.

"We need to talk," he said.

"About what?" I drew back, expecting to hear more bad news.

"Marry me," he said.

I stopped breathing. How many times had I fantasized about this? A ring dropped into a champagne glass, a band playing our song, a man on bended knee. He'd said the right words at the worst possible time. Barb was dead, and her daughter was upstairs in Aunt Bluette's room.

He pulled a black velvet box from his pocket and raised the lid, revealing the biggest diamond I'd ever seen. It was round, bracketed by two pearls.

I glanced up. Something didn't feel right about this. "You just happened to have an engagement ring in your pocket?"

"It was in my suitcase. I fetched it when you checked on Emerson."

I stared back down at the diamond. "When did you buy it?"

"I didn't. See, it's my grandmother's ring. An O'Malley heirloom. I'd wanted to give it to you yesterday during lunch. But everything went crazy."

"It still is."

"We can't wait until our lives settle down. Because they might not. When we find a quiet moment, we've got to take it."

My lips cracked into an "oh shit" smile. I wanted those moments, too.

But I was scared that marriage would ruin all the good things we had. I was even more scared of myself, of all of the pits and holes and quirks that I kept hidden inside me.

Before I could protest, he slid the ring onto my finger. The diamond swung around, heavy as an ice cube, and knocked against my pinkie.

"Maybe you can wear it on a chain until you have it resized," he said.

A chain? My throat narrowed. I was totally going to ruin this moment. But I had to speak my mind. "I need to think about this," I said in a croaky voice.

"Take all the time you want. No matter what you decide, I want you to have this ring."

"Oh, I couldn't. It's an heirloom."

"I want you to have it. I'll never love another woman the way I love you."

A question had been sitting in the back of my head since last night. "Why?"

"Do you really have to ask?" A smile broke over his mouth. "I love how you hum to yourself when you ice a cake. I love how your hand feels in mine. I love your kind ways, and that little gap between your front teeth. I'm a flawed man, but I love you, Teeny. And I always will."

His hands skimmed my cheekbones. A shiver ran down my neck. My heart pounded against my chest wall. This ring was more than jewelry or an heirloom; it was an emotional U-turn for him. My Coop was moving deeper and deeper into gray areas.

I wanted to say, *Yes, I'll marry you*, but I couldn't shape the words. My hesitancy wasn't about him. It wasn't about love. It was about me. Marriage wasn't like a chicken casserole, a recipe you made every Friday night until you, or your partner, got sick of it. Then you cooked something more exotic, like Shrimp Belvedere. Unlike food, a marriage ought to last forever. That's a lot to ask for nowadays, but I still wanted it.

My mama would have said, *Quit thinking about recipes. Shut up and kiss him.*

So that's exactly what I did.

six

Early the next morning, clouds gathered over the orchard, and the air held a metallic bite. I didn't want to lose Coop's ring, so I put it on a gold chain that I found in my old jewelry box.

When I stepped into the foyer, he lifted my hand. He didn't ask about the ring, but I could tell he was worried.

"It's right here." I reached inside my collar and lifted the chain. The diamond swung down like a wrecking ball. I'd just tucked it back into my collar when Red came down the staircase, smoothing his wiry hair.

"Sheesh, I just lied to the kid. She thinks we're going to McDonald's for breakfast."

I stepped closer. "Maybe we should tell her the truth."

Coop caught my arm. "Lester said she'd run away."

"What the hell." Red pulled out his keys. "It's a lose-lose situation for everybody."

Ten minutes later, the four of us got into the van. I scooted across the backseat and leaned against Coop. Emerson climbed in next to Red. She looked spiffy in a red polka-dotted sun suit.

"After we eat breakfast, let's buy a satellite dish," she said. "I'm missing *Shark Week*."

"We'll see, kid. A muscle twitched in Red's cheek. He turned onto

Oglethorpe Square, where the Monday morning traffic moved sluggishly around a horse-drawn buggy.

Emerson smoothed her pigtails. "Hammerheads eat squid."

"They also eat other sharks," Red said.

He drove over the metal bridge. Straight ahead, the pharmacy stood out against the leaden sky, the windows glowing with an eerie green light. The wind stirred the poisonous oleanders that lined the sidewalk in front of the store, and white petals skated down the pavement.

A Georgia Genetics van was parked near the corner. Red pulled in beside it.

"Why are we stopping here?" Emerson sat up straight. "You said we were having breakfast."

"We will." Red squeezed the steering wheel. "Afterward."

"After what?" She spun around, glaring at me and Coop. "What's going on?"

"Your daddy asked us to bring you here," Coop said.

"Again?" She pounded her fist against the roof of the van. "You tricked me!"

"I'm the one who lied, kid," Red said.

She whipped her head around. "You poo-poo head."

I squeezed Coop's hand, a "quick, do something" gesture.

He sat up straight. "Lester arranged a special test, one that will show if I'm your real dad. A technician will swab the inside of your cheek. Mine too. Don't be afraid. It'll feel just like a lollypop."

The fierce gleam in her eyes told me that Emerson Philpot wasn't scared of Q-tips or strange men. She was petrified of not being loved.

"I know lots and lots about DNA," she said. "I better not be Mr. Philpot's child. I can't stand him. He takes me for granite."

Red's lips twitched. "Granite's a stone, kid."

"Don't call me that. I'm not a baby goat. And I'm *not* letting anyone take my spit."

Red lifted her out of the front seat, ignoring her pitiful screeches. He carried her into the store. Two men in lab coats waited beside the old-fashioned soda fountain. One guy was bald and sunburned, and his hands hung down like boiled lobsters. The other man had flat, flounder-like feet.

Emerson immediately hushed when Lester strutted down the aisle. He looked like an Abercrombie & Fitch advertisement. His khakis had knife-sharp pleats. His narrow face was dominated by a tall forehead that put mine to shame. His bulging hazel eyes zeroed in on Emerson.

She curtsied, her fists extended. Then two index fingers jutted up.

"Stop making those gestures," Lester said.

She tucked her hands behind her back. "Where's Mrs. Philpot?"

"We'll discuss that later, sugar."

"When can I go back to Chatham Academy?"

"Soon." Lester tugged one of his butterfly-shaped ears. "Real soon."

My stomach cramped. We'd waited too long to tell her about Barb. When Emerson found out we'd withheld the news, she'd feel even more betrayed. *You can't lie to a child,* Aunt Bluette used to say.

Emerson darted to a counter, grabbed an umbrella, and swung it dangerously close to a Preparation H display. "I want an Egg McMuffin and a latte."

"You're too young for lattes." Lester pulled a handkerchief out of his pocket and patted his glistening forehead. "But I'll buy you a McMuffin if you let these nice men swab your mouth."

"No." She pushed the tip of the umbrella into the display, and three Preparation H boxes toppled to the floor.

"Sugar, the swab test isn't painful," Lester said, but he winced dramatically, causing Emerson to recoil. What was wrong with him? And why wasn't Coop taking up for her? He just stood there, looking off to the side. We had the opposite problem of King Solomon and the two mothers. If anyone offered to split Emerson down the middle, neither Coop nor Lester would object.

Oh, come on, Teeny. Offer to adopt her.

Coop lifted his finger. "Excuse me, but is this a court-ordered test?"

"Mr. O'Malley, I'm not any happier to see you than you are to see me. I'm quite aware that you're an attorney. But a court order isn't mandatory. If the results are in your favor, I won't fight you for custody. Nor will I seek financial compensation for the last ten years and nine months."

I blinked. Didn't he know Emerson was listening? My throat burned as I choked down a slew of angry words. Not too long ago, I'd promised Jesus I'd try to be a better person, but I wanted to tie Lester to a chair and feed him Cuckoopint Cobbler, made from noxious berries that caused diarrhea and projectile vomiting.

Emerson's jaw moved convulsively, as if she were chewing ice. "Don't talk about me like I'm not here. Just for that, you're not getting my spit."

Lester's cheeks turned pink. "Don't make me sedate you."

"I'd like to see you try." She swung the umbrella, and more boxes tumbled to the floor.

The flounder man shuffled forward. "It's not an invasive test. We'll just collect a buccal sample—that's the inside of your cheek. We'll just swab it and it'll be over in a second."

Emerson dropped the umbrella. "Can I try it on you?"

"Why, certainly." The technician smiled, showing crooked teeth, each one lapped against the other like slate shingles.

Emerson walked over to him and plucked the swab from his hand. "Bend over, Mister. I'm just gonna cram this doohickey up your craw. It'll be over in a second."

"Stop acting like a monkey," Lester said. "Apologize to the nice man."

"No. He looks just like Hannibal Lecture." Emerson put her hands over her eyes.

"You pronounced it wrong," Lester said grimly. "Now get over here and open your Grand Canyon mouth."

Emerson slammed her head against Coop's stomach. "Daddy, help me. The lambs are screaming! Make them stop!"

Red snorted. One side of Coop's mouth slanted up, like he was holding back a grin. He patted Emerson's shoulder.

"Stop laughing," Lester said. "You're just encouraging her."

Didn't he see how scared she was? I crouched beside her. She lifted her face from Coop's shirt and winked.

"I saw that," Lester cried. "She's just like her mother, a drama queen."

Emerson moved away from Coop and scowled at Lester. "You're a drag queen!"

God, I loved this girl.

"Stop the theatrics." Lester turned to the technicians and snapped his fingers. "Let's get this over with. Fix another swab."

The techs prepared another kit. Lester sat on the edge of a stool and parted his lips. I imagined Barb's tongue inside his mendacious mouth and I felt sick.

"Next," the technician called.

Emerson sucked in her cheeks. Before the adults could react, she pushed over the Preparation H display and shot out the door. A blast of clammy air swept up the aisle and stirred the sale banners that hung from the ceiling.

Lester drummed his fingers on the counter. "I *knew* this would happen."

"Shouldn't we go after her?" Coop moved toward the door. Lester vaulted off the stool and stepped in his path.

"Don't trouble yourself," Lester said. "You might as well go after a typhoon. You'll never find her. When things don't go Emerson's way, she runs off. She'll be fine, trust me."

He walked to the ruined Preparation H display. "Look at this mess."

My chest felt too tight. I didn't doubt Emerson's ability to hide. I was worried about the slippery roads. What if she darted in front of a car? Or ran into someone she knew? I knew how gossip worked in this town. By now, the news about Barb would have made the rounds. Someone might offer their condolences to Emerson. I couldn't let her hear about Barb that way.

"A ten-year-old girl is missing!" I cried.

"No, she's hiding. Big difference." Lester faced the back of his store. "Kendall? I need you to fix the hemorrhoid display."

Do something, Jesus. Please give Lester a rectal fistula.

He turned back to the technicians. "How much longer can you boys wait?"

The lobster guy frowned at his clipboard. "Fifteen minutes," he said in a "be here or else" voice.

"I'll find Emerson," Coop said. "Red, give me your keys."

Red handed him a key chain. Coop kissed my cheek and ran out the door. Lester sighed and lifted a box. "He's not a hero. He's just stupid."

I couldn't hold back another second. "You're more concerned about a hemorrhoid display than your missing daughter."

"Go ahead, cut me down. But I'm a decent person. I'm not having a ménage à trois at a peach farm. Like *some* people."

In the rear of the pharmacy, a door opened, showing a glimpse of a stock room, the shelves overflowing with Halloween merchandise. Plastic pumpkins, costumes, and fake tombstones. A petite girl with spiked black hair stepped through the door. She had pale, freckled skin, the kind that burned and never tanned. Pinned to her shirt was a plastic name tag: KENDALL MCCORMACK, CASHIER. The last time I'd seen her, she'd been Emerson's age. I'd been her babysitter. Now Kendall had D-cup breasts and a frog tattoo on her right arm.

"Reach me that box," Lester said, snapping his fingers at her.

"Why, I'd be happy to." She stepped in front of him and leaned over, giving him a full view of her black thong.

"I ain't sticking around for this sideshow," Red whispered in my ear. "Let's me and you take a quick look around the building. The kid can't have gotten far."

But Kendall had overheard us. She straightened up, then she plucked a vinyl poncho from the shelf and handed it to me. "I'd hate for you to get wet, Teeny."

"Don't I get one, too?" Red asked.

She ignored him and leaned over, giving Lester another X-rated view. Red marched out of the store. I pulled on the rain gear and ran after him.

"Good luck," Lester called in a snotty voice. "You'll need it."

Red and I passed a shoe store. The rain blew sideways, flattening the azaleas and banana trees. Traffic had pulled off to the side of Pennsylvania Avenue. We rushed between the cars, our shoes filling with water. We crossed over to Rowan Street and gazed toward the bridge, where muddy water churned around the steel pilings.

I grabbed Red's arm and my fingers slid down his damp flesh. "You don't think she fell into the river?"

"Nah, she's hiding somewhere." He wiped his palm over the glass dial of his watch. "We got thirteen minutes to find her. Then the DNA guys will leave."

We slogged past the bridge and headed down Hyacinth Avenue, past Dickens's Books, where the store's cat, Pip, stared out the rain speckled window.

"We need a freaking Amber Alert," Red said.

I thought of the river again, and I let out a pre-asthma hitch. I'd left my pocketbook on the counter, and my inhaler was tucked inside. But I'd lose precious time if I ran back to the pharmacy. I drew in a mouthful of watery air and forced it down my throat.

Red tugged the edge of my poncho. "You need your inhaler. Let's head back."

"No, let's keep going."

"She don't even like you."

"But *I* like *her*."

"No, you pity her."

"Her mother's dead. Her legal father is an asshole. And, she might be Coop's child."

Red scraped his hand over his face, flinging off water. "But she ain't yours."

I reeled backward. If he'd slapped me, I couldn't have been more hurt. "No, she isn't. But I know how it feels to be alone."

"Oh, I get it," he said. "You're identifying with the kid. She's motherless. Just like you."

I shook my head. He didn't understand the first thing about me. I did want children, a child army, and I didn't care if they were bios or adopted.

"I've made peace with my mama," I said. "I'm just trying to find Emerson before she drowns."

"You're setting yourself up for heartache. What will you do if she's Philpot's kid? He won't let you be Aunt Teeny."

"He might."

"You can't fix your hurt places by trying to fix hers."

"That's not what I'm doing."

"Yes, it is."

I lifted my fist. "Don't head shrink me, Red Butler Hill."

"It's Red to my friends, girlie. You know that."

We trudged around the block, checking every alley, and circled back to Pennsylvania Avenue. The rain had slowed and the air smelled fresh, but the thickness of it made it even harder to breathe.

Red looked at his watch again. "We've got fifty-nine seconds until the techs split."

I struggled to pull in a breath, my shoulders heaving. "I don't care about the DNA test. I just want to find her. She could be in danger."

"You're endangering yourself. You're almost in respiratory arrest." He grabbed my shoulders and steered me toward Pennsylvania Avenue. "Come on, girlie. We've still got one minute."

seven

The rain stopped while we walked back to the pharmacy. The Georgia Genetics van was gone. I cut around Red and hurried into the store. Lester was gone. Kendall sat on a stool, flipping through *Brides* magazine. "You all find Emerson?" she asked without looking up.

"Negative," Red said.

"No one ever does." Kendall licked her finger and turned a page. "Lester got called away. Something about the funeral. He said to tell you that he'd set up another DNA test."

I couldn't answer because my throat was closing. I grabbed my purse, dragged out my inhaler, and took a puff.

Kendall flipped another page. "Your boyfriend called. He had a flat tire and he's waiting for Triple A. I'm supposed to give you all a ride home."

The leather screaked as she slid off the stool. She pulled a Hello Kitty key ring from her pocket. "Most of these keys are Lester's," she said, her face swelling with pride.

"He must trust you," Red said.

"Yeah, I'm the only one he trusts. He even let me pick the code to his burglar alarm. It's my birth date—ain't that cool? My car's out back. It's brand-new, a black Mazda. You all go on. Just let me tell Norris I'm leaving."

"I'm here," a deep, nasal voice said.

I turned, and a tall, gaunt man glided forward. His eyes were pale green, the size of guinea eggs, and they bulged from their sockets. He lifted a bony, raptor-like hand and swiped it over his broad forehead.

"I'm Dr. Norris Philpot," he said. He spoke as if his mouth were filled with grapes, and he pronounced Norris like Norrith, squishing the Ss. "Didn't you used to work at Hoot-erth?"

I nodded. Years ago I'd waited tables at Hooters. "I'm surprised you remember me."

"I ate there every Friday night." His lips parted, and a glossy strand of saliva stretched between them. "I tipped you extra."

Kendall jingled her keys. "I hate to rush you all, but we need to scoot."

Red looked relieved and pushed me toward the back door. Norris blocked my way. He gave me a bordering-on-seductive smile that triggered my gag reflex. "What are you doing thith Friday night?" he asked.

"I'm busy." I shook my head. "Sorry."

"Name the day and I'm yourth."

I was too startled to answer. I let out a fake wheeze and grabbed my inhaler to cover my revulsion.

Red nudged him aside. "She's got a boyfriend."

"I'm talking to Teeny, not you." Norris twisted around him and gripped my shoulder. "What about tomorrow night? We could thee a movie and go dancing."

While he talked, his raptor claw kneaded my flesh. It felt creepy, and I shrank back.

"Hey, let her go." Red's voice carried a switchblade-edge.

"Thay out of it," Norris said.

"Move your hand, athhole," Red said.

Norris's claw rose from my shoulder. He pointed at Kendall. "Get that rattlethnake out of here."

Kendall talked nonstop while she drove toward the farm. "I used to babysit Emerson," she said. "What a brat."

"I thought she went to a private school," Red said.

"She came home on holidays and for two weeks every summer. Lester was so impressed with me, he hired me to be his cashier. But I do a little of everything. I'm his right-hand man."

Red chuckled. "I just bet you are."

"When Lester and I get married, I'll make Emerson go to a public school. It was good enough for me. Besides, she needs a home life."

I sat up straight. Kendall and Lester were getting married? Was she making this up? Or were they having an affair? Why would a cute girl get mixed up with a self-righteous pharmacist? He was twice her age. And, until Barb's death, he'd been married.

Red stiffened. "You having a fling with Philpot?"

"Kinda. Sorta." She slapped her graduation tassel, and the blue threads jiggled.

"Can you define kinda-sorta?" Red asked.

"I haven't slept with him," Kendall said.

"So it's a platonic thing?" I asked.

"Platonic?" She looked confused. "Is that a type of enema?"

"An affair," I clarified. "Romance minus the sex."

"I guess Lester and me are platonic. But we know each other in itty-bitty biblical ways."

"What would you call itty?" I asked.

"I can't tell you in front of a man." She shot a wary glance at Red. "But I can assure you that I haven't sinned."

"Of course not." Red made an obscene hand gesture.

Kendall pressed her lips together, and her jaws clenched as if she were grinding hard candy. "For your information, Mr. Man, I know what the Bible says about fornication. And Lester and me haven't gone that far. I'm saving myself for marriage."

Right, I thought, remembering the peep show she'd put on for him by the hemorrhoid display. I wasn't interested in sin. I wanted to hear about her relationship with Emerson.

"I'm the very opposite of Barb," Kendall said. "She slept with anything. Why, she even banged my cousin. He laid her carpet and then she laid him. If she saw a dick, she'd hop on and ride. That's why everybody called her the Train."

She'd spoken about the Train in the past tense, as if Barb had died months ago. I leaned forward. "Has Lester told you what happened to his wife?"

"Yes, and I was so shocked. Can you imagine hanging yourself with panty hose? What was she thinking? Only fat ladies wear hose in the summertime."

Red's eyes narrowed. "Is that how she did it?"

"That's what Lester said." Kendall glanced over her shoulder and grinned at me. "It's so good to see you again, Teeny. Remember that time you babysat me and I lost a tampon up inside me? A lot of people would have laughed. But you drove me to Dr. O'Malley and he took it out. I appreciate how you took me seriously. So I'm gonna give you a hint. I saw how Norris was eyeing you. Which isn't surprising. He used to be an eye doctor. But he lost his medical license, and he's kinda dangerous."

Red snorted. "What did he do?"

"Oh, I can't tell you that. I'd die of embarrassment. If you want to know what happened, talk to Zee Greer. She works at Baskin-Robbins. Just stay away from Norris. He's a bad skirt chaser. But that's all I'm gonna say. I can't speak ill of my future brother-in-law."

Kendall lapsed into silence. Ten minutes later, she swerved down my driveway. Gravel pinged against the fenders, like bullets hitting a tin can.

After she left, I walked onto the porch. The storm had left behind a glossy dampness and water still dripped from the eaves. I groped inside my purse for the house key. From the corner of my vision, something red streaked across the porch. The wooden glider jerked, then it banged against the side of the house.

"Who's there?" I yelled.

Red lunged onto the porch so fast, he bumped into the glider. It wobbled backward, the chains squeaking, and surged forward. In the middle of the seat, a puddle of water skated across the wood and dripped over the edge of the swing, the drops scattering in all directions, fine and prickly, like needles.

Emerson stepped around the corner of the house, her polka-dot dress stuck to her legs. "It's just me," she said in a small voice.

"Jesus, kid," Red cried.

"We've been out of our minds over you," I said. "How'd you get here?"

"Hitched a ride with an old lady." Emerson squeezed her braids, and water dribbled down. "She had a cast on her wrist for carpool tunnel syndrome."

Red lifted his hands above his head. "Why'd you run, kid?"

"Because I felt like it." She stuck out her tongue.

"Lester will get your DNA," Red said.

"Not unless he traps me and gives me roofies."

She knew about roofies? I unlocked the door and stepped into the foyer. Sir and T-Bone pranced around me, pausing to sniff my dress and shoes. Once again, they'd escaped from the parlor.

Emerson's teeth clicked. "Burr, it's cold in this house. I better put on dry clothes or I'll catch Ebola." She darted past the curio cabinet and up the stairs, setting Aunt Bluette's Precious Moments figurines to trembling.

I started after her, but Red pulled me back. "Let her go, homegirl."

"Shouldn't we let Lester know that she's safe?"

"Like he cares. Give Kendall a chance to drive back to the store and call her. She'll be more than happy to pass the message along."

"Red, I like you, but you've got to stop telling me what to do." I squirmed away from him and bolted up the stairs. I stopped outside Emerson's door and knocked.

I heard a rustling sound, then her door opened. She still wore her damp dress, and she looked old and wizened. "Are you going to yell at me because I runned away?"

"No."

She scraped her toe over the rug, tracing flowers in the pattern. "Then why are you here? To spy on me? Report my crimes to Mr. Philpot?"

"I wouldn't do that."

"Yes, you will. I want Coop for a daddy, and you want your booty call."

I stared down at her, amazed that her small body could be filled with so much worry.

A bump moved in her throat. "If you have sex with Coop, you *could* make a fetus. And I'll be left out."

I cupped my hand over my chest, feeling the outline of the diamond ring. She was still fear biting. The only cure was to bake something warm and sugary—food heals, food cures.

"Right now, I'm going to make a peach pie," I said.

"Don't change the subject. I know all about sex. And don't say I'm too young. I'll be eleven soon. Mrs. Philpot said I'll be dating in four years. She told me everything about boys." Her eyes narrowed. "So don't tell me you and Daddy aren't you-know-whatting. Even bedbugs do it."

"I'll be in the kitchen if you need me."

"As if."

The minute I headed down the hall, she ran after me, clutching the hedgehog to her chest. Aunt Bluette would have compared Emerson to a Nutty Buddy cone—a tooth-breaking layer of hard chocolate and chopped nuts with a shivery-sweet center.

Red leaned against the counter, drinking a Diet Coke. "What you fixing to make?"

"Something with bacteria," Emerson said from the doorway.

Red laughed. "Thought you was gonna change clothes."

"I changed my mind instead."

Red turned to me. "What're we having for lunch?"

"I was thinking about a nice risotto, salad, baked potatoes, mayonnaise biscuits, and peach pie with a lattice crust."

"You guys are nuts," Emerson said. "All you think about is food."

While she traipsed around the kitchen, I phoned Coop but got turfed straight to voice mail. I left a message about Emerson. When I hung up, she was right beside me. She tucked the hedgehog between her knees and held out two rubber bands.

"Teeny, will you braid me?"

"Sure." Using my fingers, I divided her hair into three sections. I remembered how Aunt Bluette used to gently run a brush over my possumy curls. She used to keep a little TV propped on the kitchen counter, and we'd watch true crime shows. In one episode, the cops had needed a serial killer's DNA, and they'd bagged a hairbrush.

As I gazed at Emerson's clean scalp, I saw how easy it would be to pluck a strand. Without hesitating, I grabbed a glistening hair and tugged. It popped free, long and curly, with a tiny filament at the end.

Emerson shrieked and the hedgehog thumped against the floor. When she saw what I was holding, she slapped my hand. The hair went flying. We reached for it at the same time, but she was quicker. Cupping the hair in her fist, she raced down the hall.

"You almost had it, homegirl." Red picked up the hedgehog.

The toilet flushed, and seconds later Emerson skidded back to the kitchen. She jerked the hedgehog from Red's hands.

"Relax, kid. I ain't gonna take your toy."

"But Teeny would." Keeping her eyes on me, she twirled the hedgehog by its ears. "Traitor. Jezebel. Witch."

I just stared. Her lips twisted into a giant snarl. "Why are you always looking at me?"

I shrugged. "You're cute."

"And you're a hair-pulling bitch." She shivered, and fine bumps appeared on her arms.

Red pushed away from the counter. "Don't call Teeny names."

"She's a hooker."

"Jesus, kid. I ought to wash out your mouth." Red's ears turned scarlet.

"Wash your own. You took the Lord's name in vain. That's a whole lot worser than what I said."

Red's mouth opened and clamped shut. I waved my hand to show that I wasn't offended.

Emerson lifted her braid, dragged it through the air, and traced an indecipherable word. "Know what I wrote? I wrote Teeny's middle name. It starts with a B and ends in H."

"You only got one letter right," I said. "My middle name is Bluette."

"Isn't that the French word for 'bite me'?" She stomped out of the kitchen and ran up the stairs.

"Sheesh," Red said. "I ain't ever heard a little girl talk trash. Why's she doing that?"

"You've got a psychology degree. Figure it out." I pushed a straw basket into his hands. "And while you're at it, fetch me twelve ripe peaches."

He pushed open the back door and strode toward the orchard. I opened the cabinet and pulled out ingredients. Minutes later, a floorboard creaked in the hallway, then Emerson stepped into the kitchen, wearing a pink one-piece swimsuit. Cat's eye sunglasses and flip-flops completed the ensemble. She tottered across the room, dragging a quilt and humming to herself. She seemed to have forgotten about the hair-pulling incident.

"Wow, don't you look fancy," I said.

"Thanks. It was a gift from my dorm mother at Chatham Academy." Emerson straightened her sunglasses. "I'm going to lie in the sun for a while."

She flung open the back door and pranced down the steps.

The phone rang. I answered with a muffled hello.

"Teeny, this is Lester."

I imagined his thin, little mouth pressed against Kendall's. Had Barb known about the kinda-sorta affair? That would explain why she'd left Bonaventure. But it didn't explain why she'd killed herself.

"I was just about to call you," I said, and bumped my lie count up to twenty-four. "Emerson is with me. She hitched a ride to my farm."

"Super dooper," he said. "I'll pick her up tonight. Let's say eight-ish. But don't tell her I'm coming—unless you want her to run off again."

"I won't." I hung up. If only I could feed him a Bitter Apple Pie, a time-honored Templeton laxative. I wouldn't give him a lethal dose, just enough to cause unstoppable diarrhea. If he had to sit on a commode for a few days, Emerson could stay with me.

I glanced out the window. She was stretched on the quilt, listening to her iPod. I felt sad to my bones. Her whole world was fixing to change, and I couldn't do a thing to stop it.

eight

To make a peach pie, you need two crusts—homemade or store-bought. It helps pass the time if you hum. Aunt Bluette used to sing "Down to the River to Pray." Brush the lattice top with melted butter and sprinkle with sugar. Bake in a 350-degree oven for 45 minutes. Serve with ice cream and a praline pecan garnish.

I'd made this pie ever since I could reach the stove. Some cooks thought it was too sweet and syrupy; others claimed it was bland. Like my aunt always said, "One person's sugar-rapture is another person's sugar hell."

Coop showed up just as I took the pie from the oven. While the dogs leaped around him, he braced his arms in the kitchen doorway. His hair curled around his neck like chocolate shavings. "Something smells delicious," he said.

I smiled. He'd been through an ordeal, but he could still appreciate home cooking. Why was I so hesitant about marrying him?

Red glanced up from the newspaper. "You get my tire fixed?"

"Had to get a new one," Coop said. Light streamed through the window and hit the hard line of his jaw. He bent down to pat the dogs.

Red lowered the paper. "Those tires are brand-new."

"When I was looking for Emerson, I must've run over a nail."

"Yeah, maybe." Red's top eyelids flattened, giving him an owlish look.

Coop glanced up, and I could have sworn that something passed between them, something they didn't want me to know.

They didn't notice when I walked out the back door. The storm had left behind a crisp, green varnish that smelled of pine needles. Birds flitted in and out of trees. A plane droned across the sky.

"Aunt Bluette?" I whispered. "Tell me what to do. I don't know what it takes to raise a child."

But neither did Lester. He hadn't wanted Emerson to know about the DNA test; I'd honored his wishes, but she'd still run away. Now, in just a few hours, he would take her home, and I'd promised I wouldn't warn her. Even a hardened adult couldn't take that much deception in a single day. How could Emerson stand it?

Tell her the truth.

I walked toward the quilt and the faint sound of a Black Eyed Peas song drifted up. She lifted her sunglasses. "Move, Teeny. You're blocking my rays."

I squatted beside her and plucked out her earbuds. "I'm sorry I pulled your hair."

"I'm sorry you interrupted my music."

"I need to tell you something, but you've got to promise you won't run away."

She sat up. "Okay. Maybe. It depends."

"Your father is picking you up tonight."

Her chin jutted out. "But I'm already with my father."

"I'm referring to your legal daddy."

" 'There can be only one,' " she said. "That's from *Highlander*. It's a neat movie. You ever watch it?"

"Many times."

"You're pretty cool for a skeezer."

I shrugged. "Nah, I'm just a film buff."

"Well, Miss Buffy, when is Mr. Asshole coming to pick me up?"

"Eight o'clock."

"Dammit." She slapped the quilt. "I knew this was coming. Coop's a lawyer. Can't he do something?"

"Lester has legal rights."

"Legal schmegal." She gave the quilt a karate chop. "What about my rights? For all intensive purposes, a child should have rights."

My brain was stuck on *intensive purposes*, one of my favorite malapropisms. I chewed the edge of my mouth, holding back a smile. "Not until you're eighteen. Then you'll make your own decisions. Good ones and bad ones. But at least they'll be yours. In the meantime, you can't keep running away."

"But the Philpots piss me off."

"Each time you run away, you're hurting yourself."

Her eyes wobbled. "How?"

"I don't mean to scare you, but a thousand things could happen. You could fall and bump your head. And you should never, ever hitch a ride with a stranger."

"I know that. But I was so mad."

"Hey, I understand. Lester made me mad, too. But you can't let your anger be bigger than your common sense."

"I don't want to go home with him. I like it here. Can't you talk to Mr. Philpot?"

"I can try." But I knew he wouldn't listen. Just this morning he'd accused me of turning the orchard into a love shack. He wouldn't want his daughter exposed to a bizarre ménage à peach.

"I bet you won't try hard," she said. "Because you don't like me."

"Wrong."

"Huh, you think I'm a brat."

"You work hard at it." I pressed my finger against her belly. "Inside, you're Marshmallow Fluff."

She giggled, then reached for my hand. "I shouldn't have called you a bitch."

I forced myself to give her a stern look. "Just don't do it again."

"Why? 'Cause you'll get mad?"

"This isn't about me. When you call people names, it doesn't hurt them, it hurts you."

She grimaced. "How?"

"Words have power. They can make you feel good inside or they can have a bite. And when you call someone a bitch, in a weird sort of way, you become a bitch. What you say about others is how you secretly feel about yourself."

She pretended to gag. "That's the suckiest thing you've ever said. If I called a squid a butthole, it would still be squid. And I wouldn't turn into a butthole."

"You'd be one on the inside." I rubbed my forehead. I was going about this all wrong. She'd seemed liked a mini-adult, but now I realized she was still a child. And I was trying to make her grapple with mature concepts. I took a breath and started over.

"People are a lot more complicated than squid. We feel love, hate, jealousy. Some are honest. Others can't tell the truth to save their lives. Mostly, people are a mixture of good *and* bad. Some are sweet. Some are tart."

"Like a smoothie?"

"Right. But it's not your job to judge the smoothie."

"How am I supposed to know the difference between good and bad if I can't judge?"

"You watch and learn, just like you study animals. Then you put it all together and decide what kind of girl you want to be. Kind people teach you to be caring and thoughtful. Gossips teach you to hold your tongue. Selfish people teach you how to be generous."

I didn't know where these words were coming from, but they felt true. I wasn't just talking to Emerson, I was talking to myself.

She sighed. "I don't know what a bitch is, but I felt bad after I called you one. I might not show it, but I'm easily hurt."

"We all are, honey."

"Even the Philpots?"

"Yep."

"Mr. Philpot isn't coming over for a while. I've got time to soak up some rays." She tugged my hand. "Why don't you lay out with me? Not to be rude, but you could use a little tan."

Lester's silver Mercedes pulled into the driveway at eight-thirty. He got out, his brown suit waffling around his long legs, and frowned at the house. *Den of iniquity,* his eyes said.

I led him into Aunt Bluette's cozy parlor with the rag rug, pictures of dead Templetons, and the old walnut hi-fi, where vinyl records rose up in black columns. He sat on the sofa, twisting his hands together, casting suspicious glances in my direction.

"Where are your boyfriends?" he asked.

"In the backyard, fighting a duel."

My answer seemed to disappoint him. He undid the top button on his collar, and light brown hairs sprang out around his Adam's apple. "It's so hot outside," he said. "My throat's parched. Could I trouble you for a glass of iced tea?"

On my way to the kitchen, I passed by the stairs. Emerson had been in the bathroom for twenty minutes. What if she'd planned to escape? She could climb out the window and shimmy down the trellis. My stomach twisted. I ran up the stairs and knocked on the door.

"You okay?" I called.

"Can't a girl primp in peace?" she yelled.

I ran back down to the kitchen and fixed the tea. Lester hadn't asked for pie, but I didn't want to be rude, so I cut a slice anyway, and set it on a china plate.

Even assholes needed comfort food.

I resisted the urge to garnish the dessert with a passion flower, which is slightly poisonous but only if you eat the roots or seeds. It can also be used to rid the body of worms.

The fork rattled on the plate as I walked back to the parlor. The room was quiet as a burial chamber, except for the walnut clock on the mantel.

Each decisive tick said, *Time's up*, a reminder that my short stint at mommyhood had ended.

I set Lester's tea and pie on the table. He lifted the glass, ice tinkling, and drank; his throat clicked in rhythm with the clock. T-Bone lumbered into the room; Sir was right behind him.

Lester lowered the glass. "Yick. Will they bite?"

"Not unless you do," I said.

Red and Coop walked into the room and sat in the green velvet chairs across from Lester. The three men glared at one another. No introductions. No greetings. I positioned myself by the pocket doors and kept an eye on the stairwell. The bathroom door was still closed.

"I just left Eikenberry's Funeral Home," Lester said, looking pleased with himself. "I picked a mahogany casket with a waterproof liner. The viewing is Tuesday. Six to nine. I'm having a tasteful graveside service on Wednesday."

"What would be untasteful?" Red pressed his fingertips together.

"Who are *you*?" Lester blinked.

Red badged him. Lester held up his hand and showed his teeth, like Béla Lugosi shying away from a crucifix. Then he lowered his arm. "How do I know if that badge is real? You could've bought it anywhere."

"It's real," Coop said. "He works for me."

Lester smirked. "Is he working tonight? Or enjoying Teeny's opulent hospitality?"

"I'm on duty 24/7." Red paused. "How'd you get your wife's body released so soon?"

Lester ran his finger around the rim of his glass. "One of my friends called the Sweeney coroner. Then everything moved faster."

"You must have important friends," Red said.

"A few." Lester smiled. "Not to brag, but I've been to the governor's mansion several times. I've attended fund-raisers with Ted Turner and Newt Gingrich and Jimmy Carter."

"Did one of them call the coroner?" Red asked.

"You can drop the sarcastic tone." Lester's eyes widened until they resembled two fried eggs. "I'm just trying to explain how I dealt with the coroner."

"I'm surprised that Sweeney has a corner," Coop said. "It's a podunk town. Six traffic lights. Three detectives. A volunteer staff fingerprints the jaywalkers."

"Sorry that my wife didn't ask your opinion about the best place to be murdered." Lester's hand hovered in front of his mouth, as if to call back the words. A red flush crept up his steep forehead.

Murdered? I gripped the pocket door until my knuckles turned white.

Coop leaned back in his chair, his foot scraping against the floor. "Did you say *murdered*?"

Sweat beaded on Lester's forehead. "The Sweeney police are calling her death a suicide. I can't help what the coroner thinks."

"What does he think?" Red asked.

"Ask him yourself. I know that Barb killed herself. She left a suicide note, an empty bottle of merlot, and an empty bottle of pills. She liked antidepressants, stimulants, downers. She thought she was exempt from adverse drug reactions. There's no telling what the toxicology screen will show. That's what started this whole 'she might have-been-murdered' mess."

Coop's knee jogged up and down. "Sorry, you've lost me."

"I phoned the coroner this morning to see if he'd done a tox screen. The answer was no. He'd already finished the autopsy and he was satisfied that Barb had hung herself. I could tell that he didn't care about her drug problem. He was on his way out the door. Going to Pinehurst, North Carolina, to play golf."

Lester talked fast, his eyes shifting back and forth.

"I threatened to call the governor," he continued. "The coroner checked her again, and that's when he found the thing in her head. But he was just getting even with me for messing up his trip."

Coop's knee went still. "What thing in her head?"

"A subdural hematoma. That's a blood clot inside the skull. A slow leak. Like she'd been struck in the back of the head and a vein bled slowly.

Or she could've fallen. It wasn't a serious injury. It wouldn't have been fatal. Even the coroner said so."

"Did the police notice that your wife had a head wound?" Red asked. "They should have seen it at the crime scene."

"Haven't you heard a word I said? The injury was inside her brain. No scalp laceration No blood. Just a hematoma inside her skull. How this adds up to murder is beyond me." Lester spoke in a flat and emotionless voice, but a pulse throbbed in his neck. "If she'd had a broken hyoid bone, then I could understand the coroner's paranoia. But she just had a head injury."

Red gripped the sides of the chair, his fingers sinking into the plush velvet. "I'm confused. If the coroner suspected homicide, why did he release the body?"

"Nobody has said the word *homicide*, okay? The coroner just said her death looked suspicious."

"But he still let you take her body out of the morgue?" Red asked.

"There is no morgue. He works out of a room in Sweeney Hospital. I showed up this afternoon with the funeral home people. The coroner was gone. Nobody was there. So the guys from Eikenberry put Barb in the hearse. I didn't know anything was wrong until an hour ago. My cell phone rang. It was the coroner. He wanted me to return Barb's body. He wanted an expert to examine her. I told him to stick a golf club up his rear end, that it was too late. Barb had already been embalmed."

Red slumped in his chair. "Sheesh."

"It's not my fault that Sweeny doesn't have a proper place to do autopsies," Lester said. "If the coroner had wanted to keep Barb, then he should have locked that room. Or maybe he should have hired an assistant. But no, Dr. Bigshot was more worried about missing his connecting flight in Charlotte. Apparently he was at a travel agency when I showed up at the morgue. Then he went to dinner. He wasn't worried about Barb. He was stuffing himself with steak and baked potatoes, or whatever people eat in Sweeney."

"Have the police been notified?" Coop asked.

"About what? A bump on the head? The coroner's mistake? The embalming?" Lester spread his arms. "I don't know what they know. But I'm not a dumbass. I've talked to my personal attorney."

"And?"

"He said, 'The hay is in the barn.' That's Bonaventure-speak for it's too late to call in a forensic pathologist. You should know this, Mr. O'Malley. After Barb's body left the morgue, it was contaminated with all kinds of DNA. The funeral home driver. The embalmer. The lady who fixes dead people's hair and makeup. If an expert came to the funeral home right this minute, it wouldn't matter. The embalming procedure destroyed evidence. If the expert found something—a stray hair or fiber—the evidence would probably be dismissed by a judge."

"You seem to know a lot about forensics," Red said.

Lester gave him a chilling stare. "I'm just repeating what my attorney said."

"You need to let the state ME decide what he wants to do," Coop said.

"Mr. O'Malley, my wife was capable of anything. She was a bipolar drug addict."

"That doesn't mean she wasn't murdered," Coop said.

"She wasn't. I'm tired of discussing this." Lester glanced at his watch. "What's keeping that child? Teeny, go fetch her. I need to get home. My friends will be bringing cakes and casseroles. I need to be there. I shouldn't make people wait."

Red sat up straight. "Mr. Philpot, why did your wife wait a decade to question her daughter's paternity?"

"She was just being Barbish." Lester twisted his wedding ring, gold with tiny diamond chips. "She didn't do anything unless it benefited her in some way. She didn't care who she hurt. The day she broke the news, I was sitting at the breakfast table, eating grits. And she said, 'Lester, pass the salt. And Emerson isn't your daughter.'"

"That musta been a shock," Red said.

"A big one."

"Bet you wanted to throttle her."

Lester blinked. "What are you insinuating?"

"Nothing," Red said. "But I'm sure the police will want to know where you were the night Barb disappeared."

"I was in Bonaventure. Mama and Norris can vouch for me. They've been living with me ever since Barb moved out." Lester smirked. "Anymore questions, Serpico?"

"You sure don't act like a man who's just lost his wife," Red said.

"I may not seem grieved, but I am. I was a good husband and father. You can't imagine the effort I put into Emerson. After she was born, Barb had post-partum depression. She tried to kill herself—twice. She was too unstable to care for an infant. I got up at the butt-crack of dawn to feed the baby and change her diapers. She was a difficult child. I endured her tantrums. The trash talk. The endless button pushing. What thanks did I get? Double ought zero. Zilch. Nothing."

Red flashed a sympathetic, good-cop stare. "If I were you, I'd be pissed."

"I was. And I still am." Lester grabbed his fork and dug into the pie. Tiny crumbs drifted between his stretched-out knees.

"Sounds like Barb made you do the grunt work," Red said.

Lester nodded vigorously. "She did."

"You had a right to take a piece of ass on the side."

Lester lowered his fork. "How did you know about that?"

Red waved off the question. "Maybe Kendall wanted more. Or you wanted more from Kendall. But she wouldn't put out, would she? Not while you were married."

"I know what you're doing. You're trying to say that I had a motive to hurt my wife. It's a darn lie. It's worse than a lie. It's slander. Because I wasn't having a real affair. Lester Philpot's penis hasn't been inside Miss McCormack."

"Has Lester's penis been anywhere else?" Red asked.

"Why, how dare you."

"Hey, you brought up your penis. I didn't."

"You're a crude little man." Lester threw down his fork and it skittered across the coffee table.

"Where was Kendall Saturday night?" Red asked.

"In my house. Ask Mama. She didn't want Kendall there."

Coop shook his head. "I called you a dozen times the night Barb went missing, but you didn't answer. Not until Sunday morning."

"Mama turned off the ringers. She likes her beauty sleep. I didn't know that Emerson had been abandoned on Sullivan's Island. Or I would have driven up there and rescued her."

"So you knew that Barb was staying at Sullivan's Island?" Red's gaze was unflinching.

"I'm not answering any more questions." Lester folded his arms.

"Just one more." Red smiled. "Why did you send Emerson to a boarding school?"

"To protect her."

"From what?" Red asked.

"Barb." Lester scrubbed his hand over his hair until it stood up like frayed wires. "She tried to kill Emerson."

nine

Lester shifted uncomfortably on the sofa. "Few people know what a neglectful mother Barb was," he said. "But Lester Philpot knows. Lester Philpot saved Emerson's life."

"What happened?" I asked.

"Emerson almost drowned," Lester said. "She was five. Barb was sitting at an umbrella table next to the pool. She was fitting a puzzle together. I don't know why Emerson took off her water wings or why Barb didn't hear the splash. And I don't know what made me go outside. If I hadn't, Emerson would be dead. I saw her little body on the bottom of the pool. I dove in. Pulled her out. Blew air into her lungs. Brought her back to life. Barb never stopped working on that damn puzzle. She had this way of blotting out the world."

Coop shut his eyes. But Red looked skeptical. I was caught somewhere between shock and gratitude. It was a horrible story, but at least he'd saved Emerson.

Lester tugged his earlobe. "After that, I couldn't trust Barb. And for good reason. She was taking a lot of Xanax. She didn't keep track of Emerson. I got phone calls from people who lived blocks away from my house. They'd found Emerson wandering the streets. I hired a nanny, but Barb drove the poor woman away with nonstop demands. I pulled strings and got Chatham Academy to admit the child."

"What about when Emerson got older?" I asked. "Why didn't you bring her home?"

"Barb acted so sweet when it was just the two of us. She'd take her happy pills and put on a sexy outfit. It was just easier to leave Emerson at school. She was miserable with us. If things didn't go exactly her way, she'd run off. She disappeared every single Thanksgiving, just when we got ready to leave for the restaurant. I can't remember a Christmas morning without calling 911. But she always came back. That's why I didn't get upset at the drugstore. You can drop Emerson in Times Square, give her a quarter, and she'll survive."

An old ache broke loose in my chest, and I wanted to cry—not for myself but for Emerson. I drew in a teaspoon of air, and I could have sworn I smelled Lily of the Valley. It was Aunt Bluette's signature scent, and an effective poison.

Lester's gaze shifted to the hallway, as if he'd detected my aunt's perfume, too. "Barb and I weren't a family in the traditional sense," he said, looking back at Coop. "But we did our best. I was devastated when I found out that Emerson might not be my child. Barb told me that she'd never loved me. She said she'd always loved *you*. She swore that you loved her. You destroyed my family."

Coop's shoe hit the floor, and the slow, rhythmic tapping began. "That's not true. I didn't know she was in South Carolina until yesterday."

The upstairs bathroom door squeaked, and Emerson stepped into the hall. She walked down the stairs, her blue checkered dress billowing. Her braids had been replaced by two slightly damp pigtails. Instead of the hedgehog, she clutched a white straw handbag.

A pulse ticked in my throat. I wanted to stop all the clocks in this house and pull her into my arms and say, "Don't worry, honey. I will love you. I will be your aunt Bluette."

Emerson walked past me. Lester stood, the corners of his mouth slanting down. They glared at each other.

"I want to talk to Mr. Philpot alone," she said.

I hated to leave, but Red and Coop guided me into the foyer. Coop shut the pocket doors and took my hand. The dogs ran onto the porch and scattered into the shadows. The evening air pooled around us in deep blue baskets.

Red paced along the sidewalk, his stubby arms swinging. "I want to know more about this masked guy you saw, Teeny."

I gave him a quick description. "He had a key to her house," I added. "What if he killed her?"

"What was the motive?" Coop stubbed the tip of his shoe into the gravel. "When I talked to the Sweeney police today, they said a woman fitting Barb's description had checked into the Motel 6 at two a.m."

"Was she alone?" I asked.

"Yeah."

"What if a robber followed her to her room?" I asked. "On the drive down, she could have stopped on the interstate for gas or bite to eat. Maybe she flashed a wad of cash. Someone could have stalked her."

"Or she could've killed herself," Coop said.

"In Sweeney?"

"We might never know the answers." Coop pulled a roll of Tums from his pocket.

Red threw a rock. "Philpot could have hired someone to whack her."

"Why?" Coop slid a Tums into his mouth.

"Revenge. He was pissed at Barb. And he was banging another woman. Did you notice how he referred to himself—and his penis—in the third person? Guilty people often do that. It gives them distance from the crime. The dude is hiding something."

Like a mask? I walked to Lester's Mercedes and opened the door. I honestly didn't think he would hurt Barb, but he was tall and skinny. Just like the man I'd seen at her house.

"Teeny, get back here." Coop said.

I ignored him and clicked open the glove compartment. Registration. Auto manual. Kleenex box. I checked under the seats. Nothing. Not even a gum wrapper. Lester sure was tidy. I hit the trunk release, then hurried around the car. Spare tire. Jack. Jumper cables. I shut the trunk lid and walked back to the men.

"What were you looking for?" Coop asked.

"A Bill Clinton mask."

His jaw tightened. "If you'd found one, it would be inadmissible in court."

"I just want answers. Because if Barb didn't kill herself, her murderer is out there. It might have been the guy in the mask. I didn't see his face, but I can identify his skinny body in a police lineup."

All the color left Coop's face. "This is my fault. If I'd told you about Barb, you wouldn't have gone to her house that night. You wouldn't have seen anything."

The screen door creaked and Lester shuffled outside. I looked behind him, expecting to see Emerson trudge out with her backpack and hedgehog, but the porch was empty.

"Well, I told her about Barb," Lester said. "I didn't go into detail, of course. I just explained that her mom had passed away. Emerson wants to see you, Teeny. Can you make it fast? I've got all those neighbors waiting to bring me food."

Oddly enough, I knew why he was in a rush. Even if he wasn't mourning for his wife, he still had to honor Bonaventure's traditions. The whole town was into death. The locals had turned bereavement into art. They cooked food that was soothing, easily transportable, and fed the multitudes. All day long they'd baked funeral casseroles, wrapping them in tinfoil, their names carefully Scotch-taped to the bottom of each plate. More than a little hubris was involved, because folks wanted to get credit for their offerings. Lester would need to keep track of who'd brought what, because each dish required a handwritten thank-you note.

"Why don't you go home and tend to your guests," I said. "Emerson can stay here."

Lester stared at his watch, as if all of his options were spread out on the glowing dial. I knew what he was thinking. He could leave Emerson with me, a peach skank, or he could go home and say all the right things to his neighbors. "I guess it's okay," he said.

Coop moved between me and Lester. "We'll take good care of her," he said.

Lester pulled out his handkerchief and mopped his forehead. "Just bring her to the funeral home tomorrow afternoon. Come around four. That way, I can show her Barb's body."

Coop winced. "Won't that be traumatic for a child?"

Lester shoved the handkerchief into his back pocket. "Sorry to disappoint you, Mr. O'Malley, but you're not part of the decision-making process. Just bring her to Eikenberry's. After the visitation, I'll take her home and get a DNA sample. Even if it requires Valium and a small army. When we know the truth, we can get on with our lives."

I felt a tug inside my chest. He kept referring to Emerson as *her.* If only I'd put that passion flower into his pie.

He took out his wallet, peeled off a wad of twenty-dollar bills, and forced them into my hands. "She'll need an appropriate outfit. Take her to the mall. Buy what she needs."

I pushed the money back. "Emerson is grieving. I'm not dragging her through a mall. Surely she's got a dress at your house."

"Nothing that fits." Lester shrugged. "Her clothes are at Chatham Academy."

I put my hands on my hips and gave him a "don't you dare mess with me" look. "Send Kendall to the mall. Tell her to buy a dark dress, size ten. And dress shoes. Nothing colorful or cutesy."

His nostrils flared. "Yes, Your Grace. Anything else?" He didn't wait for my answer. He got into his Mercedes and drove off.

"You got any hard liquor, homegirl?" Red asked.

"Not a drop. I better check on Emerson." I ran into the house. She sat on the sofa, her head bowed. Her tummy pouched out, as if her inner marshmallow were rising to the surface. She glanced up, her eyes flat and dry. "Mrs. Philpot died. She's really dead."

"I'm so sorry." I pressed my hand to my midriff and took a step closer.

"My guinea pig died at Chatham Academy. Squeaky went to sleep and didn't wake up. Mrs. Philpot's just like Squeaky. She's really, really gone."

I folded my hands and waited for her to continue.

"I'm parentless. Just like an amoeba. They don't have moms and dads. Amoebas are their own parents."

I almost blurted that I was parentless, too, but this wasn't about me. Aunt Bluette had known when to talk and when to be silent. Some things couldn't be fixed with words. Many a time, I'd sat in the parlor the way Emerson was doing and my aunt would shut the doors and go about her business. When I got ready to talk, I'd go find my aunt.

Emerson rubbed her eyes. "Where's Mr. Philpot?"

"He went home."

Her face brightened. "Without me?"

"You're staying here tonight."

"Just tonight?"

I nodded. I couldn't bring myself to mention the viewing.

"I'm a tired, little amoeba. And I'm going to bed." She slid off the sofa and walked past me. When she reached the foyer, she broke into a run and stomped up the stairs. I sat there a minute, breathing in her soap-and-herbal-shampoo smell. Then I walked back outside. Red and Coop stood in the yard, their hands jammed in their pockets, watching the house as if it were on fire.

"How's Emerson?" Coop asked.

"Sad." I walked over to him. "She's gone to bed."

"I need bourbon." Red rubbed his eyes. "Lots and lots of bourbon."

ten

Thirty minutes later, Red and I pushed a cart through the Aisle Liquor Store. The name was a pun—*I'll Lick Her*. It had opened three years ago after church ladies and old-timers had finally lost the battle to keep Bonaventure County dry and pious.

I bent over a wooden rack to study merlot bottles, and a warm hand caught my elbow. I spun around and looked up into Mary Queen Lancaster's wrinkled face. She'd been one of Aunt Bluette's friends, a square, solid woman, with sharp blue eyes that took in everything. If you wanted to hear the latest gossip, ask Mary Queen. She owned a landscape company on Savannah Highway, but when she wasn't delivering mulch, she read tea leaves. The sign in front of her house read, A DIRTY BUSINESS.

She patted her grizzled hair, and I saw a cast on her wrist. "Carpal tunnel syndrome," she said, smiling at Red. "Is he one of your new boyfriends?"

I shook my head. "A friend."

"That's not the impression I got from Emerson Philpot. I gave her a ride to your farm yesterday."

"Teeny's just a pal," Red told her.

"Does that mean you're available? 'Cause I like younger men. But I don't like young women who make fools of themselves." Mary Queen shot me a glance. "I don't mean to meddle, but since Bluette ain't here to set you straight, I will."

"About what?" I folded my arms, bracing myself for a lecture.

"Emerson's a cutie. But I'm praying that she isn't Coop O'Malley's child. If she is, you better watch out for them Philpots." Mary Queen picked up a bottle of Wild Turkey, glanced at the label, and cut her gaze to me. "Norris used to be my eye doctor. Thanks to him, I've got new corneas. Of course, that was before he got into all that trouble."

"What did he do?" I asked.

"A patient accused Norris of rape. It happened right after you moved to Charleston. The Philpots kept it out of the newspaper, but I've got my ways of hearing things." She set the Wild Turkey bottle in her cart.

"Who did he attack?" Red asked.

"A pretty waitress from the Sweet Pea Café. It was a he-said-she-said situation." Mary Queen sighed. "There wasn't enough evidence to charge Norris, but I'm quite sure he raped her. Before it happened, I read her tea leaves. I saw a skinny line in the bottom of her cup, like angel hair pasta, but now I'm thinking it was a penis."

Red didn't comment, but his eyes said, *She's a Loon.*

"I'm not trying to be cute," Mary Queen said. "Any man who rapes ought to lose his penis. I wish I'd warned the girl."

"So how did Norris lose his license?" Red asked.

"The waitress reported Norris to the state medical board. Apparently it wasn't the first time. They jerked away his license. Ordered him to attend a sex school in Arizona."

"Did he go?" I asked.

"Not yet. He's working at the drugstore, hounding the female customers." Mary Queen set a Beefeater gin bottle into my cart. "You'll be needing this, Teeny."

Coop was in bed when Red and I got home. I tiptoed across the room and sat on the edge of the mattress. I watched him sleep, and my heart slipped out of rhythm for a second, beating a wild bongo beat. We'd always had good rhythm and bad timing.

He stirred. "Teeny?"

I smoothed back his hair. "I'm glad you're awake. I ran into one of my neighbors at the liquor store. She told me why Norris isn't practicing medicine. He raped a woman."

"Alleged rape," Coop said.

"You know about it?"

"My dad mentioned it a while ago." His hand drifted over my hair. "I don't want you to worry. I want you to think about my proposal."

"I am."

"Have you ever loved someone so much that it hurts?" he asked. "That's how I feel about you, Teeny."

"You've loved before," I whispered.

He put his hands on my face. "Not this way. Not ever this way."

His words sent a reckless desire streaking through my head. For the first time that evening, I took a deep, calming breath that actually left me feeling more relaxed. I kissed him over and over, weaving my hands through his hair, and then we were under the covers and nothing was between us. His chest was pressed against mine, our hearts whooshing, as if a thousand doors and windows had flung wide open.

The next morning, I sat in the window seat and thumbed through my vocabulary book. I picked out *jejune*, which means "sophomoric and silly." I turned to the Cs and put my finger on a random word. *Certitude.* "Certainty, sureness, assurance."

A car roared down the driveway. Kendall's Mazda shot around the curve and parked beside the yellow van. She got out of her car and straightened her dress, a black, cobwebby A-line. She dragged three shopping bags out of the backseat and dumped them on my front porch.

"I've been shopping my fool head off," she said. "There's a sale every Tuesday at Miss Pitty's Boutique, so I went hog wild. But the clerks were so rude. They acted like Lester had sent a dingo to dress his baby. You know what I'm referencing? That movie set in Australia with Meryl Streep? And a—"

"Dingo ate her baby," I finished.

"Exactly!" She reached into the largest bag and pulled out an ebony rayon dress. It was long-sleeved, with built-in gloves.

"Isn't this the darlingest thing you ever saw?" she asked.

"Hmm," I said. A spider could wear this to a tarantula's funeral. A jejunish spider. I opened another bag and lifted a black dress. It looked too fussy for Emerson.

"Taffeta," Kendall said. "It's got pizzazz, don't it?"

I searched the other bags, but all I found were patent leather shoes, lacy socks, and hair bows. I was so disappointed, but at least this dress didn't have gloves.

After Kendall left, I dragged the bags into the kitchen. Coop stood by the sink, washing a frying pan. Steaming platters of link sausages and scrambled eggs sat on the table. I was impressed that he'd cooked.

He flicked a tea towel at my rear end. "Let's go back to bed," he whispered.

It was tempting, but I'd already smelled food. "There's a time for everything, O'Malley," I said. "A time to make love and a time to eat pancakes. Besides, Emerson and Red are upstairs."

Coop lifted a wicker basket and steered me out the back door. The dogs loped ahead of us, streaking across the grass. "Where are we going?" I asked.

"It's a time for peaches."

I couldn't resist the orchard, so I let him pull me along. Morning sun blazed through the leaves, and the air smelled like burned sugar. The branches webbed above us, forming lacy, green nets.

Coop stopped between two Elberta trees. "Tell me about the peaches," he said.

The names slipped off my tongue like sweet talk. "The trees by the creek are Sunbrites and Shepard's Beauty." I moved in a circle, pointing. "Elbertas, Galas, Summerladies."

"I remember coming here with my dad," Coop said. "The rows were filled with ladders. The pickers were singing 'Abide with Me.' And you were up in a tree, singing with them."

I briefly shut my eyes. I remembered how the air had strummed with bees and hymns. *Abide with me through clouds and sunshine, Lord, abide with me.* Coop squeezed my arm. "It's so good to see you smile," he said.

I reached up into a branch and tugged at a ripe Elberta. It snapped free. I held it in front of Coop's mouth. His teeth sank down and juice trickled over his lips. A golden drop held on his chin and shimmered.

"It's so sweet," he said, pushing the fruit toward me. I wrapped my hand around his hand and guided the peach back to his mouth. Keeping his eyes on me, he bit deeper. I touched his throat at the exact moment he swallowed.

"Your turn," he said, and put the peach into my cupped palms. The wind rushed through the rows, and I could have sworn it carried a voice.

Trouble's coming.

My hands sprang apart as if I'd released a bee, and the peach thumped to the ground. I'd never been able to see the future like Tallulah, nor could I read tea leaves like Mary Queen. My bad feelings never had the decency to tell me what might happen. But I just knew trouble was coming.

Since this was our last day with Emerson, I let her pick what she wanted to do. I'd expected her to ask for a satellite TV dish or a Happy Meal. But she said, "Take me to Pinocchio's Toy Mart."

Ten minutes later, I stood with Coop and Red in the middle of the stuffed animal section. Emerson ran down the aisle, her face incandescent. She zoomed past the Barbies and stopped in front of a row that was crammed with riddle books and jigsaw puzzles. She grabbed a copy of *The Cipher Book* and walked to a display table where a Noah's Ark puzzle lay under glass.

"I thought she'd go straight for the dolls," Red said.

"Her mother was into code breaking and anagrams," I said.

He lifted a stuffed rat. "So it's a hereditary thing?"

"A learned thing," I said.

Coop picked up a stuffed gopher and it gave a little squeak. "Barb used to write me encrypted letters."

My lips slid into an "oh shit" smile. I remembered her diary and the horrid things she'd written. I also remembered the time she'd stolen pieces from her father's Pacific Ocean puzzle. If Mr. Browning had suspected her of pilfering, he'd never said. Once, he'd glanced up at me, his blue eyes flat and empty. "You should join us, young lady. Puzzles train the mind to be Machiavellian."

Barb had instilled the love of game playing in her daughter—not as a shared hobby, not to bond, but apparently to raise a cunning child.

Coop and Red helped Emerson carry her selections to the cash register. I made a loop through the store, searching for masks. Since it was August the Halloween merchandise hadn't been set out, and I only found a carnival mask and a hard plastic one, the kind favored by actors in horror movies.

A clerk passed by, her arms loaded with American Girl dolls. I hurried after her. "Miss? Do you sell Bill Clinton masks?"

The clerk turned, and her thick eyeglasses slid down her nose. "No, sorry. But Philpot's Pharmacy stocked them last Halloween."

I could hardly breathe as I walked to the checkout counter. Coop and Emerson watched the clerk slide the puzzle boxes into shopping bags. I pulled Red aside. His expression changed from boredom to skepticism as I told him about the mask.

"That proves nothing," he said. "You've got to stop this, Teeny."

"But when we were at Philpot's Pharmacy, I saw Halloween stuff in the stockroom."

"So? Did you check the shelves? Or do you have X-ray vision, girlie?"

"The stockroom door opened. I saw plastic pumpkins."

"But no Bill Clinton mask, right?"

"Let's go to the store. I'll keep Norris busy and you can look through the stockroom."

"Are you nuts? If Norris catches me, I could be arrested."

"But if we find that mask, it could mean that Lester was at Barb's house that night."

"No, it won't." Red shook his finger in my face. "If you find that mask, you got nothing—except a lawsuit."

"My gut tells me that Lester wanted her dead."

"You're gut is wrong, girlie."

I folded my arms. One way or another, I'd find a way into Lester's stockroom. The mask didn't hold the answer, but it was a piece of the puzzle. The puzzle that lay behind Barb's death.

eleven

The bells at Our Lady of Perpetual Succor Church tolled four times as Red steered the van toward Eikenberry's Funeral Home. The sprawling yellow clapboard house sat on the corner of Arkansas and Locust—Corinthian columns, mint green shutters, and a deep front porch. It was the nicest place in town to say farewell to the dead. But Eikenberry's had another purpose: it was the birthplace of gossip.

Red turned into the shady parking lot. It was empty except for Lester's Mercedes. Emerson's eyes got big, but she didn't say a word until we'd climbed out of the van.

"Did you know that lizards bob their heads before they attack?" she asked us.

"I thought it was courting behavior," Coop said.

"They're trying to scare off the other lizards." Emerson drew her hand into a claw. "It's a power play."

He smiled but didn't comment.

"I'm more interested in rats," she said. "You can flush a rat down a toilet and it'll live."

"You tried it?" I asked.

"No, but if Mr. Philpot was smaller, I'd flush him." She strode to Lester's Mercedes, her dress fluttering like crow feathers, and kicked the front tire.

When we stepped through the rear door of the funeral home, a blast of cold, rose-scented air rushed up my nose. The décor was just as I remembered: Persian rugs, antique tables, and crystal chandeliers. Coop and I turned into a corridor, where a framed Confederate flag was draped on the wall, next to photographs of Robert E. Lee and Stonewall Jackson. A portrait of Josh Eikenberry hung on the opposite wall. The picture had been made a few years ago, before a ski accident had left him paralyzed.

Emerson walked ahead of us, swinging her arms. I glanced into a kitchen, where the counters were heaped with foil-wrapped pans. Red nudged my arm. "Does Eikenberry's serve meals?" he whispered.

"No," I whispered back. "Just cookies and coffee."

He gave me a questioning look, but I turned away. I didn't want to be overheard in this gossipy place. Nor did I want to explain that the foil packages were for Josh. Because then I'd have to mention the ski accident, and Josh didn't like anyone to bring that up. Not the church ladies who fussed over him. Not the unmarried women who brought him homemade chicken and dumplings.

I stepped into the wide foyer. It was lined with doors; each one was named after a Civil War general. I dreaded seeing the room where Aunt Bluette's coffin had been displayed. Before her death, she'd requested that Eikenberry's handle her funeral arrangements. Josh had met me at the front door in his wheelchair, a sympathetic smile on his face. He'd greeted me warmly, as if he'd never groped me on that long-ago date. He'd helped me select a funeral package. He'd also arranged to have a peach tree planted in Azalea Park in my aunt's honor.

Coop's hand slid around my waist. "You okay, Teeny?"

Before I could answer, Josh steered his wheelchair toward us, the low whine of the motor echoing in the chilly foyer. The chandelier shone down on his thick, auburn hair, turning it the color of new pennies. The dial of his Mickey Mouse watch caught the light as he adjusted a blanket over his legs.

"I see you've brought the young lady." Josh smiled at Emerson. "What a cutie pie."

She lifted her pigtails and sketched something that looked suspiciously like an F and a U. I hoped she'd written *funeral*, but then she drew a C.

Josh pointed to a room with double doors. "Little Miss Philpot, your daddy asked me to escort you to the Stonewall Jackson Room."

His chair scooted forward, leaving two deep tracks in the carpet. As he steered toward the room, Red bolted forward. "Here, I'll get the doors."

"No, no. I'm fine." Josh pushed a button on his chair and the doors sprang open.

"Like magic," Emerson said.

"No." Josh chuckled. "Just modern technology. The funeral home has Wi-Fi. There's even a complimentary computer in the refreshment room."

"Woopy doo," Emerson said.

I looked past Josh, into the viewing room. White wooden chairs were lined up in tidy rows. Lester sat in one, not too far from a mahogany casket—it was huge, the size of a sideboard. I almost expected to see its glossy surface covered with silver serving pieces.

Emerson tugged Coop's jacket. "Aren't you and Teeny coming?"

He looked so sad, but he just patted her shoulder. "We'll be right here if you need us."

"But I do need you."

I squeezed my hands, wishing he'd tug her pigtails and say something about rats. Even a "you can do this" smile would have been helpful.

He kept on patting her shoulder. "You need a moment with your mom," he said. "Just you and her."

Emerson shook her head. "Don't make me go in there. I'm scared of dead people."

I tried to hold still, but my scalp twitched as if fire ants were crawling through my hair.

"Little Miss Philpot?" Josh called from the doorway. "Come on. Let's get this over with. You can have a cookie afterward."

"I don't want your damn, dead cookie," she said.

Coop led her to the door. He squatted beside her and whispered something. She nodded, folded her arms, then stepped into the room. Josh clicked a button, and the doors closed.

"Why's he in the chair?" Red asked.

"Last winter he wiped out on a double black diamond trail in Aspen," Coop said. "He's paralyzed from the waist down. He was making progress in rehab, but his father talked him into coming home."

At the other end of the foyer the door to the Longstreet Room opened, and Josh's uncle stepped out. Amos Eikenberry lifted a bony hand and smoothed three gray hairs on his scalp. His deep-set blue eyes blinked compulsively. The locals called him Mr. Winky, but he was so good natured, he referred to himself that way. He glanced over his shoulder, smiled at me and Coop, then turned into the Beauregard Room, where Aunt Bluette had been laid out.

"Who's the blinking dude?" Red asked.

"Mr. Winky," Coop said.

"Like the Winkies in *The Wizard of Oz*?" Red began to hum. "*Oh-E-Oh, Yo Ho—*"

He broke off when a muffled screech came from the Stonewall Jackson Room. "Let me go," Emerson cried. "You poo-poo head!"

I grabbed Coop's arm. "What are they doing to her?"

"Think I should go in?" He cast a panicky glance at the doors.

I nodded and gave him a little push. Another screech rose up. "I won't kiss a dead lady. Ack, I'm choking! Quick, somebody do the Heineken Remover."

I heard Lester's low, humming voice. Then Emerson said, "Shut the freaking lid or I'll sue."

The double doors creaked open, and Josh's chair shot out of the room. His eyes were rounded, as if he'd just spotted a typhoon.

"I'll cuss if I damn well please," Emerson cried. "It's the only way I can make grown-ups listen."

Josh's head bobbed violently, making me think of those lizards

Emerson had mentioned. Lester stepped out of the room, dry-eyed and calm, as if he were experienced with funerals and dead wives. Emerson ran after him, swinging her arms from side to side.

"Stop!" she screamed. "I command you to answer my question. Why aren't there any flowers?"

Lester tugged the edges of his jacket. Without looking at Emerson he said, "I requested donations to the Prostate Cancer Society."

"But that's *your* favorite charity," she said. "Mrs. Philpot would've wanted beaucoup flowers."

Josh looked surprised. "Why, Lester. I didn't realize you had cancer."

"He doesn't," Emerson said. "But he worries all the time about getting prostrate cancer."

"It's pros*tate*," Lester said. "Not pros*trate*."

Josh wheeled closer to Coop. "Are you and Teeny staying for the viewing?"

Lester gave the undertaker a malignant stare. "I'm sure the lovebirds have other plans."

And leave the birthplace of truth and slander? Miss all the gossip? "No," I said. "We don't have plans."

Emerson spun around, her lips spread into a smile.

"You're a precious little girl," Josh said. "And lucky. You've got two daddies. I wish I'd had me a spare."

She stopped spinning and glared. "Too bad you're not a starfish," she said. "Then you could grow new legs."

"Emerson!" Lester cried.

"It's quite all right," Josh said. "She's just a child. She knows not what she does."

Red looked as if he'd just stepped into a gopher hole. But the poor man had only seen the barest glimpse of Bonaventure. Weird, shimmery vibes were as normal as the church bells that gonged in the distance, calling the faithful and the fanciful—not to prayer service, not to Bible study, not to confession, but to the weekly bingo game.

• • •

Mr. Winky unlocked the plastic thermostat covers and cranked up the air-conditioning. "Hurry up, Vlado," he called to a short, blond man. The duo turned into the hall and vanished.

Minutes later, Josh parked his chair beside the front door and directed people to the appropriate viewing room.

I sat in the middle of the Stonewall Jackson Room, squished between Coop and Red. The Philpots were up front, but I couldn't see Emerson because there were so many people between us. All around us, mourners perched in the white chairs, their voices rising and falling like musicians tuning their instruments in an orchestra pit. The chandelier dimmed for a second, and the voices gathered strength, building into an overture.

Bonaventure's finest rumormongers had gathered in front of me, and they were warming up, tweaking and plucking words, tuning the language.

". . . strangled herself with Hanes pantyhose."

". . . control-top L'eggs."

". . . crotchless tights from Frederick's of Hollywood."

The conversation snapped off when Kendall McCormack stepped into the room. Her hair was spiked into the Statue of Liberty style, a local favorite on prom night. She lurched down the aisle on four-inch heels, her black minidress grazing the tops of her thighs. Her glossy black fingernails picked at a long strand of pearls that hung around her neck. When she spotted Lester she released the pearls and tottered over to him. She whispered something. His head wrenched back, as if she'd thrown a Rocky Road Pie in his face. He snatched her arm, his fingers sinking into her flesh, and he escorted her back up the aisle.

"This is less than six degrees of separation," Red whispered. "You and Coop. Coop and Barb. Lester and Barb. Lester and Kendall. In an indirect way, all of you have boned each other."

My gaze drifted to the far side of the room. Norris rose from a chair and slithered toward the casket. He was quickly surrounded by four elderly, bespeckled men, who kept gesturing at their eyes. An old woman joined them and smacked her cane against Norris's leg.

Suddenly I couldn't breathe. I touched Coop's arm. "I'm going to the powder room."

I ignored his worried look and squeezed past him, into the crowded aisle. When I got to the vestibule, it was jammed, too. The front door stood open, letting in a blast of warm night air. I eased my way to the porch. City crickets shrilled from the oak trees, as if shocked by human beings and their strange death rituals.

A blond man got out of a rocking chair, his ponytail streaming over his shoulder, and stepped into the light. His eyes were dark green, the exact color of champagne bottles, and thickly lashed. He wore a beige linen jacket, tight jeans, and scuffed brown cowboy boots.

"Teeny Templeton?" His voice was deep and clear, one hundred percent pure swamp rat.

God no. Not him. Not tonight. Not Son Finnegan.

I stepped back. The crickets fell silent, as if waiting for my response.

"Don't act like you don't remember me." He laughed, but his eyes said, *Peter the Denier.*

Hell, yes, I remembered every overendowed part of him. Son, not a nickname for Sonny or a misspelling of the sun. When he'd been born, his mama, Cissy Finnegan, hadn't been able to think of a suitable name, so she'd written *Son* on the birth certificate.

"When did you get back in town?" I asked. Did he still have washboard abs and a gorgeous ass?

"I was just about to ask you the same thing," he said. "But since you beat me to it, I'll go first. I've been in Iraq. I moved home this past spring. I tried to look you up, but I heard you'd moved to Charleston."

"Iraq?" I said. "You looked me up? I haven't seen you since I was twenty."

"Yeah, those were good times. Just me and you working together in the orchard."

My brain went on a fact-finding mission. There had been some scandal about Son's dad. . . . The file dropped into place. His daddy had died in the state penitentiary for cattle rustling, and his mom had taken in laundry and cleaned houses.

"I was an army surgeon," Son said. "I clocked a lot of hours reconstructing faces. Now, I'm tweaking. Eyes, noses, Botox."

I cut my gaze at his broad shoulders and sharp green eyes. All those years ago, we hadn't been able to keep our hands off each other. He'd been an older man, twenty-six, in his last year of medical school, and he'd given *roll in the hay* an all-new meaning. Son and I would meet in my aunt's barn after the pickers had left for the day. Hours later, we'd emerge, our bodies gleaming with sweat as if we'd been swimming. Just when I'd started to feel something for him, Aunt Bluette had put an end to the budding romance.

"I've got a brand-new office near Bonaventure Regional," Son was saying. "I'm board certified in plastic surgery."

"I'm glad for you." And I was. He could have turned out like the other Finnegan boys, breaking into houses to finance their meth addiction, but Son had used his smarts to rise in the world.

"Your turn." He leaned into me. "Why are you in town? I don't suppose your visit has anything to do with Barb Philpot's little girl?"

I felt an "oh shit" smile coming on, and I instantly repressed it.

"Surely you're not surprised that I know about you and Coop and Barb." Son wiggled his brows. "If PhDs could be handed out for gossip mongering, every citizen in Bonaventure would have a diploma."

"No comment," I said.

"You've been hanging out with too many lawyers. Let's get out of here and have a drink. Catch up on the dirt."

"No thanks." I had the feeling that someone was gawking at us, and I glanced over my shoulder. A piano teacher was talking to the mayor. I started to chastise myself for being paranoid when Norris stepped around the mayor. I thought of the woman he'd raped, and I made a fist. But Norris wasn't looking at me. He ran down the porch steps, putting me in mind of a tall possum. He scuttled past two Sweeney policemen and scurried to the parking lot.

I squinted at the officers. Surely they weren't here to pay their respects. Did this have something to do with the coroner's belated findings?

Son caught my arm, then looked down at my fist. "Is something wrong?"

"No." *Yes, I just saw a predator with sharp teeth, a pointy nose, claws, and (I wouldn't be surprised) a bald tail.* My fingers sprang open, and I smoothed my palm down the side of my dress.

Son pressed two fingers against my wrist. "Your pulse is doing a Texas two-step. I asked you for a drink. Not your blood."

I pulled my hand out of his grasp.

"What's wrong, Teeny? You look pale. Can I get you a glass of water?"

I glanced away. Did he think I was having a panic attack over him? I reached inside myself and searched for a tranquil spot, the one Aunt Bluette had helped me find so long ago.

Think about black bottom pie. Think about red velvet cake. Think about Hershey's sauce trickling over a scoop of mocha chip ice cream.

There, much better. I gave Son a real smile. "I wouldn't mind some chocolate."

"I'll buy you a Godiva store. But O'Malley might not like it."

"Just give me the candy and nobody'll get hurt." An ancient image replayed in my mind, Son pulling a sweat-soaked shirt over his head, his muscles moving under his tanned skin, and me pinching the metal tab of his zipper, sliding it down halfway.

He put one hand on the wall and his ponytail swung between us. "Want some advice? Don't put all your peaches in one cobbler."

"If you were a peach, I'd purée you in a Waring Blender."

"No, you'd eat me." He winked.

I looked under his arm and saw something that made my lungs feel like shrunken pods, the kind that wither in hot sun. Coop stood two feet away, his arms crossed, foot tapping the wooden porch in an unmistakable "what the hell are you doing" rhythm.

twelve

I turned away from Son and bumped my knee against the rocker. It banged against the house. My heart was beating just as hard.

Do something, Teeny. Channel Doris Day. She-Who-Can't-Be-Lied-To is about to tell a whopper.

"Coop, there you are." I waved, but cracks ran through my voice. I'd missed Doris by a thousand miles.

"I thought you were in the ladies' room." Coop's foot went still. He gave Son a scornful look.

If I told a lie, I'd have to raise my tally. So I gave Son a pleading look. "Take care, Dr. Finnegan."

"You, too, Miss Templeton." He pulled my hair. "And try not to purée any peaches. That's too brutal."

Coop slipped his arm around my waist and drew me across the porch, but not before I saw Son's lips curve into a machete-sharp smile.

"What were you and Son Finnegan talking about?" Coop asked.

"He was in Iraq." That wasn't an answer, but it was the truth. Sort of. Lord, my mouth was dry. I looked over Coop's shoulder. "Where's Red?"

"He's coming."

"Give me two minutes," I said. "I want to say bye to Emerson."

"Sure, but we're meeting my parents for dinner."

"We are?"

"Mother called while you were in the ladies' room. I didn't think you'd mind. But if you do, I can cancel."

"No, no, no." Had I just told lie number twenty-five? Dr. O'Malley had always been kind, but Miss Irene hadn't liked me since that day I'd hollered in church. I went ahead and raised my tally, then I walked back to the Stonewall Jackson Room.

Emerson's grandmother, Helen Philpot, stood near the coffin. She was tall and big-eyed, a killer tennis player with muscular forearms and leathered skin. Her bouffant, apricot-tinted hair was curled to perfection, and she reminded me of an entry at the Westminster Dog Show.

Emerson leaped out of her chair and grabbed my hands. "Bad news, Teeny. I'm not coming home with you and Coop."

Helen rolled her eyes. "Oh, for heaven's sake, Emerson. That's not bad news for *them*. Sit back down in that chair and be still."

"No," Emerson said.

Helen raked her manicured nails down the sides of her navy jacket. Emerson recoiled, as if she'd felt the sharp sides of those talons, and plopped in a chair.

Helen turned to me. Her irises looked like chopped green olives. "You must be Teeny Templeton."

"Yes, ma'am."

"Emerson won't stop talking about you. Thanks for taking care of her." Helen tucked her arm into mine and guided me toward the casket. "Do you play tennis?"

"Not in a while."

"Barb used to play. She always made foot faults. She made them in real life, too. Thanks to her, I might not be a grandmother." Helen frowned at the mahogany casket. The upper lid gaped open. Inside, Barb's head rested on a white satin pillow. A scarf was draped around her neck.

I glanced away.

"I never liked Barb," Helen said. "She was tricky. Even in death she looks like she's up to something. And she was always in motion. Like a great white shark."

Barb had once bragged that her lineage went back to Attila the Hun. I wondered how she'd handled Helen.

"I've got Emerson's things in the van," I said. "Shall I fetch them?"

"How clever of you to change the subject. You'll make a fine lawyer's wife. Unless you're just Cooper's rebound woman." Helen's voice held a fleeting edge of sweetness, like sugar water dribbled over gravel.

I stiffened. Helen had nailed one of my biggest fears.

She patted her hair. "I was surprised to hear he'd gotten divorced. He's half Catholic, you know."

"Yes, ma'am." I shifted my gaze to the other end of the room. The Sweeney policemen were talking to Lester, who kept swiping a handkerchief over his forehead.

Helen pulled me into the far corner, out of Emerson's earshot. "Are you worried that Cooper will turn out to be her daddy?"

"Not at all."

She stared hard at me. "Either you're a liar or you're in love. But don't worry. It's highly unlikely than he's related to that child. She's got gray eyes, but other than that, she doesn't look like the O'Malleys. She sure doesn't look like a Philpot. And you know why?"

"No, ma'am."

"Almost eleven years ago, Barb went into labor on Curry Island. It was early September, hot as blazes. We were gathered at my beach house, eating oysters and boiled crabs. Right in the middle of dessert, Barb's water broke. When we got to the little hospital, it was pandemonium. The nurses put the patients on cots. Some of the poor dears gave birth in the hall. Barb got preferential treatment because Lester knew who to call."

Something broke loose in my chest, as if a hard little egg had cracked. If I didn't hold real still, it would shatter. "But Emerson said that her birthday was in December."

"That's what the poor child thinks. But she was born on September fourth—a scant seven months after the wedding. Barb was afraid people would call Emerson a bastard, and they would have. So Lester hired a big-shot lawyer to fix everything. Emerson got a new birth date. Highly illegal, of course. But we went along with it. We had to. We thought Emerson was our baby."

I pulled in a breath. The egg in my chest tore open, and feathered things banged against my ribs. Everything Emerson knew about herself was a lie.

Helen stepped closer. "The OB ward was understaffed the night Emerson was born. I parked myself beside the nursery window and watched a nurse take off the babies' ID tags and put them in a heap. I tried to keep track of Emerson's tag, but the nurse saw me gawking and shut the curtains. After that, I couldn't be certain if we'd gotten the right baby."

"You could've checked footprints," I said.

"Oh, we did. But one baby's prints got on all the records. So Lord knows where Lester's real child is—or Coop's." Helen's bony fingers closed on my wrist. "Barb and Emerson stayed at the beach house for a few months. Then they returned to Bonaventure. The gossips never said a word. Wasn't that nice?"

I nodded.

"Every time I go to Curry Island, I drive by the elementary school and look for a tall, green-eyed girl. I haven't found her. But I know she's out there."

Her words slashed around me. Lies. So many lies, each one sticky-sharp. I must have flinched, because she abruptly let go of my hand. I moved away from her and walked to Emerson's chair.

"I've got to leave, honey." I smoothed her pigtails. "Give me a call sometime. My number's in the phone book."

I expected her to say "as if," but she sprang out of her chair and wrapped her arms around me. "I'll really miss you. And tell my daddy that we have unfinished beeswax."

I stepped out of the funeral home, into the warm night air. I had the nagging feeling that I'd forgotten something, but I couldn't think straight. My head was filled with Helen's prickly words. The humidity sluiced around me, and I could feel my hair tighten and curl. I reached up, making sure my bobby pins were in place.

My thoughts scattered when I saw Coop. He stood at the end of the porch, leaning against a wooden column. He smiled at me. "Ready?"

I slipped my hand into his. As we walked toward the parking lot, I told him about Curry Beach. His eyebrows went up, but he didn't comment. I smoothed my hair again, but this time the pins flew out and clattered against the asphalt. Coop bent down to gather them; I hunkered beside him. He slid a bobby pin into my hair.

"There you go," he said, his hand lingering on my cheek, giving off the faint scent of pine-and-cotton.

I pushed down my worries about Emerson and forced out a smile. "Where are we having dinner?"

"Mother made reservations at Heads 'N,' Tails."

Now I'd totally lost my appetite. Heads 'N' Tails was a trendy restaurant in the historic district, and items on the menu used every piece of the animal.

When we got to the van, Red said, "Sit up here with me, girlie."

Coop helped me into the front seat, then he got into the back. From the radio, Drowning Pool whispered the opening lyrics to "Bodies," and Red turned up the volume. The pins wouldn't stay in my hair, so I plucked them out. I pulled down the rearview mirror. My image bore an uncanny resemblance to Emerson's hedgehog, which, I suddenly realized, was still in the backseat, along with her backpack. So that's what I'd forgotten. But it gave me the perfect excuse to see her again.

Red drove around Oglethorpe Square, the van's tires bumping over the cobblestones. We parked by The Little Savannah, a popular bistro, where customers were lined up on the sidewalk. Across the street, rosy floodlights washed over the stucco façade of Heads 'N' Tails. The building resembled a plump roast in a butcher's case.

Red spread his arms. "Look at all the tourists laughing and carrying on. They don't seem worried about being mugged. Bonaventure must have a low crime rate."

"We've got our share of criminals," Coop said. "But no one ever hears about them. The tourism council created a brand—" 'Bonaventure is a smaller, safer Savannah.' "

This was true. The *Gazette* was written by staffers with MFAs in creative writing. The crime log was carefully zany: a unicycle had either been stolen or borrowed; a man in a frog suit had eaten all the seedless grapes at Piggly Wiggly; a woman had forced her cheating boyfriend to eat habanero peppers, and he'd filed assault charges.

On our way to Heads 'N' Tails, a tall, angular woman in a white nurse's uniform walked toward us, her blond hair jutting up like cockatoo feathers. Her turquoise eyes blinked wide open. "Teeny!"

"Dot!" I blasted out her name. My mock enthusiasm matched her seemingly genuine joy. I looked up. She towered over me like a swing set. "I haven't seen you in—"

"Eight years. It's taken me that long to get an MA in nursing." Dot was talking to me, but her eyes were on Coop and Red. She was taller than both of them.

"Eight years?" I repeated, shaking my head. I could have gone another eighty without seeing her. She knew about my tortured romance with Son Finnegan.

Dot couldn't keep still. She smoothed one hand down her flat chest; then she fingered the gold praying-hands brooch that was pinned to her collar. Her gaze slid to Coop, then back to me. "Where are you all off to?"

"Dinner with my folks," Coop said.

"I won't keep you." She darted a look at me. "Give me a call, Teeny. I'd love to catch up."

I nodded, and my lips slammed into a smile.

She walked off, her narrow hips switching back and forth. Red stared until Coop hit his arm.

"I can't help it," Red said. "She's pretty."

"But skinny," Coop said. "I thought you like big-chested women."

"You don't know what I like." Red flashed a mysterious smile.

We stepped into the Heads 'N' Tails lobby. The air smelled pleasantly charred, with a hint of fennel and caramelized onions. The brown-eyed hostess glanced up from a podium and smiled at Coop. "Your parents are already here, Mr. O'Malley."

The hostess plucked three menus from a stack and led us into the dining room. It was U-shaped, with zebra-striped walls, a red ceiling, and a black-and-white marble floor. Smoke curled beneath the track lighting, floating over the empty tables and a small dance floor. In the corner, a band played Leona Lewis's "Run." My favorite heartbreak song.

I looked around for exits—you never know when a restaurant will catch on fire—but didn't see any. I spotted Irene O'Malley, and my stomach cramped. Her chin-length brown hair was pushed back with a blue band that matched her eyes. She was an older, stouter version of Coop's first wife, Ava, which made me wonder if he had a type.

"Hello, Teeny," Dr. O'Malley said. He rose to his feet, candlelight glancing off his salt-and-pepper hair. My heart pounded in the roof of my mouth as Coop seated me next to his dad. Coop pulled out the chair beside me and sank down next to Irene. I breathed in her perfume, Eau du Bitch. Did she know Coop had given me a diamond ring? I still wore it on the chain, but it was hidden by my dress.

"Why, Teeny," she said, drawing out the Es and the N in my name. "I haven't seen you since the summer you dated Coop. He brought you to our pool party, and you wore a red polka-dot bikini." She broke off and touched the back of her head.

"Nice to see you again, Miss Irene." I tried not to remember that party. I had, as usual, dressed wrong for the occasion. I'd assumed a pool party had meant we'd swim, but the guests had worn shorts and sandals. I'd wanted to make a good impression on Coop's parents, so the night before the party, I'd given myself a home permanent, taming my ungodly frizz into glossy, dark blond spirals. Unfortunately, I'd left a curler in the back of my hair.

Now, all these years later, I was pretty sure I'd committed another beauty faux pas. I touched my hair, and sure enough, a lone bobby pin jutted out. I plucked it out.

Irene turned her gaze on Red. "Mr. Hill, how long have you been working for my son?"

"Two years. Before that, I was a homicide cop. Cold cases. Stuff like that." He lifted his finger and pulled an imaginary trigger. "Boss and I get along like mashed potatoes and sour cream."

Irene leaned forward. "Who's the sour puss? You or Coop?"

"We're a good team." Red looked at his menu.

"A word of caution," Dr. O'Malley said. "Avoid the pan-fried goat brains—even if you like fennel and garlic."

Irene tilted her head, the tips of her pageboy swinging like scythes. Her blue gaze impaled me. "Teeny, you look just as fetchin' as ever." She turned to Coop. "But do I know *you*?"

Coop looked embarrassed. "What have I done now?"

"Hmph," she said, and lifted her wineglass, the burgundy swaying. "Your daddy told me you were in town, but I didn't believe him. Because if *my* son came to Bonaventure, he would have visited his mother."

She pronounced *mother* like a native Bonaventurian: *muh-tha*.

"I apologize," he said.

"Your grandmother is in town," Irene said. "She'd like to see you, too."

"Why didn't she join us for dinner?" Coop glanced at the empty seat beside Red.

"You know how Minnie is. She can't leave those damn Chihuahuas." Irene toyed with the gold buttons on her suit. "She's cooking beef Wellington tomorrow night. Ava used to love it. But *you* used to love Ava."

His cheeks reddened. "I've never been fond of British cuisine," he said.

"Not even English trifle? We're having that for dessert." Irene set down her wineglass.

Coop's right shoe slapped the floor ten times.

"Are you trying to send me a message in Morse code?" Irene asked. When he didn't answer, she kissed his cheek, leaving a red smudge. "Lighten up, Poopy-Coop."

"I'll try, Mommie Dearest," he said.

"Flatterer." She grabbed her purse and stood.

All three men scrambled to their feet. She flipped her hand. "Sit, sit. I'm just going to the ladies' room, not Antarctica. See y'all later."

She bustled away, giving off gusts of perfume, her wide hips easing between the tables. Most Bonaventure women traveled in packs, but she hadn't asked me to join her. I should've felt offended, but I was relieved.

Coop reached for my hand and squeezed it. "Mother isn't always that way."

"Which way?"

"A helicopter mother."

The hostess walked by our table. She was followed by a man with green eyes and a blond pony-tail.

Dammit. Son of a bitch. I was totally busted.

thirteen

I held the menu in front of my face and forced myself to study the entrées. Rooster Heart Tartare, garnished with garlic pods and cockscombs. Porcine Testicles with Crostini. Five-Brain Portobello Burger. The cheapest item was french-fried entrails.

Our waiter drifted around the table, setting out flatware, his bald head gleaming in the candlelight. I lowered my menu and looked up at him. He handed me a tiny calico bag that was tied with a red ribbon. A fragrant, herby smell rose up.

"Compliments of the chef," the waiter said. "It's Herbes de Bonaventure. Kinda like Herbes de Provence, but without the lavender."

He gave everyone at the table a bag. "The cocktail du jour is the greyhound," he said.

Red's face turned chalky. "Please tell me it don't have a real dog in it."

"No, just vodka and grapefruit juice." The waiter grinned.

"I'll have one," I said.

"Me too," Dr. O'Malley said.

"A glass of milk for me," Coop said.

"From which animal?" the waiter asked.

"You pick," Coop said.

Irene returned from the ladies' room, her lips freshly dipped in red. Coop leaped up and pulled back her chair. From the next table, Son winked. He pointed to the dance floor, then to me. I looked away and rearranged my knife and spoon. Was I flattered? A little. Alarmed? Totally.

Coop glanced at Son, then back at me. I was relieved when the waiter set down our drinks. I took a bracing sip of the greyhound.

Irene cut her gaze to Son's table. "Is that Dr. Finnegan over there? What a handsome fellow he is. And a marvelous plastic surgeon. Why, just last week, I sat next to him at a cookout. We had a *long* conversation. He asked about you, Teeny. I told him I hadn't seen you in a decade, not since my party. You had a darling little curler in your hair."

My mouth went dry, and I took another swig of the greyhound. So what if I'd slept with two men in this restaurant? The Baptist in me said, *Slut.* My backsliding part said, *Nobody's keeping a tally.*

The waiter returned with something that looked and smelled like homemade bread. Coop sliced off a hunk and reached for the butter—at least, I hoped it was butter. I kept rearranging my fork and spoon, wishing I could readjust my past just as easily. I'd fix it so that Barb was alive and Son was her old lover. Emerson could be their daughter. I'd give O'Malley and me a brown-eyed, dark-haired child named Coopette.

Red polished off his drink. "So, Teeny. What's the story on your nurse-friend? The one with the hair."

Dr. O'Malley and Irene set down their drinks. "Who?" they asked.

"We ran into Dot Agnew," Coop said.

"Her?" Irene's nostrils twitched as if she'd caught a bad odor. "Didn't her *muh-tha* used to breed budgies?"

"What the heck is that?" Red asked.

"Parakeets," I said. "Mrs. Agnew made bird recordings, too."

"I don't care about the mother." Red smiled. "Tell me about the daughter. I didn't see a wedding ring. Is she single?"

"Ring or no ring, don't get mixed up with her," Irene said. "She's got a bit of a reputation."

This was true. Though I'd lost touch with Dot, her romantic history had been chronicled in the Bonaventure *Gazette*'s society pages. She'd been married, divorced, married, divorced. From the gossips, I'd heard about her in-between men: bikers, dirt movers, musicians, bankers, doctors, pilots, and even one of her divorce lawyers.

"What kind of reputation?" Red asked. "I noticed she had a pin on her collar. Praying hands. Is she religious?"

"Dot won those hands when she was fourteen," I said. "She appeared on a radio show called *Name That Bible Verse.*"

"I remember that," Irene said. "The disc jockey couldn't stump Dot. She won an all-expense-paid trip to visit Oral Roberts University."

Irene's mouth twisted into a sardonic smile, though I was sure she didn't know the rest of the story. Dot had dated juvenile delinquents, hoping to reform them. *Repent,* she'd tell the boys, *so your sins may be wiped out. Acts 3:19.* Then she'd beat them off in green pastures, near the valley of the shadow, and their rods and staff were comforted.

Red looked disappointed. "So she's churchy?"

"She's a born-again skank," Irene said.

"I might marry her." Red looked Irene in the eye. I knew for a fact that he liked zany, free-spirited women as long as they didn't veer into loon territory. But he hated bitches.

Another silence descended. I finished my greyhound. I needed a stronger drink: a double martini, heavy on the Beefeater, a gin-soaked olive skating along the bottom of the glass.

Irene's eyes widened. "Oh, goodie. Here comes Dr. Botox."

Son angled toward our table, moving more like a cowboy than a physician. His cattle-rustler genes wanted to make trouble. He stopped beside my chair.

"How you doing, Dr. O'Malley? Miss Irene." His gaze skipped over Coop and Red, then settled on me. "Teeny."

Only Son could make my name sound like a four-letter word. The candle on our table sputtered, and light rippled over his teeth, giving him a vampy look. My lungs felt ripe and plump, as if they'd turned into mutant spaghetti squash, packed with seeds and stringy flesh, the skinny girl's substitute for pasta. It's low-cal and edible, but nothing like the real thing.

He chatted with the O'Malleys about yesterday's storm, then he gave me a quick two-finger salute. Instead of returning to his table, he left the restaurant.

Irene looked offended. "Was it something I said?"

Our waiter set a domed platter in front of her. He raised the lid with a flourish. There, on a curly layer of romaine, lay three hamster-like bodies, skinned and headless, butter dripping from their tiny claws.

"Perfect." Irene lifted her fork and knife.

Coop brushed his mouth against my ear. "Anything you want to tell me about Son Finnegan?"

Not unless I was under oath. Not unless he pulled it out of me with sharp tweezers.

"He worked for Aunt Bluette one summer," I said under my breath. And we made love until I was limp and breathless. He had to run to the house and get my inhaler.

"It's not polite to whisper," Irene said, and sank her teeth into a hamster.

fourteen

When we got home, I ran straight to the bedroom to fetch my emergency stash of chocolate. In the center of the floor, a trail of bikini panties led from my overturned suitcase to the bed. My little girl pillow with the daisy-print was topped with a black lace bra. Gardenia blossoms circled my green plaid nightgown. White gunk was splattered over it. A Nokia cell phone lay in the center of the bed. Was it my phone? It wasn't playing *The Twilight Zone.* All I had to do was press a button and I'd find out. But I knew the truth.

The guy in the mask had found me.

I opened my mouth to scream, but a rasp shot out. This wasn't a panic attack, it was real asthma, and I was going down. Where was my inhaler? In my purse.

I bolted from the room and skidded into the hall. The kitchen loomed ahead, a rectangle of cozy light. I tried to suck in air, but my throat was locked. Black slashes churned in front of me, a plague of locusts. I battled them away and lurched through the doorway.

"Teeny, what's wrong?" Coop's brows came together.

I swerved past him, stopped by the counter, and snatched my purse. I turned it upside down. Keys, lipstick, inhaler, wallet clattered across the Formica surface. The noise startled Sir, and he scooted under the table.

A wheeze tore out of my throat as I grappled for my Ventolin. But I couldn't stop shaking. Coop pushed the inhaler between my lips and pressed the button. Tart vapors shot against the roof of my mouth.

"Deep breath, Teeny. Good. One more."

I hadn't seen his eyes this wide since he'd fallen off that old merry-go-round. Back then, he'd been worried for himself. Now he was worried for me.

"Baby, should I call my dad?"

No baby. No dad. I couldn't form words, so I shook my head. I'd be mortified if Dr. O'Malley saw the lurid mess in my room. My panties had been laid out neatly on the floor, like they'd been pinned to a clothesline. And what was that sticky stuff on my gown?

Coop put the tip of the inhaler into my mouth. I pushed it away. "Phone," I said. "Gown."

Each word held in the air, white-hot, like steam hissing from an iron.

"Breathe." Coop made me take another dose of Ventolin.

My lungs were starting to open up, but I could feel my pulse bumping under my jaw. I grabbed his finger and tugged him to the bedroom. He stepped gingerly around my panties, as if braving a piranha-filled river. I flattened my shoulders against the wall and gulped air.

Red stood in the doorway. "Sheesh, is that Teeny's phone? How'd it get here?"

"A prowler," Coop said.

Red laced his fingers together on top of his head and wouldn't meet my gaze. My bronchial tubes dilated a bit more, and I drew in a huge, ragged breath.

"I lost my phone at Barb's rental," I said in a croaky voice. "Now it's *here*? The guy in the mask did this. He killed Barb, and now he wants to kill me."

I lunged for my phone, but Red caught my arm. "Geez, don't touch nothing, homegirl."

An hour later, a skinny policeman showed up. Officer Dale Fitzgerald had graduated from Bonaventure Senior High last year. He was slow moving and precise like all the Fitzgeralds. It was ten o'clock by the time he'd taken our statements, dusted for fingerprints, and bagged the evidence.

After he left, I pulled on rubber gloves and marched to my bedroom. I ripped the sheets off the mattress, then I sprayed it with Lysol. The smell triggered another breathing attack, but it was too soon for another dose of Ventolin, and besides, I felt sick to my stomach. When Templeton women get upset, we vomit, but I forced myself to keep moving.

I shut the bedroom window and locked it. Next, I shook out a Hefty bag and stuffed the sheets inside. Laura Ashley, 300-count, one of my garage sale finds. I dragged the bag to the laundry room, threw the linen into the Maytag, and added a box of 20 Mule Team Borax plus bleach.

Deep breath. Come on. I gripped the sides of the washing machine and stared at the old mural Mama had painted. It depicted zombies attacking Graceland. The violent art flowed over and under the shiny red cabinets. A mob at the gates. Elvis and Priscilla on the roof, throwing guitar picks at the crazed fiends while Lisa Marie hurled fried chicken.

The washing machine thumped, giving off sharp chemical odors. Coop walked up behind me. As he stared at the laundry room walls, his eyes got bigger and bigger. Bless his heart, he didn't comment about the mural.

"You shouldn't breathe these fumes," he said. He took my hand and led me out of the room. "Let me fix you a drink."

"I don't want a drink." I wished I lived in Iceland. Emerson and I could study volcanoes.

Coop opened the front door. "Take a big gulp of fresh air."

I knotted my fingers in my dress. "I'm scared."

Coop hugged me. "I'll keep you safe."

Was it really that easy to keep someone safe? I pressed my face against his shoulder.

"You're shaking," he said. "Maybe you should lie down."

"I can't sleep in my room." I lifted my face and gazed up at him. His hair stuck up in tufts. I smoothed them down. "I'll sleep on the sofa," I said.

"I'm not leaving you alone." Coop shut the front door and locked it. He took my hand and guided me to the parlor sofa. As we curled up together, the dogs padded into the room and stretched out on the floor. I forced myself not to think about the prowler.

A wedge of moonlight fell through the curtains and washed over the rug. Coop's foot knocked against the sofa's wooden arm. The thumping got louder and louder, beating a horrifying rhythm.

Game. Set. Match.

The next morning, Red helped me drag my mattress into the front yard. "Don't look so scared, homegirl. Whoever broke in your house is playing with you."

I kicked the mattress. "A guy leaves his DNA on my gown, and that's playing?"

"I studied the crime scene. Your phone was posed. Like a body. Your panties weren't in a messy heap. They were arranged in a straight line. Gardenias represent secret romance. The dude was leaving you a love letter."

I looked up at the ashy-hot sky. It wasn't even nine o'clock, and the sun was already burning my shoulders. "What's the worst that can happen?"

Red patted my shoulder. "Worst-case scenarios are as likely as a coconut falling on your head. Don't freak out just yet."

We stepped into the kitchen. Coop stood in front of the stove, forking up bacon. In his other hand, he held an iPhone to his ear. "Yes, sir," he said, then paused. "No, sir. It won't happen again."

Sunlight fell in pinstripes along the table where Coop had set out paper towels, mismatched dishes, and chipped coffee mugs. Red dug into the link sausages, scrambled eggs, and French toast.

Coop shoved his phone in his pocket and frowned. "We've got trouble. You want the medium-bad news first? Or the really bad news?"

"Sheesh." Red dragged a stubby hand over his face.

"Hit me with the really bad news." I sank into a chair and tucked my feet around the rungs.

"I couldn't sleep last night," Coop said. "I decided that you need to tell the Charleston police what you witnessed at Barb's rental."

I nodded vigorously. "My thoughts exactly."

He sat down next to me, his right shoe clicking against the floor. I counted ten thwacks, then his other leg began to shimmy. I leaned over and squeezed his knee.

"Deep breath, Coop. What did the police say?"

"I couldn't make that call, Teeny. Just a few months ago, your ex-boyfriend was murdered. The police thought you killed him—and this was before you inherited his mansion on Rainbow Row and all that beachfront property."

I didn't like being reminded of those dark days. I pulled my hand away from his leg. "The police found his murderer."

"Some of the detectives still think you're guilty."

"Is that why you didn't call them the night Barb went missing?"

He nodded. "I was more scared for you than I was for her."

"I could have called them, too." I inhaled so sharply, my head jerked. "But I didn't. For the same reason."

"What's going on, Boss?" Red asked.

"I phoned the ADA in Charleston."

"ADA?" I asked. It sounded like a diet for sugar diabetes.

"Assistant district attorney," Coop said. "I didn't mention you. I told him a woman from my hometown had abandoned a child on Sullivan's Island. And the woman had committed suicide. The ADA knew all about it. Apparently the Sweeney coroner made a big fuss. That's why the police showed up to Eikenberry's. They had a court order to remove Barb's remains. The coroner says the time of death doesn't match up with the time Barb allegedly checked into the Motel 6."

Red blew out a sigh. "So she was killed on Sullivan's Island?"

"It looks that way." Coop's foot went still. "An article ran in the paper, asking for any witnesses to come forward. So far, no one has called about a man in a Bill Clinton mask. But a Sullivan's Island teenager called the tip line. Claimed she saw a suspicious woman in her yard. She said the woman had frizzy blond hair and wore a scuba suit. She told the teenager that a man was chasing her."

I slumped in my chair. "That was me. I should have asked her to call 911. But I was scared."

"You would have been a suspect."

"For telling the truth?" I said, my voice lifting at the edges.

Coop rested his elbows on the table and stared at his empty plate. "Why would the police chase a phantom in a mask when they had a stalker-girl? If you told them what you'd witnessed, you'd be admitting to trespassing and voyeurism. The police would charge you with stalking. That's a felony in South Carolina."

I shuddered. "The police are smarter than that. They'll keep their options open."

"It's not about smarts," Coop said. "It's about facts and logic. Eye witnesses. There's the truth of what you saw and the truth of what the teenager saw. All that matters is how the police interpret these truths."

"What am I supposed to do? I saw a freak strangle Barb. Now that freak is after me."

"Eventually we'll have to talk to the police. But first, I want to dig a little. While I'm digging, I want to keep you safe."

"But it's wrong to withhold information from the police," I said.

"It's an unconscionable situation for everyone—except Barb's killer."

"I'll say."

"The truth is a prickly thing, Teeny. Honesty is in the beholder's eye." Coop's hand closed on my knee. My own foot began to shake. All my life, I've been a truth seeker. I'd thought of myself as a gray-area girl, but I'd defined the truth in the narrowest possible terms.

"An eye witness saw you on Sullivan's Island," Coop said. "She can testify about your strange clothing and behavior. This places you in the vicinity of the crime. Sure, it's absolutely the right thing to tell the police what you witnessed. But it's the wrong thing for you. Because your statement will give you a motive for killing her."

"How?"

"You'll have to tell the police why you went to her house that night. You'll admit that she taunted you. You'll admit that you and Barb argued. You'll tell them that your boyfriend might have fathered Barb's child. The police will think you and her were rivals. And—"

"I still have to tell them what I saw."

"But you don't have to do it today, homegirl," Red said. "Where you go, trouble follows. The cops won't look for a skinny dude in a Clinton mask. They'll zero in on a blonde with big hair. They'll get a search warrant. They'll find the scuba suit at the Spencer-Jackson House. Game over."

"Red's right," Coop said. "This will turn out poorly for you."

"You too, Boss."

Coop shook his head. "I don't care about me."

"You could be disbarred. You can't be Teeny's lawyer and boink her at the same time."

"Actually, I can," Coop said. "A while back, I looked this up in the ethics rules. If the *boinking,* as you put it, began *after* I represented Teeny in a legal matter, then yes, ethical charges could be filed against me. But Teeny and I have been intimate for a while. If she pays me a small retainer fee and asks for legal advice, I can represent her. What she tells me is confidential. Lawyer-client privilege. Because the relationship preceded the representation."

I put my hand over his hand. "Name your price, O'Malley."

"Give me two bucks, tell me what you saw through the window, and ask how you can avoid incriminating yourself." He smiled, then his eyes turned the color of tarnished silver. "Before we do that, you need to hear the medium-bad news. My boss called. He's threatening to fire me if I don't come to the office today."

A shivery feeling moved through my chest. "How long will you be gone?"

"Overnight. Maybe longer. Mr. Robichaux wants me to handle a divorce for an art dealer." Coop nodded at Red. "You're doing surveillance on his wife. Teeny can stay with my parents until I get back."

"No." I stood up so fast, the chair wobbled.

"You can't stay here by yourself," Coop said. "Not after last night."

"I'm coming to Charleston."

"Bad idea, homegirl," Red said. "Every cop in the Holy City is looking for you."

I felt dizzy and gripped the table.

"Don't scare her, Red." Coop guided me back to the chair. "I ought to quit that damn job and stay here with you."

"If you quit, then I'm out of a job, too." Red shoved a piece of toast into his mouth. "Let Teeny stay with your folks. I'd like to see a pervert break into your mama's house. She'd cut his balls off and sauté them."

"True." Coop slid a Tums into his mouth. "You can't stay by yourself, Teeny. And you really need to avoid Charleston."

"I'll be perfectly fine at the Spencer-Jackson. I've got a burglar alarm."

"And what happens when your sketch appears on television?" Red asked.

Coop poured syrup on his French toast. He didn't mention his mother again, so I took his silence as a sign that he'd capitulated. Red broke off a piece of bacon and fed it to Sir.

Coop set down the syrup jar, then reached for my hand. "Teeny, listen to me. I just want one thing in life. To wake up with you every morning. I want to make sure that happens."

"I don't want you to quit your job on account of me."

"I don't want you in jail—or hurt." He squeezed my hand, and something passed through me. Love, guilt, fear. So much fear.

"Teeny, my mother's house is a fortress."

"Why would she need one?"

"My parents' house got burgled a few years ago. Mother believes the criminals will return, and if they do, I pity them. She's taken karate lessons. Installed video cameras and alarms. That's just how she is, pugnacious and paranoid." He gave my hand another squeeze. "You won't have to stay long. Just a few days. Then I'll be back."

"Does Irene know I've got a bulldog?" *Does she know about the O'Malley ring?*

"Mother likes animals."

Right, when they're on a platter. I was afraid to stay by myself at the farm. I had many sleepless nights after Aunt Bluette had died. And the Spencer-Jackson House scared me.

"Okay." I slumped in my chair. "I'll stay with your mother."

Coop looked relieved. "I'll come back as soon as I can."

Red pushed away from the table. "If we hope to be in Charleston by noon, we better drop Teeny at your folks' house and scoot."

I sat up straight. "I'll drive myself."

"How?" Red spread his arms. "You don't have a car."

"Aunt Bluette's truck is in the barn."

Coop gave me a long, level look. "You're sure it runs?"

I opened the drawer, fished out the keys, and tossed them to him. "Check it out."

Coop tried to leave T-Bone with me, but the dog sensed what was going on. He leaped into the backseat and wouldn't come out, not even when I tried to lure him with bacon. Coop kissed me good-bye and climbed into the passenger seat. Red tooted the horn, then the van moved down the driveway. I felt an urge to run after them, the way Dorothy Gale had chased after the Wizard's balloon. *Come back! Come back! Don't leave without me!*

The brake lights turned red, and the van stopped. Coop got out and ran back to me. He gathered my hair into his hands and pulled me close, giving off new smells, soap and pancake syrup.

"I love you, Teeny."

"Love you, too."

"I know you're worried about my mother, but you can handle her. My grandmother will help you. Minnie O'Malley might be old, but she's tough."

"Does she know karate, too?" I smiled.

"Verbal judo is her specialty. If you need me, call. I'll tell my boss to take a hike."

"You're not a quitter, O'Malley." I grabbed his shirt and pulled him into a kiss.

After he left, I remembered that Emerson's stuff was still in the van. Sir gave me a worried look. His pink tongue was caught between his lips, and his eyes said, *Big mistake. You shoulda gone with them.*

"Don't worry," I said. "All the Templetons are hard-wired for disasters."

Sir's tail wagged.

"Blizzards, burglars, drought, oil spills, cancer, treachery, liars."

I heard the phone ring. I dashed back inside the house, skidded to the kitchen, and grabbed the receiver. I just knew it was Coop. "Hey, come back," I said. "You've got the hedgehog."

Silence. "I must have the wrong number," a girlish voice said. "I'm trying to reach Teeny Templeton."

"Speaking."

"This is Kendall. I need to see you. In private."

I sighed. I wasn't in the mood to discuss her romance with Lester. "This isn't a good time, honey. I'm on my way out the door."

"But you have to listen." She lowered her voice to a whisper. "Barb was murdered. And I know why."

fifteen

My stomach tensed, and I gripped the phone tighter. "I can't help you, Kendall," I said. "If you've got suspicions, call the police."

"They'd think I was batshit crazy. You're the only one who ever listened to me. That's why I called. Plus, you're boyfriend is a lawyer. We might need him. See, I found evidence this morning. I was vacuuming Lester's bedroom and the Electrolux sucked up the edge of the rug. Then it sucked up a paper. It was a computer printout. It had a list of organs and how much they sell for."

A picture took shape in my mind, a carved cherry pipe organ like the one at First Baptist. "Was she buying or selling?" I asked.

"I don't know."

"If she was selling, the organs would be at her house, right?"

Kendall sighed. "I've been to the house a lot and never saw any. But I didn't look in the refrigerator. She's got a Sub-Zero. She could've fit several organs in there."

"An organ won't fit in the fridge." I wove my fingers through the phone cord.

" 'Course it would. Wait, do you think I'm talking about a musical instrument? No, no, no. I mean human organs. Eyes. Skin. Teeth. Veins.

Creepy stuff like that. Barb's got a long list with prices. Gosh, an Achilles tendon sells for $2,000."

I jerked my fingers out of the phone cord. She might as well have said the Philpots were reptilians from outer space. "Barb wouldn't sell black market organs."

"She used to work in medical records at Bonaventure Regional. When I saw the printout, I thought it was job related. So I called her old boss. She told me that the hospital doesn't do transplants. But even if they did, Barb wouldn't have been involved with organs. She was just a coder."

"A what?"

"Her job was to match a bunch of numbers to an illness. The medical records lady told me that the code for diabetes is 2501. There's a code for everything. It's for insurance companies."

"So?"

"Don't you get it? Barb was selling body parts, and the job got her killed. I want to come over to your house and give you the printout. Your boyfriend can check it out."

"He'll need more than a printout." I paced in front of the window, stretching the phone cord behind me.

"What more does he need?" Kendall asked.

"I don't know. Some kind of proof that she was selling organs."

Okay." She sighed. "I'll see what I can dig up."

"Maybe you shouldn't. What if Lester is involved?"

"Seriously? He'd never do something mean like that. He won't let us put out rat poison at the store. He uses sticky traps and sets the rats free. They just run back into the store."

"If Barb was selling body parts, Lester would know about it. She'd have to explain the extra money she was earning. If Lester won't kill a rat, he sure wouldn't mess with the IRS."

"No, he wouldn't. Lester's worried about money. His business is sucking. The new Walgreens is about to bankrupt him."

"Hold on. Lester wouldn't be worried about money if his wife was selling tendons."

"He might not have known about it. He's real upset over his cash flow problems. Saturday morning, he and Norris got into a fight—right in the middle of the drugstore. It's a good thing no customers were there. Norris drove off. He didn't turn up until the next day. He looked like he'd been up all night. I guess he went to a massage parlor."

My thoughts whirled. Barb had disappeared last Saturday night. The man who'd choked her had looked thin and rangy. Just like Norris. Could he have killed her? But why?

"What if the printout didn't belong to Barb?" I asked.

"Who else would hide something like that?"

"Norris. He's an eye doctor."

Kendall snorted. "He don't like hard work. Cutting people up would be hard."

"Norris knows how to remove corneas. Maybe he stuck that printout under the rug."

"That's not his style. Barb's the one who hides things. Norris is into sex. There's only one part of the body that interests him, and it can't be sold on the black market. Have you talked to Zee Quinn, the girl who works at Baskin-Robbins?"

"No."

"See? Nobody listens to me. But you'll listen if I get more proof, won't you?"

"I guess."

"Fine. I'll get it and then I'll come straight to your house. And you can give it to your boyfriend."

She hung up. I put my head in my hands. If Barb had been selling black market organs, Lester knew about it. Maybe he and Barb were selling, and Norris was doing the surgery. A family operation. But where were they getting cadavers?

I was still in my nightgown, so I ran upstairs and rummaged in Mama's old closet. I put on a red blouse, a skirt that was patterned with cherries, and red cowboy boots. Then I went downstairs to wait for Kendall.

Thirty minutes later, I was pacing by the front door, glancing every few minutes at the driveway. What if Kendall had made this up? She was in love with a freshly widowed man. And his brother had been missing from Saturday morning until Sunday at noon.

I went over that night again. What if Norris had gone to Barb's rental? All this time, I'd had trouble understanding how my phone had gotten from Sullivan's Island to Bonaventure. Now I knew. Norris Philpot had been wearing that mask. He'd found my phone.

An hour went by, and I decided I couldn't stay in that house another second. I packed a bag, then I hooked a leash to Sir's collar. I grabbed the truck keys and we walked to the barn. The old Ford rose up like a humpback whale, gray-black with white pits in the fender. I yanked open the door, and searing air curled out, stinking of oil and sour milk. Aunt Bluette had been a packrat. I pushed a rusty Thermos to the floorboard.

"Hop in, Sir," I said, giving him a little boost. I tossed my suitcase into the truck bed, then I climbed into the front seat. The engine turned over with a thump. Halfway to the Piggly Wiggly, I passed a wrecker that was towing a black Mazda. A graduation tassel dangled from the rearview mirror.

Kendall's car.

I pulled off the road and told Sir to stay, then I scrambled out of the truck and waved both arms at the wrecker. The brakes screeched, and the driver poked his head out the window.

"Is this Kendall McCormack's car?" I called.

The driver pushed back a Georgia Bulldogs cap, revealing damp red curls. "Yessum. Her Mazda's totaled."

The back of my throat started to ache. "You're sure?"

"That it's totaled?" The driver's eyes widened.

"No, are you sure it's Kendall's car?"

"The police did a DMV check. The Mazda is registered to Kendall McCormack." He made a *tsking* sound. "Looks like she got drunk and wrecked."

"Drunk?" I said. "This early in the morning? I just talked to her. She was sober."

The man leaned out of the tow truck's window, the morning sun gleaming against his hair. His eyes were bloodshot, as if he'd been awake since the Eisenhower administration. "I ain't passing judgment, Miss. I'm just repeating what I heard."

"How bad was she hurt?" I knotted my hand against my stomach.

"Can't say for sure. By the time they called for a tow, the paramedics done took the girl to the hospital." He wiped the sweat off his forehead with a dirty hand. "When I showed up, a few responders were still here. They didn't mention no fatalities. Maybe she got banged up?"

I stepped toward the Mazda. "May I take a peek?"

He looked up at the sky, his mouth twisting into a bow. While he made up his mind, the heat from the asphalt leeched through my boots, stinging my bare feet. I stamped my foot, trying to blunt the pain.

The driver snapped to attention. "Well, I reckon it won't hurt. Just make it quick."

I ran over to the Mazda. The front fender was crushed. The windshield was cracked on the driver's side. Blood was splashed over the dashboard and the driver's seat. She'd been hurt real bad.

My legs wobbled, and I grabbed the door handle to keep from losing my balance. I didn't like blood. But this wasn't the moment to wimp out. I forced myself to take another look. I didn't see the printout she'd mentioned. A Hello Kitty key chain dangled from the ignition. And one of those keys went to Philpot's Pharmacy. I leaned into the car, snatched the chain, and shoved it into my pocket. I hurried back to my truck and waved at the driver, hoping he hadn't seen what I'd done.

The tow truck rumbled by, dragging the Mazda. I felt weak when I saw Kendall's shattered windshield, and I buried my face against Sir. He gave me a few halfhearted licks, reminding me that the body count would rise if I didn't get him some water.

I drove home and put Sir in the parlor, where it was cool, then I went straight to the phone and dialed Coop. He answered on the second ring. I filled him in on Kendall's strange call, the list of organs, her wreck, Lester's finances, and my suspicions about Norris.

"The printout and the wreck are mutually exclusive, Teeny. You have no proof that Barb or the Philpots were involved in illegal trafficking."

"For once, instead of thinking like a lawyer, can't you think like a criminal?" I stamped my boot on the floor. "Norris lost his medical license. Lester's drugstore is bankrupt. Barb liked jewelry. They had motives."

"For?"

"To run a chop shop for human body organs. Innocent people don't hide a price list of corneas under the bedroom rug."

"*If* there's a list." He paused, as if to let his words resonate. "Go to my parents' house. I'll try to drive back to Bonaventure tomorrow."

But I wasn't going to the O'Malleys' just yet. After Coop and I hung up, I dialed the hospital and asked the operator to page Dot Agnew. Two minutes later, a familiar voice said, "Teeny, I was just thinking about you. But I'm late for a meeting."

"Oh, okay. Listen, if you get a minute, will you check on a patient? She's in Bonaventure Regional."

"Oh, honey. I can't do that," Dot said. "I can't tell you about our patients. Hospital policy, you know. But I can put you through to the patient's room. What's the name?"

"Kendall McCormick."

There was a slight pause. "What happened. Did Lester finally get her cherry?"

"You know about that?"

"Everyone in town knows. Kendall has a big mouth. Seriously, why's she in the hospital?" Dot laughed. "Did she lose another Tampax inside her?"

I gripped the phone. "I shouldn't have told you that."

"Back then, you told me everything. And I do mean *everything*. Oh, Teeny. Don't be angry. I'm sorry I poked fun at the McCormick girl. I didn't realize you all were still close."

"She was on her way to my house when she wrecked." I felt swimmy-headed and propped my hand against the wall. If I hadn't told Kendall to get proof, she wouldn't have wrecked. But I couldn't tell this to Dot. She'd have me slapped into a straitjacket.

"Oh, sweetie," Dot said. "I wish I could help. But I'd lose my job."

"Don't explain. I know about rules." I grimaced. Boy, did I ever know.

I ran back outside to the truck. I had to see if Kendall was all right. I drove to the hospital and bought a tin of cookies in the gift shop. Chocolate chip pecan, dipped in white chocolate. A volunteer directed me to room 312.

I stepped into the elevator, and a group of LPN students swarmed around me. The overhead speakers crackled and a nasal voice said, "Code Blue, room—"

The doors glided shut and the voice snapped off. The students talked about a tonsillectomy. That morning, a sixteen-year-old boy had gone into cardiac arrest and died.

The elevator dinged, and the students rushed out. Hospital personnel raced past them and disappeared around a corner. Another nurse ran by, pushing the Code Blue cart.

The students followed the rapid-response team, and I followed the students. They stopped outside room 312. A plump, middle-aged woman was trying to push her way into the room, screaming Kendall's name.

A student put her arm around the woman. "Let's go to the visitors' waiting room, Mrs. McCormack," the nurse said. More members of the trauma team bolted down the hall and swung into Kendall's crowded room.

The student led Mrs. McCormack away. I lowered my hand to my purse, feeling the outline of the Hello Kitty key chain. If I gave them to Kendall's mother, the memento would push her over the edge. The poor woman was already in shock.

I was feeling pretty stunned myself. Pictures of the Mazda's shattered windshield kept flying through my head like bits of glass. My hands shook so much, the cookies rattled inside the tin. I made up a new recipe called Please-Don't-Die Peach Vinegar. Take a cup of chopped peaches and add white wine vinegar. Strain through cheesecloth, over and over until the liquid is clear; pour it into sterilized jars. Add a cinnamon stick to each jar and put them in the fridge. Steep two weeks. Remind yourself that anything can turn bitter. All it takes is time and coldness.

I walked back to the elevator in a daze. The metal doors slid open, and Son Finnegan stepped out.

sixteen

Son's eyes widened when he saw me. His shoulders went back, and he stood even taller, adding three inches to his height. He adjusted his lab coat. A stethoscope was coiled in his pocket like a garden snake. Pinned to his collar was a button that read: BEST DOCTOR OF THE YEAR, THE ENTERPRISE.

"We keep running into each other." He grinned. "It's fate."

"I just came to see Kendall McCormack." I glanced over my shoulder. "But a trauma team went into her room. Can you find out what happened?"

"And violate patient confidentiality?"

I pointed to his button. "You think rules exist for people who like rules."

"You've got a point. But let's talk in my office." He steered me past the nurses' station into a storage closet. IV poles rattled as we squeezed into the tiny space. He shut the door and leaned against it.

"Nice office," I said. "The medical décor is spot on."

"Your boots are the perfect accessory." He pushed away from the door. "God, you're beautiful. Your eyes are still the color of Irish whiskey. And when you're thinking hard, they widen a little, and—"

"Can you find out if Kendall's going to live or die?"

"Sure. On one condition. Have dinner with me tonight."

"You know I can't."

"I'm asking you to dinner, not an orgy."

"I'd feel safer at an orgy." An image flickered behind my eyes, Son and me rolling together in the orchard, our bodies slick with dew and sweat.

"What are you scared of, Boots?"

"Rats and bees," I said, silently adding, Norris, Lester, Irene O'Malley. Son Finnegan.

"Stay here and think about dinner," he said. "I'll check on the Code Blue."

After he left, I sat on the floor and pressed my forehead against the cookie tin. I hadn't told Coop everything about me and Son. Not that it was a disgrace. In my whole life, I'd had four lovers. That might sound like a lot until you compared it to other things. Would you only try on four pairs of shoes in your whole life? Would you only eat four Lindt Truffles?

A long while later the door opened, bringing in a gush of cold, medicinal air, along with Son Finnegan.

"Kendall was admitted this afternoon with a concussion and a scalp laceration," he said. "All tests were negative. No skull fracture. No intracranial bleeding. But she had a blood alcohol of .12."

"Is that high?"

"Yeah. According to the nurse's notes, she was talking crazy. But she was alive. Twenty minutes later, the patient's mother went to the cafeteria, and while she was gone, a nurse stopped in the patient's room to take her blood pressure. The patient was unresponsive. The nurse called a code. I guess that's when you walked up."

"But I talked to Kendall before the accident. She didn't sound drunk."

"A blood alcohol level doesn't lie." He helped me to my feet, and I handed him the cookie tin.

"There's more, Teeny. Your friend's not going to make it. The docs are working hard, but they can't get a heartbeat. There's no telling how long she went without oxygen. She's probably got massive brain damage."

I felt light-headed and forced myself to breathe through my nose.

"Why would Kendall have coded in the first place? She's young and healthy."

"A small bleed might not have shown on the CT. Or the radiologist could've missed it."

"What would a small bleed do?" I asked.

"The brain would swell. And the pressure would kink off the arteries that feed the brain. The patient would stop breathing and go into cardiac arrest."

"I'd hate to be a patient here."

"Why?"

"Too many people are dying. I heard the nursing students talking about a botched tonsillectomy. A sixteen-year-old boy died."

"It's a hospital, Teeny. Bad shit happens." His forehead puckered. "Last week I lost a twenty-two-year-old patient. She sailed through the breast augmentation. Nurses found her dead during a routine vital sign check. Cold and blue. Pupils fixed and dilated."

"What killed her?"

"The post showed zip. I've lost two other patients. Both were young women. But I'll explain everything over dinner."

I shook my head. "Coop and I are together."

He glanced at my left hand. "I don't see an engagement ring."

I lifted the necklace.

Son peered down at the diamond. "No wonder you've got it on a chain. That ring would fit Sasquatch."

"It's a family heirloom."

"Cooter's too cheap to buy you a ring that fits?"

"Coop, not Cooter."

"We ought to talk about this so-called engagement. If you're afraid to be seen in public with me, I'll bring dinner to your house."

"I'm staying with Coop's parents."

He drummed his fingers on the cookie tin. "Oh, come on. One chicken dinner won't kill you. It'll be strictly business. Cooter head won't know."

"But I will."

"You're still attracted to me."

"Not anymore."

"Then why are your nipples hard?" He lifted one hand from the tin and pointed to my blouse.

I glanced down. Two hard nubs jutted against the cotton fabric. I pushed past him, flung open the door, and rushed into the hall.

"Teeny, wait!"

I bolted down the stairs, out the front door, into the hospital parking lot. Heat waved over the pavement, distorting the cars. A white van sped by. Black letters were written on the van's side: BIOSTRUCTURES.

I climbed into my truck. The steering wheel burned my palms and I let go. Dammit, I had no business coming to the hospital. And I'd made things worse by asking for Son's help.

First things first. Get out of the parking lot. I rooted under the seat, found a pair of socks, and pulled them over my hands. Then I started the engine and drove to the Square. My plan was to talk to the woman at Baskin-Robbins. Maybe she knew something about Norris. Something that could link him to Barb. Because I felt certain that they'd been selling body parts.

I was a sweaty mess by the time I stepped into Baskin-Robbins. The frosty air felt good, rippling over my hair. A young, brown-eyed woman stood behind the glass counter, running a damp cloth around the ice-cream bins, her hairnet bulging with dreadlocks. She looked to be in her early twenties, close to Kendall's age.

"Get you anything?" she asked me.

"I'm looking for Zee Quinn."

"I'm her. What's up?"

I stared at the glass case, as if my thoughts were on ice cream rather than the illegal sale of corneas. "Got anything low cal, Zee?"

"Not much." She laughed, and her dark eyes swept over me. "How about a smoothie?"

"I'm allergic." I patted my hips. "I break out in fat."

"Girl, you ain't big. Get you a Peach Passion Banana. It's made with fat-free vanilla yogurt."

"Sold."

Her smile widened, showing a slightly crooked front tooth. "You won't be sorry."

While she made the smoothie, I ran through options. I could get to the point and ask if Norris was a homicidal maniac, but Zee didn't know me. She might not talk.

"Kendall McCormack told me to look you up," I said.

"Yeah?"

I leaned over the counter. "She said you might help me."

"With what?"

"Norris Philpot."

Zee's hand shook as she set my smoothie on the counter. "That'll be $9.44."

I looked up at the menu. "Um, I thought a large smoothie was $4.99."

"When I get upset, my dyslexia gets stirred up. Plus, I forgot to add tax."

I handed her a five-dollar bill and change. "I had a little incident with Norris."

Zee's gaze sharpened. "What'd he do to you?"

"He asked me on a date. He was very persistent, but I turned him down."

"Smart move on your part."

"Kendall told me that you had a run-in with him."

Zee stared at me a long moment. "Why do you care?"

"Because I'm a little freaked out. Is he dangerous?"

She looked over her shoulder. "Lucy, watch the counter for me. I'm taking a break." Zee turned around, her hairnet shaking. "Meet me outside."

I plucked napkins from the box and hurried out the door. She stood beside a stone picnic table, her arms crossed. "Girl, I'm going to tell you something, and you can't tell anyone. Not your mother or your daddy or your best friend."

"Don't have any of those. But I can keep my mouth shut."

"Okay, then." She folded her arms. "A year ago, I was helping my auntie clean her garage. I got a splinter in my eye. She took me to Dr. Philpot. He had a fancy office with a surgery room. He put me to sleep. When I woke up, a tiny white dick was in my hand. And the dick belonged to Dr. Philpot."

I opened my mouth. *Chu-chu* sounds came out of my throat.

"At first, I thought I was having some sort of drug-induced nightmare." Zee spat on the pavement. "Then he started moving my hand. I don't have to tell you the rest."

"Did you confront him?"

Her eyes filled. "I should've broke that ding-dong in two. But I just lay there, pretending to sleep. Let him do his thing. From what I hear, it could've been worse."

"He raped a woman, didn't he?" I dabbed a napkin over my face.

"The police didn't do nothing about it."

"Pervert. I think he broke into my house." I told her about my cell phone, the gardenias, and my soiled nightgown.

She wiped her eyes. "That sick mutherfucker."

She spat again. "You'll be all right. Don't let his skinny white ass get near you."

That sounded like a good plan. She went back inside. I carried my smoothie around the corner, into the shady arcade. I dropped coins in the pay phone and told the operator I wanted to make a collect call to Coop O'Malley. You'd think I'd asked for a year's supply of free martinis. I was pouring sweat when she finally put me through. Coop accepted the charges.

"I've been ringing you for over an hour," he cried. "I was just about to make Red turn the van around."

"I'm okay."

"Please tell me you didn't go to the hospital."

"Just for a second."

"Dammit, Teeny. A criminal broke into your house. You shouldn't be gallivanting around town. It's not safe." He yelled so loud, I held the receiver away from my ear.

When he stopped shouting, I explained about Kendall's Code Blue, skipping over the part about Son. I also told him about Norris and Zee Quinn.

"Hearsay," he said. In the background, I heard a knocking sound, as if he was beating his fist against a dashboard. "If you keep asking questions, he could file harassment charges. Where are you now?"

"Oglethorpe Square."

"Go to Mother's right now. She's expecting you."

Great. Just what I needed. An evening with my biggest fan. I exhaled harder than I'd intended.

"Teeny, I know you're upset about your friend. You wouldn't be you if you didn't care about people. But I need to know you're in a safe place. Just put up with my mother until I get there."

Not without a cattle prod. But he sounded so upset, I promised I'd try. After we hung up, I threw away my melted smoothie. I went back to the farm, intending to collect Sir. But I was shaking all over. I couldn't stop thinking about Kendall. And what about that printout? What were the chances that Norris had worn that Bill Clinton mask?

Before I faced Irene O'Malley, I needed to collect myself; instead, I went into the parlor and put a stack of records on the hi-fi. I knew I could count on Elvis and "Jailhouse Rock" to give my mood a boost. Sir and I went upstairs. We both stretched out on Mama's old bed. A dormer window looked out into the front yard, showing a wash of blue sky.

I wished I'd had time to make peach preserves. The recipe is simple, but the process is tricky. Cooks should never attempt to make jam if they are in a sour mood. The fruit will grab hold of bitterness. If the cook is upset, the lids won't seal. Unless you wish to be poisoned, you'll have to eat your jam right away. Hot preserves are just like anger: When the mixture cools, it sucks out the oxygen in the jar, bends the lids inward, and creates a protective seal. Nothing can seep into your preserves. Or you.

I stopped thinking about food and hummed along with Elvis. Sir snored. Then I fell asleep with my boots on.

seventeen

I awoke to the sound of a growling bulldog. I opened my eyes. The dormer window was backlit with leaden dusk. The Elvis music had stopped playing. How long had I slept?

A car rumbled down the driveway. I leaped out of bed and jerked back the curtain, expecting to see Coop. But a navy Jaguar pulled in next to my truck. Son Finnegan climbed out, holding brown paper sacks.

My pulse beat behind my eyes. I ran downstairs, skidded to the porch, and collided with him. The bags crumpled, giving off the smell of fried okra. I lifted my chin, trying to seem taller. "I told you not to come," I said. "Why didn't you listen?"

"Why is a mattress in your front yard?"

"Leave."

"Not until you eat. Didn't know if you still liked red wine, so I got white, too."

I spread my arms, blocking the door. "Take your fried okra and go."

"You've got a good nose, Boots."

"If you aren't gone in two seconds, I'll sic my dog on you." I waved at the screened door. Sir pushed his flat muzzle against it. "He hates tall, blond doctors," I added.

"Yeah, he looks ferocious." Son looked at the dog. "Hey, puppy. I brought sustenance. Ask your beautiful mama if you can have a chicken tender."

Sir licked the mesh.

"Traitor," I said.

Son reached around me, opened the door, and strode into the house. He set the bags on the dining room table.

I rushed after him. "You should've called."

"And spoil everything?" He pinched my cheek. "After dinner, we can go over my patients' charts. Then we need to talk."

"I don't have time."

"Since when?" His hand lingered on my face. "If you had to pick between O'Malley and a chocolate pie, you'd pick the pie."

I jerked away. "I'm spending the night with his parents. I've got to leave now."

"Be glad I brought wine." He winked. "You'll need it."

"I'm not having dinner with you." I breathed through my mouth, trying not to smell the okra and chicken and corn bread.

"I love it when you're caught between food and anger, Boots." He lifted a Styrofoam carton from the bag.

"Quit calling me Boots."

"You used to like it."

"I lied."

"Your nipples say otherwise."

I folded my arms over my breasts. Son opened the carton, revealing plump, batter-fried chicken strips. They had a nutty, bacony smell. My mouth filled with saliva, and the craving for good food threatened to trump my common sense.

He grinned. "Which cabinet holds the dishes?"

I hated to encourage him, but I could already imagine my teeth sinking through the chicken tender. "Right behind you on the sideboard."

While he set the table, I couldn't resist opening the other Styrofoam boxes. Fried jalapeño grits, batter-fried green beans, pecan pork nuggets, grilled Georgia shrimp, Vidalia onion rings, and strawberry shortcake. I blinked at the onion rings, and my rudeness vanished. I swooned, imagining the sweet, translucent ribbon caught inside the crunchy coating.

"I asked them to put the whipped cream in a separate container," he said. "Think it'll melt, or should we eat dessert first?"

He looked so distraught, I couldn't stop smiling.

"Go ahead, laugh," he said. "See if I care."

He moved toward me, and Sir cut in front of him, showing his teeth. All the hairs on the dog's back stood up.

Son leaped back. "Talk about a delayed reaction. Jesus, what'd I do?"

"I warned you."

"Here, puppy." Son clapped his hands.

The bulldog pounced on Son's ankle and bit into the beige trousers. "Jesus, get him off."

I rushed over to Sir and worked the fabric out of his teeth. Just last month, I'd taken him to a canine training class, and I tried out a command. "Leave it!"

Sir's broad head stopping sawing from side to side and he spat out the trouser. I patted his head. "Good Sir. Good boy."

Son rubbed his ankle. "Shit, it's stinging. Why'd he attack all of a sudden?"

"He's never done it before. He must've smelled the badness on you."

"I love it when you sweet-talk me." Son winked.

"Thanks. Did he break the skin?"

"Nah, I'm okay." He lifted his trouser and ran his finger over raised, pink marks. "But I've got bad news about your little friend."

"Kendall?" I dug my fingernails into my palm. She was dead. I just knew it.

"She didn't make it, Boots. I'm sorry."

I'd been expecting the worst, but hearing the words made me slump over. I gripped the side of the table to steady myself. "It's not right for young people to die. It's just not right."

"No, it's not." Son put his hand on my shoulder.

The bulldog lunged again. I dropped to the floor, grabbed Sir's collar, and pulled him against me. His fur stood up like stiff, white threads. I wanted to hear about Kendall, but I'd have to put Sir in the bedroom.

And I didn't trust myself to be alone with Son. The summer he'd worked at the orchard, he'd seduced me in ten minutes. But that was a long time ago. Now I could handle him, right?

I stroked Sir's head. "If I put up my dog, will you stop flirting?"

"I'm not flirting, Boots. I'm just trying to feed you."

My gaze passed over Son's Gucci loafers, up to his hands, then I studied his face. His ponytail was caught in a leather strip, and the blond curls fell down his shoulder. I swallowed. Big feet, big hands. Big . . .

Don't think about the rest of him.

I pulled Sir into my arms, grunting, and toted him to my defiled bedroom. I set him on the floor and walked around the room, gathering up my old chocolate supply. I put it in the top of my closet. When I was satisfied that the room was dog-proofed, I tossed him a stuffed duck. He looked away, disgusted.

"I do not feel sorry for you." I shook my finger. "Try to behave."

I went to the kitchen and found a wine opener in a drawer. In another drawer I found a Band-Aid and a crumpled tube of Neosporin. From the parlor, I heard Billie Holliday singing "Lover, Come Back to Me."

I frowned. Son was making himself at home. I stepped into the dining room just as he returned from the parlor.

"Your hi-fi is a relic," he said.

"Whatever." I handed him the Neosporin and the Band-Aid. He dabbed ointment on the bite marks and watched me fill our glasses with merlot.

"To the Georgia Bulldogs." He raised his cup. "And your bulldog. Even though he's a biter."

I raised my cup higher. "To all dogs."

"You'll love the food," he said. "It's upscale Southern."

It did smell ambrosial, so I didn't need prodding. I sat at the far end of the table, near the kitchen door in case he pulled anything. We ate in silence, forking up the delicacies, while in the background, Billie sang about tangled love.

I'd just polished off the chicken nuggets when the kitchen phone rang.

I moved slowly, weighted down by grease and carbohydrates. Thanks to my shortness, there's no margin for diet errors and nowhere to go but sideways. In my next life, I hoped I was tall with a fast metabolism, but until that happened, I would have to unbutton my skirt.

When I lifted the receiver, no one was there. I heard a crackle. I hung up and walked toward the dining room. The phone trilled again. I skated back into the kitchen and snatched the receiver.

Silence.

If I'd been alone, I would have been alarmed, but Son and his food had left me stuffed and serene. I dropped the receiver into a drawer and hurried back to the dining room. He put down a half-eaten green tomato slider. "Who keeps calling? Cooter or Mama Cooter?"

"Wrong number," I said.

"From the wrong guy." Son speared a triangle of pastry and held it out. "Try the Guinness turnover."

I took the fork out of his hand and raked my teeth over the tines. The turnover was sweeter than I'd expected, almost as good as a fried Twinkie, with a salty aftertaste.

"Do that again," he said. "That thing with your teeth."

I dropped the fork and it clunked against the table.

"Aw, don't be offended, Boots. I love a woman who knows how to eat." He opened another carton. Inside was a luscious sponge cake, vanilla pudding oozing from the center onto fresh strawberries.

After we finished dessert, I felt more sociable. I undid the second button on my skirt and took another sip of merlot. "Okay," I said. "We've had dinner. Tell me about Kendall."

"Her X-rays were negative." He leaned back in his chair and stretched his arms over his head. "No skull fracture. CT was normal. No bleeding. No brain swelling."

"But I saw her car. Blood was everywhere."

"She had a scalp wound, and those things gush. She probably had a concussion."

"Are they fatal?"

"Not unless she had an occult bleed. That means hidden."

While I gathered plates and empty cartons, Son went to his car and fetched the medical charts. He came back and set them on the table. I sat across from him.

"You can come closer," he said. "I won't bite."

"But I could."

"I've had my shots. Come on, Boots. It's easier to explain the medical information if you aren't sitting way over yonder."

He was playing with me, using the charts as bait. "I can see fine," I said. "Let's get started. The O'Malleys are expecting me."

He crossed the room in two steps. Before I could run away, he lifted me from the chair and slung me over his shoulder. Blood rushed into my face. A burning-hot pulse drilled against the top of my head.

"You're a Cro-Magnon!" I clawed the back of his shirt, but my fingers hit solid muscle. I raised up, my hair streaming into my face, and slapped his arm. He set me in a chair. Then he moved behind the chair and leaned over me, clamping his arms against my arms. Using his legs, he pushed my chair closer to the edge of the table. His hard, ropy muscles twitched, and I felt a pulsebeat throb against my flesh.

He pressed his lips against my ear. "Remember how it used to be, Teeny?"

No, I didn't want to remember anything. I pushed down an image of him standing in the barn, pulling down his tattered jeans. I thought of Oleander Pudding, Arsenic Apple Turnovers, and Sausage-Stuffed Death Cap Mushrooms.

"Finnegan, if you don't back off, I'll kick your ass."

"Keep talking dirty." His breath kicked up my hair. "I swiped confidential charts just for you. I broke the law, Boots."

"It was your idea." My chest sawed in and out. "Not mine."

"Don't hyperventilate. The charts are from my office."

"If you don't let me go I'll take out an ad in the Bonaventure *Gazette.* It'll say, 'Son Finnegan stole hospital property.'"

"So? I'll rent a billboard. It'll say, 'Son Finnegan loves Teeny Templeton.'"

I stopped squirming. He released one of my arms and slid the folders in front of me. He opened the first chart and flipped back the cover.

"Ingrid Robertson. Twenty-two years old. Breast augmentation. No complications during surgery. No post-op complications. Private pay, so no insurance company was screaming at me to discharge her. Third day post-op, the night nurse found her cold and unresponsive. A Code Blue was called, and the trauma team responded. I arrived ten minutes later and took over. Couldn't get a pulse. I called the code after forty-five minutes—that's a long time, Boots. But she was so damn young."

"What was the cause of death?"

"I wasn't sure what happened. The clinical cause of death agrees with the autopsy about half the time. We don't always know why people die. But the coroner thought that Ingrid had gone into cardiac arrest, secondary to PVCs."

"PVCs? What's that?"

"Premature ventricular contractions. It means the lower chamber of the heart, the ventricle, contracts before it should. PVCs can be deadly."

He closed the chart and lifted the next one, going out of his way to rub against my arm.

"Valerie Atwood. Age thirty-two. Liposuction. Normally this is an outpatient surgery, but I admitted her because she had difficulty urinating post-op. She wasn't on a cardiac monitor. Someone from dietary brought her lunch tray and found Ms. Atwood unconscious. A Code Blue was called, but we lost her."

"More PVCs?" I asked.

"Probably. Nothing turned up on the autopsy. No pulmonary emboli. No abnormalities. The official cause of death was cardiac arrhythmia. But nothing in the nurse's notes supported this theory. Her pulse had been regular."

He opened the third chart. "Brianna Connors. Age forty-eight. Tummy tuck. Expired second day post-op. Autopsy revealed nothing, but the coroner suspected a fat embolism. The review board agreed with the path report.

But if I have any more unexplained deaths, the medical staff might start to question my abilities."

"Maybe they already have." I tried to push his arms away, but he hemmed me in tighter.

"I may not look it, but I'm a conscientious doc. Even so, the mortality rate in plastic surgery is one in one hundred thousand. I've had three deaths in six months. That's high. Statistically, this shouldn't be happening."

"Have other doctors lost patients?"

"Sure. Including Cooter's daddy. Last month, Dr. O'Malley admitted a twenty-six-year-old man for a third-degree burn on his arm. I was brought in to do a skin graft. The patient recovered and was scheduled to be discharged. When the nurse came to get him, the patient had expired."

"All these patients were young and healthy," I said.

Son tucked my hair behind my ear. "After I saw you today, I did some checking. Bonaventure Regional's mortality rate is higher than it was last year."

"Wouldn't this alert someone to investigate?" I asked.

"Only if the death rate climbs." Son's hand moved to my neck. "I've got some theories about these deaths. One, act of God. Two, nursing error. The wrong medication or too much medication. Three, Angel of Death."

"Someone at the hospital could be killing patients?"

"More likely, it's a combination of God plus one overworked nurse. Most nurses are as smart as the docs. I bet two-thirds are smarter. But they can't be everywhere at once."

"True." The air between us crackled, and a jolt moved up my arms, into my breasts. I wondered if he kissed the same way, if he still had that little trick where he blew on the belly button.

I leaned away from him. It was wrong to be attracted to another man. It was wrong to feel this way when Kendall was dead.

From the hi-fi, Def Leppard sang "Pour Some Sugar on Me." When Mama had been at her craziest, she'd paired this song with Judges 9:11 and a recipe for candied violets.

"Don't move away from me, Boots," Son whispered against my neck. "Don't you remember how good it was? I love you. And I never stopped."

My throat felt tight and full, as if I'd swallowed the Savannah River. He started to kiss me. I turned my head, and his lips glanced off my cheek.

"You're wasting your time with Little Deuce Coup," he said. "You know his problem, don't you? He can't resist a woman in distress. It's his kryptonite. The minute he realizes how strong you are, he'll be gone." He got in my face. "The least you could have done was respond to my letters."

I frowned. "What letters?"

"The ones I wrote after your aunt ninja'd us. Did your aunt throw away the letters?"

"What letters? She didn't throw away any letters." But maybe she had. To get me away from Son, she'd sent me to Chamor Island, a tiny island off the Georgia coast. It was shaped like a bear claw pastry, but it smelled of sulfur. Wild horses ran down the empty beach, crocodiles bellowed from the swamp, and mosquitoes drank my blood. Inside the brown wooden house, Aunt Bunny played with her Ouija board, and my cousin Ira built talking Jesus dolls. But Ira made up sacrilegious things for Jesus to say: *Thou shalt eat oysters during an R month. Thou shalt not kill doodle bugs. Thou shalt not spit on the floor.*

"I tried to find you, but I didn't know where you'd gone," Son said. "I had to go back to med school in September. But I wrote you letters. I used a fake return address. I used an alias, Parker MacArthur. I named it after that song you loved. 'MacArthur Park.' I mailed the letters from Atlanta. I bet your aunt burned them."

Now my throat felt bigger than the Atlantic Ocean. Yes, I'd been fond of Son, I wasn't denying it, but now, everything was different. *I* was different.

From the bedroom, my bulldog howled. Son bent closer and brushed his lips against my ear. "You may think you love him, but he's wrong for you. I speak your dialect. We're country people, you and me. We don't put on airs. We don't try to be something we're not."

I couldn't argue with him. These same worries rang in my head all the time, a warning sound like a buoy in a storm.

"I'll always be waiting for you, Teeny. And if there's one chance in hell that I can be with you, I'm taking it."

Behind me, the floor creaked. Then a familiar voice said, "What's going on?"

eighteen

Coop stood in the doorway, his arms loaded with flowers and a sheaf of papers. Son and I broke apart. A burning, scalding pain spurted out the top of my skull. "I didn't hear you come in," I said, rubbing my forehead.

"Who can hear anything over Def Leppard?" Son said.

I introduced the men, but they ignored me and glared at each other. A muscle jerked in Coop's jaw. He set down the bouquet and the papers, which looked like mail. He turned his blue, bottomless gaze on me. "Why didn't you go to my folks' house? What's *he* doing here?"

"I asked him to check on Kendall."

"Are those medical records?" Coop gestured at the stacked charts. He turned to Son. "I'm sure you're familiar with the Health Insurance Portability and Accountability Act?"

"HIPPA?" Son asked. "Sure."

"And you still brought private medical records into this house?" Coop spoke quietly, but his voice was shaking. "These patients could sue."

I tried to ignore the thrumming pain in my scalp. "I asked Son to break the rules," I said, emphasis on rules. "And he did."

Coop pulled a Pepto-Bismol bottle out of his hip pocket, wrenched off the cap, and drank.

Son tucked the charts under his arm. "You don't have to defend me, Teeny. But I appreciate it. If you need help, you know where to find me."

I sank onto the chair and the toes of my boots pointed inward.

Son turned into the hall. "See you around, Counselor."

The screen door clapped against the frame. Sir's barks echoed, as if he'd fallen into the bottom of a well. I wanted to climb in with him. Coop took another long swig of Pepto-Bismol, and the chalky smell drifted over to me. He capped the bottle, tucked it under his arm. As he lifted the mail, his hard gaze swept over my trembling hands.

"You didn't need Finnegan's help. I told you my dad would check on Kendall."

"She died."

"Oh, no." He looked down at the floor. "I'm so sorry. What happened?"

I started with Kendall's wreck and ended with Son's visit. "I feel responsible for what happened to her. See, she wanted to show you the printout. But I told her she'd need more proof. She went looking for evidence. That's when she wrecked."

Coop's eyes softened. "Stop blaming yourself."

"Don't blame Son for coming over. I was upset about Kendall. I asked for his help."

Coop's foot tapped the floor. "Why him? A guy you barely know."

"I didn't say I barely knew him."

Coop's eyelashes fluttered. "Is he an old boyfriend?"

"We dated eight years ago. Briefly. Then we broke up."

"What happened in between?"

"The usual. I was twenty-one years old. What were you doing at that age?"

"Point taken." He looked up at the ceiling. "I'm just trying to understand why you asked for his help. Why didn't you ask me?"

"I called you. Twice. Both times you told me to go to your mother's house. I wanted to know why Kendall died, and Son found out."

"He broke the law, Teeny."

"But he's never lied to me."

Coop jerked back, as if I'd shoved him. I couldn't pull in a full breath. My breastbone ached all the way through to my spine, like I'd fallen on the sharp end of a meat thermometer.

Air. I needed air. I ran to the kitchen, snatched my inhaler, and sucked in the bitter fumes. A floorboard creaked, and Coop stepped into the room. He dumped the flowers, the mail, and the Pepto-Bismol bottle on the table. His eyes circled my face. "You're upset."

"I'm perfectly calm." I took another hit of Ventolin.

"A paradigm of serenity." He glanced at the counter, where I'd lined up empty Styrofoam containers. His mouth opened, then clamped shut.

From the bedroom, Sir let out another howl. I moved toward the hall, but Coop caught my arm. "Stay. You need another dose of Ventolin. I'll get the bulldog."

I set my inhaler aside. I'd already had two doses; I couldn't take another for six hours. I buttoned my skirt. Then I lifted the phone out of the drawer and put it in the cradle. I heard the staccato sound of bulldog breath, and a second later, Sir bounded into the kitchen.

"Why was he in solitary confinement?" Coop spread his arms in the doorway.

"He bit Son."

Coop laughed. He bent down and patted Sir's head. The tension between us seemed to lessen. "Where's T-Bone?" I asked.

"With Red."

"Are you hungry?" I asked. "Let me fix you a sandwich."

He glanced at his watch. "We'll get something to eat at Mother's."

"It's too late." I wasn't referring to time. It was too late for Kendall. Too late for Barb. Maybe too late for me and Coop. "I'm staying here tonight."

"What am I going to do with you, Templeton?"

I shrugged. He opened the back door and walked into the dark yard. He put his hands on his hips and gazed up at the stars. His shoulders slumped, as if the whole sky had fallen on him. I felt so guilty. He'd driven all these miles to make sure I was safe. He'd brought flowers. And

I'd eaten fried okra with Dr. Botox. I started to go after Coop and put my arms around him. I wanted to tell him I was frightened. And when a Templeton gets frightened, we try to act brave. Never mind that we take bravery too far. That's what I'd done. By trying to do the right thing, I'd done the wrong thing.

I put the flowers in a vase and set them on the counter. The phone rang, and I lifted the receiver. An unfamiliar, whispery voice said, "Itheeyou." It sounded formal, Old English words, *I thee you.* No, not Old English. A lisp.

"Norris?" I said. "Is that you?"

There was a decisive click, and the line went dead.

I flew in and out of dreams, ugly winged nightmares that stung me over and over, leaving a nagging pain in the back of my mind. I awoke with my fists knotted in the sheets. Morning light fell through the windows; bright shards cut across the floor and slashed over the bed.

Coop sat in a chair, lacing his shoes. His hair was combed, and water marks outlined his brown curls. I fumbled on the nightstand and grabbed my inhaler.

"Hey, you're awake." He stood. "You and Sir have to go to Mother's right now. I've got to be in Charleston by noon. I'm meeting Red. He's setting up surveillance."

Part of me wanted to stay in Bonaventure so I could be near Emerson, but the other part wanted to be away from Son Finnegan. "I'm going to Charleston."

He shook his head. "The police are looking for you."

"Your parents live only a few miles from the Philpots. I don't want to be that close to Norris. I know he called me last night."

"You can't be sure."

"Yes, I am. He broke into my house and left my phone. And dirtied my—" I took a puff from my inhaler. I wanted to believe Norris had worn that mask. Otherwise, I'd always be scanning faces and thinking, *Is he the one?*

Coop sat down on the bed. "Red talked to a Charleston detective. A witness saw Barb having a drink with a tall, rangy guy the day before she went missing. They were acting pretty cozy."

I drew a stick figure on the sheet. "Norris Philpot is skinny, just like the guy in the Bill Clinton mask."

"Or she could have picked up a guy in the bar. Maybe he noticed her jewelry. He could have followed her home, intending to rob her. That would explain the mask."

"But he had a key to her house."

"You're trying to build a case against Norris, but you've only got conjecture." He smoothed my hair. "Let me protect you, Teeny. My parents' house is the best place for you right now."

"So you keep saying."

"Whoever broke into your house is a damn coward. He doesn't want an audience. My mother and grandmother will be there. There's a cook and a housekeeper. With all those people around, you'll be safe. I'll be back tonight."

"That's too much driving. Your truck is in worse shape than mine. It's a six-hour round trip. You could wreck."

"I'd walk over a thousand scalding hot french fries to get to you." He paused. "I see that smile, Teeny. You can't hide it. Come on, give me another one."

A long while later, we got dressed and went downstairs. The kitchen door stood ajar, letting in a blast of heat. Emerson sat at the table, surrounded by the mail that Coop had brought last night. A blue envelope had been opened.

"How did you get in?" I cried.

"I've got my ways. You can't get rid of me." She lifted her arm. A chain stretched from her wrist to the chair. "Unless you've got the key to these handcuffs."

nineteen

Sunlight streamed through the kitchen window, glinting on Emerson's cuffs. She still wore the black taffeta dress that Kendall had bought. She was waiting for Coop and me to say something, but a snug band had wrapped itself around my chest.

Coop knelt beside her. "Where'd you get those cuffs, princess?"

"It's a secret." She smoothed her free hand down her stained, wrinkled dress. One edge of the stiff petticoat hung down, beggar lice stuck to the netting. Hadn't the Philpots noticed that she'd worn the same outfit for the last two days? Weren't they taking care of her?

A wedge of light hit Coop's face, outlining the edge of his jaw. "How did you get into the house?"

"I used Mr. Philpot's Visa card. The lock popped open." She glanced down at the handcuffs. "I got these from Red. They're the icky, old-fashioned kind. I prefer the twist-tie ones."

I thought Coop was going to lecture her about theft and delinquency, but he folded his arms. "I hope you stole the key, too."

"Maybe." With her free hand, she lifted a stained paper bag from her lap. "Anybody want a funeral cruller? I brought éclairs too."

The strap around my chest loosened. If she'd swiped the doughnuts from the Philpots' kitchen, then she hadn't been roaming the countryside for days.

Coop pushed back his hair, the way he always did when he was flustered. "Teeny, where's your phone book? I've got to call Helen Philpot. She's probably frantic."

"She's not." Emerson lifted her chin.

I peeked under the table. Her ankles were crossed primly; her shoes and socks were coated with Bonaventure County's sandy loam, perfect for growing onions. "Why are you still wearing this outfit?"

"I didn't have nothing to change into. My stuff is still in Red's van." She pushed the doughnut bag aside and lifted the blue envelope. "Is this your mail, Daddy? 'Cause you got a letter from Mrs. Philpot. She mailed it from South Carolina."

Coop stopped looking for the phone book. He crossed the room in three long strides. He tried to snatch the envelope, but she pushed it into my hands. The seal had been ripped open, and a blue paper jutted up. I glanced at the postmark: Mount Pleasant, South Carolina, Saturday August 9. I recognized Barb's handwriting—boxy, all capital letters. She'd addressed the note to Coop's house on Isle of Palms.

"Go ahead and open it," Emerson said.

I pulled out the blue paper and spread it on the table.

SEAPORT COED,
EMAIL RUB INTO. CLAMEL TOAD DEUCE
FOYER MANAGE TRASH. ALIEN WILL PIX.

A BUSHEL FETCH NEUTER
CHALET OWES NULL
CLOUDS FOURTEEN

SUICIDE SOLEMNER

VALOR EBB
XXOO

Suicide solemner? Manage trash? I glanced at Emerson. "What's this? A joke?"

"No, silly. They're anagrams."

A muscle twitched in Coop's jaw. "She used to write me letters like this back in high school. She sent them after we broke up, too. I couldn't decode them. I never got past *Seaport Coed.*"

"It means *Dearest Coop,*" Emerson said. "*Valor Ebb* is *Love Barb.*"

"You and your mother just happen to have the same talent for solving anagrams?" I asked.

"No, she teached me," Emerson said. "After every lesson, she gave me ice cream."

"But I thought you were never around her," Coop said. "You went to that school."

"The Philpots made me come home for holidays. I had to crack anagrams to find my presents on Christmas morning." Emerson wrinkled her nose. "So do you want me to decode the letter or not?"

"That's okay," Coop said. "I can look up the anagrams on my iPhone."

"It'll take you thirty minutes to type in the phrases on those tiny keys. I can decipher it in a flash. Let's cut a deal."

Coop shook his head.

"But the clues lead to a treasure. Don't you want to find it?" She snatched the letter and began to read out loud. "'Dearest Coop. I am in trouble. Call me after you decode the anagrams. I will explain. Love, Barb.'"

Trouble? I shook my head. "I'm confused."

Emerson sighed. "Give me a pencil and scrap paper and I'll make you a cheat sheet."

I found an index card and a pen in the drawer. I set them in front of her. She lifted her free hand and began to write.

SEAPORT COED = DEAREST COOP
EMAIL RUB INTO = I AM IN TROUBLE
CLAMEL TOAD DEUCE FOYER = CALL ME AFTER YOU DECODE

MANAGE TRASH = THE ANAGRAMS
ALIEN WILL PIX = I WILL EXPLAIN
VALOR EBB = LOVE BARB
A BUSHEL FETCH NEUTER = CLUES BENEATH THE FUR
CHALET OWES NULL = CLUES ON THE WALL
CLOUDS FOURTEEN = CLUES UNDERFOOT
SUICIDE SOLEMNER = MORE CLUES INSIDE

Emerson tapped *A Bushel Fetch Neuter.* "This means *clues beneath the fur. Chalet Owes Null* means *clues on the wall.* And *Clouds Fourteen* means *clues underfoot.* And so on and so forth."

"Yes, I can see that. But what does it mean?" Coop asked. "What's *underfoot?* Which wall was she referring to? What kind of trouble was she in?"

"She never said." Emerson set down the card. "But it's real clear that she wanted you to find something. Maybe we can find it together?"

I remembered the printout and sat up straight. Did Barb have a fur coat? If so, she might have left a note in the pocket.

Coop gave her a stern look. "How do I know that you're telling the truth? Maybe you didn't solve these anagrams. Maybe you're making up phrases."

"Take the letter to a cryptologist. Then I want a full apology and a double order of fries."

"You can't stay here, princess." Coop shoved the letter back into the envelope, along with Emerson's cheat sheet. "I'm going back to Charleston this morning, and Teeny is staying with my family."

"Can I stay with them, too? Because your people are my people."

"My mother isn't good with children," Coop said. "And if I don't leave right now, I'll be in trouble with my boss."

Emerson reached into the doughnut bag, fished out a tiny brass key, and unlocked the handcuffs. After they drove off, I found the envelope on the floor. It must have slipped out of Coop's pocket. I stuffed it in the silverware drawer. What clues had Barb meant? Would they prove she'd been involved in a chop shop? Was she reaching from the grave to implicate the Philpot brothers?

I massaged my forehead. I always thought better in the orchard, so I grabbed a basket and walked outside. Clouds drifted low over the trees. A mockingbird swooped down the row, its shadow rippling over the grass. The wind kicked up, bending the weeds. I took a breath.

Peaches. This was the smell of home, of a childhood that had been bruised in places but was still whole and mostly sweet. But I missed Charleston: the bells of St. Michael's, horse drawn carriages, and the way afternoon light cast a rusty sheen over harbor.

I loved Bonaventure, too. Emerson had given me a new reason to stay. I'd promised Coop that I'd go straight to his mother's house, but I wasn't quite ready to face Irene. So I lingered in the orchard a few minutes longer.

She needs a little sweetness, Aunt Bluette's voice whispered. *Take Irene some peaches.*

I smiled. Maybe I could fix an I'll-Make-You-Like-Me Fruit Salad, with oranges, cherries, apples, peaches, and passion fruit. Make a sugar syrup and pour over fruit. A touch of lemon juice gives backbone to the syrup.

I loaded my basket and walked back to the house. The phone was ringing, and I snatched it up, praying I'd hear Coop's voice. *You've got heartburn, and I've got a burning fear in my heart*, I'd say. Let's make it stop. We'll book a guided tour in Ireland. A stone cottage, an iron bed, a snapping fireplace. The name of the tour will be the Ring of Kerry Meets the Ring of O'Malley.

"Teeny Templeton, is that you?" a nasal-voiced woman asked. "This is Angie Trammel. Can you bake a cake for my daughter's bachelorette party?"

"How'd you know I was back in town?" I asked.

"Mary Queen Lancaster mentioned it," Angie said. "I desperately need a cake."

"I wish I could help, but my baking supplies are in Charleston. Besides, I only do basic layer cakes. Nothing fancy."

"Don't be modest, Teeny. Mary Queen was singing your praises. Me and my daughter will be at your house in ten minutes."

"Sorry, I won't be here," I said, but she'd already hung up.

Sir and I were on our way out the front door when the Trammels' white Cadillac roared into my driveway. I reluctantly showed the ladies to the parlor, and Sir sniffed their heels as if they'd both stepped in doggie doo.

They refused my offer of coffee.

"I'm on a colon-cleansing diet," Angie said. She was a middle-aged version of her daughter Suzy. Both women raked their red fingernails through shoulder-length black curls.

"Oh, Mama, hush." Suzy flapped her hand. The sun glanced off her rhinestone-studded t-shirt, sending a dazzle around the room. Sir pounced on the rug, trying to trap the light with his paws.

"I'll need more than a colon cleansing before Suzy's wedding gets here," Angie said, fanning herself. "The damn thing's jinxed."

"Mama, quit exaggerating," Suzy said. "Only two bad things have happened."

"Yes, but trouble comes in threes. I'm just waiting for the third one to show up." Angie cupped her hand around her mouth and leaned toward me. "First, the groom's blood pressure medicine took away his manhood—"

"Mama!" Suzy cried.

"Well, it's the truth. How am I supposed to get a grandchild? Randy might as well be sterile. I could just cry." Angie twisted one of her curls around her thumb and turned to me. "The second bad thing is so awful. Suzy's wedding dress, a full-beaded gown, the most beautiful dress ever created, is being altered by Clair-Beth Butts." Angie paused to load her lungs.

I gave the mother/daughter pair an I'm-sorry-I'm-out-of-time smile and made a big show of checking my watch. "About the cake . . ."

"It's Kendall McCormack's fault," Angie launched back into her story. "If she hadn't died, her cousin Clair-Beth could have finished altering Suzy's wedding dress. But she hasn't touched her needle. Said she just knew she'd nick her finger on every bead and cover the dress with hundreds of bloodred polka-dots."

Suzy's hands fluttered like a bird. A bird that had just eaten some poisoned wedding cake. "Some people are saying Kendall was drunk. Others are saying it was an unfortunate accident. But she didn't drink."

A prickle ran down my spine.

"That's true," Angie said. "Kendall was allergic to alcohol. One sip of wine, and her face would turn pink as a baboon's butt. She'd break out in hives, too. She couldn't even get near cooking sherry."

"She wasn't supposed to fornicate, either, but she did," Suzy said.

"I think Lester drove Kendall to the bottle." Angie wrinkled her nose. "He was too old for her. It's so sad about his wife. First, I heard she killed herself, and now they're saying she might have been murdered. At least, that's what I heard at the viewing. I was standing right by Lester when the Sweeney police showed up. Personally I think Lester killed Barb and made it look like suicide."

Suzy leaned forward. "Or maybe Norris did it."

I caught a breath, then slowly released it. Never mind that I shared their opinion; the Trammels were rumormongers, and they would repeat everything I said. But my desire to pump them for information was greater than my fear of slander.

"Why would *he* murder *her*?" I asked.

"Revenge." Angie patted my hand. "Barb and Norris used to be lovers, you know."

I felt a buzzing in my throat, as if I'd swallowed a wasp. "Seriously?" I asked.

"It was a scandal," Angie said. "If you want the lowdown on Barb, talk to Emma Underwood. She used to be an art teacher. Now she's got Alzheimer's. Didn't your mama take lessons from her? Lordy, Emma used to know all the gossip. And she was particularly interested in Barb Philpot."

"Visit Miss Emma early of a morning," Suzy said. "Her memory is better before lunchtime."

"Does she still live on St. James Square?" I asked, picturing the blue house on the corner of Louisiana and Juniper. Her backyard faced the O'Malleys' pool and gazebo.

"Yes." Suzy thrust a thick pile of computer printouts into my hands. Each one showed a photograph of a risqué cake.

"I like the one of the nude sunbathing couple," she said, and handed me the instructions. "You'll need to make the penis out of marzipan. I want a nice, big one on my cake."

"Eek," Angie said. "I couldn't eat a marzipan unmentionable. Why don't you get Teeny to bake you a cute beach cake instead. She can put candied shells all over it."

"I want the penis cake," Suzy said.

"I can't make that." I shook my head. "I don't have the training."

"It's a freaking cake," Suzy cried. "How much training do you need?"

"It takes skill to make sugared genitalia." I struggled to keep a straight face. "If you want a red velvet cake with cream cheese icing, I'm your girl. But when it comes to fondant body parts and flesh-toned icing, I'm sadly lacking."

I gave the Trammels the phone number of a Savannah cake lady. They reached for matching Louis Vuitton bags and left. I could already hear the little beep-beep from Angie's cell phone as she punched in the number.

Sir was staring at the floor, as if waiting for the sparkles to return. I wandered through the house, checking locks and pulling the window shades. After talking to the Trammels, I was even more convinced that Norris had worn that Bill Clinton mask. If Norris and Barb had been lovers, maybe they'd also sold body parts.

But at least I wasn't dealing with an unknown enemy. At least the enemy had a face and a name. Just knowing this made me feel calmer.

The kitchen phone rang and I hesitated before picking it up. I wasn't sure if I could take any more craziness. I answered with a curt hello.

"Hey, girl," Dot said. "Don't bite off my head. I guess you heard about Kendall?"

"Yes."

"I feel so bad that I didn't help you."

"Forget it."

"You sound depressed. I know what'll perk you up. Let's go to the Tartan Hair Pub today. You can get a makeover. My treat. "

I lifted a hunk of frizz, tempted to accept her offer. "Thanks, but I'd better pass."

"Oh, come on. You'd be so cute if you thinned your hair a little. A new style will give you a new outlook. So will a pedicure. When's the last time you had one?"

I slipped my foot out of my boot and stared at my toes. "Never had one."

"Oh, my god. Are you freaking kidding me?" Dot cried. "How do you expect to hold on to Coop O'Malley with gross toenails? Meet me at the Tartan Hair Pub in ten minutes."

"Can't. I've got to be somewhere." But a pedicure did sound nice.

"This is an emergency beauty intervention," Dot said. "If you don't show up, I'm coming to get you."

"I'll be there." I hung up. If Coop learned I hadn't gone to the O'Malleys', he'd be upset. But maybe improving my looks would improve his mood. No, I was just stalling. Because I didn't want to stay with Irene.

I unzipped my suitcase and dragged out my vocabulary book. *Debacle.* A catastrophe, fiasco, or calamity. I put Sir in the parlor with his toys and a water bowl.

On my way out of the house, I grabbed a roll of Scotch tape. I locked up, then I climbed onto a wicker table and placed a strip of tape over the screen door. I patted it against the frame. If Norris tried to break in while I was gone, the tape would come loose. James Bond had used a hair in *Dr. No,* but he'd done that in a hotel room. Out on the porch, a gust of wind might dislodge the hair. A false alarm would feel like a real one, so I hoped the tape would stick.

I wasn't in a hurry to get a pedicure, so I knelt beside the porch and picked wild daisies. I felt a powerful longing to set them on Aunt Bluette's grave.

I pulled into Bonaventure Cemetery. Tourists milled around the tombstones, photographing the cherubs and old-timey monuments. Many of them dated back to the Revolutionary War and they were engraved with epitaphs from the Bible; but one tombstone always drew tourists.

A lady in a red dress aimed her camera at a black granite marker. Carved into the stone was XAVIER ST. CLAIRE, PHILANDERER.

I walked past the monument. In the distance, a hearse cruised through the narrow lane, followed by a row of cars with bright headlights. They were headed toward a maroon tent, where Vlado and Mr. Winky were setting up chairs.

I stopped in front of Aunt Bluette's marker and set the wildflowers on the grassy mound. She'd thought up a special epitaph before she'd died. I ran my fingers over the rose granite, tracing the letters.

STEP SOFTLY, AN AUNT LIES HERE.

A shadow fell over the grass. I looked up. Son Finnegan smiled down at me. He wore sandals, cut-off jeans, and a Burberry shirt. He held a dozen yellow roses. "Well, if it isn't the cute cemetery chick."

"Don't you ever work?" I said.

"Not if I can help it." He grinned. "I'm not stalking you. I came to see Mama. She's just over yonder."

We walked to Cissy Finnegan's stone. It was black granite, heaped with ceramic frogs and angels. Son propped the roses against a smiling toad. "Can I buy you a latte?"

At first, I thought he was talking to the frog, but then he looked up at me.

"Quit trying to feed me." I glanced past him. In the funeral procession, I saw Irene O'Malley's red Eldorado.

Now she would know I'd been in the graveyard with Son.

He rose to his feet, the wind kicking up his ponytail. "Like it or not, Boots, we have unfinished business. If your aunt had shown you my letters, we might have ended up together."

"There's a tiny hole in your logic," I said. "If you loved me so much, you would have found a way to tell me. Other than letters."

"So much was happening in my life. I was in my last year of med school. I lived at the hospital. They owned my ass. And afterward, I did an internship in Boston. A five-year surgical residency in Los Angeles. A fellowship took two more years. Then I was putting soldiers' faces back together." He looked up at the sky. "I wasn't a monk. I had lovers. But in my whole life I loved one woman. I'm looking at her right now."

Sweat trickled down my back, sliding just beneath my dress. "It's too late, Son. I don't want to be hurtful. But I'm in love with Coop."

"Big mistake. Because his mama is a cannibal. How can you love a man who takes marching orders from a female Jeffery Dahmer? Irene has ruined every relationship Cooter has ever had."

"That's a lie. She had nothing to do with Coop's divorce."

"I sat next to her at a cookout. She polished off a dozen baby back ribs. In between bites, she told me how she got rid of Ava—isn't that the wife's name? Then Irene started bitching about you."

A cramp flickered in my belly. "What did she say?"

"Hurtful things."

I grabbed his shirt and pulled him closer. "Tell me."

"She called your hair a lethal weapon. I stood up for you. Then she asked if we'd dated. I denied it, of course. But I don't think she believed me."

Great. Perfect. I was spending the night with a paranoid, burglar-hating, flesh-eating woman who knew all about me and Son.

"It'll never work out, Boots. You and Cooter are too different. The farmer's daughter and the doctor's son. You say tomato, he says tomahto."

I reached up to pat my bangs, and I shot him a bird that only he could see. Then I left.

twenty

Halfway to the hair salon, I burst into tears. I pulled the truck over to the side of the road; heat boiled through the window. It had been just this hot the summer Son Finnegan had worked at Templeton Orchard.

I remembered the day Aunt Bluette's sharp eyes had caught me chatting him up. "Back to work, Mr. Finnegan," she'd said, a wobbly smile caught on her lips. She steered me into the house, and her smile morphed into something sharp and toothy.

"Stay away from that boy." She wagged her finger. "His daddy is in the penitentiary."

"At least he's got a daddy," I said. Then, spitefully, I added, "And a mama."

Aunt Bluette's eyes filled, but the tears just stayed there, shimmering on the edges of her lashes. "I won't let you date him. He's trash. Do you hear me?"

"Yes, and I don't care."

"It'll never work, Teeny," Aunt Bluette said. "Your mama and Son's mama hated each other. They wrangled over a man."

"I'm not my mama. And Son isn't his father."

"I don't want you to get hurt again." Aunt Bluette blinked, and tears ran down her wrinkled face.

I felt so ashamed that I'd sassed her. I hugged her as hard as I could. "Son won't hurt me."

"There's all kinds of hurts," she said. "Just all kinds."

Every afternoon, Son and I waited until Aunt Bluette drove to town, then we met in the hayloft. What I felt for him was sweet and tender, just like the last peach of summer. And I wasn't giving him up.

Dot Agnew was home from college that summer, and she devised a plan for Son and me to meet. "Tell your aunt that you're going on a church retreat with me," Dot said. "Then you and Son can have two whole days together."

For the first time in my life, I lied to Aunt Bluette. I added it to my annual tally, then I packed a bag and ran off to Hilton Head with Son. We got a room at the Seaside, a blue building with white Adirondack chairs out front. We didn't put on our suits, just ran down to the beach. It was a blazing hot afternoon. Old ladies sat beneath striped umbrellas. Babies played in tide pools. Son pulled me to the edge of the water. He kneeled in the sand and drew a giant T + S.

He got to his feet, his green plaid shirt filling with wind, and clasped my hands. "I love you, Teeny."

"Love you, too."

"I'm gonna marry you someday. Will you wait for me?" His wet hand slid down my cheek and caught in my hair. The surf rushed between our feet and swept over the T + S, scrubbing out the letters. I leaped onto his shoulders and he spun me around. He carried me back to the hotel, pausing every two seconds to kiss me.

Cissy Finnegan stood outside our door, flanked by Son's tattooed brothers. Aunt Bluette and the Baptist preacher were behind them. All the breath left my body, as if a fist had slammed into my chest.

"You little fucker," Cissy yelled. She flew at Son, slapping his face and arms.

"How dare you run off with Ruby Ann's daughter!"

Thwack, thwack, thwack.

"You ain't messing up your doctoring career."

Aunt Bluette pulled me away from Son. He tried to run to me, but his brothers held him back. Cissy spat on the floor.

"Damn Templetons," she said.

Aunt Bluette and the preacher dragged me to his Buick. I was crying so hard, my nose was running. I felt a cool hand against my shoulder.

"I'm so sorry, Teeny," Aunt Bluette said. "But you'll thank me someday. When you find true love, you'll thank me."

The preacher didn't drive back to Bonaventure. They went south, past Savannah, down I-95 toward St. Mary's. During the ferry ride to Chamor Island, I slumped on a bench, sobbing, while they discussed corn bread.

"Bacon grease is the secret ingredient," Aunt Bluette said.

"Jalapeños change the flavor entirely," the preacher said.

"So do chives," she said.

"There's hundreds of recipes," the preacher said. "Hundreds of ingredients. No need to get stuck on one."

I realized they weren't talking about the versatility of cornmeal. This was a food parable, and they were telling me that I'd find love again. All kinds of love.

I spent a month in Aunt Bunny's cottage, and when I returned to Bonaventure, Son was gone.

A giant neon clover sat on the roof of the Tartan Hair Pub. The parking lot was empty except for a gold Corvette, which I assumed belonged to Dot.

I got out of the truck. The shop's interior was done up in green plaid and Irish bric-a-brac—leprechauns, pipes, and clover. Green mirrors and chairs lined both walls. A row of hairdryers sat in the middle of the aisle. Four sinks were in an alcove. At the last sink, Dot's long legs jutted out of a plastic cape that was printed with shamrocks.

She lifted her head and waved. "Mr. Sheehan, just give Teeny the works."

Mr. Sheehan was in his sixties and wore a tight, hunter green bodysuit. He put a finger to his lips and walked around me, his shoes clicking on the tile floor. "Define *works*."

"I just want a pedicure," I said.

"You need highlights. Straightening. Maybe lowlights . . ." His voice trailed off, then he shook his head. "No, highlights won't show up in that bush."

He lifted a clump of my hair. "Are you part Aborigine?"

I shrugged. Honestly, I didn't know. My daddy could have been anyone.

Twenty minutes later, Dot was getting a comb-out, but I was sitting in Mr. Sheehan's chair, my scalp burning from the straightening solution. I gritted my teeth and took a hit of Ventolin.

"The smell is formaldehyde, doll," Mr. Sheehan said. "Years ago, funeral homes used it to embalm people. But it got outlawed."

It was against the law to put formaldehyde into a dead person but not on my hair? "How much longer?" I asked.

"Five more minutes," Mr. Sheehan said, then bustled off.

The front door opened and Norris Gallagher walked in, looking like a skinny Jesus. He wore a white Izod shirt, white shorts, and white tennis shoes. He was all legs and eyes. A few strands of hair protruded from his bald head. How could a salon help this man?

As his gaze circled the room, I slid off my chair and ran to the bathroom. My hair gave off a tart smell that burned my throat. I lowered the toilet lid and perched on the edge. Surely Norris wouldn't require a shampoo. He'd be gone in five minutes, right?

I cracked open the door and breathed clean air. A beautician was shaping Dot's bangs into long question marks. Across the room, Norris sat in a chair, facing the mirror. A girl with a nose ring crouched behind him, shaving the back of his neck. Mr. Sheehan stood in the middle of the store, his hands splayed on his hips.

"Where's Teeny?" he asked.

"The bathroom," Dot said.

Norris turned his head, and the nose-ring girl shrieked, "Yikes, don't move. I almost sliced off your ear."

I shut the door and locked it. I heard the clickety-click of Mr. Sheehan's shoes. "Time's up, doll," he called.

"I'm sick."

"Would you rather be sick or bald?"

I didn't answer.

"You need rinsing. Or you'll look like an extra in *Night of the Living Dead*."

"One minute!"

"I'll give you two. After that, I can't be responsible for what happens."

I cringed. Can't be responsible for what? I knew about perms—they were, oddly enough, a cure for uncontrollably curly hair—but hair straightening was a new concept. Did I need a neutralizer?

I bolted to the sink and rinsed my hair. Fumes curled up, tart and peppery. Spots churned behind my eyelids. I lifted my chin, and water slid down my neck. I gulped a mouthful of formaldehyde. Where was my inhaler? In my purse. And my purse was next to Mr. Sheehan's chair. I gagged. Now I knew why formaldehyde had been banned.

Mr. Sheehan banged on my door. What's going on?"

"You said to rinse," I called. "So I rinsed."

"You need a neutralizer. Or you'll end up fried." The doorknob spun. "Open up."

Which was worse—a singed scalp or a face-off with Norris? I thought of Zee Quinn and her hand on his private parts. Then I imagined the shocked look on Irene O'Malley's face when she opened the door and saw my bald head.

"I can't hear you," I yelled.

I heard Mr. Sheehan walk off. "Dot?" he yelled. "What's wrong with your friend? Is it that time of the month?"

I looked in the mirror. I was a dead ringer for Samara, the demon girl from *The Ring*. All I lacked was a dirty white nightgown and a stone well. Samara wasn't dead, she was just pissed off. Even demons have bad hair days. I pictured her slithering through a television set, her grimy hands scrabbling against the floor. All she wanted was a comb, maybe a detangling lotion, and Mr. Sheehan better have it or else.

Outside my door, the footsteps returned, pounding out a *coming to get you* rhythm. A scratchy-scrapy noise started up, as if Mr. Sheehan were dragging a fingernail file over the wooden door. The door came off the hinges. Mr. Sheehan set it aside, as if it were no heavier than a curler. He pulled me out of the bathroom, towed me to a sink, and rinsed my head, all the while talking about baldness and chemical breakage. Finally, he shut off the water.

"Oh, my god. Oh. My. God."

I raised up, water pattering down the front of my plastic cape, and turned. In the bottom of the sink, a blond rat's nest clogged the drain.

"Am I bald?" I cried.

"You've still got plenty of hair. Don't stress it and maybe it won't fall out."

A towel engulfed my head. I shoved it out of my eyes as he led me past Dot and a goggle-eyed Norris. Mr. Sheehan pushed me into a chair and turned on a blow dryer.

When he finished, my hair was flat as roadkill. When the Lord had given me curly hair, He'd known what He was doing because it had suited my round face. Now, sleek, honey-colored panels fell past my shoulders, accentuating my flat head and the signature Templeton ears.

Mr. Sheehan spun my chair around. Norris's chair was empty. Dot stood off to the side, patting her freshly coiffed head. "Poor Teeny. Let me treat you to a pedicure. You'll really need one now."

"Later," I said. "I'm on a bad-beauty roll."

The nose-ring girl swept up Norris's hair. It resembled wild rice. I looked over at Dot. "How well do you know Norris Philpot?"

"Well enough. He chased every nurse at Bonaventure Regional. He hates me because I reported him to administration."

"Norris and I grew up together," Mr. Sheehan said. "He drank from a sippy cup too long and it ruined his mouth."

"A sippy cup wouldn't do that," Dot said. "Unless he sucked it until he was twenty."

Mr. Sheehan lifted a hunk of my hair. "If you hadn't pulled this stunt, your hair would've had a little oomph."

I rose from the chair and a blond clump drifted to the floor.

"Don't comb it," Mr. Sheehan said. "Don't wear a ponytail. Don't even look at it, and maybe it won't fall out."

On my way back to the truck, Norris popped around the corner of the building. His scalp gleamed in the noon sun. His whole head had been shaved.

"Hello, Teeny," he said. "Your eyeth are tho pretty."

Eyeth. A chill ran through me. Was he selling body parts or collecting corneas as souvenirs? I gave him a wide berth, but he stepped in front of me.

"Let me take you to dinner."

Sweat trickled between my shoulder blades. "I'm engaged. And I'm in a hurry."

"What a cute non thqueter." A raptor claw dropped in front of his crotch. "You make me tingle."

I ran to my truck, climbed inside, and drove home with the windows rolled down, praying the air would blow off the formaldehyde stench. Loose blond strands blew around me like tiny worms. The odor was still with me by the time I stepped onto the porch and checked my Scotch tape booby trap. It was intact, unlike my hair.

When I got inside, Sir trotted down the hall, grunting to himself. I thought I'd put him in the parlor, but the pocket doors gaped open. He looked up at me, twisted his head, then howled until spittle flew out of his mouth.

"Knock it off. It's your mother." I checked all the doors and windows. They were locked. But I didn't feel safe in this house. On my way to the foyer, I stopped in front of the hall mirror. I looked like somebody had poured a bucket of honey over my head. Ignoring Mr. Sheehan's advice, I gathered the stiff strands, trying to shape them into a ponytail. They immediately sprang out.

Great, just what I needed. Rigor mortis hair. At least it wasn't a climatic disaster like in *Day After Tomorrow.* Or flesh-eating bacteria. In a few months, I'd be my old, frizzy self.

Unless someone was hiding upstairs. No, that was foolish. I didn't know what kind of car Norris drove, but when I'd sped down Savannah Highway, a Mercedes with tinted windows had passed my truck. He could have parked it behind the barn. I remembered how easily Emerson had slipped through the kitchen door, and I felt sick to my stomach. It would be a relief to hide out in a fortress.

I fastened the leash to Sir's collar, then I grabbed the peach basket.

"Come, Innocent One," I said. "Time to face Momzilla."

twenty-one

It was mid-afternoon by the time I turned onto Mississippi Avenue. The O'Malleys' white house faced Hanover Square, and tourists were taking photographs of the spitting fountains and the Revolutionary War–era sundial.

A plump, elderly woman met me on the front porch. She had silver, chin-length hair, and her straight bangs were held back by rhinestone barrettes. She wore a Rolling Stones t-shirt and black leggings. Her tennis shoes looked as if she'd rolled them in glitter, and they were tied with green organdy ribbons. In each arm she gripped a barking Chihuahua.

"Y'all quit yapping," she cried in a shrill, nasal voice. The Chihuahuas fell silent and trembled. The woman turned to me, her silver-blue eyes crinkling at the edges. "I'm Minnie O'Malley. You must be Teeny."

"Yes, ma'am. Nice to meet you." I held the peach basket in one hand, Sir's leash in the other. He shrank away from the Chihuahuas, his nails scratching over the brick porch.

"God love him," Minnie said. "He looks like a manatee. Can I give him a treat?"

Without waiting for my reply, she shifted both Chihuahuas to her right arm and pulled a cheese cube out of her pocket. The Chihuahuas whimpered.

"Hush, or I'll feed you to the bulldog," she told them. She leaned over and waved the cheese in front of Sir's nose. He gave her a rapturous look. She fit the cube gingerly into his mouth, then she raised up.

"Come on in and get out of this heat," she said, and pulled me into the foyer.

I'd been on Coop's porch before, and in his backyard, but I'd never set foot inside his house. The foyer was large and airy, with a black-and-white checkerboard floor and a curved staircase. Minnie sniffed. "I smell peaches."

I lifted the basket. "Elbertas."

"What's that other smell?" Minnie asked. "Have you been to the hair salon?"

"Why, yes ma'am. I just left the Tartan Hair Pub."

The Chihuahuas sneezed. "Caesar and Cleo have delicate lungs," Minnie said. "Hold on while I put them up."

She turned into an arched hallway. I immediately began looking around. A burled grandfather clock stood on one wall and emitted an irregular click, like a faulty heart valve. Next to the stairs, an ornate gold table held a cherub clock. Off to my right, French doors opened into an oak-paneled study, where antique clocks were lined up on the mantel, all of them ticking out of rhythm.

I looked down at Sir. "No wonder Coop is always worried about the time," I whispered. The dog ignored me and gazed toward the hall. The Chihuahuas howled in the distance. Minnie rounded a corner and smiled.

"Well, what do you think of Irene's décor?" she asked.

"Pretty," I said.

"Huh, it looks like she robbed a Horchow outlet. You don't want to see this place at Christmas. Lights on the roof and in the windows. It's enough to cause corneal abrasions."

She squinted at my hands. "Well?" she said. "Where is the O'Malley diamond?"

Something in her tone made me think of the Hope Diamond and its bloody history. I lifted the chain and dragged out the ring.

"Welcome to the family!" She flung her arms around me. My hair slung forward, releasing toxic puffs.

She drew back. "The diamond is an O'Malley heirloom, but the pearls are new. Did Coop tell you the story behind them?"

"No, ma'am."

"Why, that bugger. My grandson can be such a coward. He's probably afraid you'll laugh at his story. A little fear is acceptable, but cowardice is dorky. I'm misquoting Ghandi, but what the hell."

I didn't care who'd she'd quoted. I already loved Minnie-of-the-Ring.

She leaned closer. "If I tell you about the pearls, you've got to swear on Mary Magdalene and the saints that you won't repeat me. Because one day Coop will tell you this story, and he hates it when I preempt him. So you'll need to act real surprised or he'll know I beat him to the punch."

"I won't tell."

She tucked her arm through mine and pulled me toward the hallway. "When he was six, the whole family went to Sea Island for my birthday—we've got a little place there. We ate raw oysters for lunch. They're the food of love and sex, you know. Anyway, Coop found two pearls inside the shells. Fat Irene wanted to make them into earrings, but when she discovered that one pearl was smaller, she lost interest."

When Minnie had attached "fat" to "Irene," I'd almost laughed, but I caught myself in time. I lifted the necklace and studied the ring. One pearl was definitely larger. Why hadn't Coop told me? He knew I loved family stories, mine and everyone else's.

"Coop gave the pearls to me," Minnie was saying. "I had the O'Malley diamond reset. I promised Coop that when he grew up and fell in love, I'd give the ring to his bride. I can't tell you how many women he's been through. I thought for sure Ava would wear my ring. It would've fit her big, British finger. But it stayed on mine. Now it's hanging around your sweet, little neck. Well, I see why. You're a dainty thing. Small boned like a Chihuahua. But prettier."

I cupped the ring in my hand, trying to decode Minnie's words.

Coop hadn't loved Ava enough to give her the O'Malley ring? I moved under the chandelier, and light glanced off the diamond. The stone seemed to say, *No, Coop didn't give Ava the ring. But he didn't tell you about the pearls.* His failure to share this story wasn't a lie, but it felt like an important omission.

"This is an epic occasion," Minnie said. "And it calls for a drink."

She led me and Sir into Dracula's library. Oil paintings hung on the bloodred walls, each canvas featuring ruined castles and rabid dogs. Through the bay window, a swimming pool reflected streaking clouds.

I sat down on a white silk sofa, and Sir flopped down on my feet. Minnie walked to a coffin-like bar. The shiny, black granite counter was empty except for a potted shamrock, its leaves folded tightly, as if praying that someone would remember to water it.

"What's your poison, Teeny? We got everything."

"I'm not sure." I glanced at the shelves behind her, where liquor bottles and crystal glasses were lined up according to shape and size. My gaze stopped on an oak keg. They had Guinness on tap?

"I'm in the mood for a dirty martini," she said. "Want one?"

"Please." I set the peach basket on the coffee table. Minnie dropped ice into the martini glasses. She lifted a pitcher and dribbled water over the cubes.

"So, tell me," she said. "Is Coop a good lover?"

She set the glasses inside a small freezer. I'd never discussed sex with an older woman, not even Aunt Bluette. So I ignored the question.

"Oh, come on. It's just us girls." Minnie poured olive juice, vermouth, and gin into a shaker. "One time I took a Magic Marker and wrote *I Love You with My Whole Heart, Body, and Soul* on Jack O'Malley Senior's tallywacker. I signed my full name, too, Mary Francis Minerva Donoghue O'Malley. Jack was my husband."

She crossed herself, then a smile lit up her wrinkled face. "Could you write that on my grandson's privates?"

"With room to spare," I said.

"I'm not one bit surprised." Minnie laughed. She opened the freezer, dumped the cubes and water into the shamrock, then she finished making our drinks. She put them on a tray and walked toward me, her tennis shoes sparkling.

"The key is to drink fast." She handed me a glass, then lifted hers. "May the hinges of our friendship never grow rusty."

"Here's to Irish men," I said.

"Amen." She downed her drink and burped. Then she walked back to the bar. "Want a refill?"

"I'm good."

"Yeah, you better stay sober or Fat Irene will get pissed." She mixed another martini. "I never understood why Jack Junior left the Church to marry a frigging Baptist. And a preacher's daughter to boot. It broke my heart."

"I'm Baptist," I said a little defensively.

"So is Coop." Minnie shrugged. "I'm not against all Protestants, even if they do everything ass backward. I'm against Fat Irene. She is so full of herself. Why, she acts like she's discovered the cure for bird flu."

Minnie refilled her glass. "Fat Irene is only fifty-eight, but she's in bad shape. High blood pressure, high cholesterol, and highfalutin ways. She eats way too much salt and sugar. She's got type two diabetes. She's taking the pills now. But she doesn't test her sugars and she doesn't eat right. She'll be on the shots pretty soon. I'd like to take a needle and stick her in the butt myself."

"I didn't know she was ill."

"My gripe isn't her health," Minnie said. "My gripe is her personality. Can't blame diabetes on meanness. People say she's paranoid about burglars, but she's really a control freak. And she's too law-abiding. When Coop was eight years old, she made him memorize *Robert's Rules of Order.* She taught him to make lists, too."

"He still makes them," I said. "The front of his refrigerator is crammed with Post-it notes."

"Poor kid was a nervous wreck. When he was little, Fat Irene was always yelling at Jack Junior. Pitching fits. Breaking the crystal. I'm not saying Jack Junior was a saint. He might have fooled around with a nurse or two. But he was a good father."

I sat up straight. The O'Malleys had been dysfunctional? "Dr. O'Malley was a ladies' man?" I asked.

"And a workaholic. I thought for sure Jack Junior and Irene would get a divorce. Apparently Coop did, too. He became the perfect son. Never gave them a bit of trouble. Followed every rule. He thought if he behaved, his parents wouldn't fight."

"He's still trying to be perfect." I traced my finger over the rim of my glass.

"Yes, he's a Boy Scout."

"I was a Brownie and a Girl Scout."

"Did you have a slew of badges?"

"Just one. The Make It, Eat It badge."

"Coop had every single one." Minnie sighed. "Fat lot of good it did him. Those badges were a bunch of crap. But I can't blame the Boy Scouts for the way Coop turned out. You know his big failing?"

Situational ethics, I thought. When he gets into a sticky spot, he lies. I started to nod, then shook my head.

Minnie plucked the olive from her glass and tossed it over her shoulder. "He equates being wrong with being bad. He thinks nobody will love him if he screws up."

"I'll love him."

"His ex-wife said that, too. Don't worry, I'm not Ava's fan. Never was. I knew from the get-go they'd never make it." Minnie frowned. "But poor Coop got swept into all that British bullshit. Ava's people go back to William the Conqueror. She tried to dominate Coop. But you're wearing the ring. You know what it says? His heart is yours. If you want it."

"I do."

"Then get him to loosen up. Make him listen to Ozzy Osbourne. 'Breaking All the Rules' is a good song. Or R.E.M's 'Losing My Religion.' "

I repressed a smile.

She waved at a wide-screen TV. "You didn't come here for Coop-

Scoop, did you? You came to hide from a pervert. So let's kick back and relax. Any special show you want to watch?"

"The Weather Channel would be nice," I said.

"You don't seem like a forecast junkie."

"I like to know when storms are coming."

She clicked a button on the channel changer, and the screen filled with churning water. "Oh, poo. It's 'Tumultuous Thursday.' Let's watch something less depressing."

Was it Thursday? I'd lost track of time.

Minnie settled on the Syfy channel. *Tin Man* was playing. "What the hell is this?" Minnie cried, waving at the TV. "Why does that guy have a zipper in his head?"

"*Tin Man* is an updated version of *The Wizard of Oz,*" I said.

"Does it have tornadoes?"

"Yep."

"I can't catch a break from shitty weather." Minnie sat down next to me. "A storm is coming, Teeny. A storm called Fat Irene."

I thought she was joking until I heard a rustle of silk. A second later, Coop's mother strode into the room. She wore a mud-brown muumuu, the fabric printed with crocodiles and palm trees.

"Teeny, so nice of you to finally join us," Irene said, spitting out the word *nice.*

"Don't be rude," Minnie said. "Teeny is wearing the ring. She's practically family."

Irene gave me a look that dismissed me as daughter-in-law material. Her nostrils opened like valves. "Do I smell chemicals?"

"It's your horrible perfume." Minnie flashed an impish grin, then she opened her cigarette case.

"You shouldn't smoke," Irene said. "It leads to bladder cancer. You'd hate wearing a Depends."

The women's eyes locked. Irene was the first to look away. I didn't want her to see my quick smile, so I lowered my chin. My hair swung forward, giving off a formaldehyde stench.

On the big television, the screen showed Dorothy Gale in a wicker jail. She was talking to the guy with a zipper in his head. "Here I was thinking this nightmare couldn't get any weirder," Dorothy said.

Minnie pinched my leg. "It wasn't weird till Fat Irene crashed the party."

"I heard that," Irene said.

"Good." Minnie lit a cigarette.

"Now who's being rude?" Irene asked.

Minnie leaned against me. "I'll say one thing for Irene. She's a damn good eater. But she likes to eat things with hair and teeth."

"A high compliment coming from you, an anorexic," Irene said.

Minnie blew a smoke ring. "What's for supper?"

Irene smoothed her hand down the crocodile dress, as if composing herself. When she finally spoke, her voice held the perfect blend of Southern manners and fangs. "Pork chops, mashed potatoes with pan gravy, string beans, glazed carrots, and jalapeño cornbread."

Minnie smiled. "You should swallow an Orlistat. That pill will suck the fat out of your food and blow it out your ass. Then you'll be the one wearing a Depends."

Irene gave her a chilling gaze, then she turned to me. A finely honed intelligence shimmered behind her eyes. They were so much like Coop's, I couldn't breathe.

"We heard about your troubles," she said.

I repressed an urge to grab my dog and bolt from the house.

Minnie blew another smoke ring. "Bad news travels through Bonaventure like the fat in Irene's blood."

Irene straightened the needlepoint pillows on the sofa, giving each one a karate chop. "Coop said a prowler broke into your house."

"Yes, ma'am." I put one hand on my neck. It was slick with perspiration.

"Quit yes mamming her," Minnie said. "She ain't the holy mother."

Irene hacked the pillow next to me. She stared at my necklace. "My son is worried about you."

Minnie lifted an ashtray and stubbed out her cigarette. “It’s scary when a pervert leaves a cream puff on your bed.”

“How many martinis have you had?” Irene asked.

“Not nearly enough,” Minnie said.

Irene gave her a warning glance. “You promised you’d behave.”

“I lied.” Minnie raised her glass. “To older whiskey, younger men, and faster horses.”

In the distance, the banished Chihuahuas howled. Irene pressed her fingers to her temples and squeezed. “If those dogs don’t hush, I’m having their vocal chords cut.”

“I’ll report you to PETA,” Minnie said.

“And I’ll make sure you end up in a nursing home.”

“Excuse me, Teeny.” Minnie rose from the sofa and marched off.

Irene’s big breasts heaved beneath her muumuu, the fabric quivering as if the crocodiles had come to life.

“So, Teeny, how did you manage to attract a pervert?” Her tone was brusque, tinged with doubt, as if I’d been visited by aliens.

My mouth went dry. “It wasn’t intentional.”

“You sure know how to cause trouble,” Irene said. “Coop might lose his job. But he’s not worried about that, he’s worried about *you*.”

I dragged in a breath, but the air wouldn’t move past my throat. I shoved my hand inside my purse and found my inhaler.

Irene sidled closer. “I expected you here last night. But you’ve got those slow-moving Templeton genes. I saw you at the cemetery today. You were chatting up Son Finnegan.”

“I was just putting flowers on my aunt’s grave.” I took a sip of Ventolin.

“From my perspective, it looked as if you were putting the moves on Son.” Her voice sounded different, smooth and silky, like cream slithering over oleander blossoms. The way she’d said *Son* made my pulse throb in my lips.

“Normally I’m open-minded and understanding,” she continued. “But I resent having to babysit you and that bulldog. I don’t want either of you in my house or my life. The last thing I need is for your pervert to show up."

I couldn't imagine her being scared of doodly squat, but I was shocked by her tirade. I'd be better off at a hotel, one that accepted dogs. I got to my feet, tugging on the leash. "Come on, Sir. Let's go."

She pushed me down. "You aren't leaving until I say so."

"You just said I wasn't welcome."

"No, but I'm ignoring the voice inside my head, the one that's telling me you're a gold digger. I'm ignoring my distaste for all things Templeton. But I promised Coop that I'd watch over you. If you leave and the pervert gets you, my son will blame me. I won't let your false pride come between me and Coop. So you *will* stay here until I say otherwise."

God, what a bitch. "I'm your prisoner?"

"Save the theatrics. You're just like your mother. She was sweet on my husband. Always dragging you to his office on some pretense or another."

"I had asthma," I said.

"And your mother had hot pants."

"She's not here to defend herself. Don't talk about her." I shoved my inhaler into my purse, my hand shaking. I understood why Irene was attacking me, but why was she going after my mother? I couldn't remember a single time when Ruby Ann had been inappropriate with Dr. O'Malley. She'd been terrified of doctors.

Sir gazed up at me with worried eyes. He hated conflict. I wished Emerson was here to offer crocodile trivia. Did reptiles swallow their hatchlings or was that a myth? No wonder Coop had to-do lists, ulcers, and tapping feet. "I don't know what my mama did to make you hate her so much, but I apologize on her behalf."

"I don't accept *in absentia* apologies," Irene said. "One night Jack and I stayed up all night, fighting about your mother. He finally admitted that he found her attractive. Not that it did her any good. Jack loved *me*."

Did she see all women as rivals? How could I convince her that I wasn't a threat? "I love your son," I said.

"Such pretty words." She smirked. "I'll make you eat them."

Minnie would have said, I'll make you eat a Lipitor. But I held my tongue.

Irene heaved a sigh, and suddenly her dress was alive, a squirming mass of scales. "If Barb Philpot's child has Coop's genes, you won't stick around."

"I'll help him raise her."

"More pretty words." Irene put one hand behind her ear. "Do you hear that sound? It's Barb. She's twirling in the grave."

twenty-two

In the morning, Sir and I wandered downstairs. A housekeeper with a Spanish accent directed me to the sunroom. Light slammed through six arched windows which overlooked the pool. On the far wall, a buffet table had been set up, hotel-style. Country ham, biscuits, fruit, and pastries. A note lay against a silver coffee pot.

Friday, August 15
Dear Teeny,
Hope you enjoy your solitary breakfast. It's the last peace you'll have for hours! When you're finished, get ready to rock and roll! We're hitting the spa, the boutiques, and the chocolate shop!! My treat. See you in the foyer at 9 a.m.
Minnie
XXOO

I pressed the letter to my chest. All my life I'd wanted a Minnie. I didn't know if it was safe to traipse around town, what with Norris lurking, but I had an idea that he wouldn't mess with her.

While I ate breakfast, I read the Bonaventure paper. The obituaries had a cryptic write-up about Kendall McCormack. A memorial service would be held tonight at the Eikenberry Funeral Home. In Bonaventure-speak, a memorial service was a severely abbreviated funeral.

I didn't know how abbreviated until that evening, when I turned into the Longstreet Room. As I walked down the aisle, two elderly women glanced at me and whispered. I'd spent the day with Minnie, and now I looked like a hooker.

I spread out my fingers. My nails were glossy red. My hair had been layered, conditioned, and teased, which only emphasized the stick-straightness. At a chic dress shop, Minnie had picked me out a short, black sleeveless dress and four-inch heels. She'd insisted I wear the outfit to the memorial service.

"Don't look so scared," she'd said. "The prowler won't get you at the funeral home—too many witnesses. And don't worry about Irene. She won't be home tonight. She and Jack Junior are having dinner at Heads 'N' Tails. If Coop phones, I've got your back."

When I refused, she rolled her eyes. "I want to introduce the bulldog to Caesar and Cleo," she said, smiling down at her Chihuahuas. "Sir won't bond with them if you're around."

Now, I glanced toward the front of the Longstreet Room, expecting to see Kendall laid out in a walnut casket; but a gold resin urn sat on a table, flanked by potted ferns and framed photographs.

She'd been cremated? I felt a buzzing in my chest, as if wasps were trying to sting their way out. Aunt Bluette used to say, *Trouble takes and takes and takes. And it gives nothing in return but heartache.*

Mrs. McCormack sat in the front row. Her lips puckered, relaxed, then puckered again, as if she were trying to whistle.

"Sorry about your daughter," said a woman in a purple hat.

"Kendall just banged her head a little," Mrs. McCormack said. "She was doing fine. Yelling at the nurses to discharge her. Then somebody called the room and said a meal was waiting for me in the cafeteria. Stuffed peppers, my favorite. I was just gone a minute."

I wondered if the caller had lisped. Whispers rose up from the corner of the room where several women discussed Kendall's supposed intoxication.

"Impossible," said one.

"The blood test got mixed up," said another.

"I heard she ate too many bourbon balls."

"The only balls she ate were Lester's."

Kendall might be alive if I hadn't told her to find more proof. After she'd talked to me, where had she gone? To someone she'd trusted. I looked around for Norris. He'd left the Philpot's mansion the night Barb had gone missing. He'd taken a financial hit after he'd lost his medical license, but he could have raked in tax free dollars by slicing off corneas. Maybe he also had a gardenia bush in his backyard.

A chill ran up my neck. If Kendall had shown him Barb's printout, he might have slipped alcohol into her Coca-Cola. But why not just kill her? Why put her in a car? I was even more puzzled by Mrs. McCormack—why had she opted for cremation?

Lester shuffled past me, casting sneaky glances at each row. Part of my brain said, *Let him pass*, but the other, wilder part said, *Put the squeeze on him.*

I grasped his arm. He stared down at my hand, as if it were covered with leprosy sores, then he glanced at my hair.

"I didn't recognize you," he said. "You look different without the chicken fluff. Are you wearing a wig?"

I released his arm and stepped backward. "I'm so sorry about Kendall."

"Yes, it's sad." He looked at me a beat too long. "Say, I really do like your hair."

Bile scorched the back of my throat, triggering my gag reflex. He'd lost a wife and a girlfriend, but he wasn't shaken? "I'm just surprised that Kendall was drunk," I said.

He didn't answer, just twisted his wedding ring. The metal had cut into his flesh, leaving a red circle.

"Wasn't Kendall allergic to alcohol?" I asked.

"I wouldn't know about that." He shifted his body, pointing his feet toward the door, like he couldn't wait to escape.

He raked his hand across his forehead, leaving a damp streak. "I hate to break your heart. But you're not O'Malley's only love. He's a cocksman. Before he hooked up with you, he dated a brunette lawyer. A real looker. A Charleston blue blood. Rich as the pope. Word on the street is, they're still together. Sneaking around behind your back."

A zinging pain shot through my head. What brunette?

Lester gave me a triumphant stare. "You think I'm lying, don't you?"

I nodded.

"The minute Barb told me that Emerson might be O'Malley's child, I began checking him out. So I know all about that brunette lawyer. They say her name is Chlamydia Smith. If I were you, I'd be extra careful. Because it's my understanding that venereal diseases are making a comeback."

I wanted to ask him about the brunette, but I had a feeling that he was baiting me. "How's Emerson?"

He rubbed his nose, as if he'd caught a whiff of something rotten. "Imagine the worst and multiply it times a thousand. Tell Coop-the-cocksman that I got the DNA sample today. I should have the results soon. Until then, can you bring Emerson's damn hedgehog? She's asking for it."

"It's in Charleston."

"How'd it get there? Never mind. Just get it back, will you?"

He started to walk off, but I thought about Emerson's real birthday. I knew what that DNA test would show. I pinched his sleeve. "No matter what happens, I'd like to be a part of Emerson's life."

He stared, his face unreadable, then he pulled his sleeve out of my grasp. He worked his way down the aisle and stood in front of Kendall's urn.

On my way out of the funeral home, I got caught in a bottleneck. A girl with Goth-black, shoulder-length hair was talking to Zee Quinn.

"Wonder if Kendall was a closet drinker?" the Goth-girl asked Zee.

"Nuh-uh." Zee patted her dreadlocks. When she saw me, she smiled.

"I hate it when young people die," the Goth-girl was saying when I walked up. She yawned, revealing three gold studs in the center of her tongue.

"I'll tell you what's weird," Zee said. "Kendall was scared of fire. Why would her mama cremate her?"

"You'd think Mrs. McCormack would've known how Kendall felt," the Goth-girl said. "But she was clueless."

"Where you getting this information?" I asked.

"I work here." The Goth-girl looked down at her glossy black fingernails. "I do hair and makeup. Plus, I do odd jobs. I went with Vlado to the hospital the other day to fetch Kendall's body."

"Vlado?" Zee asked. "That Russian guy?"

"He's an embalmer." The Goth-girl pointed to Mr. Winky's assistant, a young fellow with short blond hair and stubby legs. "I love his accent."

"You were telling us about Kendall," I prompted.

"We brought her to the embalming room, and Mrs. McCormack was waiting outside the door. She wanted me to use a light touch with Kendall's hair and makeup. No eye shadow or rouge. Mr. Winky came in and told me to quit. He said Kendall was going to be cremated. I didn't believe him, but he showed me a document."

I touched the Goth-girl's arm. "What did it say?"

"That Kendall wanted to be cremated. Mrs. McCormack didn't know a thing about this document. But it was legally binding. She had to go along with it."

"How did Mr. Winky get the document?" I asked.

"Mr. Philpot gave it to him," the Goth-girl said.

"And who told *you*?" Zee asked.

"Vlado." She fanned herself and grinned.

My pulse beat in the roof of my mouth. If the Philpots were involved in black market organs, and I believed they were, they would do anything to conceal their activities. If Kendall had shown Barb's printout to Lester, he wouldn't have patted her on the head and told her to rearrange the Preparation-H display. He would have gotten her drunk and put her into the Mazda, hoping she'd drive into a telephone pole.

No, she might not have wrecked. Maybe he'd put her behind the wheel, then he'd gotten into his Mercedes and chased her, nudging her car off the road.

But what if a witness had seen him? In any event, Kendall had survived the wreck, only to die in the hospital. Had one of the Philpot brothers gone to her room and smothered her? Injected her with something that would stop her heart? But why take so many steps to kill someone? Lester had a whole pharmacy at his disposal. If he'd wanted to eliminate Kendall, he could have given her a fatal dose of insulin or epinephrine. So maybe I was an alarmist, and he was innocent.

One thing still bothered me. How many twenty-year-old women thought about cremation? How many of them put their burial preferences in writing? I drew in a sudden breath. What if the document was fake? Maybe Lester *had* injected Kendall with a drug, and he'd feared the coroner would order a toxicology screen. That happened all the time on *CSI: Miami*.

The Goth-girl was still talking about the cremation. "Vlado and I were supposed to take Kendall's body to the crematorium, but Mr. Philpot wouldn't let us. He arranged for a crematory to pick up Kendall."

So here was a freshly dead body with corneas, teeth, tendons, and bones. Why hadn't the Philpots killed Kendall at the pharmacy? They could have harvested her body parts. Instead, they'd produced a possibly fake cremation document.

I inched closer to the Goth-girl. "Do you remember the crematory's name?"

"Never heard of it," she said. "It's in another county."

Zee tossed her head, rattling the beads. She looked over my shoulder and frowned. I turned. Norris stood in the vestibule glaring at us, then he dipped back into the crowd.

I ran to the parking lot and bumped smack into Son Finnegan. His gaze swept from my hair to my dress, then back up to my face. "Wow," he said. "Just . . . *wow.*"

I shoved him away, my hair swinging. "Are you stalking me?"

"No, but Norris Philpot is." Son pointed at the funeral home.

I whirled. Norris stood on the porch, waving his raptor claw, the neighborhood bird of prey in a suit and tie. But his eyes said, *No escape.*

twenty-three

My heel caught on the sidewalk and I stumbled forward, barely saving myself from slamming face-first against the cement.

"Hey, Boots," Son called. "It's not my fault you got man problems."

"Go away, Finnegan." I veered into the parking lot. Lester's Mercedes sat in the first row. I walked around it, checking the bumper for dents or black paint. But I only saw a few dead bugs. This car hadn't been used to force Kendall's Mazda off the road. But I didn't feel calmer.

I got in my truck and stabbed the key in the ignition. The engine shuddered and let out a whinny that hurt my ears. I stamped my shoe against the accelerator as if I were crushing spiders. The engine backfired and the truck jolted forward.

Son stepped in front of the truck and spread his arms. I hit the brake. He walked through a thick veil of exhaust and leaned against my window.

"You're getting on my last nerve, Finnegan."

"But we need to talk. Another patient died today. A healthy thirty-year-old woman. She went into cardiac arrest after liposuction."

"I don't want to hear about it." I gripped the steering wheel. "I'm sick of death."

"Then why do you hang out at the funeral home?"

Good question. "So do you."

"I've got my reasons. Let's go to Bunratty's Pub and I'll explain."

I imagined an ice-cold mug of Guinness, a clover stamped into the foam, Celtic music playing in the background, Son and me sitting in a booth. I loved Coop, but I couldn't ignore the glimmer of lust I felt for Son—what if it turned into something stronger?

"The O'Malleys are expecting me," I said.

He pushed in a little closer. "For supper? Is Irene planning to stick an apple in your mouth and serve you as the main course?"

"Step away from the truck or I'll run over your toes."

"It's Friday night. You shouldn't be alone with a flesh-eating bitch." He pushed a scrap of paper into my hand. "It's my phone number, not a love letter. Just in case you change your mind."

I tucked the scrap into his pocket, then I smashed my shoe against the pedal. The truck blasted out of the lot, backfiring and spewing smoke. I stopped by the deserted 7-Eleven and bought a bag of M&M's. On my way to the parking lot, the back of my neck tingled, and I had the oddest feeling that someone was staring. I turned brandishing my M&M's.

No one was around except a striped tabby cat. He flicked his tail and trotted away.

I took the scenic route to the O'Malleys' house, driving down streets named after deadly flowers. Every few seconds, I glanced in the rearview mirror to make sure no one had followed me. From the radio, Lady Antebellum was singing "I Need You Now" and I got so blue, I almost ran over a trash can.

I parked beside the O'Malleys' carriage house, pulled off my high heels, and walked barefoot around the gazebo. Eerie blue light radiated from the swimming pool, casting jagged streaks over the patio. I wanted to eat chocolate and tuck my feet under Sir's warm belly. But when I got closer to the house, I froze. The kitchen door stood open. So much for state-of-the-art security.

Gripping my shoes to my chest, I stepped inside the house. Sir didn't rush out to greet me, nor did I hear the distant hum of conversation. The house had an empty feel. "Minnie?" I called.

No answer.

Sir trotted into the kitchen and butted his head against my legs. "Where's Minnie?" I asked. The bulldog yawned, revealing his pink, ribbed mouth.

"So how did it go with the Chihuahuas?" I asked him.

He showed me his teeth. I reached into the M&M bag, dragged up a red candy, and slipped it into my mouth. Sir licked his lips, tags clicking.

"Sorry, buddy," I said. "Chocolate is deadly to dogs."

He tilted his head and gave me his "you shouldn't be eating it either" look.

"That's true," I said. "But you'll still love me if I weigh two hundred pounds and wear turquoise muumuus, right?"

Sir raised his hind leg and licked himself.

"Fine," I said. "I'll move to Italy and meet a white-haired chef named Alejandro, who'll feed me homemade ravioli."

Sir's head shot up, the undershot jaw quivering, as if he were tasting that ravioli. "I'll hire an artist to paint my curves and dimpled thighs. We'll make love in the kitchen and drink too much wine. We may even raise bulldogs."

The phone rang. I swallowed a gob of chocolate and answered with a garbled hello.

"It's me," Coop said. "I called earlier. Minnie said you were asleep."

I didn't want to get my new best friend in trouble. But how could I expect honesty from Coop if I lied? "I went to the funeral home." I swallowed again, and the rest of the candy went down like ground glass.

"To spy or pay your respects?" Coop sounded amused, not angry.

Just in case I was misreading his tone, I said, "Kendall was cremated."

Silence.

If I mentioned her fear of fire, he'd call it hearsay. If I brought up Emerson's DNA test, he'd think I was meddling. If I accused the Philpot brothers of skinning corpses, he'd tell me to take a sedative.

"There's something odd about Kendall's cremation." The words blasted out of my mouth before I could stop myself. I told him how Lester had derailed the funeral by producing an anti-casket document. I was just getting warmed up about the Philpots' possible chop shop when Coop stopped me.

"The Sweeney police arrested a man for Barb's murder."

My knees buckled, and I leaned against the counter. "When?"

"This afternoon."

"Do the police have the right man?"

"He didn't have an alibi. Barb's jewelry and credit cards were in his pockets." He paused. "And he had a Bill Clinton mask."

"Who was he?" I shut my eyes, expecting to feel a huge wave of relief, but my insides were knotted.

"A twenty-nine-year-old meth addict. He lived in an apartment near the Motel 6," Coop said. "A big gardenia bush in the backyard. Surgical equipment in the kitchen."

Would a murderer leave those items lying around? And why had the police decided to search his house? I tried to rustle up some enthusiasm. "Did he confess?"

"No, but the police are satisfied. So am I."

"Was this the man I saw at Barb's? And the guy who broke into my house?"

"I'm confident that he is. But you'll have to go to Sweeney next week to see if you can ID him in a lineup. So I'm sending Red to Bonaventure. He'll be there later tonight."

"What about the Charleston police? Do I need to talk to them?"

"I've already discussed this with the ADA. He'll meet you in Sweeney."

I ate another M&M. "I thought Red was on surveillance."

"We found a replacement."

"I don't understand. If the murderer is in custody, why do I need a babysitter? Why did you pull Red off your case?"

"Minnie said that Mother has been acting up. I thought Red could act as a buffer."

"But there's no reason for me to stay at your mother's house. I can leave, right?"

"I don't want you to be alone."

"Why not?"

"I don't want to scare you, but the suspect could have an accomplice."

"What makes you think that?" I exhaled a little too forcefully.

"I'm just being cautious."

This was his *semper paratus* coming out. I understood that part. But I also wondered if Coop was making sure that I stayed away from Son. Or maybe he didn't want me to turn up unannounced in Charleston, interrupting him and Chlamydia Smith. I thought of a third reason: what if the man in Sweeney was a hired hit man or a stooge? Someone the Philpots had set up to hide Norris's role in Barb's murder. I pushed aside my theories, and a raw longing took their place.

"I miss you," I said. "When are you coming to Bonaventure?"

"Not for a week. Maybe longer."

I shivered, remembering Lester's comments about the pretty brunette lawyer. "Your boss sure is keeping you busy," I said.

"I've got two meetings in the morning."

"But tomorrow's Saturday."

"Mr. Robichaux set up the meetings."

Would the brunette be joining them? "I saw Lester tonight," I said. "Have you mailed Emerson's stuff?"

"Red's bringing everything tonight."

"Great. I'll pop some corn. We'll have a pajama party." I didn't want Red. I wanted Coop to be my co-conspirator, to feed me chocolate and help me nail the Philpot brothers for Barb and Kendall's murders.

After we hung up, my necklace felt too tight, as if the weight of the slender chain had cut off my air.

The next morning, I put on my boots and a dress that had deep pochets. Red was waiting in the kitchen. "I got the kid's hedgehog in my—" He broke off, his throat convulsing, tiny ripples waving across his neck. "What the hell happened to your hair?"

"I'll tell you on the way to the Philpots' house."

They lived in Musgrove Square, just past All Saints Church and the Prince of Wales Pub. Red parked in front of a raspberry stucco house. The front gate stood ajar, and a man pushed a lawn mower over the grass. I grabbed the hedgehog and Red got the backpack. We walked to the front porch and rang the bell.

The door swung open and Helen Philpot aimed a raptor claw at a discreet sign. "Whatever you're selling, I'm not interested. Didn't you see the 'No Soliciting' sign?"

"I'm Teeny Templeton. We met the other night at Eikenberry's?"

"Yes, yes. Of course." She looked at my red cowboy boots, as if to say, *You went out in public like this?*

I glanced past her into the wide foyer. Sunlight slashed through five French doors, each one framed by poofy silk draperies. Beyond the doors, I saw a swimming pool with waves cutting across the surface. I thought of Lester diving into the water to save Emerson, and I wondered if I'd misjudged him.

"Lester asked me to drop off Emerson's belongings," I said, and lifted the hedgehog.

"How kind of you."

A French door opened and Emerson ran in, slinging water onto the floor. She tugged at the straps of a navy, one-piece bathing suit. "Get me a towel, Mrs. Philpot," she called.

"Look on the table behind you." Helen did an eye roll. "Kids."

Emerson lifted a wet pigtail and sketched illegible letters. When she saw me, her mouth opened wide, showing her gums and teeth.

"Teeny!" She ran over to me, her feet slapping against the parquet floor. She pulled the hedgehog from my hands and kissed it.

"Here's your clothes, too." Red set the backpack on the floor.

Emerson turned to me. "Kendall got put into a jar. They cooked her."

A blue vein appeared on Helen's forehead. If I hadn't seen the quick rise and fall of her chest, I would have thought she was holding her breath. "Don't be disrespectful, Emerson," she said.

Red shuffled his feet. "That's how children handle grief," he told Helen. "Kendall's death was a trigger for . . . anyway, they need to talk about their feelings."

Helen made a small, exact noise in her throat. "Sorry, I didn't catch your name."

"He's Red Butler Hill," Emerson said. "He's a detective. He's got gun."

"As in Scarlett and Rhett?" A smile flickered at the edge of Helen's mouth.

"Yes, ma'am." Red nodded. "But it's spelled like the color red. My mama is a big fan of Margaret Mitchell, but she can't spell."

"I'm a fan of good manners." Helen folded her arms. She still hadn't invited us to come inside. My gaze passed over a carved gilt table. I squinted at a hand-painted mural on the staircase wall. The figures seemed to depict the Battle of Atlanta. In the upstairs hall, a headless statue stood in an arched niche. Someone, doubtlessly Emerson, had drawn blue polka dots over its legs. That made me relax. But I still didn't understand how a pharmacist could afford such finery. I'd gone to an antiques show in Charleston a few weeks ago, hoping to find a kitchen table, and I'd been astonished at the prices.

My heart started beating in the back of my throat. Just because the Sweeney police had arrested a man for Barb's murder didn't mean the Philpots weren't selling teeth and tendons. With so much at stake, they could have hired someone to kill Barb.

Emerson tugged Helen's arm. "Can Teeny and Red stay for lunch?"

"Not today. I've got a tennis game."

"They can babysit me," Emerson said.

"Another time."

I glanced around the foyer again and saw gold cherubs painted on the domed ceiling. Now, more than ever, I believed that Kendall had found a printout with a list of human organs. I believed that the printout had led to her murder. And what about Barb's anagrams?

Clues beneath the fur. Clues on the wall. Clues underfoot.

I stepped closer to the mural, scrutinizing the figures.

Helen walked up behind me. "It's interesting, isn't it?"

"It stinks," Emerson said.

Helen gave her a look that said "I'll deal with you later," then she turned to me. "Barb started this mural on a whim. But she made such a mess, she had to call her art teacher for help. Most of this is Emma Underwood's work."

I nodded. This was the second time I'd heard that name. A sign that I should investigate further.

I heard a car turn into the driveway, and I glanced over my shoulder. The funeral home van stopped under a live oak, moss trailing down like dirty fingers. Mr. Winky climbed out of the front seat, walked to the rear compartment, and pulled out an urn.

"Oh, for the love of god," Helen said. "What now?"

Mr. Winky lurched onto the porch and held out the urn, his eyelids flapping like startled birds. "Where do you want me to set her?" he asked Helen.

"Her?" Helen cried.

"Kendall McCormack's cremains," Mr. Winky said.

"You mean, her ashes?" Helen fanned herself.

"Yes." Mr. Winky's right eyelid went still, but the left one jerked like a hooked trout. "Mr. Philpot said to deliver the cremains."

"He didn't tell me," Helen's fingernails scraped through her hair. "I'm sure it's a misunderstanding. Kendall's mother should get the ashes."

"Why don't you call your son?" Mr. Winky started to put down the urn.

"Take it back!" Emerson dove into the man's stomach. He toppled backward and the urn flew out of his hands. The vessel hit the floor and shattered. Beige granules spilled between Emerson's feet, fine dust particles rising toward her wet ankles.

"Gross!" She swiped at her legs.

I reached down to brush off the ashes, trying not to be creeped out. I'd never seen cremains, but I'd expected it to resemble whole wheat flour. This stuff was gritty. The clay-colored specks were too perfect, each one the same size. I raised my hand and blinked at the gray residue that clung to my fingers.

"It looks like kitty litter," Emerson said.

Red hunkered by the urn. He pinched some grit between his fingers and held it to his nose. "It's not scented."

Emerson lifted a damp pigtail and squeezed water over the granules. "Look, it clumps," she said.

"Sheesh, don't touch it," Red cried. "It's evidence."

"Of what?" Helen asked.

Mr. Winky stood in the doorway, his eyelids flapping double time. "It's ashes, I can assure you," he said.

A drop of perspiration hung from the tip of his nose.

"Doesn't look like human ashes to me." Red folded his arms. "Does Eikenberry's have a crematory?"

"No, we use the one near the river," Mr. Winky answered. "But Mr. Philpot talked the McCormacks into using an out-of-town crematorium."

"He did not," Helen said. "Lester wasn't on speaking terms with the McCormacks. He wouldn't dare discuss Kendall's burial with them."

"But your son had a document," I said.

"What document?" Helen asked.

Red nudged my arm. "Hush, Teeny."

"I want to know about this document," Helen said in an imperious tone.

"Ask him." I pointed to Mr. Winky.

He gave me a baleful look, then he dragged a handkerchief from his pocket and wiped his nose. "I never saw the document," he said. "But Opal Brabham did. She's our cosmetologist."

The Goth-girl? I felt more confused than ever. Who should I believe? Mr. Winky had every reason to lie because his credibility was on the line. I'd met the Goth-girl once, and she'd repeated her story in front of me and Zee Greer. Why would Opal lie in front of witnesses?

Emerson blew on the litter, watching it scatter.

"I'm calling the police." Helen stepped away from the open door and walked to the gilt table. She lifted a French phone and dialed 911.

Emerson tugged my dress. "Am I in trouble?"

"No, sweetie." I squeezed her hand.

"It sounds like the crematory messed up," Mr. Winky said. "You should report them to the state board of funeral home directors."

At least he was admitting that a problem existed.

After Helen explained the situation to the 911 operator, she hung up and snapped her fingers at Emerson. "Up to your room. Now. We've got a busy afternoon."

"But I want to see the *CSI* stuff," Emerson said.

Helen slung the backpack over Emerson's shoulder, then she steered the girl to the banister. Emerson walked halfway up the stairs and sat behind the railing.

"Dammit, I don't have time for this," Helen said. "A broken urn is on my floor. And the police are on their way. How will I ever get to my tennis match on time?"

Five minutes later, Officer Dale Fitzgerald showed up. He agreed the debris bore a striking resemblance to Precious Cat Clumping litter. "I've never been called to investigate a case of missing cremains," he said.

Emerson poked her face through the railing. "The dude on *CSI* would bag it," she said.

"Here in Bonaventure, the rule is, *SIC,*" Fitzgerald said. "Sorry I Can't."

"Just get on with it," Helen snapped. "Or you're the one who'll be sorry."

twenty-four

After much hemming and hawing, Officer Fitzgerald phoned the police chief, who was vacationing in St. Augustine with his family. It was decided the remains would be photographed, collected, and sent to a forensic expert in Atlanta. Then Fitzgerald escorted Mr. Winky to the station, presumably for questioning.

Helen shooed me and Red to the porch, as if we were leftover bits of urn, and slammed the door. We got into the yellow van.

"I told Coop something was wonky about Kendall's cremation," I said. "And he blew me off."

"Don't jump to conclusions. The crematory might have misplaced Kendall's ashes."

"Misplaced Kendall's ashes? Doesn't seem likely. And if the crematorium was reputable, they wouldn't fake it with kitty litter."

"The local police will handle this. And the funeral home board will get involved."

"I thought you hated crime."

"True crime. Not true grit." He steered the van away from the curb, into the dappled sunlight that fell around Musgrove Square.

I glanced back at the Philpots' house, wishing I'd taken a closer look at that mural. Had Barb stashed more notes in her house—or did

Lester have records at his store? I had Kendall's keys, and the alarm code was her birth date. But if I wanted to sleuth I had to get away from Red.

"Okay, the urn thing is weird," Red said. "But mistakes happen."

"So do murders."

"You don't know if Kendall was murdered."

"Why was Lester in a hurry to get her cremated in the first place? If she isn't in the urn, where is she? And what about that guy the Sweeney police caught? Maybe someone paid him to kill Barb."

"How did we get from ashes to a hit man?" Red asked. "That's a leap, even for you."

I decided to take a different approach. "What did you think of the Philpots' mansion?"

He whistled. "I bet they hired Tony Soprano's decorator."

"I bet it took a lot of money."

"Yeah? So?" He shot me a suspicious glance. "What you getting at?"

"How can Lester afford that house? Musgrove Square is the most prestigious part of the historic district. The houses almost never come on the market. When they do, the prices start at one million."

"That's not a huge amount. Even for a small city like Bonaventure. Lester probably has a killer mortgage."

"Can you find out? Kendall said that Lester was worried about his finances. Business is drying up at his pharmacy."

"He's probably being hammered by the all-night Walgreens. Kroger and Publix have drugstores, too."

"Yet he's paying tuition at Chatham Academy. He drives a Mercedes. Barb had a BMW. He swings a fat mortgage. I'm just wondering how he manages."

"I'll look into it, homegirl. And I'll check into the urn, too."

I nodded, but my mind whirled. I had an idea that the kitty litter would just be swept away and we'd never hear another word about Kendall's cremains.

Unless I found proof.

. . .

Ten minutes later, Red and I were sitting in the O'Malleys' shady gazebo. Above us, a ceiling fan chopped through the humid afternoon air. I pictured the urn, then I tried to imagine what Chlamydia Smith looked like. To soothe myself, I invented a drink called If-I-Can't-Have-True-Love, I'll-Buy-A-Bigger-Dress-Size: vodka, coffee liqueur, Hershey's Syrup, crème de cacao, crushed ice, and chocolate ice cream. Place ingredients in a blender and pulverize. Ponder the chemistry of food and romance. If love can be frozen, will it still be love? True love isn't smooth, it's lumpy; but if you own a quality blender, you can make this drink in three minutes.

"You're thinking up shit," he said.

"Just a recipe." I put my elbows on my knees. "But I'm baffled."

"About the recipe?"

"No, all this other stuff. First, Kendall found a printout about black market organs. Now she's dead and her urn is full of kitty litter."

"We've been over this," he said. "The crematory screwed up."

"But what if it's not an error? What if litter was deliberately put into that urn?"

"Well, that's fraud. It's happened before, right here in Georgia. A crematory was broken. The operator didn't fix it. So he passed off dirt and cement powder as the remains. Threw out the bodies like trash. One was stashed in a rusted hearse. Others were dumped into a pond. The owner got a twenty-year prison sentence."

"Can't you call the GBI?"

"And tell them what?"

"A corpse is missing!"

"Misplaced until proven otherwise. Knock off the questions. Let's go inside and eat pie."

"How can you think about pie when people are dying? Barb. Kendall. And Son Finnegan lost a patient today."

"Maybe he'll find her."

"This isn't funny. What if patients at Bonaventure Regional are being murdered for their organs?"

"Sheesh, here you go again. If something like that was going on at a hospital, somebody would know. Transplants require a team. There's strict laws, too. At the most, the crematory committed fraud. They prolly hoped the family wouldn't know what cremains looks like."

I lifted a hunk of hair, pretending to examine it, but I was really hiding my face. I was afraid Red would glean my thoughts. "You're right. It's a mixup."

He gave me a wary look.

A door slammed and I glanced at the house. Irene and Sir strode past the swimming pool, their reflections moving in the blue water. Irene wore a flowing chartreuse tunic and matching slacks. She held Sir's leash with two fingers, as if the leather might be radioactive.

"She looks pissed," Red whispered.

Irene's lips were drawn into a tight line. Oddly enough, Sir's were, too.

"Where's Minnie?" I asked.

Irene stared at my boots as if the red leather had been tooled out of human hearts. "We had an altercation over her Chihuahuas. I made her go back to Savannah."

I clenched my hands. "I'm sorry to hear it."

Irene handed me Sir's leash. "The next time you disappear, will you please leave a note?"

"Teeny can come and go as she pleases," Red said. "Barb Philpot's murderer is in custody."

"I heard." Irene's lips were glossy red, as if she'd recently bitten into a small, quivering rodent. "I thought we could all breathe easier, now that Teeny's prowler isn't lurking. But I just talked to Coop. He's not feeling well, and he wants you to stay at my house for a few days."

I looked up at her. "What's wrong with him?"

"His ulcer is giving him fits."

"I don't see the connection between his gastric problems and why I've got to stay in this house," I said.

Her gaze flickered over me as if she were studying a diagram of a cow in a butcher's shop. "How dare you speak to me in that tone. My son never had an ulcer until he took up with you."

My throat constricted, not from my asthma but from all the angry words I was holding back. If I stayed at Casa Too Much another second, I'd tell Irene what I really thought of her, and I loved Coop too much to disrespect the woman who'd birthed him.

I got to my feet.

"Where are you going now?" Irene said.

"A walk." I led Sir out of the gazebo.

"I'll go with you." Red scrambled after me.

"Don't be late for lunch," Irene called. "I'm having it sent over from Heads 'N' Tails." Irene spun around, her tunic billowing, and stomped toward her house.

Red followed me down the cobbled driveway, to the corner of Hawthorne and Mississippi. A tour bus was parked by the curlicue gate to Hanover Square. In the heat-waved distance, water spilled from a fountain. Red moved toward the entrance to the Square. I was still feeling an adrenaline rush from Irene's verbal smackdown, so I went in the opposite direction, toward Hawthorne Street.

"You ain't going to the park?" Red asked.

"I want to be alone," I called over my shoulder. "Go back to the O'Malleys'."

"Look, don't let Irene upset you," he said. "She's a control freak."

She was a freak, all right. I cut down Louisiana Street. It was just behind the O'Malleys' house. I could hear Red puffing behind me, but I kept going. I stopped in front of a blue house with gargoyles on the roof. UNDERWOOD was spelled out on the cast iron mailbox. Miss Emma Underwood had been diagnosed with Alzheimer's. How much would she remember?

Clues on the wall.

With luck, Miss Emma could tell me about Barb's mural—and Barb. I led Sir up the cobbled walkway and rang the bell. Behind the door, chimes played "Georgia on My Mind."

Red staggered to the porch, his cheeks flushed, but before he could interrogate me, the door opened and a stout nurse with short auburn hair smiled at us. Pinned to her chest was a nametag: FRAN BELCHER, R.N.

"Hi, there," she said. "How can I help you?"

I introduced myself and explained that my mama used to take art lessons from Miss Emma. "I stopped by to see how she's doing," I added. "I won't stay long."

From inside the house, an aristocratic voice called, "Who is it, Nurse Ratched?"

The nurse led me and Red through a gloomy foyer that smelled of Vicks VapoRub and tea bags, into a bright solarium. An elderly woman in sunglasses stood in front of an easel, dabbing paint onto a canvas. Behind her, the wall was strewn with colorful handwriting.

Fran Belcher Slept with My Plumber was scrawled in bold, red print just below *Fran Belcher is a thief.*

Miss Emma lowered her sunglasses, revealing small brown eyes. "I saw y'all earlier in the O'Malleys' gazebo." She waved her brush toward a window. The view showed Miss Emma's yard. The overgrown grass melted into Irene's clipped lawn. A curved path led to the gazebo.

Miss Emma looked from me to Red to Sir. "What a delightful trio—a girl, a dog, and a lion man."

Nurse Belcher folded her arms. "It's not nice to spy on people, Miss Emma."

"It's not nice of you to point out my failings to Dorothy and Toto." Miss Emma flicked her paintbrush at the nurse, then she cast a speculative glance at Red. "I just love cowardly lions."

"Don't be offended," Fran said. "Five minutes from now, she'll think you all are actors on *General Hospital.*"

"That's a lie. *General Hospital* doesn't have a bulldog." Miss Emma tilted her head and her dangly earrings caught the light. "Fran, go fix us something cold to drink."

"Fix it yourself." Fran crossed her arms.

"You're fired." Miss Emma said. A drop of blue paint slid off the tip of her brush and hit the floor. "Leave this instant."

"Oh, shut up," Fran said. She pulled an emery board from her pocket and buffed her nails.

Miss Emma turned to Red. "You, lion man. Go outside and break me off a tree branch so I can switch my nurse's legs."

Red grimaced. He'd once told me that he hated female backbiting worse than stakeouts.

Fran shrugged. "In five minutes, the bitch won't remember what she said."

Miss Emma set down her brush. She moved to a coffee mug that held a set of Sharpies. She plucked out a blue pen, uncapped it, and stepped closer to the wall. In bold letters she wrote, *Fran called me a bitch!*

Red pulled the leash from my hand. "Teeny, stay as long as you like. The mutt and I will be at Dr. O'Malley's."

Fran showed them out and didn't return. Miss Emma dragged the Sharpie over the F in *Fran,* then she added a smiley face with horns. "Girl, what's your name again?" she asked.

"Teeny."

"Are you the O'Malleys' new maid?"

"No, ma'am." I hesitated. "I'm engaged to their son."

"That's scandalous." Miss Emma drew a question mark on the wall. "Coop's just a boy."

"He's grown up," I said gently. "He just turned thirty-one."

"He used to go steady with that trashy majorette." Miss Emma set down her Sharpie. "Barb Browning. She married that druggist. What's his name?"

"Lester Philpot," I said.

"Barb took art lessons from me. Not a speck of talent. Her skills lay elsewhere. She could put together a thousand-piece puzzle in no time at all. And she constantly wrote in her diary. Even during art lessons. She carried that thing with her everywhere."

Miss Emma reached for her brush, dipped it in a red pot, and drew an apple on her canvas. "Every time Barb came here for a lesson, she'd write and write. If Coop was home from college, she'd spy on him. One day she caught him sitting in the gazebo. It was an icy December afternoon. Barb walked out my door and didn't bother to put on her coat."

I turned to the window. In the distance, I saw Red and Sir walk around the gazebo, toward Irene's house.

"Coop wasn't wearing a coat, either," Miss Emma said. "Barb went straight to him and took off his clothes and seduced him. And in all that cold, too. I tried not to watch. After a while, Coop got up and pulled up his pants and left. Barb stayed behind. She wrote and wrote in that diary. And she didn't come back to my house."

A tremor started in my fingertips and moved up my arms. "What year was this, Miss Emma?"

"Child, I don't remember. Dates don't stick with me. But I'm sure it was the year I put up a manger scene. I swapped baby Jesus for a blue Smurf figurine."

I could totally see her Smurfing the manger.

Miss Emma tapped a finger against her chin. "But I think Coop was a freshman in college. He and Barb were broken up. Irene was so pleased." Miss Emma dipped her brush into a pot of blue paint and drew a tiny Smurf. "Right after Valentine's Day, Barb up and married Lester Philpot. Everybody said she was pregnant."

The tremors moved from my arms into my jaws.

"I've never seen their daughter." Miss Emma dabbed her brush in black paint and drew a frowning devil face on the Smurf. "I expected to see her when I painted Barb's mural. I believe the girl was at school. Barb didn't write in her diary, either."

I edged closer to Miss Emma. "Did she say why?"

"She stopped keeping a diary after the child was born. Barb had the baby blues. But she still put together those puzzles."

"I saw the mural," I said. "When did you paint it?"

"Two years ago." She pointed to the wall, toward a long pastel column.

In the middle, she'd written, *Painted BBP's mural—Battle of Atlanta.* The date was scrawled beside it.

Two years and one month ago.

Miss Emma drew a black doodlebug on her canvas. "Even then, my mind was starting to get foggy. So I listed my freelance projects. I was real excited to paint the Battle of Atlanta, but Barb didn't know her history. She painted what she wanted. Thank goodness she chose an inconspicuous spot. She worked in one area, halfway up the staircase. At the curve. I hope people don't think I painted it."

I was barely listening. Eleven years ago, Coop had been a freshman at the University of North Carolina. He and Barb had broken up for good that autumn. But if Miss Emma was right and he'd slept with Barb that December, he could be Emerson's father. When the DNA test came back, Lester might have no choice but to let the child live with Coop. And me.

"Girl?" Miss Emma snapped her fingers. "What's your name again?"

"Templeton." My voice was barely a whisper. Poor Miss Emma. Her memories were tattered, as if moths were flying inside her head, chewing holes in the past.

"I've heard that name before." Miss Emma painted fangs on the doodlebug. "I used to know something about Barb's diary. But I can't remember. If it comes back to me, I'll write it on my wall. Or I can ask my housekeeper. Fiona cleans for the Philpots, too. She knows all their secrets. She said Barb ripped the pages out of her diaries and put them somewhere. She kept the pages she wanted and burned the rest in the BBQ pit."

I sighed. Fiona McTavish had died two years ago—a hit-and-run driver had plowed into her on California Avenue. I told Miss Emma good-bye, promising I'd give my regards to Irene, then I walked back to Hanover Square.

Lunch was served in the solarium, but I stayed in the kitchen and ate graham crackers. I thought about Coop's ulcer—why hadn't he mentioned that he'd been feeling poorly? Or was Irene trying to goad me?

A swooshing sound rose up as Sir padded around the room, dragging his leash over Irene's throw rugs.

Clues on the wall, clues beneath the fur, clues underfoot.

I felt certain that Barb's anagrams referred to organ harvesting. She'd worked at the hospital, with access to patients. She could have been part of a black market ring—without Lester's knowledge. Maybe the Philpots weren't involved. But why had Lester pushed for Kendall's cremation?

I needed to study the mural and look under Barb's rugs. Her closet was probably filled with fur coats. But how could I get inside the Philpots' mansion? I could wait until they were gone. I'd hidden Kendall's Hello Kitty chain in the truck. Maybe one of the keys would fit. But if the burglar alarm went off, the police would swarm to Musgrove Square.

Still, I had to try. As the smell of Irene's sweetbreads wafted into the kitchen, I found a notepad and wrote: *I'm taking Sir for a ride.*

I grabbed his leash and we raced out of the house, into the sweltering, pine-smelling air. By the time I stopped in front of Barb's house, I had a plan. If everything worked out like I hoped it would, I'd know the identity of her killer.

twenty-five

Sir trotted down the Philpots' sidewalk, straining at the leash. Before I could ring the bell, Helen flung open the door as if she'd been waiting on the other side. She'd changed into white Bermuda shorts and a crisp, sleeveless t-shirt. A tote bag dangled from one hand, a key chain from the other. The foyer was spotless, not a trace of the urn fragments or spilled litter.

"You're back already?" she said. "What did you forget? Because I was just leaving."

Behind her, the French doors stood open, and wind stirred a gauzy curtain. She glanced over her shoulder. "Emerson, for the last time, get out of that pool!"

I heard a splash. Then Emerson yelled, "I told you to go without me. So go!"

"Oh, for Pete's sake." A fine net of perspiration stood on Helen's upper lip. She dumped her tote bag on the floor and everything spilled—sweatbands, metal racquet, water bottle, tennis balls, and a towel monogrammed with a black P. Philpot, petty, puzzle.

"I ought to leave the little monster," Helen said, shoving the items back into the tote.

I stubbed the tip of my shoe against the porch trying to distract myself from the ache in my chest. A long time ago, my mama and I had taken an unexpected road trip from Tybee Island to Myrtle Beach. At night she'd dumped me with strangers. If free sitters weren't available, she parked me in a motel room by myself.

Quit crying, Teeny. I'll be back in a few hours. Put the "Do Not Disturb" sign on the door. If anybody knocks or rattles the knob, start barking. Robbers are scared of dogs.

"I'll stay with Emerson," I said.

Deep lines slashed across Helen's forehead. "I hope you've had rabies shots. Little Miss Know-it-All is in the pool, but she's not alone. She went behind my back and invited some neighborhood kids. Nothing but tiny hoodlums."

"I like kids."

Helen's forehead puckered. "Are you sure you want to babysit? I'm in a tennis tournament. A round robin. I could be gone for hours."

"My whole afternoon is free," I said. "Take your time."

"I suppose you could use the practice. Emerson could end up with Coop. But I still think she belongs to someone on Curry Island. We should have the DNA results any day now." Helen slung the tote bag over her shoulder. "I'm sorry if I was rude earlier. I wasn't happy to see you at first. I'm upset about that damn urn. And I was ticked off about that document you mentioned. I called Lester, and he doesn't know about it."

My knees began shaking. "I was mistaken," I said. "I'm so sorry."

"Lester is upset. He's had so much tragedy in his life. He had a promising baseball career until he hurt his shoulder." Helen lifted her key chain. "My son has suffered. Everyone in this family has suffered except for Barb and Emerson."

Helen looked down at Sir. "Will he tinkle on Lester's walls?"

"No, ma'am. He's housetrained."

"He better be, or I'll send you the cleaning bill." Helen rushed out the front door.

After I heard her car drive away, I set down Sir's leash and walked up the staircase. I paused in the curve that Miss Emma had mentioned.

A cherub statue sat on a low ledge. Faux ivy looped around and behind it, then trailed up the wall.

I pushed it aside. It took a minute to find the exact spot where the art teacher's precise images ended and Barb's cruder ones began. Bucolic clouds hovered over a street that did not, to my recollection, exist in Atlanta. Barb had painted a replica of downtown Bonaventure, with its pastel buildings nestled around the Square. Lester's green pharmacy stood across the bridge. On the sidewalk was a stick family. One figure had long blond hair and wore a sequined majorette costume. Beside the woman was a blue-eyed man with dark bangs. Next to him was a little blond child with a wide mouth.

The next thing I saw made me gasp. Scattered behind the little family were two dismembered stick figures. One had frizzy hair and stubby legs. She wore an apron. The other figure had long brown hair and resembled Ava O'Malley, Coop's ex.

Barb had painted this scene years and years after she and Coop had broken up. I imagined her squatting in this curve, leaning toward the ledge, illustrating key events from her past. She'd painted her mural in a hard-to-see spot, below eye level. Her tall husband couldn't find her handiwork unless he bent over, shoved aside the statue, and clawed away the silk ivy.

I squinted at the mural. A flash of red caught my attention. Just outside the square green pharmacy, body parts were lined up on the sidewalk. Eyeballs, bones, teeth. Attached to each one was a price tag. A trail of blood led into the store.

My heart slammed against my ribs. *Clues on the wall.*

A shrill cry rose up from the pool. I straightened up and ran down the stairs. I grabbed Sir's leash and led him to the patio. Three small children stood in the shallow end of the pool, tossing a beach ball.

Emerson spotted me and waved both hands. She scrambled out of the pool. "Teeny! You came back."

"Helen is playing tennis. I'm babysitting you."

"I'm so glad." Emerson started to wrap her arms around me, then she hesitated. "I'm all wet."

I pulled her against me, feeling her cold body mold itself against me. Two small boys pushed in around us. "Let's play hide-and-seek," the taller one said.

Emerson introduced them as the Gallagher twins—Reed and Alex, though I couldn't tell them apart. They seemed younger than Emerson, and so skinny, their rib bones threatened to poke through their skin.

"Alex's got a missing front tooth. It makes him lisp like the Asshole-Who-Can't-Be-Named." Emerson pointed to a boy in green swim trunks. "Reed's got a chicken pox scar on his forehead."

She scooted away from me, reached for a towel, and blotted her face. "I've been through hell," she said, her voice muffled by the terry cloth. "Mr. Philpot and his lab rats got my saliva. They snuck up behind me and did a blitz attack."

"I'm so sorry, honey." I helped her dry off.

The Gallagher twins bounced on the balls of their feet. Alex stuck his finger in his nose. Reed pointed at Sir. "Lady, what kind of dog is that?"

"English bulldog." I reached down and patted Sir's head.

"Quit talking." Reed shoved his brother. "I want to play hide-and-seek."

Emerson thumped my arm. "Teeny's it."

"One, two, three," I said. The children scattered into the house. "Four, five, six."

Still counting, I led Sir back inside, past the staircase. Giggles drifted down, followed by, "Shhh!"

"Ten, eleven, twelve . . ." I felt overwhelmed by the sheer number of walls and floors. Miss Emma had said that Barb had hidden pages of her diary under the rug. I decided to check under the rugs first.

At the end of the hall, double doors opened into a bedroom that was bigger than my whole upstairs. The walls were bare, except for a large plasma TV. No rug. Who'd removed it? And why?

The closet door stood ajar, showing a glimpse of pastel ball gowns. Further down, I saw mink coats. I hated to deviate from my plan, but *clues beneath the fur* kept reverberating in my head. I checked the full-length coats and found nothing. Then I plunged my hand into the pocket of a silver fox jacket. My fingers closed on a cold, hard object. I dragged it up. The light hit a small brass key.

I tucked it into my bra and moved back into the hall. I lifted a small Persian rug. Nothing. So far, so good. I'd found clues on the mural and a key beneath the fur. I peered up the stairwell. Did those bedrooms have rugs? No, keep looking downstairs.

"Ready or not, here I come," I yelled.

More laughter swirled down as I passed through a living room. Chandeliers, curvy French tables. Oil paintings. But no rug. That seemed odd. Wouldn't a manse have Persian carpets? Maybe a few sisals?

Sir and I climbed the back staircase and turned into a frilly bedroom. Lilac walls, pink silk curtains, and a plush white carpet. Sir looked at the closet and wagged his tail.

"Come on, Sir," I said. They're not hiding in there."

More giggles.

I shut the door behind me. Sir and I checked the other bedrooms. Each one had the same thick white carpet on the floor. At the end of the hall, we turned into a storage room. It was piled with boxes and doodads. Everything was so dusty, I was afraid it would set off my asthma.

A few rag rugs were scattered over an unfinished floor. I moved around the room, lifting the rugs. All I found were dust bunnies. I'd literally worked myself into a corner, and I needed to think a minute. I perched on the edge of an old Windsor rocker. The chair scooted backward a few inches.

Sir trotted past me, toward a window that overlooked the front yard. "We've checked all the rooms," I told him. "Guess Miss Emma was mistaken. Barb didn't have any rugs to hide her papers, did she?"

The bulldog didn't answer. I leaned back in the chair, and it listed to the right. I rocked again, and the chair jerked. I got up. Now I saw the problem. The rocker was caught on the edge of a thick flotaki rug. I scooted the chair aside and pulled back the rug.

A flutter of white.

My pulse slammed against the top of my head. I lifted a page and recognized Barb's curvy handwriting. *Coop and I broke up last night at the drive-in.*

I slid the papers into my deep pocket, my breath coming in sharp, painful bursts. "Come on, Sir."

He wouldn't leave the window. His paws were spread on the sill, and he growled under his breath. I glanced past him and my lungs flattened. A Mercedes was parked in front of the house. Norris got out and walked to my truck.

I glanced down at my bulging pocket. I had a sudden vision of Norris dragging me into a bedroom. My stomach lurched. I dragged Sir away from the window and stepped into the hall.

Stop it, Teeny. Norris won't attack in front of a child posse. I had a perfectly good reason to be here. If he asked, I'd say, I'm babysitting. And he would answer, Gollum-like, *What's do you have in your pocketeses, Precious?*

Sir and I ran into the hall, veered into the lilac bedroom, and flung open the closet door. Alex grinned up at me.

"Where's Emerson?" I asked.

"Hiding."

I walked back into the hall. "Game over, Emerson," I called in a Mary Poppins voice.

Silence.

"She ran outside," Alex said. "She always hides in the gardenia bushes."

A sick feeling threaded from my stomach to my throat. So the Philpots had gardenias? Somehow I managed to get Sir down the stairs and out the French door. Alex bobbed at my elbow.

"Where's the gardenias?" I asked.

"This way." Alex pushed open the iron gate and darted to a bush. I had a clear view of the street. The Mercedes was empty. So was the front lawn. Where was Emerson? Where was Norris?

I smelled a waxy sweetness. I moved to a cluster of bushes, all of them sprinkled with white flowers. Emerson wasn't there. I turned to Alex. "Does she have another hiding spot?"

"She might. Want me to yell for her?"

"No, no. Let's play another game. Have you heard of 'Where's Waldo?' "

He nodded.

"Let's play 'Where's Uncle Norris'? You know him, right? He's Emerson's uncle?"

Alex nodded again.

"Listen carefully," I said. "Run around the house. If you don't see Norris in the front yard, yell, 'Clear.' Can you do that?"

He nodded. Then he sprinted around the gardenias. Sir tried to follow him, and I snatched his leash, my hand shaking. A drop of sweat hit my knee and rolled onto his head.

"Clear!" Alex yelled.

I gripped Sir's leash with both hands and crept out of the bushes. Norris stepped around the house and blocked my path. He looked me up and down. His gaze stopped on my pocket.

"Nith of you to thop by, Teeny."

My pulse ba-doomed in my ears. "I'm babysitting."

Alex crept forward. "Lady, I didn't mess up," he said. "He wasn't in the yard. He was on the front porch."

Sir lunged at Norris's pant leg. I pulled him back.

"He bites," I said.

"Then he thould be put down," Norris said.

Acid burned the back of my tongue. Norris's eyes were the size of jumbo eggs, the lids stitched with tiny bird-like veins.

"Why were you thneaking around my houth?" he asked.

"We were playing a game called 'Where's Uncle Norris,' " Alex said.

I cringed.

Norris smiled. "Why were you looking for me?"

"What? No, I don't—"

A raptor claw seized my arm. He towed me toward the Mercedes. "Let me go," I yelled.

"Thut up and get in my car."

"I'm not going anywhere with you." I slung off the claw. "You freak."

Norris punched me in the mouth. The blow knocked me to the ground. I lay on the grass, too dazed to move, my mouth filling with the taste of copper pennies.

A shadow fell over the grass. "Get up," Norris's disembodied voice said.

I shook my head.

"Were you thpying on me?"

I ran my tongue over my lip. It felt huge. "I wathn't thpying."

"Bitch." He snatched my arm. "Come with me."

I sat up, gingerly touching my mouth. Emerson ran into the yard. "Don't you hurt, Teeny," she yelled.

Norris ignored her and grabbed my arm. Sir dove into my lap, his fur bristling, and glared up at Norris.

"I'll kill that thupid mutt."

Footsteps pounded in the grass. Emerson dropped to her knees beside me. "Teeny, your lip."

"She was thnooping." Norris stepped back. "I'm taking her to the police."

Emerson and Alex helped me to my feet. Nothing felt broken, but my mouth throbbed. She glanced back at Norris. "Why'd you hit her? You big popeyed ape."

"I didn't hit her, I juth tapped her."

"I saw you." Emerson shook her fist. "Norris, you're a conehead. An ostrich's eye is bigger than your brain."

"Thut up."

"You could fit an ostrich in your forehead." She spat. "Alex, run inside and call 911."

"I touched my lip. It hurt worse than a bee sting, but it was swelling. Ice. I needed ice.

"I'm okay," I said. "Really."

But I wasn't okay. I'd tricked children, stolen a key and diary pages, and I'd gotten slugged by a pervert. I couldn't leave these innocent babes with him.

Norris walked alongside us. "Go into the houth, children. I need to talk to Teeny."

Emerson ran to the flower bed, grabbed handfuls of black mulch, and threw them into Norris's eyes. He staggered backward, fingers clawing air.

"Drive to the police station, Teeny!" Emerson yelled. "Go, or he'll hurt you again!"

"I won't leave you," I said.

"I can handle him." She dug her small hands into the mulch again and pelted Norris.

A green Cadillac lurched to a stop behind the Mercedes. The door opened, and Helen flew out like a white swan, her head bobbing on her long neck. Her hair was damp at the roots, feathered at the tips. She flung off her sunglasses, looking from Norris to me, then she ducked back into the car and pulled out her tennis racquet.

"Norris, damn you," she cried. "Did you hit that woman?"

He rubbed his eyes. "Yeth, but—"

"Are you insane? Two neighbors have called me! You attacked a woman in front of witnesses." She sprinted across the grass and slammed the racket against his ear.

Whap. Whap. Whap.

"Mama, no." He yelped. "Pleath."

"Quit sniveling!"

Whap, whap, whap.

Norris wrenched away from her grasp and ran around the house. Emerson and Alex grabbed more mulch and chased him. Helen walked over to me, swinging that racquet. The skin around her eyes had turned white.

"Miss Templeton, I am so sorry. I didn't raise Norris to hurt women.

Please don't have him arrested. He's going to a clinic in Arizona next week. But they won't take him if he's got pending assault charges. You need to leave before the police get here. I'll pay your medical bills. I'll do anything."

"Just be kind to Emerson," I said.

"Is that all?"

"Isn't that enough?"

In the distance, I heard a splash, followed by a loud, lisping voice that beseeched Helen to save him from Emerson's wrath.

I staggered to the truck. Helen helped me put Sir inside. I got into the front seat, flipped down the visor, and looked at the mirror. No broken teeth. But an upper incisor felt loose. My lip was so big, a chickadee could mistake it for a perch.

I drove to the corner and turned right. I wouldn't feel safe at the farm, not now. But when Red and Irene saw my lip, I'd have to tell them what I'd done, that I'd burgled the Philpots' house, and they'd tell Coop.

I drove to the library, the only place I'd felt safe as a child, and angled into a shady parking slot. I pulled the diary out of my pocket.

And read things that changed my life.

twenty-six

Barbara Browning Philpot's Diary

June 2

Coop and I broke up last night at the drive-in. All because of a green worm. It crawled real fast like it was doing push-ups all the way down his sleeve. I couldn't drag my eyes away from that worm. Up and down up and down. One minute I was in love with Coop and the next I hated him and I was gagging. How could he not know what was crawling on him? I couldn't love somebody that ignorant. But where had the worm come from? A tree or out of his body?

June 10

My friend Linnea said that Coop and Teeny Templeton went to the lake. Gag me with a spoon. That didn't take long, did it? I just wonder if that worm came from Teeny's peach farm. Maybe he's been seeing her behind my back. I hate her and I hate Coop. I hope he drives his Mustang off the bridge and I hope Teeny is with him and I hope they suffer the way I've suffered.

June 19

I wasted four precious years of my precious life on a boy who attracts worms. He was just the water boy in high school and didn't even play football. I was Miss Everything. I am destined for greatness. If I was Catholic, I'd pray to the patron saint of bad boyfriends because Coop was super bad.

June 21

Tonight I helped Father put together a Big Ben puzzle and I don't even like the British. I hid five pieces under the rug. I'm not sorry I hid them and I'm not sorry I broke up with Coop.

June 29

Teeny and Coop went to a pool party at his house. I would like to cook her in a soup pot and feed her to the O'Malleys. They would all want my recipe. Teeny isn't the only one who can cook. If someone reads my diary they will see my brilliance and know that I am bound for greatness. Even Hollywood. Even with the lack of commas my diary will make a good movie.

July 1

Coop is still dating the peach bitch. I have been thinking of ways to kill her. I could push a shish kebab skewer up her nose and her brains would leak out but I don't like blood.

I might stop keeping a diary because it's a time suck.

July 31

Today I didn't think about Coop. I went shopping with Linnea and every outfit I put on looked so cool. I should be on a soap opera or a TV game show. I wouldn't mind a job like Vanna White. I could spin the wheel for a show called I Want To Buy A Consonant.

August 2

Coop won't return my phone calls and I don't know why because he's always worshipped me. Is he screwing Teeny? Maybe I should have screwed him. Maybe I still can. But how can I get him alone?

August 8

Today is Coop's 19th birthday. I called his house and his mama answered and she made Coop talk to me. I told him I'd had a flat tire and I was afraid a rape/strangler would snatch me. I wasn't lying. I am very beautiful and men follow me down the street and I just ignore them.

When Coop showed up to fix my tire, I laid on top of him and I wasn't wearing panties and that was the end of Teeny Templeton.

August 28

Coop left for college today. He's going to Chapel Hill, NC. I cried and cried and ruined my mascara. I thought I might go blind. I'm not cut out for a long-distance romance. I'm cut out for marriage and a membership in the Bonaventure Country Club. I'm beautiful and smart and glamorous.

I'm the daughter of two professors and you don't see me in college. I'll let Coop take care of me.

September 18

Coop came home last weekend and tried to break up with me. I cried and he weakened. Linnea says he's dating a cute cum dumpster at Chapel Hill but he denied it so I did some new things to him and he shut up and went back to North Carolina.

October 31

Coop was home for the Bonaventure Halloween parade and we watched it with his parents on Oglethorpe Square. Teeny walked by. Coop smiled and she smiled back. I pretended to be sick and made Coop take me home. Mother and Daddy were still at the parade so I took off my clothes but Coop pushed me away and said, I don't love you, Barb. It's over.

I'm too upset to write another word. I might commit suicide if I can find a way that doesn't involve blood or pain.

November 2

I drove to Lester Philpot's new drugstore today and asked if he had anything for a headache and he gave me an illegal pill. He broke the law just to relieve my pain. Now that is impressive. I let him kiss me. If he gives me more pills I'll give him more than a kiss. Maybe.

November 4

I went back to Lester's for more pills and he asked me out to dinner. He has a big forehead and big eyes and I bet the rest of him is big too. For our date I'm going to wear a black angora dress and high heels and a push-up bra. Coop will be so jealous when he hears I'm dating a pharmacist.

November 10

Lester and me didn't make it to the Sailmaker Restaurant. He kissed me in the backseat of his Cadillac, which is an old man car. It was dark and he wouldn't let me touch him there but he is a good kisser so I got distracted. He got on top of me grunting and pushing and grinding and breathing. The car fogged up. I shut my eyes and pretended he was Coop. But something was wrong. I didn't feel anything inside me and then it was over and there was a grody wet spot on the backseat.

November 14

Tonight my parents went to Augusta. Lester came over and when he pulled out his you-know-what I thought it was a piece of string. He is no consolation prize. He's not. I miss Coop but he's gone, gone, gone and Lester is here, here, here. But his pharmacy is filled with pills that make me forget about his tiny parts.

November 16

I looked it up in the library and think Lester has a micro-penis. This is a real affliction. I don't see why I should be saddled with it. Just until something better comes along. At least he has good drugs and I don't have to pay for them.

November 20

I called Coop's dorm but his roommate said, Sorry, he's gone to a party with Megan. How can I love a man who doesn't love me? I will find this Megan. Then I will cut out her kidneys, but I will do it carefully so she won't die right away and then I will make her drink lots of water. And I will laugh when she can't pee. People can die that way for real.

November 24

Lester invited me to spend Thanksgiving with his parents on Curry Island. I told him I was busy, then I drove to Savannah and met a guy with blue-gray eyes. When I squinted, he looked just like Coop. He says his name is A.M. Jones, which sounds fake. I told him my name was Teeny Templeton. I went to his room and it was a relief to see normal body parts.

November 26

I went to Savannah and had sex with the Coop-look-alike. I could fall for him if he didn't wear polyester pants but you can't have everything in a man.

December 1

A.M. left Savannah and went to sell insurance in Jacksonville. But we talk on the phone every day. I am a little bit in love with him but I wish he drove a cuter car. I will think about him tonight while I am having sex with Lester.

December 5

The key to handling a man is to maintain a pecking order. Chickens have the right idea. The top chicken gets to eat first. I met A.M. in Savannah and we went to a café and I gobbled up my food. I drove back to Bonaventure and had dinner with Lester.

December 9

Drugs I Stole from Lester's Store

1. Xanax
2. Oxycontin
3. Percocet
4. Adderall
5. Ambien

December 14

I missed my period and it's too soon to take a pregnancy test. Plus I threw up. Twice. I don't want a baby. Who is its father? A micro or macro? Either way the baby will bust me wide open when it comes out and I don't like pain. So I hope I'm just late.

I have to stop writing now and get dressed for my date with Lester.

December 18

Met A.M. and told him I might be pregnant, and he promised we'd elope. I'm meeting him tomorrow at our hotel.

Things I Don't Like About A.M.

1. Travels
2. Drives a shitty Buick
3. Doesn't floss his teeth
4. Cheap clothes from Target

P.S. I have to decide if I want big money or a big man.

December 19

I am sitting in the hotel room wearing a black thong and a lace bra. I am waiting for A.M. I have been waiting all day. Where is he? When he shows up I will act kind and then I will wait until he's asleep and I will scoop out his eyeballs with a grapefruit spoon. I will look the other way when the blood runs down and his body convulses. I know what the initials A.M. mean.

A Man.

I bet he is married and who cares, he has to do right by me.

December 20

A.M. never showed up. And I've got his demon seed inside me.

December 21

I am at art class, sitting in Miss Emma's sunroom, pretending to paint clouds, but I am watching Coop. He is in the gazebo, reading a book. If only he was my baby's father. He almost could be. I'm freshly pregnant. If I sleep with Coop today, a baby will pop out in nine months and he will think he is the father. This might work.

More later.

December 22

I had Coop on his back in 3 seconds. He tried to make me quit but I was wearing the black thong and I bet he's never seen one. I forgot how huge My Lord Hugeness is. Now that is a real man. I wrapped my legs around him so he couldn't get away and then it was over and he wouldn't talk to me. He got dressed and went into his house.

Ha ha, I whispered. Just wait. I've got you now.

December 23

I can't wait to tell Coop that we made a baby. He will marry me. He is half Catholic and he will not let me have an abortion. I will get us an apartment in Chapel Hill and I will decorate it with blue and white plaid curtains. I will bake bread. I will be such a good wife.

December 28

I just got back from Savannah. The doctor said, Congratulations, Miss Templeton, you're expecting a baby. I hope words gets out that Teeny is pregnant. I still hate her for dating Coop. We'd be together if it wasn't for her.

December 31

This is the most unhappy New Years Eve of my entire life. I drove by Coop's house. He was in the yard with his crazy granny and a petite brunette with big boobies. They were holding hands, watching the granny shoot fireworks.

I needed a new babydaddy. I drove straight to Lester's drugstore. He was just closing up. I wished him a Happy New Year and wa-la, I took off my clothes.

January 4

Things I Hate About Lester

1. Tiny-meat
2. Big ego
3. Bad breath
4. Drives an old man car
5. Big eyes
6. Horrid ears
7. Ugly kneecaps
8. Mole on his right nipple

January 15

I mailed Coop a coded letter and he mailed it back. I sent another note and it came back with RETURN TO SENDER written on it, in Coop's neat-nick handwriting. I called his dorm and his roommate said Coop and his girlfriend were at a movie. The roommate told me to stop badgering Coop. He said I was pathetic. I'd like to spray-paint his body so he'd suffocate, but I'm not a cruel woman.

January 28

Will an abortion hurt? Probably. Unless they give me pain medicine. I bet they don't do that unless you have an actual baby. I want lots and lots of pain medicine. When I go into labor, I want a bikini caesarian. I'd rather have a scar than a big vajayjay.

February 3

I looked up the number for a family planning clinic. I don't want my stomach to swell and get stretch marks. I don't want big boobies and swollen feet and hemorrhoids. I've seen the heads of newborns. I might as well get pills from Lester and kill myself now because how will the fetus come out without killing me?

February 14

I am getting married today. I am carrying the child of a traveling salesman, but I am marrying a guy whose micro-peen should be in the Guinness Book of World Records. I threw up twice today. I am so nauseated I can't keep a diary. I will never write another word. I will recover from childbirth and I will go to Savannah and find lovers and babysitters. I will get over Coop. I will be child-free and famous and everyone who was mean to me will kiss the hem of my petticoat.

twenty-seven

After I finished reading the journal, I felt slimy all over, as if I'd been handling snakes. I wiped my hands on my dress. Once again, Coop had withheld critical information about Barb. Why hadn't he told me about that day in the gazebo? Was it too intimate? Embarrassing? None of my business?

Hot, sour fluid spurted into my mouth, and I cracked open the truck's door. I hated to be sick on the library's pavement, so I forced myself to gulp air. If I showed the diary to Red, he would yell at me for taking a foolish risk. He would call the Bonaventure police and make me press assault charges against Norris.

Breathe, breathe, breathe.

I'd promised Helen that I wouldn't make a fuss. My motives were purely selfish because I wanted to stay on her good side. Barb had slept with A.M. and Lester. There was at least a fifty-fifty chance that Emerson wasn't a Philpot.

Sir scooted next to me and put his head on my leg. I knew he wanted a reassuring pat, but I couldn't move. Tears ran down my cheeks, prickled over my raw lip, and curved under my chin. I don't know how long I sat there. Finally I drove to the Square and parked in front of Baskin-Robbins. It was against the law to bring a dog into the store, but I wasn't leaving him in the hot truck.

Sir strutted ahead of me into the air-conditioned store. Zee looked up from the glass ice-cream case. "Teeny, that dog can't come in here." She broke off. "What happened to your lip?"

"Gop hip." I led Sir to the counter.

"Who did this?"

"Norrith."

At the sound of his name, Zee rocked on her heels. Her eyes hardened. "That no-good, pasty-faced pervert. Did you call the police?"

"No."

Zee made an ice pack and held it against my lip. "You need to report his ass. He beat you."

"If I do, the Philpots won't let me get near Emerson." I spoke slowly, enunciating each word carefully so Zee could understand.

"You shouldn't be alone," she said. "What if Norris comes after you?"

I hadn't thought that far ahead. I couldn't go back to Irene's house. She'd tell Coop about my lip and he was sick. He didn't need any extra worries.

"I'll manage," I said.

She looked at her watch. "My shift is almost over. Keep that ice on your lip. Then we'll figure out what to do."

My hands began to shake. "Thanks, but I can take care of myself."

"Sure you can. You're like a free-range chicken. And Norris is the hawk."

Twelve minutes later, I was driving down Savannah Highway. Zee was right behind me in a blue Volkswagen. As I turned down the driveway, I began to see holes in my plan. Irene and Red were probably wondering where I'd gone. I'd need to call and make up a plausible story, or Red would come looking for me.

I pulled up to the house and climbed out of the truck. The sun was almost gone, leaving fiery, pink smudges in the clouds. An unfamiliar white van was parked on the grass. And a strange man sat in the porch swing, hunched over a laptop computer.

Zee pulled in behind me, and music drifted through her open window,

Jay-Z singing "99 problems." She hopped out of her car. "That's my cousin Asia," she said. "Like the continent. He's a microbiologist."

I stuffed Barb's diary into my pocket and followed Zee to the porch. Asia stood, gripping his laptop. He wore camouflage shorts and a UGA t-shirt. Long, hairy toes jutted out of leather sandals. His beard was short and sculpted, as if it had been dipped in espresso powder. A Glock jutted above his belt. The same gun Red carried.

"Pleased to meet you," he said.

"Likewise," I said.

To my surprise, Sir didn't bark. One of his ears swiveled toward the orchard, quivering each time a bobwhite called out, and his other ear tracked my movements.

Zee grabbed her cousin's arm. "Thanks for setting aside your busy-ass schedule to be Teeny's bodyguard."

"No problem," he said. "I just rescheduled my tai chi class."

Bodyguard? I was too thankful to speak.

"You all hungry?" Asia lifted two huge paper sacks. "I bought take-out from King Kong Chinese."

"Asia thinks food solves all problems," Zee said.

I used to think that, too. I unlocked the house. I'd left the air conditioners blasting, but this was Georgia heat and the humidity had seeped through the walls and windows, filling the rooms with a warm, weighted pressure.

Asia set the paper bags on the kitchen table and veered to the refrigerator. He put ice cubes into a dishcloth, then he pushed it into my hands. "Fifteen minutes on, fifteen off," he said.

"You hurt anywhere else?" Zee asked.

I lifted the hem of my dress a few inches. Just above my boots, my knees were cross-hatched with thin red lines, each one caked with dried blood. And I felt sleepy. I just wanted to curl up in Mama's old featherbed with my dog and rest for a few days.

"I know you're hurting, but try to eat," Zee said, opening cartons. She got a plate and spooned up fried rice, sesame balls, and General Tsao's Chicken.

Asia put his hands on his hips. "Where do you keep your forks?"

Over Zee's protests I got up and opened a drawer. I handed Asia the cutlery and started to shut the drawer, but I saw a flash of blue. I lifted Barb's envelope and walked back to the table.

"What's that you got?" Zee leaned over my shoulder.

"Barb sent my boyfriend some clues before she died. That's why I went to the Philpots' house. To see if I could find anything."

I handed the envelope to Zee and explained about Emerson, the DNA test, the diary, and the body parts.

Zee opened the envelope and pulled out the blue note. "What is this?"

"Anagrams." I traced my finger under each line, decoding the words. "I found a key in a fur coat—clues under the fur. I saw a mural in her foyer—clues on the wall. She'd painted a mural. A picture of my boyfriend—and me."

I omitted the headless part.

"Are these clues, too?" Zee peeked inside the envelope and her forehead wrinkled.

I leaned closer. Barb's blocky handwriting was scrawled inside the envelope. My heart tripped as I scanned each phrase.

ADULTS GROWLER
HOP TO
TISSUE WHIM WIT
CEDE NEPHRITIS ION UP
NASAL DYNAMICS
BECK YOLK OX
ANAL FINK BERM JINN
A THOUSAND LIVERS

I carried the envelope to the table. "I wish I had an anagram solver."

"I can find one on my laptop," Asia said.

"But I don't have wireless Internet," I said.

"My laptop is 4g / WIMAX-enabled." He sat down next to me and opened his Dell. His fingers curled over the keyboard. "What's the first phrase, Teeny?"

"ADULTS GROWLER."

He typed in the phrase. Then he whistled. "Wow, 7,215 results. Does LARGEST WOULDST mean anything to you?"

"No." I leaned toward him and scanned the list. On the fifth row, I saw DRUGSTORE WALL.

"That's got to be it," I said. "She put something on the drugstore wall."

"But why did she write two sets of anagrams?" Zee lifted Barb's note.

Asia snapped his fingers. "Could the anagrams inside the envelope possibly cross-reference the anagrams in the note?"

"Clever," Zee said. "Like Russian nesting dolls."

I handed the envelope to Asia. "Let's find out."

Asia typed in HOP TO. Only ten results. But PHOTO was listed at the top of the list.

"So she put a photo on the drugstore wall?" Zee asked.

Asia typed in TISSUE WHIM WIT and hit the return key. A long row of results came up, and nearly every other word was SWIMSUIT. At the bottom of the list I saw WHITE SWIMSUIT. Back in high school, Barb had always worn white suits because they showed off her tan.

Zee scrunched up her face. "Does this make any sense, Teeny?"

"Not yet."

A clicking sound rose up as Asia typed NASAL DYNAMICS. I half expected it to be the name of a medical company, but it turned out to be CAYMAN ISLANDS. BECK YOLK OX was easy—LOCK BOX KEY. I thought of the little key I'd found in the fox jacket.

Asia typed in ANAL FINK BERM JINN. We scanned the list. He tapped the screen, right next to FABLE MARK JINN INN.

"Could that be a hotel in the Caymans?" he asked.

The results for CEDE NEPHRITIS ION UP produced over 80,000 hits, each one beginning with CEDE. Not a single one made sense. A THOUSAND LIVERS had 10,000 possible solutions, including A HALVED SINUS ROT and A VERDANT SUSHI LO.

"We still lack three anagrams," Asia said. "Let me type in CEDE NEPHRITIS ION UP again."

Zee hopped off the table. "I wish we could get inside Philpot Pharmacy and look at the walls."

"We can," I said. "I've got a key. And the code to the burglar alarm."

I explained about Kendall's Hello Kitty key chain and how the code was her birthday.

Asia scowled. "Please don't tell me you're thinking of breaking and entering."

"We need to see what's on the drugstore's walls," Zee said.

"Are you crazy? It's Saturday night. The Bonaventure PD has extra patrol cars on the weekend. They've got to keep the tourists safe. Besides, what could you find on a damn wall?"

"Barb hid clues," I said. "I'm guessing they're in a photograph, or behind one."

"And if you find this picture, then what?" he asked.

"It may have information about the Caymans bank account. Whatever it is, I'll show it to my boyfriend. He can talk to the Bonaventure DA. They'll get a search warrant."

"I don't think it works that way," Asia said. "Where's the probable cause?"

"That's right," Zee said. "On *Law & Order*, there's always probable cause."

"There's another problem," Asia said. "We don't know if we've correctly solved these anagrams. DRUGSTORE WALL could also be GORED RUST WALL."

"It's the drugstore." I touched my lip. Damn, it hurt.

"But why did this woman put a clue on a wall that her husband sees every day?" Asia asked. "There's either a flaw in her logic or yours."

Zee's eyes got huge. "Maybe she wanted him to find it?"

"Then why did she send the anagrams to Teeny's boyfriend?" Asia asked.

I shut my eyes. Barb had used these anagrams to lure Coop, to ensnare him in her problems. She'd wanted to lead him to the drugstore wall. But I couldn't believe that she'd meant for him to see her diary.

Sir howled and ran to the front door. Asia pulled out his Glock and walked to the porch. Sir raced down the steps. Red squatted behind Asia's van, writing in a notepad.

"Hey, mutherfucker," Asia called, holding the Glock in both hands. "Why are you writing down my license tag number?"

"Wait, I know him," I said, but Asia was already drawing a bead on Red.

"Put your hands on your head," Asia yelled.

"Don't shoot." Red dropped the notepad. He lifted his hands and slowly got to his feet. "I wanna talk to Teeny."

Sir pranced over to him. Red kept his hands in the air. Asia clicked on the safety, then shoved the gun in his waistband.

Red's gaze flickered over my lip. His upraised hands curled into fists. "Who hit you?"

I crossed my arms and didn't answer. I refused to raise my lie tally over Norris.

Red cut his eyes to Asia. Then he lowered his fists until they were level with his hips.

"Don't go for your gun, Red." I walked to the edge of the porch. My words sounded muffled, as if I had a mouth full of hard candy.

"I was just worried, homegirl. You took off and didn't tell us when you'd be back."

"So?" Asia said. "Teeny's a grown woman. And you ain't her man."

"She's a trouble magnet." Red flashed a "just us boys" smile. "Know what I mean?"

Zee straightened up. "What you mean, what you mean?"

"Red, go back to the O'Malleys' house," I said.

"Girlie, I can't understand a thing you're saying." He spit onto the gravel. "You should see a doctor about that lip."

"Fluck you," I said.

"Let me interpret that for you." Asia leaned over the railing. "Take a hike."

"I ain't going nowhere." Red's gaze swiveled back to me. "I wanna know what happened to your lip."

"She fell," Zee said.

Red's chin jutted out. "Who the hell are you guys?"

"My cousin is Teeny's bodyguard," Zee said.

"What's your qualifications?" Red nodded at Asia. "You got a permit to carry that Glock?"

"Red, please leave," I said.

"Something's happened to you. Something bigger than Irene and her insults." Red took a step forward. "Don't shut me out, Teeny. Why're you trusting these people and not me?

"The lady has spoken," Asia said.

"Well, I ain't leaving. I'll sleep in my van."

"No!" My voice held in the air.

Red's eyes narrowed. "Why the hell not?"

"You'll roast," I said.

"Just don't let Irene eat me." He winked. "Well, good night. And don't let the bodyguards bite."

twenty-eight

Red climbed into his van. The engine turned over, and a plume of exhaust curled up into the darkness and vanished. Sir and I followed Asia into the house. Zee pushed in behind us.

"I'll take him a pillow and something to eat," she said. "Maybe a Thermos of tea."

Sir and I wandered to the parlor and curled up on the sofa. I heard Zee walk out to the van with refreshments. I was halfway hoping she'd bring Red back, but she returned alone. A while later, Asia went outside and set out spotlights. Light blazed through the curtains. Then he began to hammer the roof.

"What's he doing, Zee?" I cast a worried look at the window. "Do I need this much security?"

"Probably. But Asia needs light because he's hooking up a satellite dish. He wants to see a movie on Showtime."

I kept glancing out the window, expecting to see Red climb out of the van to investigate, but he didn't budge. Zee looped her arm around me. "You look exhausted," she said.

"Yeah." I inched my way up the stairs, gripping the banister for support. Sir ran ahead and leaped onto Mama's old bed. I pulled Barb's diary out of my pocket and hid it on the top shelf of the closet. I veered back to the bed and sank onto the mattress.

• • •

A dazzle-dance of Sunday morning light fell into the bedroom. Only a week ago, I'd climbed into the yellow van and started this strange adventure. I peeked out the window. Red was gone.

I found Zee and Asia in the kitchen, digging into leftover rice, ginger beef, and Ma-Bo Bean Curd.

"Your friend tore out of the driveway at six a.m.," Asia said.

I lifted the toaster and gazed at my smeary, distorted image. The edge of my mouth resembled a sleek, blood-fattened leech.

"Ice it down," Asia said.

We lolled around the house until noon, watching *The Wizard of Oz*, on AMC. Auntie Em was telling Dorothy to chill about Miss Gulch. I pressed a bag of frozen brussels sprouts against my mouth and went back up to Mama's room. I tried to work up my courage to phone Coop. I imagined his gray beach house, a wedge of blue sky, the rocking chair on his front porch, a wooden walkway that led to the sea. I imagined sunshine spilling through his French doors, washing over law books and legal pads. I imagined his phone ringing and ringing through all of that brightness.

He always spent Sunday mornings in the dining room, the newspaper spread out on the glass table, a cup of coffee at his elbow. Beneath the table, T-Bone would be stretched on the floor. I'd spent many mornings sitting next to Coop, the scent of caramel coffee wafting between us. I could almost hear the rustle of the newspaper and the thump of T-Bone's tail.

Sir seemed to sense my mood, and he pushed against me, making faint, growling noises. My hand shook as I punched in the number to Coop's house. When he didn't answer, I dialed his cell phone. Maybe he was at the beach, just him and T-Bone, no blue-blooded brunette, no picnic breakfast for two.

He answered on the seventh ring, his voice soft and scratchy as if he'd just woke up. In the background, I heard a rhythmic beeping like a microwave oven that had just finished its cycle. Beneath that noise, I heard a television.

"Hey, it's me," I whispered. "Your mother said you aren't feeling well."

A long, thrumming silence. "I'm okay. But what the hell's going on with you?"

"Love you, too, baby sweet-cakes," I said. "What's that beeping?"

He didn't answer right away. "The TV."

"Oh." But where was this TV? A hotel room? A bar? Chlamydia Smith's apartment?

"Teeny, why did you run away without telling Mother and Red where you were going? How'd you hurt your lip? Who is this bodyguard you hired?"

"You've talked to Red."

"He's worried. Who are your new friends?"

"Asia Greer is my bodyguard. He's got an MA in microbiology."

"How'd you meet him? At a germ convention?"

"Drop the attitude, O'Malley."

"I'm just curious. Normally, you don't trust anyone."

"I do, too."

"You don't like the meter reader on Rainbow Row."

"He's flirtatious."

Coop ignored me and barreled on. "Yet here you are, letting a strange microbe man watch over you. Red mentioned a young woman, too. Who is she?"

"Zee Greer. Norris molested her."

Coop let out an exasperated sigh. "Sounds like you've teamed up with someone who hates Norris."

"No, I've teamed up with someone who doesn't hate me."

"What does that mean?"

I almost said, *Your mother hates me, and Red thinks I'm a loon.* But I refused to be a whiny bitch. Besides, I was almost telling a lie. I couldn't break into Philpot's Pharmacy if Red was babysitting me.

We lapsed into silence, nothing but the background beeps and canned laughter from his television. "How did you hurt your lip?" he asked.

"It's okay. Really."

"I'm glad to hear it. But you haven't answered my question."

"Where are you, O'Malley? And don't lie. Because I know you're not home. I called your house."

"Tell me who assaulted you, and I'll tell you where I am."

My stomach tensed. I could give a watered down version of the hide-and-seek game at the Philpots', leaving out Norris's attack. Or I could skip to the diary. Another option was to enlighten him about the clues Zee had found in Barb's envelope. I picked the diary. "I found the clues underfoot," I said.

Another long silence. "And?"

"Remember how Barb used to write in her diary? She'd hidden some of the pages under the rug in her guest room. I found them. She wrote about you. Did you make love to her in the gazebo?"

I heard a sharp intake of air. "I meant to tell you about that."

"Sure. Are you addicted to sins of omission?"

"I couldn't find the right time to bring it up. After the incident with the prowler, I was only thinking of your safety." He paused. "How did you get inside Barb's house? How did you know where to look?"

"Don't try to change the subject. We're talking about your inability to share your problems with me."

"I don't want to burden you."

"Aunt Bluette used to say that worries shared are worries halved. I can deal with your secrets. Even if they're ugly, I can deal with them."

"I can't. It's too hard for me, Teeny."

"I'm not asking you to tell me every little thing. Only if it affects us."

"Tell me about this diary," he said.

He was changing the subject again, but this time I heard a note of exasperation in his voice.

"I found it under a rug." Since I was hell-bent on truth-telling, I told him about the new clues. Cayman Islands, the lockbox, the key, the white swimsuit. "Barb left you those anagrams for a reason. If I find the clues on the drugstore wall, they might prove that the Philpots are harvesting organs."

"Whoa," Coop said. "Stop right there. You can't look for anything."

"But I think she's hidden a document at Lester's store."

"If this document exists, it would be fruit of the poison tree."

"What poison? What tree?"

"You illegally searched the Philpots' house."

"No, I didn't. I was babysitting."

"But you found the diary, right?"

"Yes."

"And you took it."

"Mmm-hum." I didn't like his tone.

"The diary is the tree. If it leads you to a document, that's the fruit. The judge would throw out the evidence."

"Can't you get a search warrant and search the drugstore? I'm positive that Barb hid something on the wall."

"You don't understand. No judge would sign a search warrant. He would ask why I thought this document was at Philpot's Pharmacy. And I'd have to tell him about the improperly seized journal."

I balled my hand into a fist. *Dammit. Son of a bitch.*

"Ask Red about the exclusionary rule," he said.

"Never mind that. What about your lies?" I swallowed. "Why do you keep hiding things from me?"

"I'm afraid I'll chase you away. That's the last thing I want. I may be a liar, but I'm a liar in love."

"You keep saying that, but I want evidence. Why do you love me?"

"Because I feel it."

"So when did it start? You didn't love me when we were teenagers."

"No, but you were my touchstone. That summer we dated, I was on my way to loving you, but Barb came between us. I went back to her for the worst reason. Because of hormones. Then I grew up and the law made me cynical. I'd lost the ability to feel joy. I was numb. And yet, I was scared. Always scanning the horizon for danger. But when I walked into that pub last June, I saw a beautiful woman who smelled like peaches and vanilla. And calmness poured over me. I fell smack in love."

"A psychiatrist would say that we make our own joy, O'Malley. We shouldn't depend on others to make us happy."

"That's why people fall in love and stay in love, Teeny. A component of love is how another person makes you feel. And what I feel for you is a forever kind of feeling."

"If that's true, you wouldn't keep things from me. Because the other part of love is sharing your hurt places. Sharing things that might get you in trouble. You have to trust me, Coop. Then I'll trust you."

"I can't promise that I won't hide things from you. But I'll try. I'll try real hard. It's just about impossible for me to open up. I'm so scared of—" He broke off. There was a rustling sound, followed by a murmur. "Teeny, I've got to go. I'll talk to you later. I love you."

He hung up. A cold pain filled my throat, as if I'd swallowed a mouthful of sorbet. Wherever Coop was, he wasn't alone. Over the beeping, I'd distinctly heard a woman's voice.

Later that afternoon, Zee went to Queen of Tarts on Dogwood Avenue. She brought back a spinach quiche and tiny buttermilk pies. Between my busted lip and my bruised pride, I'd developed a ravenous appetite. We polished off the pies and watched *Mulholland Drive* on HBO. By the time it ended, dusk had pooled in the yard and lightning bugs skimmed over the grass. Zee turned the channel and found *The Wizard of Oz* playing again.

I was ready for a hot bath and a cotton nightgown. I was tired of sleuthing. Tired of inventing theories. Each one seemed like a target in a shooting gallery, fast-moving and filled with holes.

Zee nudged my leg. "Let's go look at the Philpots' walls."

"We can't. If we find something juicy, it won't be admissible in court. At least, that's what my boyfriend said." I explained about the fruit of the poison tree.

"I'd still like to know what Barb Philpot hid on that wall. It might be something about Norris. Maybe she's got proof he's a rapist. Because if he is, no woman in Bonaventure is safe. Especially you. If you're afraid to go, I'll check it out. Just give me Kendall's keys. I'll look around the store. And if I find any clues, I'll leave them alone."

"What's the good of knowing the truth if the law thinks it's poisoned?" I asked. "I'm not giving you those keys. If you get caught, you'll end up in jail."

"I once had a tiny penis in my hand, and I'm still pissed off. If I can put that dirty white pervert in jail, the state of Georgia should give me a reward."

"They won't. If you find a confession signed by Norris himself, it won't hold up in court."

She held out her hand. "Give me the keys."

I briefly shut my eyes and channeled my favorite action heroines. Lara Croft, Tomb Raider, black leather, black hair down to my ass. No, I wanted to be Starbuck on *Battlestar Galactica.* A poker-playing, hard-drinking gal with great deltoids. Frack you, cylons. And frack you, too, Norris. Frack your itty-bitty-ness.

I looked up at Zee. "You're really going to Philpot's Pharmacy?"

"Yup."

"The alarm code is Kendall's birthday."

"That's easy. She and I were born the same day. June 24, 1990."

She wrote down the numbers on a piece of paper. Then she looked up. "So when I get to Philpot's Pharmacy, I just punch in 6-24-90, right?"

"Unless they changed the code," I said.

"Huh, I'll be out of there in a flash. I ran track in high school. Keep the doors locked while we're gone."

"We?"

"I'm not going without Asia." She stood. "Asia? Get in here. We're going to the drugstore."

"And leave me alone? I'm going, too." I heaved myself out of the chair, ran upstairs, and changed into black leotards and a long-sleeved black t-shirt. I grabbed Kendall's keys and hurried down to the foyer. Light from the television flickered over Sir as he watched the Wicked Witch scribble *Surrender Dorothy* across the sky.

Zee and Asia stood in the foyer. They'd changed clothes, too. Black tennis shoes, stretchy pants, and tops. We climbed into the van and drove past Philpot's Pharmacy. Asia cut down a side street and parked at the end of an alley. The area was K-shaped, and streetlights shone down on two narrow passages that angled toward side streets. Lester's store sat in the backbone of the K, between Shamrock's Shoes and Salt and Battery, a seafood café.

Asia strapped on a tool belt. Each slot held an instrument of pain, if not outright death. Pepper spray, Taser, knife, guns, ammo.

"I thought you were a microbiologist," I said.

"I am," he said. "But I also did a tour in Afghanistan."

"Braggart," Zee said.

"Quit talking. You're the lookout." He put on plastic gloves. "So look."

Zee crossed her arms, her dreadlocks shaking. "Nuh-uh, I ain't gonna be no damn lookout."

"All three of us can't go inside," he said. "What if someone drives up?"

She got in his face, nose-to-nose. "Then *you* stay and be the lookout."

He pressed his index finger against her forehead and pushed her back. "But you're a good hooter."

"Hooter?" I asked.

"As in owl. She'll hoot if anyone comes snooping around, like the popo." Asia tossed me a pair of gloves.

I put them on, then I took the key chain out of my pocket.

"Let's hope one of those suckers fit that lock," Asia said.

"Wait, Teeny," Zee said, slipping a paper into my hand. "Here's the code."

I followed him around the Dumpster, my shoes digging through loose gravel, and stopped by Philpot's freight entrance. The metal door had a brass deadbolt. I went though a dozen keys, trying to work them into the lock. Some fit but wouldn't turn; others would only slide halfway into the grooves.

My hands shook when I pulled out the next-to-the-last key. It glided through the notched holes, and the tumblers clicked. Asia opened the door, and we stepped inside the dark stockroom. Lord, it was hot. A red light blinked frantically on the alarm's keypad, and the harsh beeps hurt my ears.

"I got the door." Asia nodded at the box. "Punch in the code, and hurry."

I glanced at Zee's paper and punched in the numbers she'd written down, 6-42-90. The red light kept flashing. I punched in the code again, sweat dripping down my neck. Any second now, the siren would go off. The police would come, and we'd all be wearing stripes.

"What's wrong?" Asia called.

"The code won't work."

He ran over and looked at Zee's paper. "There's no such thing as June 42nd. She's dyslexic. She transposed the numbers."

He leaned toward the panel and tapped in 6-24-90. The beeping stopped. A green light glowed steadily on the panel. I let out a huge breath.

Asia clicked on a halogen flashlight and the beam cut through the shadows, slicing over tall wooden shelves. We found Halloween items on the last aisle. Asia's light picked out a witch's hat and a row of plastic pumpkins. I was wringing wet, and it hurt to breathe the dusty air. I riffled through the masks—Dave Letterman, Hillary Clinton, Tweety Bird. But no Bill Clinton.

I pulled out my inhaler and took a puff. "Shine the flashlight on the walls," I said.

I tracked the beam as it slid over the shelves onto the old bricks.

"There's nothing here," Asia said.

"We need to find Lester's office," I said.

"I'll watch the door, but make it fast." He pushed the flashlight into my hands. "Don't point the beam toward the windows. Somebody might see. If you hear me holler, stop what you're doing and haul ass."

I clamped my fingers over the light and hurried out of the stockroom. A rush of cold air blew over me when I stepped into the dark store. Streetlights cast an eerie green glow through the front windows. I walked toward the raised platform in the rear of the store, Lester's fiefdom. I glanced from side to side, hoping to see a door or a cubbyhole, anything that might lead to an office. I climbed the platform steps, keeping the beam low. I crept past the long desk where Lester normally stood, past tall shelves that were crammed with pill boxes.

I stepped around a wooden folding screen. The light picked out an oak roll-top desk. The wall above it was covered with photographs of Barb, Lester, Helen, and Norris. Dozens of brass plaques declared Lester to be Pharmacist of the Year, past president of the Rotary Club, and patron of the Bonaventure High Booster.

Drugstore Wall. Photo. White swimsuit.

I passed the light over the photographs. The very last picture showed a much younger Barb. She sat in a boat, her breasts spilling out of a white two-piece, her legs glossy with suntan oil. One hand gripped a blue leather book, the infamous diary.

I set the flashlight on the desk. My breath was coming in hitches now, but I didn't have time to use my inhaler. I reached for the picture, turned the frame over, and slid off the cardboard backing. A folded paper sprang up. I held it in front of the light.

It was a computer printout, with sales, dates, organs, prices. The names of tissue banks were listed, too. I searched for Barb's initials, but the printout was clean.

Sweat ran between my breasts, where Minnie's ring poked through my shirt like a tumor. I couldn't take the document. It was the poisoned fruit, and the judge would kick it out of court. Even if the list hadn't been poisoned, it didn't incriminate the Philpots. But why had Barb hidden it?

I reached for my flashlight and passed the beam around the room. I hadn't been able to decode all of the anagrams. I was probably missing a vital clue. But what?

Again, I shone the light on the wall. A small photograph of Emerson smiled down at me. I was tempted to grab it. But the pictures had been hung with mathematical precision, and Lester would notice a gap in the arrangement.

"Teeny? Zee's hooting," Asia called. "We've got to go."

I tucked the flashlight between my knees, set the document into the frame, and hung the photograph on the wall, making sure it was straight. Crouching low, I hurried around the screen, off the platform, down the aisle, into the stockroom.

Asia was waiting beside the back door. He set the alarm and locked up. We'd just passed the Dumpster when the hooting stopped. A light swept down one of the narrow passages.

"Run," Asia whispered. I heard a spit of gravel, then he sprinted around me.

I stumbled after him, my heart banging against my ribs. A light swept toward Philpot's freight door. A staticky voice echoed between the buildings.

Crap, a walkie-talkie.

Beneath that sound, I heard low voices. A second later, a squatty man stepped around the corner. The streetlight washed over Officer Percy Fitzgerald, Dale's older brother. A wide-hipped woman with a long chestnut braid crept up behind him.

"I'm not making this up," she said. "I was driving Momma to the Dairy Queen, and I seen a flashlight moving in the alley. I seen people moving."

A hand seized my elbow and yanked me against the brick wall. Asia put his finger to my mouth. I tried to pull in a breath, but all I could manage was a teaspoon of air. If I didn't stave off an asthma attack, I'd start wheezing and we'd end up in jail for sure.

Fitzgerald's light skimmed past the green freight door and washed upward, to the grimy second-story windows. Fitzgerald turned, and the white arc quivered on the ground. Then it skidded toward me and Asia. As the light swept across the brick wall, Asia pushed me down. The beam passed over our heads and moved to the Dumpster. A rat scurried across the pavement.

"There ain't nobody here, Lujean," Percy Fitzgerald said.

"Maybe we chased them off," the woman said. "Can I go now? Mama gets in a temper if she don't get her nightly Dilly Bar."

"Stay out of trouble, Lujean," Percy said, and the woman scuttled down the narrow passage and was gone.

I pressed my shoulders against the brick wall, hoping the scratchy heat would distract me from a full-blown asthma attack. My inhaler was in my pocket, but I didn't dare reach for it.

Percy's light circled the alley again. I took a shallow breath and held it. A scraping sound echoed in my head, and I realized I was grinding my teeth.

Gravel spit under Percy's shoes. He turned down the passage, muttering to himself about Lujean's paranoia.

Asia whispered, "One, two, three. Go."

I bolted to the end of the alley. The van's lights were off, but the engine hummed. Zee opened the side door, and I ran toward it. But I didn't have enough air, and a spinning dizziness took hold. I skidded to a stop, braced my hands on my knees, and gasped.

Asia scooped me up and ran the last thirty feet. He tossed me into the ice cold van, then he rolled into the backseat. With the door gaping open, Zee took off, the tires crunching over loose gravel. Asia's long arm snaked out. He caught the handle and slammed the door.

"Did y'all shut off the alarm?" she yelled, her dreadlocks swaying violently.

"Yeah," Asia said. "Get the hell out of here."

My chest sawed, as if I were still running down that alley. I lowered my head to the air-conditioning vent and opened my mouth wide.

"Then who called the police?" Zee asked.

"Someone named Lujean," Asia said. "She was driving by and got suspicious."

Zee glanced into the rearview mirror. "What's that light behind us?"

What light? I turned. Through the rear window, I saw the shadowy form of a man. A sour, wet hardness filled my throat, like I'd swallowed a lemon wedge.

Then the shadow passed under a streetlight. Percy Fitzgerald was chasing the van.

twenty-nine

A wheeze ripped out of my throat, blotting out Percy Fitzgerald's voice. "Stop the vehicle," he yelled.

Zee mashed her foot against the gas pedal. The engine misfired, and the van lurched forward and stalled. "Don't quit on me now," she said through gritted teeth.

I dug my fingernails into the upholstery, watching the light move over the Dumpsters and brick buildings. Percy was gaining on us.

"Pump the gas," Asia said.

"I'm trying." Zee stamped her foot against the accelerator.

"Stop the vehicle!" Percy yelled.

The sour lump in my throat hardened. Way to go, Teeny. Good job. I'd put everyone in danger and still didn't have proof.

"Pump it double-time," Asia yelled.

"I am, I am," she said. The engine caught, and the van blasted out of the alley. "Thank you, Lord," she said.

"Don't thank Him yet," I said. "What if Percy saw the license plate?"

"He didn't." Zee jerked the steering wheel, and the van shot down a dark street. "Before we left your farm, I smeared the tag with Hershey's Syrup."

"He'll know it's a white van," Asia said

"And he'll run a DMV check," I said.

Zee's hands tightened on the wheel. "Hate to say this, Asia, but she's right. You better leave Teeny's farm tonight. Get out of the state. Go to Louisiana and visit Auntie Ruth."

"You leave. I'm staying," Asia said. "There's lots of white vans in Bonaventure County. Percy Fitzgerald doesn't have anything on me. He isn't chasing me off."

"Did you find any poison evidence?" Zee asked.

"No," Asia said.

I didn't mention the computer printout.

"Then we didn't solve those anagrams correctly," Zee said. "We need to study them again and come back."

Zee drove back to the farm. Her headlights swept over a yellow van, and I sat up a little straighter. Red leaned against his bumper, his arms folded, his gaze openly hostile.

"What's his problem?" Zee asked.

"Me," I said.

We climbed out of Asia's van, into the heat-glazed dark. Crickets shrilled from the weeds. I heard faint barking and looked at the house. Sir ran from window to window.

Red glanced at our all-black outfits. "Let me guess. You just got back from church—Our Lady of the Haints."

"Maybe you should join us," Zee said.

"Can I have a private word with Teeny?" Red asked.

"I can take a hint," Zee said, and she pulled Asia into the house. After the door closed, Red turned to me. "You talked to the boss?"

"Boy, did I ever."

"I guess he told you what's going on?"

"You mean, the exclusionary rule?"

Red looked off into the dark orchard.

I stepped in front of him. "Is there something I need to know?"

"You should hear it from the boss."

"I've heard plenty from Lester. He told me that Coop has been seeing a brunette lawyer."

"That's bull. The boss is crazy in love with you and nobody else. He ain't got no room in his heart for another woman. Is that what's bugging you?"

"It's been on my mind."

"He told me he asked you to marry him. But you ain't decided."

"No."

"Why the hell not?"

"Because I can't trust him. He skirts around the truth. He hides facts. I can't live that way. I need the truth the way he needs rules. Go ahead, call me a loon. I never said I wasn't flawed."

"That's part of your charm, homegirl. You're not super-confident. You're not a Renaissance woman. You're really real. Your personality compliments the boss's personality. It's a pitch-perfect alignment of his virtues and your virtues. Your quirks and his quirks. Together, you guys are balanced. Think of it in food terms. What makes bread dough rise?"

"Yeast."

"Plus the right balance of sugar and warmth. It's chemistry."

"Are you sure that he isn't with another woman? Because when he called, I heard a female voice in the background."

"You might've heard a voice, but it had nothing to do with romance." He put his arm around me. "Come back to the O'Malleys'. Irene and Jack aren't home. We'll have the run of the joint."

"Where'd they go? On safari?" I smiled. "To feast upon wild things?"

"To the country club." He looked down at his shoes. "They'll be gone for hours. And we can talk."

"I'm tired of talking. I'm staying here."

"What's a matter, homegirl? I thought we were friends."

"Red, I'm tired. Just go back to Irene's. I'll call you tomorrow."

"But I've got news. I called a buddy at the GBI. A forensic anthropologist examined a sample from the urn. It was kitty litter. Human cremains should have teeth and bone chips. This stuff didn't."

"How did the litter get into the urn?"

"Don't know. But I did some checking. When a body arrives at a crematorium, it comes with paperwork. Piney Flats says it never got Kendall's body. Even if they had, it would take awhile for the cremains to cool down. But she died one day, and the memorial service was the next. That's too fast."

"So the funeral home is involved in this?"

"The GBI searched Eikenberry's. The funeral director talked to them. He says he filled out the cremation papers on Kendall. Apparently Lester arranged for Piney Flatts to do the cremation. Also, to pick up Kendall's body. But the body never got there."

I dragged my shoe through the gravel. "Has the GBI talked to Vlado?"

"Agents went to his duplex. He's gone."

"Or dead."

"Or in the Bahamas. Drinking piña coladas on the beach."

"Bet he's not."

Red gazed into the darkness, where crickets shrilled from the weeds. "I don't want to encourage your wild ideas, homegirl. But I think the Philpots are involved with the kitty litter. I'm not saying they're selling body parts. More likely, Lester didn't want the ME examining Kendall's body. He wanted to hide something. Maybe he paid the winking guy—or Vlado—to dispose of Kendall's body."

I thought of the printout she'd found under the rug. Now she was dead. I'd found a printout behind Barb's photograph. Was I next?

After Red drove off, I walked into the house. Before I had time to shut the door, Sir rushed into the hall to greet me. I reached down to pet him and a thick, cottony tiredness took hold. Behind me, through the screen mesh, the crickets stopped buzzing, as if something had disturbed them. A black, sucking silence descended.

I scanned the driveway. Empty. Then I glanced toward the orchard. The branches creaked. Between the rows, shadows snaked off into the gloom. I slammed the front door and locked it. But I couldn't shake the feeling that someone was waiting. And watching.

When I stepped into the kitchen, Asia was making BLT sandwiches. "You look shook up, Teeny."

I glanced past him, through the window. "I have a creepy feeling that something's out there."

"It's probably got four legs," he said. "But I'll check it out."

Zee stretched her arms over her head and yawned. "I saw a fox earlier."

The phone rang. Asia stepped away from the stove and lifted the receiver. "Who's calling?" he said in a gruff, "how dare you call" voice.

He listened a moment, then said, "I don't think she's here, but let me check."

He covered the receiver with a pot holder. "Son Finnegan. Says it's urgent."

"Tell him I'm gone," I whispered. What did Son want? And how did he know I was here?

"Sorry, Teeny isn't home," Asia said, then his eyes narrowed. "It doesn't matter who I am. Yeah, yeah. I'll tell her you called."

He banged down the receiver and shuffled back to the stove. The smell of bacon wafted around the room. The phone rang again. Asia sighed and lifted the receiver.

Please let it be Coop, I thought. *Please let him say he's coming to Georgia. Please let him say he was wrong about the poisoned tree.*

"Anybody there?" Asia paused. He slammed down the phone, cursing under his breath. "How's a man supposed to cook?"

I awoke early Monday morning and looked out the window. Red's van was still parked in the driveway. I put on a loose cotton dress and ran down to the porch. I stood there, arms crossed, until he got out of the van.

"Bad news," he said. "Picnickers at the lake found a dirt pile. Black hair was sticking out. It was a body. Young, white female."

"A frog tattoo?" My fists knotted against my arms.

"She didn't have much skin left," he said. "The medical examiner had trouble identifying the body."

The sweltering heat pushed in around me, but I felt cold, so cold. "Animals got to her?" I whispered.

"Possums did some damage. But they don't pull teeth. They don't slice off whole sheets of skin."

I sat down hard on the porch step, and my knees began to shimmy. "She was harvested?"

"Yeah. And somebody went to a lot of trouble to make sure she wouldn't be identified. Her fingertips were missing, and her eyes had been removed. But her breast implants had serial numbers. That's how the ME identified her."

Nausea was building in the back of my throat. No teeth. No eyes. No skin.

"You're looking queasy," he said. "I won't tell the rest."

"There's more?" I gripped the newel post.

"You really don't look good." He sat down beside me. "Maybe we should go inside where it's cool."

I shook my head. "Why did they remove her skin?"

"It's used for grafts. Collagen injections. Surgeons use it to plump up lips. Big money in that."

"Were Kendall's vital organs missing?"

"No." A drop of perspiration slid down his temple, and he wiped it off. "A donor has to be alive for a heart or kidney transplant to work. And the procedure requires paperwork. Laws are in place to prevent trafficking. But quite a few tissues can be removed postmortem. Corneas, veins, skin, teeth, tendons. Corneas are good for about ten hours. But tendons have a longer shelf life."

"Who did this to Kendall?"

"We'll find out. The GBI went back to Eikenberry's with a warrant and a team. They found some fishy-looking records. They coulda been altered. And they found discrepancies in the CODs."

"The what?"

"Cause of death. It looks like someone forged tissue donation forms, too. That takes legal know-how."

"Josh has an MBA." I loosened my grip on the newel post. "But he wouldn't have the skill to remove corneas."

"If he's involved, he probably hired a surgeon."

"Norris is an ophthalmologist."

"Yeah, but can he remove yards of skin?" Red's gaze sharpened. "I'm thinking a plastic surgeon would've been on the payroll. You know anybody like that, homegirl?"

"Son would never harvest organs and sell them," I said, trying to keep my voice steady. "He's no criminal."

"He's got the skill."

"So does Norris Philpot."

Red shoved his hand in his pocket and jiggled his keys. "When did your aunt die?"

"This past January."

Red stopped jingling his keys. "Was she cremated?"

"No." I felt sick and put one hand on my stomach.

"Who handled her funeral?" Red asked.

I hesitated. "Josh Eikenberry."

"Don't be surprised if you have to give permission for her exhumation."

"You're not thinking she was . . . She couldn't have been. She had cancer."

Red picked up a rock and threw it. "Maybe the tissue bank wasn't told about the cancer. See, a few years back, there was a case in New York and Jersey. A funeral home director falsified the COD. Said people died of heart attacks and strokes, but some were riddled with cancer. A chop shop got the cadavers and harvested the organs. The Feds exhumed bodies. Bones had been replaced with plastic pipes. The kind plumbers use. The diseased tissues went into healthy people."

I started wheezing. I reached into my pocket, grabbed the inhaler, and dropped it. The cylinder rolled down the steps. Red picked it and set it in my hands.

"There you go, homegirl. Didn't mean to upset you. Just want you to be prepared."

I was barely listening. My full attention was focused on the Ventolin. I sucked in the acrid vapor, then held my breath.

"Come back to the O'Malleys' house," he said.

I shook my head so hard, I pulled the inhaler from my mouth. I took an experimental breath, shallow but clear. No wheezing. My bronchial tubes were opening.

He nodded at the house. "Where's your bodyguard?"

"Inside."

"He's doing a shitty job. You need to be in a house with an alarm. And a loaded gun."

"Asia's got a gun."

"I ain't letting him watch you. You're a precious woman—a little loony at times. But you're irreplaceable."

I put my head on his shoulder. "I feel the same way about you."

"I know who hit you in the mouth," he said. "Emerson called this morning. She's worried. You ought to give her a call."

"I'm too ashamed. See, I found Barb's diary. She may have gotten pregnant by some guy named A.M. When the paternity test comes back, I'm going to ask Lester if I can adopt Emerson. Because he doesn't want her, and I do."

Red looked away. "You should discuss that with the boss."

"There's nothing to discuss. Either he's in or he's out. But I don't want to alienate the Philpots. If I cause trouble for Norris, the family will close ranks. And Emerson will be raised by body snatchers."

"Let's go to the O'Malleys'. I'll keep you safe. And I'll fix you some lunch, too."

All this talk of death was wearing me to a frazzle. "I don't know. I shouldn't leave the farm unattended."

"Ask your bodyguards to stay. Come on, let's see how it goes. You've got to be in Sweeney this Friday morning for the lineup. If Irene's house starts to wear on your nerves, we'll come up with another plan."

Since Irene wasn't home, I wandered upstairs, down a long hall that had floor-to-ceiling mirrors. I found Coop's old room at the end of the corridor. White walls, twin beds with white quilts, black mattress ticking on the windows. Everything was stiff and formal. *Robert's Rules of Order* was on the bookshelf, next to *The Right Stuff* and tennis trophies. Black-framed photos lined one wall. Punctuality awards. Pictures of him and Ava. They looked happy.

I found my way back to Dracula's den and sat down on the sofa. In the distance, the phone rang, and I heard Red's gruff voice. I clicked on the TV. *Wild at Heart* was playing on Showtime. Sailor and Lula were doing the big nasty in the Big Easy.

Red handed me a cup of peppermint tea. "You look tense," he said, then leaned over to scratch Sir's ear.

"I am."

"Maybe you should read Zen philosophy."

"I'll try anything." I took a sip of tea.

"You ever heard of Bruce Lee? He's an actor and a karate expert. He said water doesn't have a shape. It's free flowing." Red wove his hands through the air. "But if you pour water into a vase, the water assumes the shape of the vase. They're a single entity. If the vase shatters, the water runs everywhere. It's shapeless. Chaotic. When things get tough, do what Bruce says. Be water, girlie."

"I can't be what I'm not."

"Think you're tough, don't you?" He grinned.

"I aim to please." I smiled. "Who was that on the phone?"

"Don't ask. You'll just freak out."

"I'm already freaked."

"A bass fisherman found two bodies in Lake Bonaventure," he said. "One was Vlado the Russian. The other was the cosmetology girl. Both had ligature marks on their hands and ankles. Whatever was holding them down in the water must've come loose. And the bodies floated up."

A painful gas bubble was growing in my chest, pressing against my ribs. I raised the cup and inhaled the gut-calming peppermint.

"The state ME is down here. A crew is exhuming bodies from the

Bonaventure Cemetery. The docs are doing posts in a big plastic tent." Red paused. "The DA will offer Mr. Winky a deal. He'll talk before it's over. I'm guessing that the Russian put Kendall in that shallow grave."

"But who put Vlado's body in the lake? Josh is in a wheelchair. He couldn't do it. Winky's in jail."

"There's no telling who's involved."

"Like the Philpots?"

"The Feds haven't found any evidence that links them."

"I might have." I told him about the printout I'd found at the pharmacy.

"Inadmissible, girlie," he said, and launched into a diatribe about the exclusionary rule. I raised my hand.

"Save it. I may break in that store again. I haven't cracked all of those anagrams. Barb left something on that wall, and she wanted Coop to find it."

"You're not above the law."

"I don't care. The day Kendall died, I told Coop that someone was harvesting organs. He blew me off. And I was right."

"Do you want to be right? Or do you want to be happy?"

"Quit using psychology on me and act like a detective. Barb's murder is connected to the chop shop. So is Kendall's. I bet the Sweeney police arrested the wrong man."

"Maybe. A witness saw Barb arguing with a man. They were in a Sullivan's Island bar."

"Coop told me about that."

"The police are gonna show the witness pictures. The Philpot brothers, Josh, Winky, the Russian, and Son Finnegan."

I set down my cup a little harder than I intended, and it banged against the saucer. "I saw that man in the mask. He was tall and skinny. Son has muscular thighs. And Vlado was stumpy."

Red stuffed his hands into his pockets. "Before you go postal, hear me out. The GBI questioned Dr. Finnegan. He admitted that he and Barb had rubbed no-no parts. Then his lawyer showed up, and the doc stopped talking."

The gas bubble in my chest burst, spilling acid into my throat. Son and Barb had been lovers? My pulse beat in my ears, *train, train, train.* Barb had been the engine, and Son was the caboose.

Red was watching me. "Finnegan could be mixed up in this, homegirl."

"Why don't you test his DNA and see if it matches the sample that was left on my nightgown?"

"That's another thing I wanted to tell you. The substance on your gown wasn't semen. It was watered-down confectioners' sugar."

While Red swam laps in the O'Malleys' pool, I watched TV. The discovery of Kendall's body had made the Savannah news, minus the gruesome details. A NewsCam tried to interview Mr. Winky outside the jail as he did a perp walk, but he pulled his shirt over his face.

The portable phone rang and I snatched it up. "Hey, Boots." Son's voice poured over me like scalding-hot lava cake.

I glanced out the window. The pool was empty. "How'd you know where to find me?"

"Drove by the O'Malleys' house and saw your truck. Bet Irene is tickled to have you around."

"Delirious."

"Is Cooter around?"

"Right beside me."

"Sneak out. We can have dinner and catch a movie."

"Stop calling me." I clicked off.

I heard a rustling noise. I looked up. Red stood in the doorway. "Was that the boss?"

I shook my head.

He leaned toward me, giving off the sharp bite of chlorine, and snatched the portable phone. He scrolled through the numbers and his eyes narrowed. "You called Son Finnegan?"

"He called me."

"How'd he know you were here?"

"Stalkers have their ways."

"It'll kill the boss if you're seeing Finnegan on the sly."

"I'd never do that. If anyone's cheating, it's Coop."

Red's mouth opened and closed. "He's not."

"Does Coop work with a brunette lawyer?"

"You mean Sherry Beth?"

"Lester said her name was Chlamydia."

"Sheesh, no. She's a nice lady. The boss isn't interested in her."

"I called him yesterday. He wasn't at the beach. Something was beeping in the background. A TV was blaring. He wouldn't tell me where he was."

Red shoved the phone into the charger. "Boss ain't banging Sherry Beth or nobody."

"Fine. Let's call him right now." I lunged for the phone and dialed the beach house. I held out the receiver so Red could hear it ring. And ring.

I hung up and dialed Coop's cell, but I got turfed straight to voice mail. Next, I called the law firm, and a curt voice told me Mr. O'Malley was out of the office for the rest of the week.

I hadn't expected that. My hand shook when I set the portable phone back in the charger. I glanced up at Red. "If you know where Coop is, now would be a good time to let me know."

He shook his head. "I can't."

"Why not?"

"I promised."

"Let me get this straight. Coop gets to know where I am, but I don't get to know where he is?"

"He's not doing nothing wrong."

"How can he take off the rest of the week? I thought his job was on the line."

"The situation has changed."

"Okay, tell me one thing. Is he alone?"

Red tucked a towel around his waist. "Not exactly."

"Who's taking care of T-Bone?"

"The mutt's in good hands. Look, I'll talk to the boss. I'll tell him you're upset. If he gives the go-ahead, I'll explain everything."

"*You'll* explain? Right." I led Sir to the truck. We got in and I blasted toward the historic district. By the time I reached Monterey Park, my thoughts had turned to murder. Everyone who'd known about the harvesting was dead. Barb, Kendall, Vlado, and the Gothy cosmetologist. True, Winky had been in jail when the last three victims had gone missing, but he probably had helpers.

Maybe one of them was Son Finnegan.

The noon sun skated through the clouds while I drove to the farm. Asia's van was gone, and so was Zee's car. I was scared to go inside the house. Sir tapped his paw against my arm, his way of saying, Let's get out of the heat.

"But someone could be in the house," I said. "It's not safe for you, either."

Sir panted, his ears twitching back and forth.

"Go ahead and say it," I told him. "You think I'm a coward."

His forehead wrinkled, making me think of that scene in *Blue Velvet* when Dennis Hopper had sniffed nitrous oxide. That movie had centered around body parts, too. I just couldn't seem to escape it. Not in movies. Not in my imagination. Not in real life.

Sir wriggled away from me. He ran to the other side of the seat and stretched his paws on the window. Over his head, I saw a column of dust move down the driveway. A gold Corvette shot around the bend and angled in front of the house.

I cranked the truck, ready to back out. Then Dot climbed out of the car, the sun glinting on her cockatoo hair. Gold crucifix earrings dangled from her lobes. Her left arm was in a sling.

"Teeny, why are you sitting in that hot truck?" she called.

I was so relieved to see her, I scrambled out of the truck. Sir hopped out after me.

"I've been calling and calling," she said. "Someone named Asia keeps answering."

"He's a friend." We walked toward the house. "What happened to your arm?"

"A rapist broke in my house last night," she said. "He crawled in through a window."

The hairs on my arms lifted. "Did he . . . ?"

"No, no. I kicked him in the balls. He had a tiny male part, but awesome upper body strength. He just about broke my arm. Then he let Mama's budgies loose just for pure meanness. I'll never catch them. I was already upset over this organ stealing ring. Have you heard about it?" She rolled her eyes. "I hate to drink in the daytime, but I need something real strong."

"I've got gin and tonic."

"Perfect. Tonic water fights malaria and limes prevent scurvy."

We went inside. While I made her a drink, she rehashed the attack. "I didn't see his face. But I just know it was Dr. Philpot."

I squeezed the lime a tad hard, and juice squirted into the air. "How?"

"Cause he said, 'Open your legth.' "

"What made him attack you?"

"I egged him on a little," Dot said. "I was in the drugstore yesterday and Norris ogled me. Asked me for a date. I told him to kiss my asth. Normally I don't smart off to people, especially to alleged rapists. But he was so obnoxious, I couldn't help myself."

From the driveway, a car door slammed. Dot jumped. "It's him," she whispered. "I just know it."

I grabbed a rolling pin just as Asia walked into the kitchen. He set down a sack from Salad Days. "Hey, Teeny, you're back," he said. He looked at the pin, but didn't comment.

Dot gave him a dreamy smile. Asia ignored her and lifted two cartons from the bag. "You ladies hungry? I just bought some blueberry chicken salad. It's better with sautéed walnuts."

"Love some," Dot said.

He dumped walnut halves in a hot iron skillet, added a pat of butter and olive oil, then turned up the heat.

Dot gave him the once-over. "Are you a chef?"

"Microbiologist." He shook the frying pan, toasting the nuts on all sides until a smoky aroma filled the room. He piled the chicken salad into a romaine nest, then added a sprinkle of walnuts and a small cluster of green grapes.

Dot's face brightened when he slid the plate in front of her. "Praise the Lord for blueberry chicken salad," she said. "It's filled with protein, complex carbohydrates, and antioxidants."

Asia grabbed a basket and opened the back door. "I'll be in the orchard, getting me some peaches. You ladies be good."

"It's too much fun being bad." Dot blew him a kiss. "The badder the better."

After Dot finished her salad, we moved to the parlor. I paused by the hi-fi and put on a stack of records. While Elvis belted out "Love Me Tender," I curled up on the sofa next to Dot.

"This is just like old times," she said. "Me and you and Rayette used to sit in here and talk about sex, Jesus, and food. Whatever happened to old Rayette?"

"She married an electrician and they moved to Alabama," I said.

Dot propped her hurt arm on a pillow. "I hope the police catch Norris-the-rapist. Because I'm starting to wonder if he killed Lester's girlfriend. Maybe Norris tried to rape her, too. I bet he got her drunk. Maybe she escaped. Then she wrecked her car. Norris might have found out she was in the hospital. He could've sneaked into her room and killed her."

I'd been thinking along the same lines. "But he used to be on the medical staff. Wouldn't someone have seen him?"

"We have a lot of new employees. Norris could have worn sunglasses and a hat. He could pass for a visitor. All he had to do was inject a fatal dose of potassium into her IV. Insulin would work, too."

"Aren't those drugs traceable?"

"Yes. But she was cremated. Now the news is saying someone put kitty litter in her urn. And her poor little body was cut to pieces." Dot shook her head. "If murder can happen in Bonaventure Regional, no place is safe."

"After a hospital patient dies, what happens to the body?" I asked.

"Our morgue caught on fire three months ago. It's being remodeled. The deceased are transported to a holding room next to the ER. Then a funeral home picks up the body."

"So where are autopsies done?

"At the funeral home."

"Could the coroner be involved in this organ stealing ring?"

"I doubt it. Mr. Winky and that Russian boy were probably behind it."

"What about Josh?"

"Oh, honey. I don't think so. He trusted Winky. Josh didn't trouble himself with the day-to-day stuff. He just planned funerals." Dot shifted toward me. "I bet Winky was doing this on the side. And he hired Norris-the-rapist to remove corneas. I bet that lispy-lipped, murdering miscreant planned to cut me up into itty pieces. Then again, Son Finnegan is a board-certified plastic surgeon."

"But Son moved to Bonaventure a few months ago. He hasn't had time to hook up with a chop shop."

"Unless they recruited him," she said.

"Would harvesters do that?" I frowned.

"Well, it makes sense. Hospitals recruit doctors all the time. Son did skin grafts at the base hospital in Germany. He was in contact with tissue banks. Maybe he returned to Bonaventure to set up a chop shop."

"What if he didn't? What if another surgeon is harvesting the organs?"

"Remember, crime is in Son's blood. His dad was a felon. His brothers are in and out of prison."

"Son grew up poor, but he's never broken the law," I said.

"That you know of." She took off her earrings and set them on the coffee table. "I wouldn't be surprised if Norris-the-rapist and Son-of-Cissy are involved in this harvesting ring. Son has lost several young, healthy patients. He spends his money on expensive toys. He's got a Jaguar, a ski boat, and a ten thousand-square-foot house on the lake. And, he's bought everything in the last three months."

"Plastic surgeons make lots of money." I shrugged.

"Yeah, they make a killing. But even if Son's not desecrating bodies, he's a dirt bag. And you, huggy bear, aren't the best judge of men."

"The Bible says not to judge."

"I don't think He meant men. Otherwise, how's a girl supposed to winnow out the Judases from the players?" Dot waved her uninjured hand. "Let's don't talk about scary things. Remember that time we got into mama's cooking sherry and we let her budgies loose?"

"They perched on the curtains," I said. "Doody was everywhere."

"Remember how one budgie sat on the ceiling fan?" Dot twirled her good finger. "Nothing but a tiny blue dot going around and around. What dumbass named those birds? A budgie sounds like a bulge in a man's Speedos. Remember the lifeguard at City Pool? He had a bulge. I used to tease him. I'd say, 'That's a mighty big budgie you got there. Or is it a cockatoo?' Get it? One cock or two?"

It didn't take much to convince Dot to stay for supper. Zee made crab cakes and hushpuppies, Asia fixed a peach-and-watermelon salsa, red rice, sautéed spinach, and skillet corn bread. We applauded when he served dessert: poached peaches, wrapped in a puff pastry crust.

After our dirty plates had been collected, Dot reached for her purse. "I dread going home. I'm such a pussy."

"What you scared of?" Zee asked.

Dot gave Zee the short version of Norris's attack, ending with the budgie fiasco. Zee's eyes changed colors, like brown sugar coming to a boil.

A pulse flickered in Dot's neck. "I'd like to shove a rattlesnake into Norris's sigmoid colon. I'd sew his rectum shut."

"I'll help," Zee said.

"You ladies need to relax," Asia said. "Karma will stomp him into the dirt."

Dot rubbed her sling. "What if he comes back tonight and finishes me off? I can't fight him off this time. Not with my hurt arm. I'd be safer at a motel."

"Don't do that," I said. "Stay here."

I put her in my old room. Then Sir and I walked across the hall and climbed onto Mama's bed. Noise drifted up from the parlor. Asia and Zee were watching *Repo Men* on HBO.

I wanted to call Coop, but I pushed my face into the pillow and forced myself to concoct a new recipe. Quit-Jumping-to-Conclusions Barbecue Rub would be fabulous on a pork roast. Blend ½ cup brown sugar, ¼ cup paprika, 2 teaspoons chili powder, 1¼ tablespoons dry English mustard, 1½ tablespoons sea salt, 3 tablespoons freshly ground pepper, and ½ tablespoon onion salt. Garlic is optional. Mix ingredients and pat onto the roast. This recipe will coat your hands, too, and you'll be unable to call your boyfriend.

I pushed down the image of the glistening roast. Then I lifted Mama's princess phone and called Red. He picked up on the first ring.

"You still mad at me?" he asked.

"This isn't a social call. Dot Agnew got attacked by Norris. She's spending the night with me."

"That good-looking dame? How many people are staying at your house? Sheesh, you ought to charge rent, girlie."

"Will you let Coop know about the attack?"

"Sure." He hesitated. "Hey, listen. It's not on the news yet, but Josh Eikenberry is missing. And, the GBI found the chop shop. A barn on the county line. Outside it had peeling red paint and a rusty roof. Inside, a state-of-the-art surgical suite."

"Who owns it?"

"Barb Philpot. She bought it six years ago."

The air filled with black globs and I thought I might faint.

"The Charleston police talked to a new witness," Red was saying. "A woman fitting Barb's description was arguing with a skinny man. Blond hair. Tall."

Keep yourself together, Teeny. I swallowed, and my throat clicked. "Son Finnegan isn't skinny. So you need to keep looking. Lots of men fit that description."

"And you need to watch yourself." Red paused. "This particular guy is a killer."

thirty

Tuesday morning sunlight blasted into my room. I put on a black J'adore t-shirt and tucked the necklace inside. Then I slipped into a blueberry-and-chocolate taffeta skirt. It had a built-in crinoline petticoat that made the skirt fan out like a bell around my ankles. The pockets were good and deep, too, perfect for tucking away candy, peaches, and my inhalers.

I tiptoed past Dot's room and crept down to the kitchen. I'd just finished making cheese grits when she walked in. "I had the most wonderful dream," she said. "Leonardo DiCaprio kissed me. Do you think he'd do that in real life?"

"Why not?" I smiled.

"Maybe he'd like me better if I got breast implants." She stared at her sunken-in chest.

"Don't be silly," I said. "You look like a *Vogue* model."

"Speaking of fashion, I love your outfit." She bent closer. "But you've got a tumor on your chest. It's poking through your shirt."

I lifted the necklace and held out the ring.

Dot's eyes blinked open wide. "That's the biggest diamond I ever saw."

"Too big."

She cupped her hand against my cheek. "Coop doesn't fit your life. But

Son Finnegan does. I hope he's not a murderer. If he's not, you should go after him. Me and you and DiCaprio can double-date."

I turned back to the stove. "Have some coffee and grits."

"Smells wonderful, but I've got to get home. I've got to feed my budgies and face my fears."

After she left, Zee wandered into the room, wearing a long Garfield the Cat nightshirt. "I don't want to worry you," she said. "But Asia saw a man creeping around your house around three a.m. We chased him, but he got away."

"What did he look like?"

"Tall. Long blond hair."

My stomach pitched. Son Finnegan had been snooping?

The phone trilled. Zee answered, and her brow tightened. She lowered the receiver. "It's some old lady named Miss Emma."

I took the receiver. "Hi, this is Teeny."

"Child, I've been trying to reach you," Miss Emma said. "I called Irene's and a man told me to call your farm. He was very rude."

"What's going on, Miss Emma?"

"I wrote something on my wall," she said. "And you need to see it."

Miss Emma stood on her porch, a black beret perched jauntily on her head. She led me into the sunroom. In the center of the wall, she'd painted a giant spider. Above the insect, she'd written two names, *Barb* and *Uma.*

I stepped closer to the wall, my taffeta skirt rustling. The spider was the size and color of a coconut, but with legs. "Who's Uma?"

"It was just on the tip of my forked tongue," Miss Emma said.

The nurse walked into the room, holding a tray. "Uma Cox," the nurse said. "She's a tarantula breeder. She lives across the street from the Philpots. A few months ago, Uma and Barb had a falling out."

"Over what?" I asked.

"Landscaping," the nurse said. "Barb was into flowers, and Miss Uma likes the scorched earth policy. You can't miss her house. It's the only one in town without grass."

I drove straight to Musgrove Square. Two police cars were parked in front of the Philpots' house. Had they come to arrest Norris for attempted rape? I squinted, hoping to catch a glimpse of Emerson, but all of the windows were shuttered.

My truck backfired, and I parked in front of Miss Uma's house, which was made out of brown stucco and sat in a patch of dirt. The yard was littered with holes, as if a giant hand had descended, yanking out the shrubbery and trees. I rang the doorbell, and an elderly woman let me in. She was dressed head-to-foot in white: shoes, socks, pants, blouse. Even her walker had been painted white. I couldn't help but smile a real smile, because this woman fit my image of the perfect grandmother. She had a hump on her back, as if someone had dropped a cantaloupe down the back of her blouse. Her thick eyeglasses magnified watery blue eyes.

"Are you Uma Cox?" I asked.

"Why, yes," she said. "Are you here to buy a tarantula?"

"No, ma'am. I just have a few questions."

"I'm always happy to discuss arachnoids." She smiled, and her face dissolved into deep furrows, the skin red and puckered like a baked apple. "Prospective tarantula owners rarely come to visit," she added. "Mainly I deal with pet stores. But I can give you a discount."

I stepped into a warm, dark hallway. A green smell rushed up my nose, making me think of forests and wet stones. In the distance, I heard crickets.

"This way, dear." Her walker scooted over the floor. I followed her into a large, gloomy parlor. White sheets covered the furniture. The windows were covered with mossy, polka-dotted draperies. Framed certificates hung on the wall: Arachnoids of the South, National Tarantula Club, The Georgia Spider Society.

She saw me looking and smiled. "I'm the vice president of the ASS. That's the American Society of Spiders? They're having a convention this year in Las Vegas, but I can't go. I can't find a house sitter. Nor can I find a repairmen. They've stomped on many a prize-winning specimen. Even I myself have to be careful. That's why I wear white."

I felt a ticklish sensation on my ankle, and I whooshed my skirt from side to side. When I didn't see a brown, furry object, I relaxed.

Uma led me into an alcove where aquariums sat on iron stands. Each tank held several inert brown objects.

"Here are my best sellers—Grammostola rosea." Uma pointed a gnarled finger at a tank. "Better known as the Chilean Rose. They're quite docile. Though if you want something feisty, I have some Costa Rican Zebra spiderlings. Don't be frightened. The tarantula has been maligned by Hollywood. They rarely bite. But if they do, it's no worse than a wasp sting. Rarely fatal."

"That's good to know." My "oh shit" smile slid into place.

"Sorry about the heat," she said. "I keep the thermostat on seventy-nine. My darlings don't like direct sun. But other than that, the G. rosea is an easy pet. I prefer them to dogs. No barking. No vaccinations. No housetraining."

I nodded. Aunt Bluette had been just as passionate about her orchard. "And spiders don't need daily exercise," I said.

"Oh, no. You can walk them," Uma said. "I know a lady who makes little bitty leashes. The cutest things you ever saw. They come in assorted colors. So you can match the leash to your outfit."

While she talked about arachnoids, I scanned the room. The polka dots on the draperies rearranged themselves. I blinked. Yes, the dots were moving.

I turned back to her. She brushed something out of her hair. A furry body plopped onto a sheet-covered chair and scurried away. "A lot of people don't see the value of owning a tarantula," she said. "But I hope you will."

"Yes, ma'am."

"Years ago, Edgar Eikenberry bought a Costa Rican Zebra for his son. It bit the boy, didn't hardly leave a mark, but Edgar threatened to sue me."

I could totally see the Eikenberrys doing this.

"And last year, one of my escaped Chileans bit a plumber. I didn't get my faucet repaired, and I had to pay for his medical bills. I've been sued many times—once for slander."

The word *slander* made my saliva turn into cement. I still hadn't discovered the connection between Uma and Barb. But if I didn't leave, and soon, the heat would set off my asthma.

I pointed at the windows. "When I drove up, three police cars were in front of the Philpots' house."

"Humph." Uma steered her walker over to the window and parted the curtains, then her lips moved. "One, two . . . I'm counting four cars. Wonder if that little girl ran away again?"

"Did the Philpots ever buy a spider for their daughter?"

"Barb tried. But I refused."

"Why?" I felt something crawl up my foot. I looked at my shoe. Nothing.

"She called my yard an eyesore. I have a time getting someone to mow my lawn. I can't do it anymore. I'm eighty-three. I can't tend to flowers or shrubs. So I had everything dug up. The grass, too."

A dot fell off the curtain and scuttled up her arm. "This spring, Barb got a petition against me. She dropped it when I threatened to tell her husband about her lover. Not that I'm a voyeur or anything. But my bedroom window looks straight into hers."

Uma gently lifted the tarantula off her arm and set it back on the curtain. "My eyes aren't what they used to be. So I used binoculars."

"I guess you saw plenty," I said.

"I hated to watch," Uma said. "But I was afraid Barb would hit me with a new petition. So I videotaped her and Dr. Finnegan. It was this position, that position." Uma flicked her hand. "And when they weren't doing gymnastics, they talked. I couldn't tell what they were saying, but it looked like they were plotting a terrorist attack."

My heart slammed against my ribs. "You're sure it was Son Finnegan?"

"He's my plastic surgeon. He took a mole off my shoulder. All he did to Barb was take off her clothes. She was a nasty woman. I hope Dr. Finnegan didn't catch a disease."

On my way out of the house, I promised Uma that I'd read up about the G. rosea. I hurried down the sidewalk, trying not to gawk at the police cars.

When I got home, the driveway was empty. I unlocked the door and Sir ran over to me, sniffing my shoes. I blinked down at him. "Do I smell like a spider?"

Definitely, his eyes said.

"Where's Asia and Zee?" I asked him.

Sir looked toward the door and sighed.

"They'll be back," I said. The petticoat was itching my skin, making me think spiders were crawling up my leg. I jerked up the skirt. No spiders. Just nerves. But I was sticky hot, so I ran up to Mama's room. I left on the J'adore shirt, then I stepped out of the skirt and put it on a hanger. I put on shorts and ran down to the kitchen.

Emerson burst through the back door, pigtails flying, the stuffed hedgehog dangling by one ear. She dove against me, smelling of sweat and dirt. I put my hand on her head, smoothing her damp hair. I thought of the police cars I'd seen at her house. "What's the matter, honey?"

"The test came back," she said, her voice muffled against my shirt. "Nobody's my daddy. Not Mr. Philpot. Not Coop. I'm nobody's child."

I knew she was waiting for me to speak, but my knees buckled as the full force of her words swept through me. She lifted her face, eyes brimming. "I want to live with you and Coop."

"I wish you could." I wanted to say more, but I held back.

"Will you talk to Mr. Philpot? Ask him if I can be your child."

I pulled her against me, feeling her fragile bones. I held her the way Aunt Bluette used to hold me.

"You bet I'll talk to him," I whispered.

"Promise?"

"I pinky-swear you." I held out my hand.

A sob tore out of her throat. She clasped her little finger around mine, then she pushed her face into my stomach again. I draped my arms around her, the stuffed hedgehog trapped between us.

"Are you gonna make me go back to the Philpots'?"

"No, but I need to call Helen. I'll ask her if you can spend the night."

"She won't let me." Emerson rubbed her nose, smearing dirt across her cheek. "Don't make me go back. Helen's like a viper. Resistant to her own poison."

"You've got half of Georgia on your feet," I said. "Let's get you cleaned up."

She held still while I ran a wet cloth over her face and neck. Then, ignoring her pleading glances, I called Helen. It hurt my heart to dial that number, but for once I was going to do things by the book. I didn't want to give the Philpots a reason to keep Emerson away from me.

Helen answered with a high-pitched hello.

"It's Teeny Templeton," I said. "Emerson's at my house."

"*Your* house?" Helen cried. "I didn't know she was gone."

"She's welcome to spend the night at the farm."

"No," she said sharply. "I'll send someone to fetch her."

"You don't have to do that. I can bring her," I said, but Helen had already hung up. I set the receiver in the cradle.

Emerson pulled out a chair and sat down. "Helen didn't know I was missing, did she?"

"She sounded upset."

Emerson drummed her fingers on the table. "You can't imagine. She went wild when the police found a cooler full of eyeballs in Norris's car. Everybody was screaming. So I ran to you."

All the air left the room. I couldn't process her words. I pictured the eyeballs trapped in small plastic pouches like the boiled eggs in the Publix deli. "Was he arrested?"

Emerson shook her head. "The police tried, but he runned away. Helen was crying. She says Norris was framed."

I remembered the three unsolved anagram in Barb's note. I found a pad and pencil in the drawer, and I wrote down *A Thousand Livers, Anal Fink Berm Jinn,* and *Cede Nephritis Ion Up.* I set the pad in front of Emerson. "Can you solve these anagrams?"

Emerson traced her finger under *A Thousand Livers* and pursed her lips. "A Dative Hurls Son? No, that's not it." She gave me a sly look. "Vlado the Russian?"

"Do you know who he is?"

"Mama's friend."

My chest tightened. "Did she have any other friends?"

"Dr. Finnegan." She yawned. "I'm hungry. If I don't eat, I'll shrivel up like a doodlebug."

"What about the other anagrams?" I asked.

"*Anal Fink Berm Jinn* is Benjamin Franklin." She pushed the notepad away. "That's all for now. I've got to eat."

While I made grilled cheese sandwiches, I glanced at the pad. Vlado the Russian hadn't been Barb's friend; he'd been an employee. As for Benjamin Franklin, Barb was probably referring to a Cayman Island bank. But what was hidden in a lock box? What about *Cede Nephritis Ion Up*? Could it be the name of a surgeon, or several surgeons?

I glanced at the notepad and picked out *Son.* Or maybe it was Noris with one R?

Emerson wolfed down the sandwiches. She wouldn't solve the other anagrams until I'd combed her hair. I gently ran a brush through it, but it was so knotted, I was afraid I'd hurt her. She gripped the hedgehog between her knees, wincing each time I hit a tangle.

"I'm sorry, honey." I bit my lip. "I'm trying to be careful."

She tipped back her head, her eyes filling poignantly with tears, and dropped her hedgehog. It bounced on the floor.

"That's okay, Teeny. You can pull all the hairs you want. Just keep me. Don't let me go."

I smoothed the brush over her snarls. The rhythmic movements jostled something that I'd forgotten. When I'd snooped in Lester's bedroom, the rug had been missing. Kendall had said she'd vacuumed a rug. What had happened to it?

"You sure do have a lot of rugs in your house," I said.

"Yeah."

"What happened to the rug in Lester's room?"

"Green food coloring accidentally got spilled on it. And some red coloring too. So Helen paid a man to haul it off."

I didn't ask how the dye had gotten there. But I said, "The rug couldn't be cleaned?"

"Helen's decorator told her to get rid of it. They were all set to buy a new one. Then this trouble with Norris happened."

I kept working on Emerson's knots. Sir eased under the table and bit into the hedgehog. I started to grab him when the phone rang.

"Yodelaheho," Red said. "I got news."

"I know about the eyeballs."

"How'd you hear that, girlie?"

"The peach trees have eyes."

"Then I guess you heard about the man in the wheelchair? Somebody poured acid on Josh Eikenberry. And Norris was spotted at the Savannah airport. They'll get him, homegirl."

I let out a huge breath. But I couldn't resist a dig. "So the only person who's missing is O'Malley."

"He'll call you tonight. Hey, I gotta go. Irene and Dr. O just got home, and we're going out to dinner.

"Moo," I said.

"Baaa," he answered.

I hung up. Sir raced past me, gripping the hedgehog in his teeth, and bolted into the dining room. Emerson popped out of her chair and ran after him.

"Give it back!" she shrieked.

I hurried into the dining room. Sir crouched under the dining room table, biting the hedgehog. Emerson plunged under the table, grabbed the hedgehog, and yanked. Sir growled, tugging in the opposite direction.

"Drop it," Emerson yelled.

Sir's jaws clamped down harder; he shook his head from side to side. The hedgehog burst apart. Bundles of money tumbled to the rug, each green pile stamped with Benjamin Franklin's portrait.

thirty-one

Sir bit into the remains of the hedgehog. He shook the critter like he was breaking its neck. Another band of money flew out.

I crawled under the table and clapped my hands. "Sir, leave it!"

He gave the hedgehog head one last, defiant shake, and a white card tumbled to the floor.

Emerson snatched it.

"What's on the card, Emerson?"

"Nothing."

I waited for her to explain, but she clamped her lips together and stared at the rug.

I lifted a green stack. It weighed as much as a slice of red velvet cake. But I wasn't holding cake. I wasn't holding money. I was holding greed. How could it weigh so little?

"Emerson, look at me. These are hundred-dollar notes. Lord knows how many. How did they get in the hedgehog?"

"Mrs. Philpot put the bundles in there when she thought I was sleeping."

Sir crept out from the table and sat in a patch of sunlight with his back to me, his fur bunching along his neck. He glanced over his shoulder and gave me the guilty eye.

I inched closer to Emerson and held out my hand. "Give me that white card."

She crossed her arms over her chest. "No."

"Fine. I'll call Lester." I started to crawl away, but Emerson snatched my arm.

"Take it." She threw the card down. "Just take everything."

The raised black print spelled out CAYMAN INTERNATIONAL BANK AND TRUST. I flipped the card. Numbers were scrawled on the back.

"That's my real daddy's phone number," she said.

"It's an account number," I said.

She tilted her head. "Does it lead to more money? Because I need it. I heard Mr. Philpot talking on the phone. He's taking me out of Chatham. He's sending me to a Christian academy in Alabama. I'll have to wear a uniform. I'll have to pray fifty times a hour or they'll stone me."

"They won't stone you, Emerson."

She grabbed my hands. "Keep me for your child and I'll split the money with you."

"Let's put everything back inside the hedgehog."

"Are you going to tell Coop about the money?"

"Yes. But not today."

Fifteen minutes later, a woman in a white tennis tutu picked up Emerson. After they left, I stitched up the hedgehog, then I put it in Mama's closet, next to Barb's diary. I cradled my head in my hands. What if Lester wouldn't let me be a part of Emerson's life? What if Coop ran off with Chlamydia Smith? Could I raise a little girl by myself? Wouldn't she need a strong male influence? I'd never had one, and just look how I'd turned out.

I didn't like unanswered questions. I liked sure things. So I went into the orchard and gathered ten ripe peaches. I came inside and made Aunt Bluette's Summer Chutney. Skin and chop peaches, taking care to remove the deadly, arsenic-like pits. Add lemon juice, peach brandy, brown sugar, honey, minced ginger and garlic, raisins and currants, peppers and spices. Mix with peach vinegar, peach juice, and canola oil. Pour ingredients over peaches and cook until the liquid is thick, about forty minutes. Cool and ladle into sterilized jars. Refrigerate. Discard after seven days, unless you plan to poison someone.

The phone rang. It was Zee. "Did you hear about Norris?" she cried. "Every policeman in Georgia is at the Savannah Airport. They've got him cornered. They're gonna put his ass in prison, and he'll never get out. Me and Asia are at Dublin's Sport's Bar. They've got live coverage. Why don't you join us?"

"Think I'll stay home. But thanks for watching my back."

"Anytime, sister. Anytime."

Dot called later that afternoon. "Are you watching the news? A SWAT team swooped down on the Savannah Airport. It's so exciting."

"I hope Norris doesn't get away."

"The sharpshooters will put a bullet between his eyes. Why don't you come over? We'll drink margaritas and watch the SWAT team whack Norris. I'm dying to show you my awesome kitchen. And don't say no. I left my earrings on your coffee table. They were Mama's. I'd hate to lose them."

She was talking so fast, I felt dizzy. But a margarita did sound nice. I couldn't remember the last time I'd had a real girl's night out. I ran upstairs, put on the taffeta skirt, rushed to the parlor. Sir was stretched out in front of the TV. The tail end of *The Wiz* was on, and Glinda the Good Witch was saying, "Home is a place we all must find, child."

I closed the pocket doors and left.

Dot lived in a miniature skyscraper, nothing but glass and steel. She opened the front door, letting out a blast of cold air. She wore enough Shalimar to cause instant respiratory arrest, but she seemed immune to the vapors. I, however, was not. I took a puff from my inhaler.

"You ought to see a pulmonologist," Dot said. She wore a black, form-fitting bodysuit that was extra tight over her crotch, showing two bulging camel toes. She'd pinned a praying hands brooch to her sling. In her free hand she held a broom, putting me in mind of the Wicked Witch of the West.

"Love your skirt," she said. "It's so poofy and stylish. Where'd you get it?"

"Mama's closet." I pulled Dot's hoop earrings out of my pocket and held them out.

"Thanks, honey bear." She put on the earrings with one hand, then she led me into her foyer. It was straight out of *Battlestar Galactica,* unfurnished except for a metal staircase.

"I'm not through decorating," she said. "I'm saving my money to buy a set of Lucite chairs for the dining room. I just love chairs. I can't quit buying them."

She set the broom beside the door, then she took my hand and pulled me into a hall. At the end was a large, ultramodern kitchen. Concrete counters. Stainless steel cabinets. A six-burner Wolf stove with red knobs—the Holy Grail of appliances. I went straight to it.

Dot laughed. "Don't pee on yourself until you've seen my Thermadore convection ovens."

"You could host a cooking decathlon." I walked past the small TV that sat on the counter. The screen showed an aerial view of the Savannah Airport parking lot. I turned away from it and faced the sink. It was stainless, deep enough to soak a thirty-pound turkey.

"Stop coveting my kitchen and let's get drunk." She tipped a pitcher over a salt-rimmed glass. The margarita mixture plopped out, resembling slushy lime sherbet. "I made an extra-strong batch," she said. "Heavy on the triple sec, a touch of PGA. I put food coloring in it too. That's why it's so green."

In the background, I heard bird calls and chirping. "Your budgies sound happy," I said.

"They do, don't they? I still can't believe that Norris set them loose. I'm just grateful he didn't bite off their little heads." She thrust her hand into a Doritos bag and pulled out a handful of chips. "Drink up before the ice melts."

I took a sip of the margarita. It felt cold against the back of my throat, the perfect blend of salty and sweet.

"It's good, isn't it?" She smiled. "If you get tipsy, you can crash in my guest room."

"I can't stay long. I need to get back to the farm."

"You expecting Coop?"

If I said yes, I'd have to raise my lie tally, and I'd been so good. An honest "no" would lead to questions that I didn't want to answer. "I love that old farm," I finally said.

"Quit trying to change the subject." She lifted her glass. "I never understood why Coop dropped you in high school. I guess Barb-the-Train offered dividends."

It felt wrong to slander the dead, so I took another sip of the margarita.

"Wasn't Coop married to a British woman?" Dot shifted her eyes to the left, as if she'd suddenly spotted Ava.

I looked, too, but I only saw a trash compactor. "They're divorced."

"Was she a blonde?"

"Brunette." I set down my glass. "Why?

" 'Cause I'm seeing a pattern. Coop screws blondes and marries brunettes. After all, his mama has dark hair."

Dot's words hit me like an openhanded slap. This wasn't the first time that I'd wondered about Coop's preferences. I lifted my glass and swallowed another icy mouthful. I had a strange feeling that something was moving on my leg. I yanked up my skirt, but I only saw a few red scratches on my knee.

"You're awfully twitchy." She patted my arm. "Your problem isn't blondness, it's farmness. You know about peaches, not haute couture. Not that I'm trying to categorize you or anything."

No, of course not. I tossed down the rest of the margarita. It slid down my throat like a slow-moving glacier. I felt my tight, little smile lock into place.

She leaned closer. "Have I offended you?"

I shrugged. In the old days I would have launched a sideways attack. I would have made a flippant remark about her sci-fi décor and asked if her designer's last name was Spock.

The doorbell echoed in the foyer.

"Drink up," Dot said, and walked to the hall. I put down my glass and started to go back to the stove, but my knees buckled. I leaned against the counter. I couldn't be drunk. Not this fast. Way off in the distance, I heard a masculine voice say, "Am I early?"

"You're right on time," Dot said. "Teeny's already here."

Footsteps. Laughter. Dot came into the kitchen, trailed by Son Finnegan. His nose was sunburned as if he'd spent the day on a boat. He wore brown loafers and tan shorts. His green plaid shirt matched his eyes.

"Hey, Boots. You ready to party?"

thirty-two

I stepped toward Son, and a rush of dizziness hit me so strong, I thought I might fall into his arms. I turned back to the counter and grabbed it with both hands. What was Dot trying to pull? I thought she disliked Son. Had I misunderstood?

"What's wrong, Boots?" He glanced at my lip, then he looked at Dot's sling.

"Did I miss the girl fight?" He winked at me. "Who won?"

"We were attacked by Norris Philpot," Dot said, and poured him a drink.

"Seriously?" He took a sip and grimaced. His gaze swept back to me. "Sorry about your lip, Boots. You all right?"

"I was until you got here," I said.

He frowned at Dot. "You didn't tell her I was coming?"

"Nope," she said.

The left side of Son's mouth angled into a smile, but the other half was still frowning. "What's going on, Dot?"

"Teeny's got love problems. She isn't sure if she loves you or Coop. So I thought I'd bring y'all together."

I realized I was holding my breath. I let it go and air rushed between my clenched teeth. "That's a lie!"

Dot's lower lip slid forward until it was the twin of mine—minus the scab. "It's the truth. You still love Son. But you're too stubborn to admit it."

"Did you set this up behind Teeny's back?" Son asked.

"Well, yes." Dot looked flustered. "I knew she wouldn't agree."

Son looked confused. "I need another drink," he said.

"Gladly." Dot refilled his glass. He turned his back on us and faced the breakfast nook, where mismatched Lucite chairs were clustered around a stainless steel table.

"I'm going home." I tucked my purse under my arm.

"That won't fix your problems." Dot yanked my purse away and set it on the counter, out of my reach. "You and Coop are finished. He may have given you a ring, but he won't marry you."

"So now you're a fortune teller?" I lunged for my purse, but she pushed me back.

"Even if you accepted his proposal, Irene won't let him marry you." Dot refilled my glass and pushed it into my hands. "Face it, you and Son are meant to be together until death do you part."

She was starting to creep me out. A long shadow fell over us. I looked up. Son leaned against the counter, the margarita glass caught in the V of his fingers.

The back of my throat tasted of rum and bile. I was totally going to throw up. "Where's the powder room?"

Dot pointed toward the hall. "Third door on the left."

I lurched out of the kitchen, but I lost count of the doors. I veered around a corner, into a bedroom furnished with more Lucite. I heard a meow. A white cat uncoiled from a white bench.

Why did she keep a natural predator around her birds? It glared at me with copper eyes. "How do you get along with the budgies?" I asked.

The cat gave me an indignant look, as if to say, *Do you see any feathers in my mouth?* It looked at my taffeta skirt and hissed. *A fashion catastrophe,* its eyes said.

A faint shred of civility prevented me from hissing back. Then I remembered I wanted to throw up, so I walked into the bathroom. I'd barely made it to the toilet before the margarita came up. On my way out of the bathroom, I got dizzy again and ended up in an alcove. Here, the bird chirping was louder, and it seemed to come from a walk in closet.

I peeked inside. White uniforms hung next to ball gowns. Clear plastic engulfed a chinchilla jacket. A jewelry case stood open, and diamond rings glittered against black velvet. Further down, a shelving unit was crammed with pill bottles. I squinted at the labels. Sonata. Oxycontin. Xanax. Another shelf held jars that were filled with colorful capsules. ROHYPNOL was written on one jar. Vials of a milky drug were lined up like nail polish.

Another sick feeling waved over me, and I put my hand on the wall. Had Dot slipped a Sonata into the margaritas? And where were the budgies? I tracked the sound to an intercom system that was set into the wall. I pressed the "open" button, and a CD disk slid out. The chirping stopped. The air was still as a tomb. I glanced at the CD label and saw MAMA'S BUDGIES written in back slanted script. My finger shook as I pushed the CD back in. The birdsong started again.

At the other end of the closet, I saw a stainless steel Sub-Zero refrigerator. Was I hallucinating? I rubbed my eyes, but the refrigerator was still there. Why did she need a Sub-Zero in her closet? To chill champagne?

I yanked open the door and light spilled out, showing a gleaming white interior. On the shelves were clear glass bottles. I lifted one. Inside, a round white globe was nestled in a rack, like a tiny pickled egg.

Only it wasn't an egg. It was an eyeball.

A dizzy vortex spun around me. I dropped the bottle. Dot worked for the chop shop, and maybe Son did, too. They'd killed Barb and Kendall and Vlado and the Goth-girl, and they were going to kill me.

I felt an adrenaline rush, fight or flight. The flight won. *Get out of here, Teeny.* I staggered out of the closet, into the bedroom.

Dot's voice echoed from the kitchen. She was talking about her marital history. But she seemed to be talking to herself, because Son didn't answer.

"My husbands come and go," she said, "but my surname never changes.

And it's a darn good thing. Can you imagine the confusion? Dot Agnew-Smithers-McMann-Alexander-Travers-Sanchez. It sounds like the scientific name for a Hantavirus."

I made my way to the foyer. I was almost out the door when a hand pulled me back.

"You're too drunk to drive," Dot said. She plucked a white hair off my black top. "I see that you've met my cat. Munchkin ate the last of the budgies. All I have left of them are Mama's recordings. But you figured that out, didn't you? Because the music stopped playing for a second."

A humming noise roared through my head, thousands of beating wings and chomping teeth, a plague of locusts. "I didn't hear any music," I said.

She pulled off her sling, then she grabbed the broom.

"You're not in Charleston anymore, Teeny." She slugged me with the broom handle and everything went dark.

I awoke in Dot's breakfast room, tied to a Lucite chair. Son sat across the table, his head lolling to the side. A rope was lashed around his chest, and his eyes were closed. Dot squatted beneath him, tying his feet to the chair. But he was her partner. Why was she restraining him?

I couldn't think straight. My head throbbed. *Cat. Broom. Eyeballs.*

The doorbell rang. Dot raised her head, the cockatoo curls trembling. She got up and walked toward the kitchen, leaving behind a lethal cloud of Shalimar. When she turned into the hall, I tried to squirm out of the rope, but it was too tight.

"Son?" I said. My heartbeat scattered, beating in my fingertips and belly.

His head jerked up.

"Were you and Dot selling illegal body parts?" My voice sounded slurry, as if words were melting on my tongue.

"You crazy, Boots?" His gaze was unfocused.

"Son, listen to me. Dot's going to kill us. Try to loosen your ropes. We've got to get out of here."

"Let me sleep, Boots," he said. "Just let me sleep."

From the hallway, I heard furious whispers, male and female, but I couldn't hear what they were saying.

"Son! Please try to get away." I twisted around in the chair, but the rope cut painfully into my breasts.

"Love you, too, Boots."

"We've got to leave." I broke off. What had I meant to say? My thoughts finned off and vanished. Something tickled my thigh. I looked down. My blue-brown pocket gaped open, and a tarantula lifted its arm. Holy crap. A stowaway from Miss Uma's house. So that's what had been itching me.

Dot stepped into the kitchen. I wanted to ask her a question, but I couldn't remember it. My thoughts darted and darted, like bait fish swimming in black water.

"You doing okay, Teeny?" she asked.

Like she gave a shit, that miserable budgie bitch. I wanted to ask what the hell she thought she was doing, but my tongue was stuck to my teeth.

"You can come in now," Dot said to the person in the hall.

Footsteps clapped on the floor. Then a tall man walked in. At least, I thought it was a man. His face was hidden by a Bill Clinton mask. A long blond wig hung in stiff curls to the man's shoulders.

I tried to suck in air, but it felt like a twenty-volume set of encyclopedias were piled on my chest. Hadn't the Sweeney police found that mask? Barb's murderer was sitting in a jail cell, waiting for me to pick him out of a lineup.

The man lifted the mask.

thirty-three

Josh Eikenberry threw the mask onto the counter and smiled, but his hazel eyes were chips of jade. He was alive?

Son lifted his head and squinted. "You look like a tranny," he said.

"Nice to see you, too," Josh said in his best "greet the mourners" voice.

"Why aren't you paralyzed?" I asked.

"Cured by Jesus." Josh stepped around the counter. He wore black pants, a long-sleeved black shirt, and hiking boots.

"He never was paralyzed," Dot said.

"That's a lie," Josh said. "I was, too."

"Just for two weeks." She turned to me. "He had spinal edema—fluid was pressing on the nerves. When the swelling went down, he was fine."

"It was the worst two weeks of my life, not counting this one." Josh sighed.

"I'll put you on my prayer list," Dot said.

"But I don't understand." I frowned at Josh. "If you weren't paralyzed, why were you in a wheelchair?"

"It's the perfect alibi," he said. "Nobody would suspect a guy in a chair. And nobody did. Not until Barb ruined everything."

"He also liked the way women fussed over him," Dot said. "Especially Barb."

Josh blushed.

Dot turned to me. "They were lovers. She wanted to punish Lester for his affair. That's why she left the business. I thought she'd come to her senses, but she had other ideas. She was going to dump her little girl on you and Coop, then she was going to leave the country."

My stomach pitched. Cayman Islands. Lockbox.

"Thanks to her, I've lost everything," Josh said. "There's a whole bunch of places that don't have extradition treaties with the United States, but they're all third world toilets. How will I ever find a decent home in Rwanda?"

"The police think you got burned up with acid," I said.

"No, that was Norris."

"Did you put a cooler of eyeballs in his car?" I asked in a shaking voice.

"I did that," Dot said. "He had it coming. He pinched my butt one time."

"But I thought Norris was slicing off corneas?" I said.

Josh snorted. "You crazy? We had a crew working for us."

I blinked. "Then who was at the Savannah Airport?"

"Nobody," Josh said. "Dot phoned the police with an anonymous tip."

"All this lying is making me thirsty." She pulled two beers from the fridge and handed one to Josh.

"Nothing like an ice cold Coors on a hot Georgia night." He slurped up the foam. "Hey, I got a new joke. What's red and bubbly? A granny in a microwave."

"You've told that one before," Dot said.

"I got a joke," Son said. "What's worse than a hundred undertakers in a trash can?"

I perked up. "One undertaker in a hundred trash cans," I said.

"That's lame." Josh turned to Dot. "They're too lucid. What'd you give them?"

"Pure grain alcohol, Coumadin, and Sonata. And, just for shits, a tiny bit of Rohypnol."

"Sonata's too weak." Josh swung an imaginary golf club.

"It worked on Kendall."

"Yeah, but you threw in a shitload of PGA. Besides, the drugs will show up in their blood."

"*If* their blood is found." Dot smiled and took a dainty sip of beer. "But we won't let that happen this time."

"You put Coumadin in our drinks?" Son cried. "You gave us blood thinner?"

"I hated to," Dot said. "It makes dismemberment so messy. But I'm just covering my ass if y'all escape."

"They won't." Josh pulled a .38 from his jacket.

I dug my fingernails into the rope and willed myself not to react.

"Put that damn gun away." Dot set down her beer. "I'm using a Taser. It's cleaner and quieter."

Josh's upper eyelid jerked, as if pulled by fishing line. "But I want to shoot Son," he said. "He's such an asshole."

"Quit whining," Dot said. "We're going to do things my way from now on. I told you not to pull that cremation stunt. And *look* what happened. You should've embalmed Kendall. But no, you had to get creative. Vlado couldn't follow instructions, either."

"But he was a psycho." Josh shrugged.

"He was stupid, and so are you," Dot said. "Maybe I should get you a shock collar. Every time you screw up, I'll give you a jolt. Then you'll learn from your mistakes."

His cheeks reddened, but he slid the .38 into his pocket.

I glanced at Son. He seemed to be dozing again.

Dot opened a drawer and pulled out a Taser. "I've got concrete blocks in the garage. Chains and rope are there, too. Open the garage door and put everything in Son's Jaguar. The keys are on the counter."

"Why am I doing all the work?" Josh's hand stole back to his pocket.

"Let's get them to the lab, okay?" Dot said.

"Anything else, your majesty?" Josh said.

"Don't screw up this time."

Josh left. Dot forced me to drink another margarita. The liquid pooled in the back of my throat. "Drink up, Teeny You don't want to be awake when Josh gets a hold of you."

I swallowed. "What's he going to do to me?"

"Yucky stuff. You'll need another margarita, trust me." She untied me and walked to the kitchen. All I had to do was bolt from the chair and run off into the night. I gripped the edge of the table and hoisted myself to my feet.

"Oh, for the love of Jesus." Dot crossed the floor in four steps and tasered my arm.

A ripple tore through my body. I stiffened and fell to the floor. I tried to get up, but my arms wouldn't move. I couldn't get a deep breath. Yet I could hear everything. And I could feel the tarantula moving in my pocket. Thank goodness it hadn't been tased.

Son's disembodied voice swirled above me. "Where'd Teeny go?"

"Teeny who?" Dot laughed. "It's a shame I have to kill you, Son. 'Cause I always had a little crush on you."

A pins-and-knives sensation shot through my hands and feet. I groaned. "God sees the sparrow," I croaked. "And He'll see you."

"God needs new corneas," Dot said.

"You won't get away with this."

"Yes, I will. The police will think you and Son ran off together."

"I'm not ready to die." I tried to lift my arm, but it was stuck to the floor.

"No one is," she said. "Only the strong and the determined survive."

I felt a tear skid down my cheek. I couldn't die without seeing Coop one more time.

Josh strode into the room, pulling on plastic surgical gloves. "I wish you'd let me put a bullet in Son's brain."

"I forbid you to leave forensic evidence in my kitchen," Dot said. "Besides, he's not going anywhere."

I flexed my fingers. "You don't have to kill Son. He hasn't done anything to you."

Dot squatted beside him and lifted his chin. His eyelids fluttered and went still.

"He's mighty cute," she said. "But the moment you told him about Kendall, he started poking in medical records. If he kept poking, he'd cause me trouble. Just think, I wouldn't have to kill either one of you if Barb hadn't tried to quit my gang. It's all her fault."

"I don't understand."

"She moved to Sullivan's Island to get away from me," Dot said. "I gave her a thousand chances to come back to Georgia. But she had other plans. So I came to her house and choked her."

I blinked. Was she saying that Josh hadn't worn that mask? "But you weren't there."

"Of course I was. I dressed up like a guy and wore that mask."

"That was *you*? How did you get a key to her house?"

"Josh got the key from Barb's rental agent. He pretended to be Lester. Told the woman he needed an extra key."

"The police will find that woman and talk to her."

"No, they won't. I sent Vlado to kill her. He made it look like a heart attack. So she won't be telling the police anything."

Tears spilled down my cheeks.

"Don't cry for somebody you never met."

"But why did you kill Barb?" My voice was barely a whisper.

"I told you. Because she quit the business. We couldn't let her walk away. She knew too much. But she was so good at what she did. So we didn't murder her right away. We negotiated. Offered her a bigger cut. But she wanted Coop—she never stopped loving him." Dot shrugged.

"You should've let her go," I said.

"She was a liability. I had to kill her. Josh didn't have the stomach for it. So I went to Sullivan's Island. But you weren't supposed to be there. You sure can run fast for a short person. If I'd caught you that night, you'd be dead."

I flinched.

"After I chased you, I went back to Barb's house. She'd regained consciousness and was packing her suitcase. I bashed her in the head with a cast-iron skillet. Then I finished packing her suitcase. I cleaned up the broken lamp and put Barb in the trunk of her car and I left."

"What if Emerson had seen you?"

"I would have killed her, too. I pulled off at a rest stop and strangled Barb. Then I headed to Sweeney. Josh and Vlado met me at the Motel 6. I put on a wig and checked in. Then we hung Barb from the shower rod. I left a note. Vlado put out pills and an empty wine bottle."

"I never dreamed it was you." I shook my head a little, trying to put it all together. Yes, Dot was tall and angular. Put a mask on her, and she could pass for a guy.

"Oh, buggar-bear, I couldn't be sure what you saw." Dot got in my face. "Then you came to Bonaventure. Josh has always hated you. He voted to kill you, but I talked him out of it. You know why? Because you were my friend. I really liked you, Teeny. So I got Vlado to put on a long blond wig and break into your house."

"Why?"

"To shake you up. To make you run back to Charleston. But you didn't."

"The icing on my gown was a nice touch."

"I thought you'd get a kick out of it."

"So were the gardenias."

"They came out of my backyard."

"You don't have to kill Son."

"Josh would be so disappointed." She smiled.

I began shaking all over. Son was going to die because of me.

"Poor Teeny. You look heartbroken. There's nothing you could have done to save yourself. I was just biding my time. Getting everything set up. I lured you to the Tartan Hair Pub so you'd have straight hair. That way, it would be harder to identify your desecrated corpse. That's why I didn't come to your house and kill you."

Dot shoved the Taser into her pocket and untied Son. "Josh, stop picking your nose and help me get Dr. Love in the car."

Son's legs wobbled as they lifted him from the chair and guided him out the kitchen door. Night air streamed in, carrying their voices. They were arguing about who to harvest first, me or Son.

I grabbed a chair leg and pulled up. Where did she keep the phone? I had to call 911. I tried to stand, but my legs buckled and I hit the floor.

Okay, Teeny. Deep breath. I rubbed my thigh, trying to get the circulation going, but it didn't seem to help. How long before I could walk? I saw a portable phone on the desk and crawled toward it, my hair swinging forward. My brain felt muddy.

Focus, Teeny.

I grabbed the desk chair and pulled up, my arms trembling. I heard a shuffling noise and twisted around. Dot stood in the kitchen doorway, her hands jammed on her hips. Josh was right behind her. I expected her to pull out the Taser, but she just snorted.

"I'll get her," Josh said. He pulled me away from the chair and hoisted me into his arms.

Dot stepped over to the counter. She opened my purse and grabbed my keys. 'I'll pull her truck around. Meet me in the driveway."

Josh's clothes gave off the harsh bite of sulfuric acid. Just like the devil would smell. As he carried me outside, I repressed an urge to pinch my nostrils.

"You're such a bitch, Teeny," he said.

"A crazy bitch," I agreed.

"A piece of trash."

"A human Hefty bag."

"You got laid by every boy but me."

I didn't bother to correct him. I was fighting for my life, not my honor. Over his shoulder, lightning scratched across the sky. A rainstorm was coming, but I wouldn't live to see it.

A garden hose lay across the pavement like a serpent. Josh stepped over it and turned toward the pebble driveway. He set me on my feet. My legs buckled and pushed me against the house.

"You want it," he said, unbuckling his belt.

Oh, god, no.

"I'm turning you on," he said. His lips parted, and he leaned in to kiss me.

I gagged. He kissed the same way he had in high school—mouth overflowing with saliva, teeth banging against mine. I tried to rack him, but my knee wouldn't bend.

He broke the kiss and tweaked my nipple. I squirmed away. His hand slid under my dress, beneath the pocket where the tarantula lay. I twitched all over, whether from the Taser or fear, I didn't know. But I couldn't stop.

"You're shaking like a bed in a cheap motel," he said. "Magic Fingers."

"And you didn't have to pay a quarter." Damn, why had I said that?

He kissed me again. *No, stop. You mustn't. For the love of God, stop.* But His eye was on the sparrow, not Teeny Templeton. It was up to me to handle this.

I dragged my mouth away. "I'm riddled with diseases," I shouted.

"Beg for it. Come on, Teeny. Beg."

My heart stuttered. Then I heard the whinny of Aunt Bluette's engine. Headlights swept over Josh and me. He let me go. I slid down the bricks, wincing as they scratched my shoulders.

Dot got out of the truck, her cockatoo hair bouncing, and opened the Jag's rear door. "Save it, Romeo," she said. "Bring her over here."

Josh hoisted me over his shoulder and dumped me into the backseat. Son was up front, his head tipped forward. Was he dead?

"Son?" I shouted. "Can you hear me?"

He groaned.

"Pay attention to *me*." Josh squeezed my breasts.

I opened my mouth to scream. Instead, I vomited. Frothy lumps hit his face, stinking of tequila. He slapped my ear hard, and I went flying across the seat. The back of my head banged against the other door.

Dot pulled him out of the car. "Don't hit her. The tissue bank won't accept bruised skin."

Josh swiped his hand over his face. "She puked on me."

She shoved him toward the house. "Turn on the faucet and clean up."

She climbed into the backseat and shone a penlight in my face. “Good, he didn’t break the skin.”

I put up my hand, blocking the glare. “How did you get mixed up in black market organs?”

She aimed the penlight at her palm; her flesh turned red and iridescent. “I used to work for a tissue bank. I flew around the country visiting hospitals. My job was to find skin donors. I could buy a whole cadaver for $6,000. But two corneas sell for $15,000. Bones in a spinal column sell for $1000. Big money in spare parts. I came back to Bonaventure and had a little chat with Josh.”

“Why him?”

“The best chop shops need a crooked funeral home director. And Josh isn’t exactly a saint. He was still in a wheelchair, but I found out that he was faking it.”

“How did you know?”

“I saw mud on his shoes.”

“So you blackmailed him?”

“Heavens no. I seduced him. Then I confronted him. I had him wrapped around my little toe. He liked the idea of making money, but he wanted to be paralyzed for a while longer—it was the first time in his life that people treated him nice. We made a great team.”

“Who else is working for you?” I asked.

“No one you’d know.” She pinched my cheek. “Your skin is soft as a peach.”

I jerked away. “Why didn’t you put Kendall’s body in the lake?”

“Vlado deviated from the plan.” She looped the chain around my ankle. “You’ve done nothing with your life, Teeny. Now you have a chance to help many people with *your* spare parts. I wish I could say the same for your bulldog. We’re just going to shoot him.”

I raised up. “No, leave him alone.”

She pushed me down. “Coop will wonder why you left that stupid dog. That makes Sir a loose end.”

My vision blurred. “You can kill me, but you’ll still be crazy.”

"And rich." She yanked off my necklace and slid Minnie's ring on her finger. "A perfect fit."

"If you get near Coop, I'll haunt your ass."

"Normally I like three in a bed. But not this time. Coop only has eyes for you." Dot tweaked my nose. "Or should I say *had*? He'll get over you. And he'll marry a pretty brunette and have children. Won't that be nice?"

She scooted out of the backseat and hollered at Josh. He stepped out of the shadows, the front of his shirt damp and transparent, showing a sunken-in chest.

"Drive straight to the lab," she said. "I'll be right behind you in Teeny's junker."

"What about Son's car?" Josh waved at the Jaguar.

"I've taken care of everything. A guy is waiting at the old sawmill with an eighteen-wheeler. The vehicles will be halfway to Mexico by tomorrow." Dot got in Josh's face. They were the same height, tall and rangy. "Make sure the bodies don't float up this time. Because I love my house. I love my job. I don't want to leave the country because you're sloppy."

"I have to leave," he said. "That's not fair."

"But you've still got a pulse. You can go somewhere else and start over. Just make sure the bodies stay in the water."

Concrete blocks. Ropes. Chains. Taser. They were going to remove our organs and sink us in Lake Bonaventure.

thirty-four

The car dipped to one side as Josh climbed into the driver's seat. The dome light pooled around me and hit the floorboard, washing over concrete blocks, chains, pliers, and a saw.

Josh put on a Braves hat that looked suspiciously like the one I'd lost on Sullivan's Island. He started the engine, and the dome light faded. I could hear Aunt Bluette's truck revving behind the Jag.

Son yawned, then sat up. "What the hell—"

Josh slugged him. Son crashed sideways and his head slammed against the window. The Jaguar's tires made a hissing noise as it sped down the driveway.

I mustered up my courage and sat up. "Josh? Why'd you kill your cosmetologist?"

"Opal? She asked too many questions."

"Who'd you get to creep around my house last night?"

"That was me. I wore a wig." Josh snorted. "Dot wanted you to think that Son was stalking you. But your fan club chased me off. So we had to lure you here."

"The Charleston police are looking for a man with blond hair. A witness saw him in a bar, talking to Barb. Was that you? Or Vlado?"

"Dot met Barb at Poe's. It was a last-ditch effort to get Barb to come back to us." He squinted into the rear view mirror. "God, you're a motor-mouth. If you don't hush, I'll stop the car and shoot you. And I really don't want to do that. I want you to be alive when I rape you."

Oh God, oh God, oh God. Not that. I shook so hard, the chains made a singing noise.

Josh turned on the radio. Snippets of music ran together as he spun the dial. He stopped on a sports station, and I heard the crack of a baseball, the roar of a crowd, then he spun the dial again and landed on WAEV from Savannah. Over the static, the Black Ghosts sang "Full Moon."

"You like shitty music, don't you, Teeny? Enjoy it while you can."

The car turned left onto Willow Street, a dark, two-lane road that led to a county highway—the road to Sweeney. Was the new chop shop located there?

Behind us, the truck's headlights swept through the rear window. Shadows skated over the floorboard. I lunged for the pliers. The Jaguar made a sharp left turn, and the pliers slipped under the front seat.

If I didn't bash Josh in the head before we reached the lab, Son and I would die. My bulldog would die. I didn't have a guarantee that Coop and Red would survive. If they started poking around, Dot would put them into the lake. Emerson would go to that school in Alabama and she'd never know how it felt to be loved.

I glanced around for another weapon. I tried to lift a concrete block, but I was still shaky and couldn't move it. I slumped against the back seat, feeling utterly defeated. Tonight, Son and I would be on the bottom of the lake, and maybe our organs would help someone; but the money was going to the Dot Agnew Foundation. She would go home, turn on her Wolf range, and heat a pot of soup. More patients would die at Bonaventure Regional because she needed to finish decorating her house. A cornea would buy new dining room furniture. A tendon would buy an oil painting. How many cadavers would buy a $2,000,000 beachfront condominium on St. Simon's Island?

I pulled myself up and grasped the back of Josh's seat, trying to crouch low. If he saw me in the rearview mirror, he'd shoot me. Straight ahead, through the windshield, a string of headlights came toward the Jaguar.

Witnesses.

I could beat on the side window and hope the driver saw me. But those lights were so far away. Josh turned on his blinker and turned down a rough-paved road. I bolted forward, grabbed his ears, and twisted as hard as I could.

"Let go!" His fist crashed into my forehead. The blow knocked me into the backseat. I sat there, too dazed to move. I was faintly aware of something moving in my pocket, a skitter-scratch. I opened the pocket, and the tarantula crawled onto the back of my hand. Maybe I should let it bite me, but no, Miss Uma had said tarantula bites weren't deadly.

Josh had been bitten by one of her pets. I prayed he still harbored a fear of arachnoids.

Again, I raised up, my eyes filling, and moved my outstretched hand toward Josh. "Oh, my god," I said. "There's tarantulas in this car. They're crawling everywhere."

"Yeah, right." Josh snorted.

I thrust my hand in front of him. He screamed. I flung the tarantula in his lap. His hands lifted from the steering wheel, and he brushed between his legs. The Jag veered off the road. I leaned over his shoulder and stretched out my arm toward the steering wheel. Just a little closer. One more inch.

The tires bounced into a hole. Branches and saplings beat against the fender. Straight ahead, the headlights picked out bark and pine boughs.

The Jaguar slammed into a tree. I heard the wrench of metal. Needles pinged against the hood. Black air rushed in around me and I was flying.

I came to in the backseat. A horn blared and blared. I smelled smoke and I sat up. Pain lanced through my thigh. Josh lay over the steering wheel.

Above him, the windshield was cracked, streaked with red. Steam hissed from the crumpled hood and scattered into the branches.

Son was sprawled against the door. He moaned, and blood streamed out of his mouth.

"Son Finnegan, don't you die on me." My fingers dug into the back of his seat. I pulled myself close to him.

"I'm hurt, Boots." He moaned again.

"Hold on." I couldn't help him from this angle, so I yanked open the back door and crawled into the dark weeds. A blast of humid air rushed over my face. As I inched forward, something jerked me back. I spun around, expecting to see Josh's hand. But it was just the chain, looped tightly around my ankle.

Trying not to panic, I grabbed the concrete block. It felt light as a biscuit. I heaved it out of the car. A warm tickle ran down my knee, and I yanked up my dress. A diagonal gash ran across my leg, in the fleshy part of my left thigh. The wound wasn't spurting. Just a deep, oozing wound.

I crept over to Son's door, pulling the concrete block with me. From the road, headlights speared through the trees and washed into the gully. Dot had found us.

I flung open Son's door. The dome light blinked on. I lifted his face. Blood streamed from his nose and mouth. But he was breathing. Bits of safety glass were scattered in his hair, and I brushed them out.

"Hurts so bad," he whispered.

I looked at Josh. His chest wasn't moving I leaned across the seat and felt his wrist. No pulse. I slid my hand into his nearest pocket and searched for the gun. Empty. I started to check his other pocket when flames spiked from the hood, sending up a dazzle of orange sparks. Smoke rolled up from the floorboard. Oh, Lord. Would the engine blow up? Where was the spider? And where was Dot? She'd been right behind us.

I scooted back to Son. "Put your arms around me."

"Can't." His shoe scooted over the floorboard. "My gut hurts."

"Son, listen to me. I know you're in pain. But the car's on fire. Come on, get out. Just lean on me. I'll help you."

More cinders spiraled up into the darkness. A circle of heat pushed against me, and I smelled burnt rubber. Son slid his arms around my neck. He didn't feel that heavy. Or maybe I had super-human strength. I pulled him out of the car, into the grass, dragging that damn block behind me.

From the road, I heard a commotion. Voices. Spangled lights.

"Holy shit," a man cried.

I led Son into the tall weeds and propped him against a tree. "I'll be right back," I said. "I'm going back for that tarantula."

Son keeled over, thumping against the ground. He dragged me with him, and I fell hard on my butt. I tried to stand. The ground rose up and folded itself around me.

A man in a Coors hat tried to pull Son from my arms. A flashlight moved over my skirt. It was dark red and sticky, warm as a wet washrag. Someone brought a fire extinguisher and aimed it at the car. Sirens drilled through the night, a black sound that chipped against my ears.

Hands lifted me up. Don't let the bedbugs bite. And don't hurt my spider. He's one heck of an arachnid.

thirty-five

Noises rushed around me. Beeping. Rhythmic clicks. The patter of water. I was lost in a forest, soon to be devoured by beetles. A disembodied voice spiraled down from the ceiling, beseeching Elena Samuels to call the operator.

Was I trapped in a department store?

The water shut off. Footsteps. A cool hand on my cheek. Two brown eyes loomed above me. "Miss Templeton, you've been in a wreck. How much alcohol did you drink?"

What wreck? What alcohol? I wasn't much of a drinker. "Where am I? What day is it?"

"You're in the hospital. It's August nineteenth. Tuesday night."

Hospital? This was Dot's killing ground. I couldn't stay here. I tried to sit up, but my head wouldn't leave the pillow. I felt swimmy-headed, and my ears were ringing.

"Don't move, Miss Templeton." She wore little white wings on top of her head. A nurse or an angel? Her voice echoed, as if it came from the bottom of hell, a hot place with rock salt and empty margarita glasses. What was the opposite of an angel? A demon?

All I could think of was Mama's recipe for Coca-Cola Basted Ham. She'd paired it with Black Sabbath's "War Pigs" and Matthew 8:31: *So the demons begged Him, saying, If Ye cast us out, permit us to go into the herd of swine.*

The demon-angel moved beside my bed. She lifted my hand and adjusted a red tube. The tube led to a purple-red bag that hung above my head. Again, the disembodied voice uncurled from the ceiling: "Doctor Braxton, call 3-East. Dot Agnew, call the emergency room."

Bits and pieces came back to me. Dot, margaritas, Son, eyeballs, Josh, the wreck. And the nurse wasn't an angel-demon. She wasn't Dot. She was someone who'd taken an oath to help sick people.

A gurney rattled past my door, wheels spinning on the tile, a sheet draped over a body.

"Who's that? Josh Eikenberry. Or Son Finnegan?"

The nurse didn't answer. I grabbed her wrist. "I know you can't tell me who's under that sheet. But if Son is alive, he's in trouble. Dot gave him blood thinner. She put it in our margaritas. I don't want Son to die. Please help him."

The nurse's face hardened. She peeled my fingers away from her arm. "How many margaritas did you drink, Miss Templeton?"

"One. But it was laced with PGA and Sonata and blood thinner." My hand dropped to my thigh. I felt a bandage, and the flesh beneath it ached. I tried to raise up again, but the nurse gently pushed me down.

"You need sutures. We're waiting for Dr. Jennings. I've got a pressure bandage on your laceration. Try not to squirm, okay?"

"You don't understand. I was drugged. Tied up. Tasered. He—he tried to rape me."

"Who?" The nurse looked puzzled.

"Josh. He's in cahoots with Dot Agnew. She's a nurse."

The nurse's eyes widened. "Miss Templeton, you're a tad confused on account of your accident."

"Dot tried to kill me and Son. Call the police."

"They're here. But you'd best not talk to them till you're sober. Try to stay calm."

How could I be calm? I'd killed a man with a tarantula. And Dot was clever and sugary. Had she gone to the farm to kill Sir? I sucked in air.

"Get the police," I said. "Send them to my farm. Dot's going to shoot my dog."

"No one is going to shoot anyone."

"I'll call the police myself. Where's a phone?"

I knew I sounded crazy. Once time Mama had gotten out of control, and Aunt Bluette had brought her to this hospital. The doctors had pumped Mama with drugs until her craziness eased. She'd just sat there like a potato, her empty eyes staring at the window.

The nurse scurried out of the room. I pulled up on my elbows. The sheet spread out like a white tablecloth. I looked like sacrificial pork tenderloin, just waiting for Dot to carve me into pieces. I couldn't stay here. She'd find me. I had to find a phone and call Red. He'd go to the farm and ninja-protect my dog.

I jerked out the IV, and blood dribbled down my hand. A dark circle bloomed on the sheet. I dangled my legs off the side of the bed until the wooziness passed. Then I slid off the gurney.

My feet hit the cold tile floor. I pressed my fist against my leg, trying to stop the bleeding, and tottered out of the room.

Light spilled down a brown tiled hall. Doors on both sides. Some open. Some closed. At the far end of the corridor, nurses gathered around a tall desk. If they saw me, they'd haul me back to bed. I stepped in the opposite direction, down another brightly lit hallway, where a baby was crying.

Don't faint. One foot in front of the other, that's a girl.

At the end of the hall, a woman in a hospital gown stood outside her door, holding on to an IV pole. "Lady, you're bleeding," she said. "How'd you get hurt?"

"I wrecked." I didn't just mean the car crash. I was broken in all kinds of ways. I looked down at my leg. Blood pattered against my toes. Dammit, I was barefooted.

I ducked into a linen closet that smelled of bleach and laundry detergent. The humming fluorescents cast a grayish light over metal shelves. I moved toward one that was crammed with scrub suits.

First, stop the bleeding. It was Aunt Bluette's voice, soft and nasal. I peeled the pressure bandage off my leg. The red wound gaped open like trout lips. I found an Ace bandage and looped it around my thigh.

Disguise yourself, Aunt Bluette whispered. I put on scrubs and a cap. Every place I touched felt sore. My face, knuckles, chest. Even my hair hurt. When I bent down to put on blue paper booties, I staggered sideways and hit the wall. How much blood could a person lose before they passed out?

I slipped into the corridor. It was empty, except for a volunteer in a pink uniform who pushed a magazine cart. From the intercom, an operator with a twangy voice said, "Housekeeping to 2-West."

My heart pounded so hard, the bosom of my scrub suit jerked. *Relax, Teeny. Nurses can smell fear.* I took a deep breath. My lungs couldn't fail me now because I'd left my inhaler in Dot's kitchen.

I stepped into the hall. It was long and blue. A light flickered above me. I checked each room. They were empty.

The intercom cracked. "Code Yellow, emergency room."

Two nurses walked by, then circled back. They stared at the patient armband that dangled from my wrist. I'd forgotten to remove it. The nurse with pale blond hair looked me up and down. "Are you lost?"

The other nurse said, "I bet she's the Code Yellow."

I ran in the opposite direction. A red exit sign glowed above a stairwell door. I opened it and raced down to the next floor. Above me, the door opened. Footsteps shuffled over the tile. I flattened myself against the wall and held my breath.

Footsteps started up again. Muffled voices. Then the door creaked shut. I clawed off my ID band and pushed away from the wall. I expected to see the nurses staring down. But they were gone.

Holding pressure against my leg, I climbed down another flight of stairs. My paper booties squeaked, as if I'd walked through a wet field. I looked down. Blood. I scooted to the exit door and crept into a hall. It was darker than the rest of the hospital. I passed by vacant rooms, the beds stripped.

Find a telephone. Call 911.

The hospital operator's voice spiraled down from the ceiling. "Code Yellow," she said.

I'd almost made it to the elevator when someone tapped my shoulder. I whirled. A woman blinked down at me, her face narrow and freckled. Perched on top of her head was a white Mr. Coffee filter. Her name tag read GLINDA REILLY, RN.

"This wing is closed." She stepped closer. "Are you new? Where's your ID tag?"

I looked past her, at a U-shaped nurse's station. "Is there a phone over there?"

"Honey, your feet are bloody. And your leg. My Lord. What in the world happened? You shouldn't be on your feet." While she talked, she steered me to a wheelchair. "I need to see how badly you're cut. I'm just going to roll up your scrub pants."

I put my hand over my leg. "Do you have a cell phone?"

"Let's get you to the emergency room."

Behind me, I felt a whoosh of air, and I smelled Shalimar.

"Glinda, call OR 6 and tell them I'm bringing the appendectomy," a familiar voice said.

Dot stepped in front of me. She'd changed into scrubs, but her Cockatoo hair was damp and spiked.

I screamed. She clamped her hand against my mouth. "It's all right, Glinda. This little gal is a tad paranoid. All her people are that way."

Glinda looked at Dot's hand over my mouth, then she looked at Dot.

"You want me to write you up?" Dot cried.

I yelled as hard as I could into Dot's hand. Murderer. Chop Shop. Killer. Then I tried to bite the fleshy part of her palm.

The nurse scurried off.

"Surrender, Teeny," Dot said. Her free arm circled around me. Then she aimed the Taser against my chest. A string flew out. Something sharp and hard slammed into my chest.

Dot pushed my wheelchair into an alcove. The abrupt movement nearly threw my limp body to the floor. She hoisted me back into the chair. Then she reloaded the Taser and aimed the red dot. I saw another flurry of white string. The blow knocked the breath out of me.

"This part of the hospital is closed for repairs. I wouldn't have found you, but you left a bloody trail." She removed two probes from my scrub top and dropped them in her pocket.

"You know what this is, Teeny?" She pulled out a syringe. It was filled with a milky substance. A white drop quivered at the end of the steel bevel.

My hands and feet throbbed, but I couldn't move. Couldn't speak.

"Propofol. Better known as Mother's milk. A real peaceful way to die. Your heart will stop. And you'll go to sleep. I wanted to use this on Kendall from the get-go, but Josh wanted to have a little fun. He was a little sweet on her. When she showed up at the funeral home with that printout, he laced her Countrytime lemonade with pure grain alcohol. It went straight to Kendall's pea-brain. Then she told everything. She kept talking about you. She said *you* needed more evidence. Josh went to call me. He left her alone for two minutes, but Kendall must have gotten paranoid. She ran off. We didn't know where she'd gone. Then *you* called and told me exactly where to find the little slut. Honestly, Teeny. You're more efficient than GPS."

Oh, no. Kendall, I'm sorry. So sorry.

I felt a tug inside my chest, right where those Taser probes had gone in. All those people dead and dismembered. All dead and gone because I was a truth junkie and Dot wanted more chairs.

She pushed up my sleeve. With her other hand, she aimed a needle at my arm. "Oh, by the way," she said. "Guess who's in jail? Lester Philpot. I put Kendall's fingers in the trunk of his car. Then I made an anonymous call to the police."

"Why did you kill so many people?" I whispered.

"I wanted to be rich," she said. "That's all I ever wanted."

Glinda walked down the hall, arms swinging, then she abruptly stopped. "Everything all right?" she asked.

Dot put the syringe into her pocket. Then she reloaded the Taser.

"Run," I cried. "Tell everybody that Dot Agnew is selling black market organs."

Dot's hand moved in a blur. She pointed the Taser at Glinda. A snap echoed in the empty hall. The nurse let out a whoop. Her eyelids fluttered and she dropped to the floor.

Dot pulled out another cartridge and reloaded. I vaulted out of the chair and slammed into her. The Taser fell on top of Glinda. She didn't try to grab it. Her muscles were still locked.

"Bitch," I said, and shoved my hand into Dot's pocket. I groped for the syringe. She made a fist and punched the back of my head. Each blow felt as light as a lemon poppy seed muffin.

"Dwarf," she cried. She grabbed my arm and shook it. The tip of the needle jammed into my finger. Now *that* hurt. I dragged the syringe out of her pocket and threw it down the hall.

"Propofol," I yelled. "She's killed patients with Propofol."

Dot raced after the syringe. I got behind the wheelchair and started running. I crashed the chair into the backs of her thighs. She tottered forward and sprawled on the tile floor.

Get the Taser, Aunt Bluette said.

I snatched it up. But Dot was ready for me. We rolled on the floor, grappling for the Taser. My booties scraped across the tile, leaving a bloody comma. Bitch wouldn't get away with it. Bitch wouldn't murder my bulldog. Bitch was going down.

She snatched the Taser. I butted her arm with my head. The Taser fell out of her hand and clattered.

I grabbed her earlobes and tore out those gold hoops. She howled. Her hands flew up to her ears. Blood ran down both sides of her neck.

I scooted on my belly toward the gun. I grabbed it and rolled over. My hands were steady as I aimed the red dot between her eyebrows.

The string wiggled. A prong slammed into Dot's forehead. She screeched. Her legs folded and she hit the floor.

Glinda sat up, grappling with a cell phone, tears rolling down her cheeks.

I was sobbing, too. I wiped my nose. A swirl of dizziness rushed around me. How much Propofol had gotten into my finger? How could a tiny puncture wound hurt more than the gash in my leg?

I sat down hard. Yet I seemed to be moving toward the ceiling. Up, up, up. So high. Right into the clouds.

Life is nothing but a peach layer cake, Aunt Bluette said. *You can't eat it in one sitting, but one day you'll cut that last slice.*

I strained to hear more, but couldn't keep my eyes open. My aunt's voice echoed, as if she were crouched inside a tin can. I tumbled in after her.

thirty-six

I dreamed that I was cooking a meal at the Spencer-Jackson House. The dining table was covered with platters of ham and chicken and steamy bowls of green beans and corn and gravy. On the walnut sideboard, a red velvet cake sat on a glass pedestal, four layers of cream cheese icing, the peaks and swirls hiding a scarlet center.

As I laid out blue-sprigged china plates, I breathed in the tang of cole slaw and baked beans. I smelled peaches, too. Turnovers, cobblers, deep-dish pies.

The smells of home.

Nature might hate vacuums, but I knew how to fill them. Home wasn't a place. Home was inside me. And I finally knew how to find it.

I heard a clinking noise, as if people were tapping champagne glasses and making toasts. Or maybe my lie tally had reset to zero. Each precise click seemed to say, *Teeny Templeton, lies are not black and white, they're pure gray. You don't need to keep a tally.*

The sound got louder. I opened my eyes. I was in a dark room. Rain ticked against a window. A nurse with gray hair moved next to the bed, adjusting knobs on a machine. She turned her head. "Do you want something for pain, sugar?" she asked.

"I want Coop."

"I'm here, sweetheart," a deep voice said.

I turned toward the voice I'd loved my whole life. Coop stepped out of the shadows and took my hand. He felt warm and alive, and he smelled faintly of pine needles. I had so much to tell him, but I couldn't shape the words. I felt like a voiceless three-year-old.

The nurse set the call button beside my elbow and left the room.

With his free hand, Coop lifted a glass and fit the straw between my lips. Water splashed over my parched tongue. I drank and drank, until my thoughts ran clear. His gaze moved up to my hair then down to the bandage on my leg.

"You look like hell, Templeton."

I spit out the straw. "Is Sir all right?"

"He's fine. He and Red are at the farm."

"What about Son?"

"The docs removed his spleen. They gave him some medicine to stop the bleeding." He glanced up at the transfusion bag, type B positive. "Don't you want to know how you're doing?"

"I'm breathing."

"You got eight stitches. It wasn't a deep cut. But the Coumadin stopped your blood from clotting."

I squeezed his fingers. "Where were you? I called your office. They said you'd be gone the whole week."

"I had a bleeding ulcer. Ended up at Charleston Medical Center."

I tried to sit up, but the pain dragged me down. "Why didn't you tell me?"

He turned away. I grabbed his chin and made him look at me. "Just tell me. It can't be that bad."

"Red and I talked about it. We were scared you'd drive to Charleston."

"I would have."

"I didn't want you on the road. I was afraid you'd end up like Kendall." A tear ran down the side of Coop's nose. "But I had another reason. A bad reason."

"What?"

"I thought you needed time to sort your feelings about Son."

"They're sorted, O'Malley." I licked my lips. They felt rough and parched. "Where's Dot?"

"Jail. She's claiming the whole Philpot family was involved in the chop shop."

"No. She set them up. She told me." I let out a harsh breath. "Is that hearsay? Fruit of the poisoned nurse?"

"She can't hurt you now, sweetheart. She can't hurt anyone."

I told him about Emerson's hedgehog, the money, the key, the margaritas, the tarantula, and the Cayman Island bank account.

He slipped his arms around me. I pressed my face against the curve of his neck. His pulse ticked against my cheek. We stayed like that a long time, just holding each other. Finally I lifted my face. "Where's Son's Jaguar? In the junkyard?"

"I suppose so." Coop leaned back, his brow wrinkled. "Why?"

"Because I want to find that tarantula. It saved two lives and broke up a chop shop. I don't want to lose it."

"You lost something else." Coop pulled Minnie's diamond out of his shirt pocket. "When the police arrested Dot, she was wearing this."

"She stole it."

"It's yours, sweetheart. I want you to keep it. Even if I'm not the one you want spend your life with."

"You *are* the one, Coop." I put my hand on his cheek. "You always were the one."

Behind him, lightning brightened the window. He put the ring on my thumb. Then he climbed into the bed and pressed his nose against my cheek. Something wet trickled onto my neck.

"Yes," I said.

"Yes, what?" he asked in a wavery voice.

"I'll marry you."

His face moved directly over mine. "I'll make you so happy. I'll break laws for you. But I'll never lie again."

"And no sins of omission." I pushed my fist against his jaw.

"Nothing but the whole truth," he said, and drew an X over his heart. "So help me God."

Whatever the nurse had put into my IV was making me chatty, and a little bossy. "Another thing, don't call me baby. Call me sweetheart. That's your especial name for me."

"Sure, sweetheart," he said in a Bogart-esque voice.

"Much better, O'Malley."

He kissed my hand. "You're a rare woman, Teeny Templeton. You showed unconditional love to Emerson. You were willing to change your life to raise her."

"I still want to." Everything went blurry as if I were under water. "She's not yours, Coop. She's not Lester's. Her father is someone named A.M. If that's his name. I read it in Barb's diary. But I know one thing for sure: Lester doesn't want her. And I do. I want to raise that little girl."

"I'll help you. We'll raise her together." He tucked my hair behind my ear. "First thing in the morning, I'll talk to Lester."

I drew his hand to my lips. "Tell him I love Emerson Philpot. And I want to be her mother."

The next morning, the nurse wheeled me out of the hospital. The sunlight felt good against my shoulders. Coop's red truck waited by the curb. He got out and rushed over. He wore cutoff jeans, and a blue shirt that brought out the color in his eyes. I got up from the wheelchair and he slid his arms around my waist.

"Lean on me, sweetheart."

The nurse's mouth puckered as if she'd sucked a persimmon. "This is against the rules," she said.

"Sue me," Coop said.

I leaned into him the way a peach tree leans in the wind. We might have missed his birthday dinner, but it wasn't too late for a cake. He liked chocolate better than red velvet, so I would bake the Templeton sheet cake, which called for bittersweet chocolate.

Coop put his hand under my elbow. "I talked to Lester."

My stomach muscles tensed. "And?"

"He's letting Emerson decide who she wants to live with."

A wide streak of joy ran through me. The truck's side window rolled down and Sir's head appeared, bobbing like volleyball. Emerson pushed in beside him, her mouth wide open.

"I told you I'd be back," she said.

I waved at her with both hands. *A truck door closes, a window opens.*

Coop and the nurse helped me into the front seat. The stitches in my leg pulled taut, but I ignored the pain. It just felt good to be alive. Sir scooted close to me, licking my hands. Emerson pressed her face against my neck. A tear ran down my chin and dribbled onto her hair.

"We've brought you a present," Coop said. He reached toward the floorboard and lifted a square box, no bigger than a toaster, wrapped in shiny blue paper.

Emerson pressed her ear against it. "It's not ticking," she said. "No need to call the bomb squad."

"Is it edible?" I asked.

"I wouldn't recommend it," Coop said.

I pulled off a wedge of paper and saw a clear plastic box. Gourmet sea salt? A Tupperware container? I peeled off the rest of the gift wrap and blinked down at a Plexiglas cage. Inside, a tarantula sat motionless on aquarium gravel.

I grinned. "Where'd you find him?"

"Emerson and I went to the junkyard." Coop bent closer to the box. "I didn't think we'd be successful. I know how to call a dog. But a spider?"

"So we whistled," Emerson said. She pursed her lips and blew a few notes.

The tarantula moved its front leg up and down like a Maestro conducting an orchestra.

I pulled Sir and Emerson against me, then I slipped my other arm around Coop. I hugged them as hard as I could. I even tried to hug the tarantula's cage.

We were together. And it was time to go home.

Teeny's Recipes

The Right to Remain Silent Salsa

Serves: 4

4 ripe Elberta peaches, peeled and chopped (discard pits)
1 cup chopped red onion
1 clove garlic, minced
2 tablespoons jalapeño pepper, minced
¼ cup chopped red bell pepper
¼ cup chopped green bell pepper
3 tablespoons chopped cilantro
2 tablespoons canola oil
2 tablespoons lime juice
1 tablespoon honey
salt and pepper to taste

Place peaches, onion, garlic, peppers, and cilantro in a bowl. In another bowl, whisk oil, lime juice, and honey. Salt and pepper to taste. Pour over peaches and veggies. Cover bowl with plastic wrap and chill at least 45 minutes. Serve with pork, chicken, fish, tacos, or pita wedges.

I've Already Hired an Attorney Chips

Serves: 4

4 pitas
¼ cup garlic oil
Sea salt
Black pepper, freshly ground

Preheat oven to 400 degrees. Cut each pita into 6 to 8 wedges and place on an ungreased cookie sheet. Brush oil over wedges and sprinkle with salt and pepper. Bake for 8 to 10 minutes or until chips are evenly browned.

Orange You Sorry You Lied Marinade

Yield: approximately 2¾ cup marinade

1 cup orange-flavored liqueur
½ cup blood orange juice
½ cup peach juice

Whisk until smooth.

Mix in:
¼ cup blood orange zest
¼ cup finely chopped, skinned peaches
4 garlic cloves (peeled and minced)
4 tablespoons stone-ground mustard
½ cup safflower oil
1 teaspoon large-grained salt (sea or Kosher)

2 tablespooons chopped fresh pepper
¼ cup chopped herbs, Italian parsley, and lemon thyme

Pour into a container and refrigerate.

This marinade is perfect for Butt Out of My Life Barbecue, Take Your Lies and Shove Them Tilapia, and Sue Me Shrimp Kabobs.

Aunt Bluette's Fresh Peach Pie

(A procedure, not a recipe)

Buy or make two pie crusts. Put the bottom crust into a 9-inch pie pan. Peel and slice a dozen ripe Elbertas. Arrange the slices in the bottom of the pie shell. In a bowl, mix ½ cup white sugar, ½ cup brown sugar, 1 teaspoon cinnamon, ½ teaspoon nutmeg, ¼ cup peach preserves, and 2 tablespoons all-purpose flour. Mix and pour over peaches. Dot the mixture with pieces of cold butter. Roll out the second crust. Using a pastry wheel, cut the pastry into strips. Lay strips on top of peaches and make a lattice design. Bake at 375 degrees for 40 minutes. Serve with vanilla ice cream. Garnish with sugared pecans.

Teeny's Red Velvet Cake

1½ cups white sugar
2 large eggs
½ cup Crisco
2 ounces red food coloring
2½ cups sifted cake flour

1 teaspoon salt
1 teaspoon baking powder
1 cup buttermilk
1 teaspon Madagasgar vanilla extract
1 tablespoon vinegar
1 teaspoon soda

Cream the Crisco and sugar until fluffy. Beat in the eggs. In a different bowl, mix the cocoa and food coloring. Add to the sugar mixture. Add cake flour, baking powder, salt, buttermilk, and vanilla extract. Blend until all lumps are gone. Add vinegar and soda. Do not beat after adding soda.

Pour into two 9-inch greased cake pans. Bake at 350 degrees for 30 minutes. Use a cake tester if you aren't sure.

Icing
4 tablespoons plain white flour
1 cup whole milk
1 cup confectioners' sugar
1 cup real butter (unsalted)
1 teaspoon Madagascar vanilla

Whisk flour and milk. Place in a saucepan and cook over a low flame until the mixture is smooth. Cool. In another bowl, cream sugar and butter. Add to the cooked flour mixture and whip until creamy. Add vanilla. Beat untl the mixture is light and fluffy and spreadable.

Variation: Cream cheese icing

acknowledgments

The author would like to thank Jennifer Enderlin, Ellen Levine, Sara Goodman, Lisa Senz, Matthew Shear, Sally Richardson, Matthew Baldacci, Sarah Melnyk, Sarah Goldstein, Nancy Trypuc, Laurie Ritchey, Shirley Hailstock, Jeanne-Marie Hudson, Andy Martin, Lori Wilde, and Lisa Davis.

Read on for an excerpt from
Michael Lee West's new novel

A Teeny Taste of Scandal

Coming Soon!

prologue

Please join us for a
rehearsal dinner
to honor
Cooper O'Malley
and
Teeny Templeton
Friday, April 20, 2013
at seven o'clock in the evening
Palmetto Place Club
Charleston, South Carolina
Hosted by Dr. and Mrs. Jack O'Malley
Regrets Only to Patsy 555-931-6665

The day before my wedding, I made a batch of I-Found-True-Love Donuts. They were the darlingest things, red velvet with white chocolate mini-chips and a splash of Bailey's Irish Cream. I had planned to bring them to the rehearsal dinner tonight, but my future mother-in-law pitched a fit. She'd booked the top floor of Palmetto Place, one of the oldest clubs in Charleston, and professionals were in charge of the menu.

Whatever.

Me, I'm just a self-taught pastry chef, not a threat to all of humankind.

So I baked the donuts anyway and planned to eat them after the party. I was tempted to whip up a batch of icing called My-True-Love's-Mom-Is-a-Hound-from-Hell. The secret ingredient is a quarter-teaspoon of jalapeño sugar, though some cooks use brimstone.

Chill, Teeny, I told myself. Then I put the donuts on a cooling rack and went outside. It was the second week in April, and azaleas were blooming all over the historic district. I live on Rainbow Row, and I couldn't help but smile as I watched a horse-drawn carriage clomp down East Bay Street. Then a puff of wind blew off the water, carrying the bite of salt and a hint of calamity.

I only had a few hours to get ready for the rehearsal dinner, and I was still wearing cutoff jeans. My fiancé, Coop O'Malley, was picking me up. His mom had insisted that we arrive early or she'd send someone to break our kneecaps. Miss Irene's threat wasn't aimed at her son. Coop is a rule-obsessive lawyer, and his childhood bedroom is filled with promptness awards and books like *Robert's Rules of Order*.

Me, I'm a slob and a hard-core foodie. Nothing but a tsunami would stop me from cooking. But I didn't want to disappoint Miss Irene. Maybe if I acted right, she would come to like me. Eventually.

I was just about to step into my breezeway, when someone said, "Teeny?"

I turned. A thin, middle-aged woman stood three feet away. I'd met her four days ago at a bizarre cooking gig. She'd told me her name was Ruby. That had been my mama's name, too, but she'd been missing for two decades, so I didn't make the connection. When I was eight years old, she'd abandoned me at a Dairy Queen. Now I was twenty-nine, and my thoughts were on my upcoming marriage. Then a detective from the Charleston PD had come to my house. He believed Ruby was my long-lost mama, and that she could be mixed up in prostitution and grand larceny, maybe even murder. The detective told me to be wary until he figured out who she really was.

But I just couldn't turn her away.

She had the Templetons' brown eyes. Her hair was five shades lighter than mine and a hundred times straighter, but a cosmetologist can do wonders with intractable curls. Ruby didn't have the family's signature ears, which resemble teacup handles. But Mama's ears had been normal.

"You don't look happy to see me," Ruby said. She tucked a blonde curl behind her perfect little ear, and her sleeve drew back, showing an EAT ME tattoo on her wrist.

"No, I'm just surprised," I said.

"I have that effect on people."

I looked up into her eyes. She was taller than me, but most people are—I'm not quite five-feet-two.

She stepped closer, glancing up and down the street. I looked, too. No tourists were on the sidewalk, and a taxi loomed in the distance.

"I hate to do this." Ruby reached inside her purse and pulled out a white handkerchief.

"Do what?" I asked.

She rushed forward and clamped the smelly cloth over my nose. A roaring sound filled my ears. Time came unhinged, and the past, present, and future coiled around me, dragging me into the dark.

When I woke up, I was sprawled in the front seat of an old Plymouth, and my left wrist was cuffed to the steering wheel. Ruby was driving.

I sat up. The Plymouth's headlights swept over cypress trees and loblolly pines. Behind them, darkness twisted out of the ground.

"What happened?" I said.

"I doped you up a little. You won't believe how hard it is to find chloroform in this town. But I know the right people."

Tears pricked my eyes. "Why are you doing this?"

"If I told you, I'd have to eat you."

"Take this handcuff off. I mean it, Ruby. Take it off."

"Relax, baby girl. The world is almost ours."

That didn't make a bit of sense. But then, my mama had always been illogical. When I was a child, she'd wrapped a man in a sheet, then beaten the hell out of him with an empty Coca-Cola bottle. It didn't take much to set her off. But I had to know what was going on.

"How long have I been unconscious?" I asked.

"A few minutes."

"Where are we?"

"The Francis Marion State Forest. A dumping ground for serial murders. So keep your door locked. Not too long ago, a pervert set a woman's car on fire and nobody noticed."

Just what I needed to hear. I gingerly touched a sore place on the back of my head. "Did you hit me, too?"

"Not on purpose. Want some OxyContin?"

"God, no."

"I got plenty if you change your mind."

My chin tipped back as I tried to pull in a breath. "I need my asthma inhaler."

"I'll get one."

I leaned against the seat, trying to figure out why she'd kidnapped me. Had I offended her? And how had she managed to put me in her car without attracting attention? Someone on East Bay Street had surely witnessed the attack. But they wouldn't know where I'd been taken.

Ruby swerved down a gravel lane, palmettoes scraping on the sides of the car, tires whomping over potholes. She parked in a grassy clearing, then cracked open her door. Humid, pine-smelling air drifted into the front seat.

My mouth went dry. "Why are we stopping?"

"I've got sugar in the trunk. Can you help me get it?"

I blinked. This was totally wacked. She couldn't lift a five-pound sack of sugar? I had to get home. I could still make it to the party. Coop had probably just arrived at my house. He would be in my kitchen, waiting for me. So would my bulldog.

"Ruby, what's going on? Why are we really here?"

"Like I said, I can't tell."

"Why the hell not?"

"If you curse, I won't take off the handcuffs."

"I won't do it anymore." I couldn't believe this was happening. She'd drugged and kidnapped me, yet she was offended by mild profanity.

She unlocked the cuffs, then grabbed my wrist and pulled me out of the car. "Gosh, you're heavy," she said. "I thought brides starved themselves."

Not if the bride is a pastry chef. I'd always wondered if my mama would find me. In my mind, I'd planned a homecoming menu: chicken pot pie, roasted asparagus, a seven-layer salad, buttered cloverleaf rolls, chocolate cake, and fresh-squeezed lemonade. I would not quiz or judge her. But now that she was here, I wanted to bite her, not serve a meal.

"Come on, now." She gripped my elbow, steered me around the car, and opened the trunk. A nubby white blanket showed the outline of a body. Long hair jutted up, black with chunky white stripes.

"You remember Sugar, don't you?" Ruby said. "She was the best hooker in Charleston. And she rocked the Trucker Prom Queen look. We'll say a few nice words after we bury her."

We? I cast an edgy glance toward the pines. How big was this park? If I ran away, would I get lost?

"Guess you're wondering how this happened," she said.

"I don't want to hear about it." The less I knew, the better. Ruby had just made me an accessory after the fact, a Class D felony in South Carolina, one that would get me slapped into the pokey. Of course, I might not get to the witness stand. Ruby could throw me into Sugar's grave, and Coop might never know what had happened. My best hope was to act tough and snarky. If I could remember how.

"Don't be scared," Ruby said. "It's just a corpse, not a flesh-eating zombie. Just think of it as a shitload of sugar."

"Enough to feed the multitudes."

"Ain't that the truth? This gal's heavier than she looks. Muscular and big-boned. She would've made a good tranny." Ruby tucked her keys in her pocket. "Grab her legs. I'll get her shoulders."

I took a half step backward.

"What's wrong now?" Ruby said.

Oh, nothing. It's not every day that I touch dead flesh.

My plan was to help her get the body out of the trunk. Then I'd run off. Just deciding this made me feel better. I put my hands on Sugar's ankles. They felt warm. Which meant she hadn't been dead very long or she was still alive, and either way, I'd had enough.

I dropped her legs and sprinted toward the trees.

"Teeny, come back," Ruby yelled. "I won't hurt you. But something might. It's dangerous around here. Rape-stranglers. Alligators. Owls. Stuff like that."

I glanced over my shoulder. In the distance, car lights spangled through the leaves. My choices were limited. Death by alligators, Momster, or an asthma attack. I'd take my chances in the forest-of-the-damned.

I hauled ass, pumping my arms, crashing through sticker bushes. All I had to do was keep going and I'd eventually find a house or a convenience store. I'd call Coop and this crazy night would come to an end. But it was just about to get crazier.

"Teeny is a delightful heroine."

—*RT Book Reviews*

"Readers already under Teeny's spell will be relieved to find everything they were hoping for."

—*Library Journal* (starred review) on *A Teeny Bit of Trouble*

"*Gone with a Handsomer Man* is fun, funny, and fabulous!"

—Janet Evanovich